You Gotta Sin to Get Saved

You Gotta Sin to Get Saved

J.D. MASON

ST. MARTIN'S PRESS ⚊ NEW YORK

This is a work of fiction. All of the characters, organizations, and events portrayed in this novel are either products of the author's imagination or are used fictitiously.

Book design by Gretchen Achilles

ISBN-13: 978-0-312-32658-6

In Loving Memory of

JOHN PAUL MASON JR.

and

Peace of mind . . . and happy endings.

Acknowledgments

You Gotta Sin to Get Saved is the final installment in an unexpected trilogy. When I penned *One Day I Saw a Black King* five years ago, I never meant to follow it up with more stories, but the characters in that book have really stuck with me, and as soon as I turned the *Black King* manuscript in to my editor, Monique Patterson, the spirit of John King's predecessors hovered around me, until I told their stories in *Don't Want No Sugar.*

After *DWNS,* I was convinced that I was through, and that I could finally put those characters to rest. Or so I thought. "Whatever happened to Charlotte?" was the last question left unanswered, and after hearing that question enough from readers, I realized that I wasn't finished with these characters or, rather, that they weren't finished with me.

In this the last book featuring the characters from my most beloved story, I can finally lay these colorful people to rest, and, I have to admit, I'm going to miss them all very, very much.

Thank you, Monique Patterson, for letting me indulge one last time in these people's lives, and to you, Kia Dupree, for all of your fabulous assistance and guidance with this project.

Hey, Sara Camilli! Picture this: Me standing in the middle of lovely meadow, with the sun shining down on me, and a lovely breeze kissing my cheecks, thirty pounds lighter and waving.

Family, friends, book clubs, thank you, and I hope you all enjoy this book, as much as I've enjoyed writing it!

You Gotta Sin to Get Saved

Keep talkin' 'bout the President who won't stop air pollution
Put your hand on your mouth when you cough that'll help the
solution

Lynn Randall sang with Mavis Staples.

She nervously tapped her fingers against the steering wheel.

She chain-smoked, and fought back the urge to vomit.

Lynn Randall was terrified, and she drove that empty stretch of backwoods road constantly glancing in her rearview mirror, praying to God that the devil wasn't following them.

She'd been driving most of the night, heading west, away from Kansas City; pushing one eight-track tape into the dashboard after another. Her eyes burned, and more than anything, she wanted to pull over and sleep, just for a few minutes. But fear wouldn't let her.

Charlotte Rodgers moaned from the back seat of the car. "You need a doctor, Charlotte," Lynn's voice cracked. "We'll stop when—when we're far enough away. When I know he ain't gonna find us."

Charlotte understood, and at least she was alive. Jesus! If Lynn hadn't gotten to her when she did—she rubbed her forehead, and dread weighted down her stomach. "What the hell was I thinking?" she whispered to herself. Bile rose up in the back of her throat. Lynn had made the worst mistake of her life, one that could cost her as much, if not more, than Charlotte, who wasn't really even her friend. She just helped her because it could've just as easily been Lynn in that position. At any given time, it could've been any woman. If he ever found Charlotte, Lynn's life wouldn't be worth a damn. She stifled a sob.

Charlotte lay in the back seat with her knees drawn to her chest. Except for the blanket she was wrapped in, she was butt-naked, rocking herself back and forth, moaning and whimpering in agony.

The inside of the car glowed golden yellow from the sun rising up behind them. Lynn had taken the same road out of Kansas City, Missouri, that she'd first come in on, damn near ten years ago, chasing behind that nappy-headed no-good Arnel. To the rest of the world, Lynn was poor white trash, born and raised, but not to Arnel.

"You got some of the prettiest eyes, girl. Pretty enough to wade waist-high in. My blue-eyed angel." She smiled just a little bit, thinking about him, even now, and after all the shit he had put her through. Loving Arnel had been her rise and fall, her pain and glory, and about the dumbest thing she'd ever done, next to this.

Her hands were still shaking. They'd been shaking all night.

Lynn rolled down the window and inhaled buckets of fresh, cool morning air, filling her lungs and washing the stench of cigarette smoke, blood, sweat, and piss from her nostrils. She wasn't paying attention and she hit a small bump in the road.

Charlotte yelped.

"I'm sorry! I'm so sorry!" She watched her squirming in agony, clutching a bloodied towel to her face. "I'm so sorry, Charlotte." Her heart beat so fast, and her hands shook even faster, as she clutched the steering wheel tightly, to settle them. "You need a fuckin' doctor! I'm gonna stop in the next town. It'll be all right! They can help you!"

"No!" Charlotte cried out. "He find me. He—oh, shhh—!" She shrank back down in the seat and curled her legs to her chest. "Tek me home, Lynn," she sobbed. "Tek me—"

Lynn didn't notice the tears starting to stream down her own face again. She shook her head adamantly. "No! I ain't drivin my ass all the way to fuckin' Colorado! That's bullshit! That's bullshit and you know it! No!"

"Lynn—" Charlotte's pitiful plea trailed off.

"No!" She swallowed and turned briefly toward the back seat. "This old car of mine can't make it that far. It just ain't gonna make it." Lynn dried her face with the back of her hand, and turned her attention back to the road. "On the Kansas side, he won't find you there. He won't even look."

"Dear Jesus!" Lynn prayed silently. *"Don't let him come looking for us. Please!"*

Her tape deck stopped playing, and Lynn ejected the eight-track tape and turned on the radio.

She turned up the volume to drown out that incessant moaning that had been driving her crazy ever since they'd left.

It had been just under an hour since she'd piled Charlotte into the car. "I got a friend in Murphy." Lynn had to practically carry the woman down the stairs after what he'd done to her. "She's good people," she continued, talking more to herself than to Charlotte. "She might let us stay awhile."

You got a penchant for niggers, don't you, girl? Act like 'em.

Talk like 'em. Even like that nigga music. Let one of 'em feel on you and ain't no decent white man gone want shit to do with you.

Her own people never understood. *Black is beautiful,* she thought to herself. Lynn just naturally migrated toward black folks, more naturally than she did her own kind, and she couldn't explain it. She never understood why, either. A black man was beautiful, strong, and long, fucking a woman so good until she cried and lost her mind all over him and gave him anything he asked for, just for one more taste, another piece, a nibble of his love.

But some black men could be the meanest mothafuckas in the world if they wanted to be. The two of them were running from the meanest one to ever walk the earth. A man like him could raise a woman up on a sky-high pedestal, like she was a gift straight from heaven, or he could snap her in two and squash her under his feet like a cockroach. Lynn shuddered.

"This just in," the radio announcer interrupted her thoughts. "The unidentified body of a black male was found this morning on the northeastern bank of the Missouri River."

The moaning suddenly stopped.

"Early reports indicate that the man may have been shot, and—oh my God! I can't—say this on the air. I can't—"

Lynn turned off the radio. Neither of them said a word. Lynn bit down on her bottom lip, hot tears filled her eyes, and she drove.

Charlotte sobbed quietly to herself all the way into Murphy, Kansas.

And a long song of surrender in blue
I remember when you took my breath away

—CHAKA KHAN, *"Papillon"*

Chapter 1

*T*he mail was late today. Charlotte glared irritably at the back of the mail truck pulling away from her curb. The snow came up to her ankles, filling her slippers and dampening her socks, but Charlotte paid no attention. She pulled her housecoat close around her, picked up her mail, then headed back inside the house.

"I get anything, Momma?" her daughter, Cammy, asked, timidly peeking her head from the front door.

Charlotte ignored her and brushed past her on the way in. She flipped through the phone bill, sales papers, the car note, until finally she came to something she hadn't expected. It was a letter, and the return address on the outside of the envelope read Denver, Colorado. Charlotte dropped the rest of the mail on the floor and stood frozen in the middle of the living room.

"Momma?" Cammy bent down to pick up the mail. "What is it?"

Charlotte fingered the envelope in disbelief. Denver, Colorado, was the place she'd come from. She'd been born there and, growing up, she dreaded she'd die there. It was the place she had left behind, and the one place she could never seem to get back to, no matter how hard she tried, and how badly she wanted to. But who in the world would be writing her from—

Charlotte sat down in her recliner, then slowly peeled the seal open, pulled out the letter, and unfolded it.

Cammy sat down on the floor next to her. "Who's it from?"

To Whom It May Concern:

I pray that this letter find its way into the hands of Charlotte Rodgers. My name is Clarice Braxton. I was adopted when I was nine by a wonderful couple with the last name of Turner, but before that, my last name was Rodgers, and my birth mother nicknamed me Reesy. I say all of this because I've never been certain that you would remember my name, or me, for that matter. It's a fear I've had ever since you left, when I was only eight-years-old.

Tears pooled in Charlotte's eyes as she read the letter, and Charlotte took a deep breath and held it for a moment. Emotions tumbled over each other; panic, then joy, and finally heartache. She'd almost forgotten and let go the memories of her two oldest daughters. Charlotte had almost given up on her baby girls. So much had happened to her through the years. Memories dirty and foul had changed Charlotte into a different woman, too afraid to recall the many lives she'd lived until now.

I've spent a lot of money searching for you, Momma, but to me it's all been worth the time and the money because in finding you, I'm hoping to fill in the missing pieces of my life, and maybe even find the closure I desperately need to move forward,

*once and for all. For the last twenty-seven years the first thought
I have when I wake up in the morning is "Why did she leave
us?", and it's the last question I ask myself before I finally fall
asleep at night. As a mother myself now, I can't fathom the
thought of ever walking out of my children's lives without a
trace, and so, I can't help but to wonder what was happening in
your life back then, to make you leave me and Connie.*

"Leave them?" She startled herself when she said it out loud.
"No," Charlotte covered her mouth with her hand. "I didn't—it
wasn't like that." Charlotte choked back tears. She closed her
eyes and tried to remember that day.

"*I've got to go.*"

She told them that, but what else did she say? She made a
promise to come back. She had to have made that promise, because Charlotte wouldn't have just left them without telling
them that. "Noooo," she said out loud, pushing aside the truth.
The girl had it all wrong, she thought frantically. Charlotte did
leave them, but she never meant to be gone so long.

"Momma?" Camille, her youngest daughter, reached out to
her mother. "Momma? What is it? What's wrong?"

Charlotte swallowed and turned her attention back to the
letter.

*I managed to find my sister Connie almost eight years ago. She
and I were separated not long after you left, and well, Connie
had it so much harder than I did. In many ways, she's still suf-
fering from the hardship of your leaving. Connie wasn't as fortunate as me, and she suffered terribly growing up. But if it gives
you any solace, if you've ever wondered, we are both fine now. I
haven't told her yet that I've found you. I'm not really sure how*

she'll take the news. In some ways I believe Connie took your leaving harder than she'll ever admit. She's too proud, and that's sometimes her downfall.

Of course, we'll be coming to Murphy to see you, Momma. I can't say when exactly. That'll depend on when Connie and I can decide on a time and when we can both get away. We need to finally see your face, and to look into your eyes, and find the answers from you that we both deserve. It's time to put the heartache and disappointment to rest. Let us have this visit to close the door, once and for all, on the childhoods we lost when you left us.

Reesy

Charlotte clutched the letter possessively to her bosom, and rocked her swollen frame back and forth in the chair. She pressed her lips together and cried quietly. A letter that started with so much promise ended in blame and disappointment. Charlotte was so young back then, and what happened to those children wasn't her fault. If they knew what she'd been through since the last time she saw them, they wouldn't point the finger at her. Reesy wrote that letter as if she'd forgotten who her mother was, and how much she'd adored Charlotte when she was a child. "Who does she think she is?" she said through clenched teeth, blinking back hot tears. She cut her eyes at Camille, sitting on the floor.

Connie had put these bad thoughts in Reesy's head. Connie was the spiteful and ungrateful one, and she whispered terrible lies to Reesy when they were children, trying to turn her against their mother. Charlotte felt relieved all of a sudden. Yes. She did leave, but it was Connie she told that she was only going to be gone for a little while. Connie had been the one, and she'd never told Reesy the truth. Connie had been such a hateful child.

"Lemme see it, Momma." Cammy reached out, but Charlotte shrugged away.

It was hard not to cry. Charlotte's bottom lip quivered, and she gave in to twenty-seven years of living without her two oldest children.

Cammy tugged gently on the letter. "No, Cammy!" Charlotte screamed. "This ain't yours," she said, clenching her teeth.

Cammy stared sadly at her mother, then lowered her head.

Charlotte glared at her. "My babies," she said, through her mouth that never opened wide enough anymore; bones and tissue had fused together, healing and leaving her face horribly disfigured. "My babies found me, Cammy. And I'm glad they did. I'm so happy they did."

She squeezed her eyes shut to help her remember their faces. Charlotte saw a blank space where her children's faces should've been. Lord! How could she ever forget what they looked like? Sadness crept up on her, stealing the joy that Reesy's letter had brought her, because she could no longer see them, or hear their voices as vividly as she once had. Charlotte had forgotten what they looked like, but then, why shouldn't she? After all, she had long since forgotten the image of her own face.

Oh, but wait a minute. She breathed a sigh of relief. There. Charlotte smiled crookedly. There, in one dark corner of her mind, she'd found them, beautiful, golden, precious little girls, like angels, like dolls, and like the kind of dreams she prayed she'd never wake up from.

She lovingly patted the letter to her chest, and watched in awe as Connie's pretty face came into view first, looking so much like Charlotte's, or at least, the way Charlotte used to look. A soft, honey-colored girl, with sandy brown hair and amber-brown eyes.

"We looked like sisters," she muttered, forgetting Cammy was nearby. Charlotte felt so proud. And she stared through the window across the room to the snow falling outside. "Like sisters." People used to tell her that all the time, and sometimes Charlotte would pretend they were sisters. Sometimes it was easier believing Connie was her sister instead of her daughter, because Charlotte had been so young when she'd had her, only fifteen. And Connie . . . Charlotte sat back and remembered how unappreciative and cold Connie could be. The way she turned up her nose at Charlotte, and rolled her eyes when she thought her mother wasn't looking.

She used to hate Connie sometimes back then, but time had brought forgiveness and acceptance of her oldest daughter. It was time for them to put their differences aside, she thought hopefully. Charlotte loved Connie, and it was long past time that Connie let go of ill feelings, embraced her mother, and admitted that she loved her, too.

"Momma?"

Cammy's sweet voice was like music. Charlotte looked at her and tried to smile. She was dark, like her father had been, but even so, Charlotte could see the strong resemblance between Cammy and Reesy.

Reesy, her baby. Her lovebug, she used to call her. Small, round, with full, soft cheeks that glowed like suns when she smiled, and Reesy smiled all the time, enough to light up a room, a house, a heart. In Reesy's eyes, Charlotte was the world. Nobody loved her the way Reesy had loved her. She was so much like Cammy, always there for her momma, doing everything in her small way to make Charlotte happy.

Despite the way her letter sounded, Reesy still believed in her mother's love, in her devotion, and she just needed to hear the truth, that Charlotte meant to come back. And that every day, she swore to herself that she would go get her girls, and they'd be together again, like she'd never left.

"I love you, Mommy."

"How much, Reesy? How much do you love your Mommy?"

Reesy spread her arms wide, then sidestepped to one side of the room, touched the wall with her fingertips, and sidestepped to the other side of the room to touch the other wall. "This much, Mommy. I love you as big as this room."

Love like that was intoxicating, and Charlotte smiled, recalling the way that child's eyes lit up every time her momma walked into the room. Too many years had passed, and Charlotte struggled to recall how she could've ever left them behind. So much had happened, but she had always meant to go back for them. Of course she did. They needed to know that. After all this time, needed to tell them that.

"They found me, Cammy," Charlotte sighed, relieved, and she stared glassy-eyed at Camille. "They found me, baby." Her crooked smile was more brilliant than Cammy had ever seen before. "And everything is going to be just fine. You'll see. My babies are coming to get me and take me back home."

Chapter 2

*D*on't kill your baby! There are other ways! Please!"
Connie Rodgers stared straight ahead as she
walked through the sparse crowd of pro-lifers
screaming and waving posters of mutilated fetuses in her face.
Pro-lifers would never go out of style, and neither would abortions. She was running on automatic, doing what came disturbingly naturally on her way to her third abortion in twenty-five
years.

It was freezing outside, but Connie refused to give in to shivering, which some might interpret as weakness or second
thoughts. She pulled the collar of her coat tight around her and
hurried inside the front door.

A pleasant-looking woman smiled at her and let her inside.
"Sorry about that," she apologized about the protestors, then
locked the door behind Connie.

Connie blew warm breath into her fists and rubbed her
hands together, following the woman to the front desk. "Connie
Rodgers?"

Connie nodded. "Yeah. That's me."

"You're about six weeks along, I see."

She shrugged. "About."

"You've been through this before?"

"Yeah," she answered simply, ignoring the woman's obvious pause leaving room for Connie to elaborate, which she never did.

Carelessness. Connie always did have a penchant for carelessness, and the price tended to be rather high at times.

"Have a seat." The woman directed her to the waiting room across from the desk and out of view of protestors. "Someone will be with you shortly."

Two younger women were already there, waiting anxiously, and looking like two scared little rabbits. Neither of them looked like they were even twenty yet. The Hispanic girl was alone, like Connie. Her gaze never left the floor. She clasped her hands tightly together in her lap, squeezed her eyes shut, and prayed silently to herself.

Connie wanted to tell her that Jesus wouldn't be caught dead in an abortion clinic, so there was no use looking for him here. But she didn't bother. Let the girl say her prayers and come out of this thing on the other side of her conscience in whatever way worked for her. Who knew? Maybe God would be decent enough to meet her on the other side of the door to drive her home.

Another girl sat clinging to her boyfriend, who looked even more afraid than she did. His hands never left his coat pockets, his knee bounced nervously up and down the whole time, and she held on possessively to him, whispering something in his ear every now and then, unaffected by his eye-rolling and obvious impatience over having to be here in the first place. He'd dump her as soon as it was over, his last act of devotion to a foolish girl he'd never meant to spend the rest of his life with anyway.

"Janine?" One of the nurses came into the waiting area, and the Hispanic girl reluctantly stood up and followed her.

"You have someone coming to pick you up?"

The girl nodded nervously, but she never said a word.

There were more painful things in the world than abortions, like root canals or rape. Connie had lived through all of them. So how come it was so hard to shake this shit once you went through with it? Like root canals or rape.

These women were young. They were probably too young to take care of babies. Or maybe, like Connie, they were just afraid to take care of babies. They had their reasons for being here, just like she had hers. All of a sudden, though, Connie's reason seemed to fade away into a fog. She wasn't too young. Hell, she was forty, with a good job, a home, even health insurance. So what was her reason for being here?

Old habits die hard. She was in the habit of getting pregnant, but of not getting a kid out of the deal. Two abortions and a give-away was her track record, and it was pathetic to say the least. But pathetic and Connie seemed to fit hand in glove sometimes. She'd lived every unfortunate childhood cliché that existed: abandonment, homelessness, molestation, prostitution. Mother-hood was a word too foreign to fit naturally into the scheme that was her life. Instinct kicked in the moment she found out she was pregnant, and the first thought that came to mind was how to get rid of it. Old habits—instead of blaming her fuckups on habits, what she needed to do was get her damn tubes tied and count it a loss.

"Samantha," the nurse was back again, this time escorting the frightened rabbit, Samantha, to one of the rooms in back of the building. Samantha started crying the minute she turned to let go of her boyfriend.

"I love you," she mouthed.

He nodded, but that was it.

Connie knew what he was thinking. She could feel the tension coming from this boy. He was drowning in it. And she knew that all he wanted was for this whole ordeal to be over with. Because then he could get back to playing soccer and hanging with his homies, and kick sweet little Samantha's dumb ass to the curb.

Connie almost laughed just thinking about it. Men were easy. Women were the ones who complicated the hell out of everything. Simplicity was the key to life. Moving forward, not looking back, sucking it up, and keeping it simple. Damn. She was beginning to sound like her man.

John King was nobody's baby daddy material, and neither one of them had any business trying to procreate. They'd been together for two years, and Connie had managed to hold onto him by the skin of her teeth. Love had something to do with their union, and the fact that they'd both found someone who was willing to be there through bad hair days or weight gains. He was there when she was happy or sad, and John just went with the flow. She didn't have to fake the funk with him, because he'd come from a dark place, too, growing up. They took it easy on each other, and Connie suspected that both of them knew this was as good as it got for either of them. Reesy called it "settling." But to Connie, it was something else, acceptance, and better than nothing.

This whole kid thing wouldn't set well with him at all. It didn't set well—period. It was a tsunami threatening to upset the balance of complacency in their world, and John had grown fond of complacency. Besides, Connie didn't know the first thing about taking care of kids. She'd tried once, when she and Reesy were small and Charlotte walked out on them, leaving them alone in the apartment. Connie tried to mother Reesy and didn't get one damn thing right the whole week they were alone. She couldn't even keep the two of them together. And her ass ended up living on the streets and eating garbage out of trash cans, so them taking Reesy from her was the best thing for that girl. In the back of her mind, Connie was always a moment away from being homeless, hooking, and eating out of trash cans. What business did a woman like that have thinking she could mother anybody?

She called herself trying to do it again with her daughter, Jade, but that little baby girl scared the hell out of Connie, and before she realized what she was doing, Connie had handed her child over to Reesy and her husband, Justin, like a loaf of bread. Eight years later, Connie regretted it. Jade had grown up believing that Connie was her aunt. It just sort of happened that way. At the time, Connie went along with it because it was the easy way out, but she paid for it now, every second of the day, and it was eating her up inside, but what else could she have done?

"Connie?" The friendly nurse was back out in the lounge, smiling and holding a clipboard in her hands. It was like an assembly line. You walked in, spread your legs, let them suck out the contents, ignored the suctioning sound, laid perfectly still, and avoided making eye contact with the nurse and doctor. Finally, in the recovery room, you reassured yourself that you'd done the right thing and that it was all for the best. At some point, relief squeezed its way in, and you shed a few tears until it was time to go home, hoping like hell that all those protestors had taken their asses home, too.

Connie smiled and stood up. She'd been through this so many times, she could've performed the procedure herself. And like before, she'd manage to dust herself off, ignore the drama churning inside her, file away her emotions, and get on with things. It was the same old lie she'd told herself too many times.

Connie slipped back on her gloves, her eyes watered, and she stood up to leave. The nurse looked curiously at her, and Connie winked and started walking toward the door. "Not today."

The pro-lifers cheered as she made her way back to her car. Shit. She couldn't help herself. Connie smiled, and even slapped one of them a high five. A woman's right to choose is just that, she concluded. And today, she'd chosen.

Connie settled into the car, took a deep breath, and dialed John's work number.

"Hey, Tank. It's Connie. Is John around?"

He wasn't going to like it, but both of them were too old to be running away from this baby thing. They were adults who'd laid together. Made together. And now, it was time for them to grow the hell up and raise a kid together. "Hey, baby," she said, taking a deep breath. "I have something to tell you."

Chapter 3

Justin Braxton might as well have been masturbating. Five, maybe ten minutes and he'd be done. Reesy watched the numbers click off of the digital clock next to the bed while her husband lay on top of her, grunting into the pillow underneath her head. *Baby! Baby! Yesssss! That's it!*

No. That wasn't it. At least, not for her. But if giving up a few minutes of sleep would get him off her back, so to speak, then so be it. The whole world had flipped upside-down on her head, and he wanted to have sex. Reesy had been thrown back in time all of a sudden, and Justin wanted to *make love*.

"You've got time for everybody else but me," he complained. "I'm not asking for a lot, Reese! Just to spend a little time with my wife. I don't see the problem."

The problem was she'd found her mother who disappeared, leaving Reesy and Connie to fend for themselves when they were children, and all of a sudden, the woman reappears again, sprouting up in, of all places, Murphy, Kansas.

And all Justin could think about was getting his dick wet. This last year and a half, Justin had changed from being her caring, supportive, understanding husband and become a sulking man with too much time on his hands, and downright needy. Reesy's patience where he was concerned stretched too thin on most days.

"Don't you get it, Justin?" Reesy was about ready to pull her hair out arguing with this man. Reesy saw no reason to have to explain herself to him or anyone else, for that matter. "Yes! I've got a lot on my mind. I've found my mother, Justin. After all these years, the woman who I thought might be dead is alive, and every answer to every question I ever had about her growing up as a child is about to be answered. Why can't you understand what this means to me? Why is it so hard for you to let me have this?"

She had the idea to look for Charlotte right after she found Connie. It had been so much easier finding her sister. Almost too easy, and the thought didn't cross her mind until the bills started rolling in that it would be so much harder to find their mother.

Avery Stallings was the private investigator she'd hired to search for Charlotte. She had hired him two years ago, despite Justin's reservations. So much time had passed, she was beginning to believe Justin was right, and that Mr. Stallings was just pocketing money he wasn't doing anything to earn, but then he surprised her one day and called her, asking her to meet him for coffee at Blackberries on Welton Street.

Reesy had been waiting for almost fifteen minutes before he finally walked through the door. Her cup of tea was nearly empty. Avery was an older man, nearly fifty, with silver hair cut close to his head and receding, and a goatee the same color. On his dark skin, it made him look dashing and sophisticated. He sat across from her, a timid smile spread across his face, and he slid a large manila envelope across the table.

"I wouldn't have been able to live with myself if I couldn't deliver this to you. Your patience has finally paid off, Reesy."

Inside was a sheet of paper with a name and address typed and centered:

```
Charlotte Ann Rodgers
4715 S. Dalton Street
Murphy, Kansas 66125
Phone number unlisted
```

Behind the sheet of paper was a picture obviously taken without the woman's knowledge. She sat in a chair on the front porch of a rundown, faded blue bungalow, her head turned to the right, so that only half of her face was visible. She was a heavy-set woman, much larger than she should've been, wearing a full floral dress, her feet crossed at the ankles, with worn slippers on her feet. Her hair was pulled away from her face, braided, and pinned on top of her head.

"It was the best picture I could get," Avery said apologetically. "That's her, Reesy. That's your mother."

Was it her? Reesy searched ageless and ancient memories for the woman she remembered as her mother, and looked deep beneath the layers of this woman in the picture, hoping to see her. Charlotte had been so beautiful. Reesy remembered how beautiful she was, and how, even now, she still saw her beautiful face every time she looked into her sister's.

"There's more," Avery continued cautiously.

Reesy put up her hand to stop him, and studied the image she held in her hand, breathing slowly as the realization gradually crept up on her, and she peeled away the layers of Charlotte in the photograph down to the Charlotte she remembered from when she was a child. The light brown of her eyes . . . the waves in her hair . . . the round tip of her nose . . . it was her. Oh, Lord

Jesus! Reesy put her hand to her mouth and stifled a cry. But she couldn't stifle the tears starting to stream down her cheeks.

"It is her," she whispered, looking desperately to Avery. "It's Momma."

He nodded, and reached across the table to hold her hand.

"I thought she might be—" Reesy choked back her most dreadful thought.

"She's alive, Reesy. And she's doing well, by all accounts," he reassured her as best he could.

"Thank you," she mouthed, smiling.

Of all the people in the world, Avery had been the one who understood what this meant to her more than anyone else. Her adoptive parents were understandably reluctant for Reesy to find her mother. They didn't discourage her, but they didn't encourage her, either, believing she'd only walk away with heartache and disappointment when and if she ever did find Charlotte. Connie thought she was crazy for even bothering to look, and whenever Reesy even mentioned Charlotte's name, Connie quickly changed the subject, or found some reason to get off the phone.

Connie and Reesy had very different memories of Charlotte. Reesy loved her mother more than anyone else in the world. She loved her enough to want to be Charlotte Rodgers, but Connie blamed their mother for the tragedy her life had become after she left them, and rightly so. But Charlotte was still their mother, and Connie needed a reunion as much as Reesy did. They all needed it.

Justin was about to cum any second now, as Reesy's mind wandered back into their bedroom. He'd complained about money, time, and attention being taken away from him.

"First Connie, and now this."

This, meaning the woman who'd given birth to her.

She really wanted to hurry up and get this over with. Reesy knew her husband too well, and with a few thrusts of her hips up to meet his at just the right moment and pace, and . . .

He kissed her, then rolled off and collapsed next to her. Justin reached over the way he always did, hoping to gather her up in his arms and hold her until he fell asleep, but Reesy was too quick for him. Instead, he pulled back a fistful of air, watching woefully as his wife slipped out of bed and disappeared into the bathroom. The sound of running water reminded him that they hadn't made love. Justin had made love. Reesy had just laid there and let him do it.

Chapter 4

Tyrell Washington was only twenty-three years old, but he'd opened up his own car repair shop a year ago. Every girl in town wanted him, but it was anybody's guess as to how Camille ended up with him. He was five-ten, about 180 pounds, with smooth chocolate skin, and locs hanging down to the top of his shoulders. He dropped out of high school when he was sixteen, got his GED, then went to trade school and got a job working in a garage across town. Now he was the boss, and Tyrell never had anybody to believe he could do it but himself.

Cammy straddled his back while he stretched out underneath her on his stomach, dozing in and out of sleep from the back rub she was giving him. He had a tattoo of a bald eagle on one arm, and paid homage to Muhammad Ali on the other. After he found out Cammy was pregnant, he promised to save the place over his heart for a portrait of their baby.

"You falling asleep?" she smiled, then leaned down and kissed the side of his face.

"Careful, Cam," he gently scolded her. "You gonna crush Junior."

She was five months pregnant, and Cammy was in no hurry

to push this baby out. It was safe inside her, and more cared for than it could ever be on the outside.

"Spreading your legs is the easy part, Camille." Charlotte fussed at her all the time about being pregnant, like it was the worst thing in the world. "Wait till it gets here. It'll worry you to death, girl." Cammy waited for it to get bad, but it hadn't. Charlotte just had a negative outlook on most things, and Cammy figured having babies was one of them.

He was beginning to get impatient with her. Tyrell had big plans of the two of them getting married, and eventually moving to Salina, or even to Wichita. She loved his dreams, and Cammy relished the way he spoke about their future together, and how they'd have more kids, a nice house, even a dog. Ty had plans of opening more shops all over the state, maybe even the whole Midwest, and down South, too. He'd even bought her a ring, but Cammy didn't have the nerve to try and wear it around Momma, knowing how she felt about Ty.

"You think you the only woman he got? You think you all he's fucking, Cammy? A boy like that got women from one end of town to the other, and you the fool, girl. Because everybody in town know but you."

She couldn't have been more wrong about him. He loved Cammy, and he loved this baby. He told her as much every time he saw her.

He turned over, and Cammy slid over to the side of the bed next to him. Tyrell gently pushed her down on her back, then raised up on his elbow and kissed her swollen stomach.

He rested his head on her, then sighed deeply. "You taking too long with this, Cammy. I shouldn't have to see you when you on your way to work or running errands for your momma. You should be here with me."

His apartment was just big enough for him, but she loved being here. Cammy had run out of excuses as to why they couldn't be together, but after all this time, he knew well enough what her reasons were. He just didn't understand them. Sometimes she didn't either, but Cammy was bound to them.

Rather than argue, she decided to change the subject. "Remember I told you that I had sisters I've never met?"

Tyrell didn't respond.

"Years ago, when Momma lived in Denver, her mother came to the house and took her children, then refused to let Momma anywhere near them."

"Wonder why," he said sarcastically.

Cammy ignored him. "We got a letter from one of them the other day. Her name is Reesy, and she tracked Momma and me down and told us she and her—my other sister, Connie, are coming to see us. Isn't that amazing, Ty? After all this time, for her to find us?"

He raised up and looked at her. "Yeah," he said, unenthusiastically. "That's sick, baby."

"I can't wait for you to meet them," she said quietly, recognizing that look on his face. She hated when he looked at her that way, as if to say he'd lost faith in the two of them together, and that he'd given up on her completely.

Ty sat up on the side of the bed and started putting his work boots back on.

"I thought you said you had an hour for lunch," she said quietly. "You going back to work already?"

Ty never said a word. He put his shirt back on, then held the bedroom door open and waited for Cammy to slip on her boots.

"I'll try and see you tomorrow," she promised, then kissed him.

Tyrell didn't kiss her back.

Cammy blinked away tears as she drove to the grocery store. He just needed to be a little more patient. That's all. When he stormed up in the house last month, demanding Cammy pack her things and come with him, he made the situation worse than it already was with Charlotte.

"You need to get the hell out of my house, mothafucka!" Charlotte screamed, waiving a butcher knife around like a wild woman.

"Put that down, Momma!" Cammy stood behind her, begging.

"You a grown woman, Cam," he said, gritting his teeth. "You free to go whenever you damn well please." Ty stood his ground, and Cammy feared that one of them would get hurt if they didn't stop all that nonsense.

"Cammy, you set one foot out that door, I swear to God!" Charlotte turned to her with tears streaming down her cheeks. Then she pointed the tip of the knife to her heart. "I can't be by myself, baby." Charlotte's lips quivered.

"Cammy! Don't fall for that shit! Aw—Cam!"

She told him that Charlotte wasn't like most people, and that she needed Cammy, maybe too much. "She's my momma, Ty," Cammy tried to explain. "I can't just walk out on her. I don't know what'll happen to her if I do."

Time. She asked him for time. She promised him she'd figure something out. But Cammy was no closer to an answer now than she ever was, and Tyrell was running out of patience.

On her way home, Cammy stopped off at the store to pick up some cleaning products. She was comparing prices on scouring powder when Tonya Stevens crept up behind her.

"Ooooweee, girl." She reached out and patted Cammy's stomach. "You getting huge!" Tonya was the monster after Tyrell. She stood back, folded her arms in front of her, and shook her perfectly coiffed head back and forth. Large gold hoop earrings brushed against the sides of her face, and she tapped a pointy-toed, orange patent-leather stiletto pump against the linoleum floor. "Damn, Cammy! When are you due, girl?"

Cammy gritted her teeth and pretended not to be offended. "I'm not due until June, Tonya."

"Damn!" Tonya wrinkled her nose. "That long? You having twins?"

Cammy shook her head. "No. I'm not that big," she said, sheepishly.

Tonya threw her hands up and laughed. "Whoa! Back up, big momma. I didn't mean no harm. I was just asking a question." She snapped her neck, and put her hand on her hip. "Ain't no reason to get all defensive."

She wasn't being defensive. Cammy bit down on her bottom lip and turned her attention back to shopping, hoping Tonya would disappear into that black mud hole she crawled out of.

"How are you and T doing?" she asked, smugly.

Cammy shot her a look.

"You know," she continued, ignoring Cammy's obvious frustration, "word on the street is, he's getting tired of waiting on you." Tonya stuck out her chest and her big ass, then sashayed past Cammy, looking down her nose at her. "I heard he's tired of that old crazy momma of yours. You don't let a man like that wait for nothing. No telling *who* he might be doing." She switched her skank self on down the aisle, then disappeared around the corner.

Don't cry, Cammy, she told herself. Cammy held two cans of scouring powder in her hands, squeezing them tightly, fighting back tears. T wouldn't want Tonya. She knew that a woman like that wasn't his type. But then, lately he hadn't wanted her, either. So what the hell was he doing?

Finding out she was pregnant with his baby was the happiest day of her life, and when she told him, Tyrell swooped her up in his arms and spun her around whooping and hollering like he'd won he lottery.

"We're gonna get married, Cammy! Shit! Ain't nothing gonna keep us apart now."

Charlotte hit her so hard across the face it nearly knocked her over when Cammy told her she was pregnant. "I told you to keep your legs closed, girl!" She'd never seen her mother so angry. "Look at what you did, Cammy! Look at this mess you did! He ain't gonna want you! All he ever wanted was that snatch of yours, idiot! That's all he ever wanted!"

"But Tyrell's different, Momma." Cammy heard the shadow of her own voice, sounding so far away and week. Tyrell said he loved her. He said he needed her like he'd never needed a woman before. He kissed her belly, and whispered his love to this baby, but all of that was a long time ago. Lately, he'd hardly even seem to remember Cammy even existed.

As soon as Cammy pulled into the driveway of the small house she shared with her mother, Charlotte bolted from the house, wearing old, worn sweatpants and an oversized t-shirt. "C'mon, Cammy!" she waived her in. "We got to hurry. We got work to do, girl!" Charlotte's eyes were lit up like ornaments on a Christmas tree. She suddenly looked ten years younger, and had more energy than Cammy had ever seen her mother have. Cammy carried both bags up the flight of stairs.

"We got to clean up! I've cleared out most of the stuff in your room. Threw some of that shit in the garbage."

"Momma?"

"Me and you can sleep in my room, and the girls can have yours," she said excitedly, practically shoving Cammy into the house.

"But I—"

"I got them sheets in the wash. You can iron them tomorrow. And I want you to scrub that bathroom floor good, Cammy. Smells like piss in there. Get you some bleach and scrub hard, until you can see your pretty face in it."

Chapter 5

nterstate 70 was a wave, and Charlotte left all her cares on the highway behind her and never looked back. She'd known Black Sam for three months, and he'd cast a magic spell on her unlike any she'd ever known, and she felt like a girl again, off on a new adventure with the freedom to start over from scratch and live her life the way she'd always dreamed.

The first time Charlotte left home, she wasn't even fifteen yet, but she wasn't afraid back then, like she wasn't afraid now of what might be waiting for her out here in the open. She'd been talking for hours, and whether or not Sam was listening didn't matter. Charlotte needed to hear herself recap her life journey to make sense of it in her head, and because she was so excited, talking calmed her nerves.

"I thought Dwayne was the one back then," she said introspectively, staring ahead at the sunrise. Dwayne Jordan was her first love—lover. "He was tall, lanky, kind of dark. He was twenty-five, and he had long skinny fingers and big feet," she chuckled. "You know what they say about a man with big hands and feet."

Sam sighed.

"Well, I'm here to bear witness that it ain't always true. But he was crazy about me, though. The first time he saw me, his eyes

damn near popped out of his head." Her voice trailed off, and Charlotte sat quietly reflecting on a time that seemed like it happened centuries ago.

She wore a pair of shorts and a halter top the day her mother, Glodean, brought Dwayne over. Charlotte was in the kitchen fixing supper for the rest of her brothers and sisters, whom she never gave a damn about. Glodean had too many kids, and Charlotte was the oldest.

"We having chicken again?" her little brother Anthony whined.

Charlotte glared at him. "If you don't shut the hell up, I'm gonna hit you upside the head with this spoon."

"Is that any way to talk to your little brother?"

Glodean never went too long without a man. This one was new, and Charlotte ignored him like she did the rest of them.

"You must be Charlene," Dwayne asked, insisting on trying to get her to make conversation.

Her little sister Karen snickered.

Charlotte finally turned around, and he stood there looking at her like she was a piece of that chicken. She put her hand on her hip and cut her eyes at him. "My name is Charlotte," she said flippantly.

His eyes traveled from her toes to the top of her head, and he winked. "Yes, ma'am."

It wasn't hard. To this day, she never quite figured out why she did it, or what she even saw in him except to have the satisfaction of knowing she could pull Glodean's man.

"Damn, girl!" he said, exasperated, zipping his pants. "Where'd you learn how to do it like that?" Glodean and the kids had gone to Grandmommy's, and Charlotte stayed home, saying she was sick. Dwayne snuck over the way he always did, and they did the same thing they always did, and he said the same thing he always said.

"I learn as I go along, Dwayne," Charlotte responded, staring at her reflection in the mirror and smoothing back her hair.

It was the truth. She'd let boys feel on her and kiss her every now and then, but Dwayne was the first one she'd let put it in all the way. It was something she needed to do, to get it out of the way. He just happened to come along at the right time. Lucky for him.

Of course she got pregnant. Her dumb ass didn't know shit about birth control, and he was too hot for what was in her pants to even think about it.

"Thinking about your kids?" Sam asked, interrupting her thoughts.

Charlotte folded her arms, cleared her throat and lied. "Yeah. I miss them already."

Before they left town, she'd told him her mother was coming to get her kids, but Charlotte hadn't seen or spoken to her mother in years. Those kids would be all right, though. She told herself that like she really cared. She expected to feel more, to worry, or to change her mind four hundred miles ago, but she didn't feel any-thing one way or another, and she wished Sam would stop bringing them up. They were big girls now, especially Connie, and she'd take care of Reesy better than Charlotte ever could. Connie was respon-sible and sensible like that. Even at twelve, she was a grown woman in a child's body.

There was no turning back for her now. Charlotte would die back in Denver, Colorado. She'd grow old too fast, shrivel up, and never know what it was to really live. She was too young for that, and she'd never let what happened to Glodean happen to her. Her mother grew old too fast, too, with nothing except a houseful of kids to show for it, and a man who didn't want her anymore, because she was fat, and dumb, and drank too damn much. She still lived in the apartment Charlotte grew up in, filled with roaches and smelling *like piss. Charlotte sighed deeply, and reached over to take Sam's hand in hers.*

"Once we get settled, maybe you can send for 'em. Once we get to Memphis and get our own place."

Charlotte smiled and put his hand to her cheek. "Sure, Sammy," she purred. "Whatever you say."

Didn't nobody slow-drag like Sam Turner slow-dragged. Charlotte leaned against his broad, hard chest, lulled into a trance, dreaming even though she was wide awake. He cocooned her, wrapped all of his body around hers, until all you could see was him. And that's just how she liked it, too, praying that not even God could break the seal between them.

"Where my sugah at, girl?" he asked in that low, deep voice of his.

Charlotte raised her lips to his, married them, and swished her tongue between his full, moist lips.

Sam bent at the knees, grinding his hard-on between her thighs, showing her how much he appreciated that kiss.

"I want it, Sammy," she whispered sensuously. "I want it bad."

"Oh, it's yours, baby. Got your fuckin' name written all over it."

Charlotte chuckled. "Just like you got your name written all over this pussy, too."

Sam sucked in his teeth and lunged into her again. "Damn! I can't wait to get you back to the room."

"I got some peoples I wanna holla at in Kansas City," he explained, taking a detour. "We gone park it there for a minute, then head on down South."

They'd been in town nearly a week now, and Charlotte was as in love with this city as she was with Sam, filled with an unexpected Southern charm, with plenty of places to party. A bluesy, funky, soul-stirring atmosphere left her feeling high all the time, and Charlotte didn't care if she ever saw Memphis.

"Disco?" Cigarette smoke permeated the room, the Isley Brothers spun on the record player from the DJ booth, and Charlotte sat comfortably on her man's lap, sipping a gin and tonic and loving every minute of her newfound freedom. "Fuck disco!" Sam shouted to two other couples sitting at the table with them in the club.

"Disco is hot, man!" one of the women shouted back, with her drunk self, sloshing her drink around in her hand. "You heard that Donna Summer?" The woman closed her eyes, threw her head back, snapped her fingers, and started singing. "I-I-I-I love to love you baby! I-I-I-I love to love you baby!"

"I like that song," Charlotte said, avoiding Sam's grimace.

"That song is bad, girl! And so is disco!" Sam shook his head adamantly. "The Temptations is bad! Curtis Mayfield is bad. Them boys over there spinning on that record player is bad as hell, and ain't none of them mothafuckas singing no goddamned disco!"

They argued. Charlotte laughed and drank, and wondered what in the world took her so long to come to Kansas City.

"You doing all right, baby?" Sam gazed lazily into her eyes.

Charlotte sighed, slipped her tongue in between his full, black lips, and drank in the juices of Sam. "Fine as wine, Sammy. Feeling better than I've ever felt before in my life." She was free as a bird. Lord! It felt good to be free like this.

He squeezed a handful of her behind and moaned. "That's what I like to hear."

All of a sudden, Charlotte threw her head back and yelled, "Aw, shit! They playing my song, Sammy." Anything by Al Green was her song. She jumped up off Sam's lap and tugged at his sleeve. "C'mon, let's dance."

"I'm in the middle of talking here, girl."

She pouted. "Please, Sam. I got to dance to this."

Sam just laughed, shook his head, and pulled his arm away. "Then go 'head and dance with your drunk ass, baby."

Charlotte was drunk, and she'd wandered off from the sanctity of Sam's lap and onto the dance floor by herself.

Lovin you whether, whether
Times are good or bad, happy or sad

Every now and then, she glanced over at Sam, watching him watching her, and Charlotte mouthed the words, singing them to him, because Sam was the only thing she'd ever needed in the world. It took running away with him for her to truly see that.

Charlotte took another sip from her glass, raised it in the air to toast him, and spun her back to Sam. He loved her ass. She felt him watching her, knowing full well she belonged to him, and when they got back to the room, she'd hand it over to him without reservation or hesitation. Even the thought of Sam's dick sent shivers up and down her spine. Charlotte was ready to fuck. When she turned around to Sam, she could see in his eyes that he was, too.

When Uncle walked into a room, people couldn't help but notice. He had a penchant for traveling with an entourage, all of them decked out in double-breasted business suits and fedoras. Tonight, Uncle looked particularly dashing in burgundy, with his pearl-handled, hand-carved mahogany walking stick and two-toned Stacey Adamses. He took his usual spot, reserved for him in the back corner of the room, and a waitress quickly made her way *over to him to take their orders before they'd even finished sitting down.*

This wasn't one of Uncle's clubs. Sam wouldn't be here if this was Uncle's place, and he damn sure needed to leave now. He turned his head, finished what was left in his glass, and searched the dance floor for Charlotte, who'd all of a sudden been swallowed up in the crowd. He dried the palms of his sweaty hands, wiping them on his pants, hoping that he'd seen Uncle before Uncle had seen him.

The cocktail waitress suddenly appeared out of nowhere and sat a drink down in front of Sam. "Uncle says hello," was all she said.

Sam nervously looked across the room at him and nodded. It was too late. Uncle had seen him. He picked up his drink and made his way over to the man's table. Sam's heart beat like a scared rabbit's. He owed Uncle money. And the dumbest thing he could've done was leave town, owing a man like Uncle anything.

"H-h-how you doing, Uncle?" he said, pissed at himself for stammering like that, and sounding as scared as he was.

Uncle smiled, his gold tooth shimmering even in the dark. He nodded. "Question is, how you doing, son?"

Uncle wasn't a gangster. He was a businessman. His business was good times. He owned nightclubs, pool halls, hos, drugs, and guns if somebody absolutely had to have one. Sam had spent a few months working for him. At one time he'd donned a business suit and fedora, and traveled in Uncle's pack until it was time to leave. That's when Sam took off, without a word to Uncle or anybody, and he just so happened to have a couple of Uncle's bills in his pocket when he left.

Sam shrugged nervously. "I been meaning to get with you," he said, hoping to sound convincing. "I believe I owe you some money." There. He'd said it. Proving to Uncle that he had every intention of paying him back. "In fact, that's why I came back," he lied.

Uncle nodded to one of his associates to get up and let Sam have his seat, right next to Uncle. Sam understood, and quickly sat down. Uncle didn't look at him. He stared straight ahead at the dance floor, eyeing that pretty little taste of honey, swirling around on it, he'd never seen before.

"You got my change?"

Sam gulped down what was left in his glass quickly. "I ain't got all of it."

Uncle glanced at him out of the corner of his eye, then turned his attention back out onto the dance floor.

"But I can get it, Uncle." Sweat beaded up on the bridge of his nose and on his forehead. "If you give me a few days, I can get it. All of it."

Uncle didn't say a word. He just nodded his head to the rhythm of the music.

"I'm sorry I took off the way I did, Uncle," Sam said. "I got a brother back in Colorado, and he was having some problems. He needed me to come out there and help him out." It was a lie, one he'd come up with on the way into Kansas City, just in case he should run across somebody who knew Uncle. Uncle was big on family, and he had a brother of his own he was close to. "He was in some serious trouble, Uncle, man. And all I knew was that I had to be there for him. So I didn't think, man. I didn't think. I just," Sam slapped his hands together, "took off! My brother needed me. So, that's what I did."

"With my five hundred dollars?"

Sam shrugged. "I didn't know I had it." He could hear how ridiculous it sounded even as he said it, and he wished he could take it back. "It was in my pocket, Uncle. I remember that I was supposed to make a drop to you, but he called before I could and—"

"Who's that?" Uncle nodded in the direction of the fine woman, coming toward them with her pretty self.

Charlotte smiled when she spotted Sam. "I've been looking all over for you." She squeezed in between Sam and the table and found her familiar spot on his lap.

"Charlotte, honey."

Honey, Uncle thought, staring at her. That name suited her. Golden like honey and sure enough, just as sweet. He licked his lips at the thought and smiled.

"This is somebody I used to work for," Sam nervously cleared his throat. "This is Uncle."

Charlotte looked at the man and laughed. "Uncle? You're Sammy's uncle?"

Uncle just smiled.

"No, baby. That's his name. Uncle."

Oh, this one was too damn precious for her own good, and Uncle realized that he'd fallen in love at first sight for the first time in his whole goddamned life.

She reached out to shake his hand, and he held it in his. "Well, it's nice to meet you—Uncle. I'm Charlotte. Sam's girlfriend."

Charlotte never noticed the look exchanged between the two men. It was an unspoken pact that was worth five hundred dollars, and some vital part of Sam's body. It broke his heart, but hell, a broken heart he could live with. Two broken legs would hurt like hell.

"Don't street her, Uncle," Sam begged him out of earshot of Charlotte before the two of them left. "Just don't turn her out."

"Got too many hos already, brotha. You let me worry 'bout what I'm gonna do with her."

"You know how I like it done, Daddy." Charlotte spread her thick thighs, inviting him in. "Give it to me, deep, Sammy!" She pushed

her finger into her hole, fucking herself before he even got his clothes off. "Hurry, baby! I'm hot to trot, Sammy!" Charlotte laughed.

Sam stood over her, admiring the sex laid out in front of him, his hands in his pockets, his hard-on straining against his zipper. He leaned down close to her pussy, closed his eyes, and inhaled.

Sam slowly unzipped his pants, letting his dick spring out in the open. Charlotte sucked in her breath at the sight of it, lifting one hand to her breast and squeezing an already erect nipple between her fingers. "I want it bad," she whispered. Charlotte reached out to him and grabbed a handful of his shirt. "Come on! Come on, now!" She pulled him down on top of her, wrapped her legs around him, and locked them at the ankles. Sam stuck out his tongue and flicked it against her lips, until she caught it and sucked it into her mouth.

He reached his hand in the small space between him and her thighs, and aimed the tip of his dick to her hot spot, then slid it all the way in, to the base, in one smooth stroke.

Charlotte moaned, then threw her head back and gasped. "Oh, yessssss!"

This was how he liked her, hot and ready to fuck all night. Sammy knew that this would be the last taste of her he'd ever get, and he was going to savor every last drop.

Chapter 6

"lex! J.J.! Hurry up! You're going to miss the bus!" Reesy dropped small bags of chips into brown paper bags and sat them on the counter.

"Can't you give us a ride, Mom?" Alex, asked, grabbing his lunch. J.J. shadowed his brother as usual.

"Yeah. Can't you give us a ride?"

"Not when there's a perfectly good bus about to pull up in front of the house, headed in your direction." She gave J.J. a quick peck on the head. "Jade!" she called out. "You'd better be getting your little behind dressed! We've got fifteen minutes!"

"Jade always gets a ride," Alex muttered, grabbing his lunch.

He was just about to leave when Reesy blocked his path, propping a hand on her hip and curling her lip. "You want to go to back to third grade, Alex? Because if you do, I'm sure we can arrange something."

"No," he almost rolled his eyes.

"No—what?" Reesy waited, patiently.

"No, ma'am."

She kissed him, too, then shooed her sons out the door, barely responding to the kiss grazing her cheek from Justin.

"Morning," he said absently.

41

"Jade?" Reesy pushed past him and rushed upstairs to her daughter's room, expecting to see her putting on her clothes, but instead, Jade sat on the side of her bed, still in her pajamas. "Jade?"

Jade looked up at her with sad eyes. "I don't feel so good, Mommy. I think I got a fever." She pressed her hand to her head to check. "I should go back to bed."

Reesy came over to her and felt Jade's head herself. "Nope. Sorry, Miss Thang. No fever."

Jade looked disappointed, and Reesy understood what was really going on. She sat down on the bed next to her daughter and pulled her onto her lap. The adults in this child's life had made such a mess of things, and now Jade was caught in the middle, and the poor thing was so confused. Reesy blamed Connie for the stresses she'd put on this child, and everybody else, for that matter.

Connie had come to Reesy and Justin about the baby before she was even born, practically begging them to take this little girl and raise her—temporarily, she told them. "I've tried to convince myself that I can do this, Reese, but—I'm not ready. Not yet. I'm terrified that I won't be good enough, or that I won't get it right."

Justin squeezed Reesy's hand in his, but sat quietly beside her. "There is no real right when it comes to raising children, Connie. You just have to love them, and that'll make you want to do your best in raising them. That's all any of us, as parents, can do. And that's natural to be afraid. I was terrified before I had my first baby."

Connie was reluctant from the start of her pregnancy, and the whole time she carried Jade, Clarice never saw her rub her stomach or get excited when the baby moved. She never made plans or even came up with a name, as far as Reesy could tell. In retrospect, even back then, Reesy had her doubts that Connie would see parenthood through to the end.

"That's not it." Connie sounded so rational and solemn. "This baby needs what I can't give it. It needs stability and family."

"You can keep your baby and still have family, too, Connie. We're all here for you. You should know that." Reesy resented Connie putting them in this situation. They had two kids of their own to raise.

Connie stared intently at her. "Clarice, I'm not ready. I wish I was. There's something missing in me that I can't put my finger on, and I don't want to subject my baby to somebody who's not all there."

Reesy and Justin stayed up most of the night discussing it. They finally agreed to take the baby after it was born, just until Connie could get right with herself. It was a day that came too late, and without meaning to, Connie had become Jade's aunt, and Reesy was her mother. It worked out fine until John came into Connie's life. All of a sudden, Connie had that missing piece of the puzzle in him, and she decided to step up and be Mommy. No matter how many ways Connie tried to rationalize it, her reasoning fell on deaf ears with Reesy, leaving her to be the one who had to try and put the pieces together for this little girl, eight years later.

Reesy found Jade's favorite seafoam-green sweater, jeans, and a pair of socks, and started to dress Jade herself.

"You got something to say to me?" she asked, slipping a t-shirt over her daughter's head.

Jade shook her head sadly.

"Because you know, you mean the world to Mommy. At least, you should know that, and I shouldn't have to remind you." Reesy was careful with how she spoke, offering reassurance to her baby that nothing in the world would ever break the bond between them or separate them from each other.

"Are you mad at Aunt Connie?" she asked, finally.

Reesy smiled. Yes. She was very angry at Aunt Connie. She was mad as hell at Aunt Connie for opening her big mouth when she should've known better.

"She should know, Reesy!" Connie said at the top of her lungs, standing in the middle of Reesy's kitchen. "She's going to find out sooner or later! And *we* need to tell her! We need to sit down and tell that little girl that—"

"You need to get over yourself, Connie," she said coldly. "She's my daughter. Not yours! You and I decided that a long time ago, together! Or did you somehow lose your memory between now and then, and forget that your ass was too selfish to take care of a baby?"

"I'm getting sick and tired of you throwing that shit up in my face all the time."

"I know what this is about, Connie. I'm not stupid. Ever since you met John—"

"This has nothing to do with him!"

"You get a damn man in your life who sticks around long enough to pay a few bills and makes some half-assed commitment, and all of a sudden you feel like you've got a family and decide it's time to close the deal using my baby!"

"She's my baby, too, Reesy! I gave birth to that little girl! Not you!"

"Yeah, and you haven't spent one day lifting a finger to be a mother to her, Connie. Now all of a sudden—"

The color flushed from Reesy's face, and her gaze fixed on

the doorway between the kitchen and the family room, where small, confused eyes stared back at both of them.

"You need to go, Connie," Reesy said quietly, never taking her eyes off Jade. Connie stood there, defiant, and ready to split that child in two, using her own selfish reasons as the sword.

"No, Reesy," she said, angrily. "Not now. I'm here and we need to deal with this."

All of a sudden, Reesy's eyes blazed red and locked on Connie. "Get the hell out of my house, Connie, or I swear to God—" Her voice quivered. "Justin!" she called to her husband coming down the stairs.

"Reesy." Connie pleaded with her eyes. "Don't do this."

"Justin! Connie needs you to come walk her to her car."

She hurried past Connie, over to where Jade was standing and starting to cry, and scooped her up in her arms. "Justin!"

She and Connie hadn't seen or said two words to each other in over a month.

Reesy finished dressing Jade. "There. Now, don't you look pretty today."

Jade didn't smile the way she normally did. "Can we go see Aunt Connie, Mommy? Can we go to her house?"

"We'll go soon, baby. In fact, Mommy's going over there real soon—to talk to Aunt Connie about something."

Jade's eyes lit up. "About me?"

Reesy's biggest fear was starting to take shape. Connie had planted a seed in Jade, one that was threatening to take root, one that would blossom into doubt and confusion in this child. Somehow, some way, Reesy needed to squash it before it was too late. She was certain that Jade hadn't really understood the magnitude of what she'd heard, and that she wasn't quite sure of what she'd heard, or how to make sense of it. It was that confusion Reesy would be forced to use to keep the truth at bay, for a little while longer, at least, until Jade was old enough to better understand the situation. Right now, she was just too young.

She dropped her daughter off at school, then turned her thoughts to Charlotte, and more importantly, telling Connie about Charlotte. Connie needed to know, and she and Reesy needed to put their differences aside, go to Kansas, find their mother, and finally confront her about why she abandoned them.

Chapter 7

Charlotte held Cammy's hand as she led her into the living room.

"Momma, it's three in the morning," Cammy complained.

Charlotte motioned for her to sit on the couch while she knelt down on the floor at the coffee table. She'd spread both pages of Reesy's letter flat in front of her, then smoothed her hand across a clean notepad of paper, with a freshly sharpened pencil perfectly aligned next to it.

"It needs to be perfect, Cammy," Charlotte said introspectively, almost as if Cammy weren't in the room. Charlotte petted the paper like she would a dog or a cat. "I have a chance to make it right," she smiled. "I can fix this, baby. And make it like it was."

Charlotte didn't look like herself. Cammy stared at her mother, trying to make sense of her expression and her tone. All Cammy had ever known about her family was sitting on the floor in front of her. Charlotte doled out bits and pieces about "her girls" to Cammy, but never enough to complete the full picture. What were they like? Why did she leave Denver?

"Glodean took my babies and never gave them back," was all Charlotte would say as to why she didn't have them anymore.

But even if she did take them, how come Charlotte didn't go after her children and make the woman give them back? How come she left town altogether, instead of staying, and waiting for them to get old enough to come to her on their own?

"Help Momma say the right thing, Cammy." Charlotte smiled weakly at Cammy. "What should I tell my baby girl?"

Reesy was her baby girl, and what did that make Cammy?

"What's in your heart, Momma?" Cammy asked quietly. "Tell her what's in your heart."

Charlotte sat quietly for a few moments before finally responding. "Love." She held tears in her eyes. Charlotte laughed out loud, and her large body nearly toppled over backwards as she clasped her hands to her mouth. "Love, Cammy! More love than I've ever felt in my entire life."

Cammy winced.

"I have never loved anybody the way I loved my baby Clarice. I have never wanted anything more than I wanted her."

Charlotte was lost in an emotional haze and it was almost if she'd forgotten that it was Cammy she was speaking to. Or maybe, Cammy thought woefully, maybe she hadn't forgotten about Cammy at all. She knew what she was saying. Charlotte just didn't mind saying those things to Cammy. After all, she wasn't Reesy.

Charlotte started writing in big, cursive letters. She spoke out loud as she did. "I love you, Reesy. Momma always has." She wrote other things, filling half the page before finally stopping again and smiling at Cammy. "You are such a help to me, little girl. I don't know what I'd ever do if I didn't have you."

An hour later, Cammy finally crawled back into bed. There'd been a time when her feelings would've been hurt so bad, she'd have cried herself to sleep. But not anymore. Cammy loved her mother more than life, but she understood her role in Charlotte's world. Charlotte was the child sometimes, and Cammy was the one responsible for taking care of her.

Charlotte watched the sun come up. The postman would be here soon, and her letter was sealed and ready to be sent to Clarice Braxton, her sweet child, all grown up now, a married woman with her own kids. Charlotte smiled proudly.

"I'm a grandmomma," she whispered.

"Get the hell outta my house, heffa!" Glodean dragged fifteen-year-old Charlotte across the room by her wrists toward the front door. "You ain't nothing but a whore! A dirty, nasty little whore!"

Charlotte kicked and screamed until her mother literally threw her out into the hallway with some of her clothes, and slammed the door shut behind her.

Charlotte sat there for what seemed like hours, but was only a few minutes. Glodean was a fat-ass pig with too many kids. Charlotte didn't like kids, and after she had this one, she wasn't having no more.

"You coming?" Dwayne stood at the bottom of the staircase, staring up at her, smoking a cigarette. "I got to get to work."

Chapter 8

$\mathcal{I}$ dream about my mother all the time." The most intimate moments between Connie and John were in the dark, lying in bed, after making love. His childhood hadn't been any better than hers, filled with lies and deception and nightmares of a woman he'd never even met. Connie thought back to a night from their past, when John finally started to open up to her, peel off his I-don't-give-a-damn exterior, and show her just how deep the pain really was. Light from the streetlamp outside filtered into the bedroom. He held her hand in his and spoke quietly about his past. "I never met her. She died having me. But I heard stories."

"What kind of stories?" Connie probed quietly.

He wasn't comfortable telling her his fears. John King was a big man, strong, tough. On the surface, he had no weaknesses, but he had plenty of them inside, insecurities and doubts that had driven him away from his grandmother's house at fifteen and back and forth across the country ever since. He ran from them, but he'd never admit that that was what he was doing. But they were always on his heels, and he carried the guilt of his mother Mattie's death with him like luggage.

"Fool raped that girl." He repeated the phrase the way he'd

been hearing it all his life. "No one ever said it to me, but they whispered it around me, like I wasn't smart enough to make sense of what they were talking about." Fool was a mentally retarded man, much older than Mattie, and John's biological father. "I never met him, either, but I look just like him, which was fucked-up, especially as a kid, because that's who my grandmother saw every time she looked at me. She saw the crazy man who raped her fourteen-year-old daughter, and since she couldn't hate him, she hated me, and blamed me for Mattie's dying."

"No, John," Connie had to reassure him. "No, you were just a kid. C'mon, baby. How could she blame you for something like that?"

For the first time since he'd started talking, John looked Connie in the eyes. "I blame me, Connie," he said solemnly. "I'm an extension of him, and I blame me. So why shouldn't she?"

The dreams he had of his mother were violent, bloody, and always ended with him waking up with a start, sweating and trying to catch his breath. Guilt drove those dreams, and the stories he'd heard growing up as a child about the monster who tortured his mother. He was an extension of that monster, and in his dreams the demon that chased after that little girl was as much John as it was his father, Fool.

The truth has a way of coming to light, though, and a year and a half ago, John had learned the truth about his parents. He followed the trail of his past back down to Bueller, Texas, and tracked down the man known as Fool. His real name was Adam, and what he found out changed him forever, and stopped the nightmares.

"Can you believe that shit?" he told Connie after he came

back from Texas. "She loved him, Connie. I mean, she dug him. My father pulled this little piece of paper from his wallet, and it had hearts and shit all over it, and she told him she'd marry him. It was still fucked-up. The girl was only fourteen, but when I met him—when I met Adam—Connie, he's a grown-ass man, but he's nowhere near as old as fourteen in the head. Know what I mean? He's a kid. And in some ways, I can see him being even more of a kid than she was."

John reconciled with his past, but in so many ways the disconnect was still there, just like it was for her, and just like it would probably always be. Connie wanted to bridge hers, though, and maybe having this baby would force her to have to do that, instead of falling prey to excuses that she couldn't be a mother because of how she grew up. Other women did it every day, and other women probably had stories like hers to tell, too, but they'd overcome their histories, and moved on. Now it was her turn, and his, too.

They'd tiptoed around each other for three days, hardly saying a word to each other. When she called him from the abortion clinic the other day and told him she was pregnant, the best response he could muster was "Oh," and after waiting about twenty seconds for him to elaborate on that with a "Baby that's fanastic! I'm the luckiest man in the world!" kind of reaction, Connie hung up the phone and neither of them had mentioned it since.

He came into the kitchen fully dressed for work, grabbed some bacon wrapped in a biscuit, took a soda from the refrigerator, then picked up his keys and headed for the door.

"John," she blurted out, with no idea whatsoever what she

wanted to say. But Connie needed to say something, and John needed to say something, and a dialog needed to finally take place.

He stopped, turned to look at her, then took a bite of his sandwich. "Yeah."

Her heart beat so fast, she felt like she'd been running a race. Connie stared desperately at him, hoping he could instinctively know the answers to the questions she didn't even know how to ask.

"I gotta go, babe," he said, taking another bite. "Or traffic's gonna get me."

Connie walked over to him. She tightened the belt of her robe, then wrapped her arms around herself and took a deep breath. "What about the baby, John? What do you think about the baby?"

John stared at her, unblinking. "I don't know, Connie," he said nonchalantly. "What do I think about the baby?"

Irritation rose inside her. "What's that supposed to mean? Do you want this baby or not?"

He threw his hands up exasperatedly. "What difference does it make? You've made up both our minds, so—what? What do you want me to say?"

Tears welled in her eyes, as reality started to get a good, strong, firm hold, and take root. "That you want it, too."

He took a deep breath, but the words never came.

"Oh . . . God, John!" Connnie spun around and finally landed on the sofa. Tears streamed down her cheeks, and she could hardly catch her breath. Of course this wasn't a surprise. The two of them were such disjointed individuals that there was no way he would want this child, and there was no reason for her to want it, either. But Connie did want this child. She wanted it more than she'd ever wanted anything because it was a part of him, the man she loved more than she ever thought she could love anyone. "Why?" she wailed. "Why don't you want it?"

John waved her off and headed for the door again. "I'm gonna be late."

"John!" she called after him. Suddenly Connie was faced with a choice. She was faced with the inevitable. If he didn't leave now, he'd leave eventually, and Lord! She was so tired of hanging on to him by the skin of her teeth. John had been an uncertainty ever since he came into her life, and Connie didn't have the strength anymore to balance on that high wire. She'd made up her mind to keep this baby, and she wasn't going to turn back this time. Connie ached from all the other times she had, and if she gave up this baby, it would kill her for good inside.

"Don't come back," her voice quivered. Connie couldn't believe what she was saying, and from the look on his face, he couldn't believe it, either. "I can't do this!" she sobbed uncontrollably. "I can't."

"You mean that?"

No. And yes. "If you don't want this baby—" Her voice trailed off.

John hesitated for a moment, caught off guard by what she'd just said. He never did do well with ultimatums or being backed into a corner. He loved Connie, but right here, right now, it didn't seem like that was enough. Shit, love was anything but enough. "I'll come back for my shit later on," he said on his way out, closing the door quietly behind him.

Chapter 9

Reesy cringed as she pulled her car up to the curb outside Connie's renovated Victorian home in Denver's Five Points. She loved her sister, but truthfully, she loved her daughter more, and there was nothing Reesy wouldn't do for that little girl, including protecting her from the woman who'd actually given birth to her. Connie had issues she would never overcome, and Reesy hated knowing the kind of life her older sister had been forced to live after Charlotte had abandoned them. But she wasn't responsible for Connie's happiness. Connie had lived through molestation and prostitution and homelessness, and that was the only thing that mattered as far as Reesy was concerned. She had *lived.* Connie had survived the worst kind of life any kid could imagine, and she'd come through all on her own. But instead of celebrating that victory and being the hero she should've been, Connie insisted on being the martyr and wallowing in self-loathing and guilt, and Reesy would be damned if she'd allow that woman the opportunity to infect her child with crap like that.

She'd been calling Connie for days with the news about Charlotte, but Connie hadn't been answering her phone. She'd called the boutique where she worked, but she hadn't been to

work, either. And her cell phone wasn't even on. Reesy apprehensively approached the house, in awe that Connie would
want to live in this part of town. Every terrible thing that had
happened to her as a child had happened here or not far from
here, and still she insisted on living in this place, a constant reminder of the hell she endured growing up. And worse yet,
she'd chosen to share it with a buffoon. Reesy despised John,
maybe because Connie loved him so much. But from what
Reesy could see, there wasn't much to love, and he was just another contrivance Connie used to remind herself that she was
unworthy of anything better.

The house was dark except for a few lit candles on the coffee
table. Connie was curled up on the sofa, turning her back to
Reesy who sat in a chair across from her. Reesy didn't even
bother to take off her coat.

Connie was sulking, obviously depressed about something.
How many times had Reesy suggested counseling to her sister,
or even that she might need medication? But Connie consis-
tently refused, insisting that she was cool and that whatever was
bothering her was no big deal. But then, that was Connie, pent
up, closed off, and distant. Reesy searched the dark apartment.
"Is John here?" Reesy asked, hoping that he wasn't.

Even after two years of knowing the man, she still couldn't
stand him. What Connie saw in him was a mystery to Reesy, but
then again, there were a lot of things about Connie Reesy didn't
get.

"Mind if I turn on a light, Connie?" Reesy started to get up.

"Yes." Connie stopped her with that one word, and never
even glanced in Reesy's direction. "I do mind."

Reesy stayed put. Obviously something was going on here.
John wasn't home, and Connie was sitting up in the dark like a

mole rat. It didn't take Reesy long to figure out that whatever was going on had little to do with her.

"Is everything all right, Connie?" she asked, genuinely trying to sound concerned. "Is everything all right between you and John?"

Connie sighed, exasperated, and finally turned to face her sister. "What do you want, Reesy?"

Of course, Reesy didn't appreciate her tone, but she swallowed her pride and made a valiant effort to keep her cool. "I tried calling, but—"

The two of them were as different as night and day. Connie was natural hair, sarongs or jeans, saucer-sized silver hoop earrings. She was eclectic and urban and a good twenty-five pounds lighter than her younger sister. Reesy, on the other hand, lived for the suburbs and soccer games with her kids, and preferred her hair bone-straight and pulled into a ponytail. Reesy was a homemaker, and loved it. Connie designed expensive one-of-a-kind jewelry, and she was an artist. If they weren't sisters, though, chances were pretty good that they probably wouldn't even be friends.

Connie turned away and shook her head. Reesy had a knack for adding insult to injury. She had no idea what was going on in Connie's life, but instinctively, she knew when to come around and dump some more bullshit on top of the situation. Sometimes Connie wondered if being reunited with her sister really was a good idea.

If Reesy was here to complain, fuss, or condemn some more, she was really wasting her time. Connie had made a terrible mistake and she knew it already. She'd let Reesy's attitude get under her skin, and Jade had paid dearly for it.

"You're not better than me, Reese!" Connie had spent the

last eight years trying not to rock the boat where that child was concerned, but the older Jade got, and every year that passed, she saw her chances of ever being more than Aunt Connie slip through her fingers, and sometimes she panicked.

"I never said I was!" Reesy spat back. "But I'm better for Jade as a mother than you are, Connie, and I won't apologize for that."

Of course she was. And Connie hadn't ever really planned on taking Jade away from the only home she'd ever known. Lord! She just wanted her to know. She wanted the world to know that someone that sweet and that special and lovable had come from her. That's all. She wanted to be able to pat herself on the back and know that she was capable of producing someone so special. That's all she wanted. Reesy's words had cut deep, though, and they rang so true. But Connie made that monumental confession in front of that little girl and Connie's heart broke when she saw the confusion and sadness in her little face. She would never forgive herself for that.

"I found Momma, Connie," Reesy said softly. Almost too softly, and Connie wasn't sure she'd heard her correctly. She turned and looked at her sister. Reesy stared back. "I found Charlotte."

"Oh, for crying out loud," Connie muttered exasperatedly. She closed her eyes and gave in to the headache she'd been fighting off all day. The sound of Reesy's voice droned on and on about her private investigator, and something about a photograph and a letter. It was too much. On top of everything else, throwing Charlotte's sorry ass into the mix was more than Connie could handle. She bolted to her feet and paced back and forth in front of the coffee table. Connie had too many thoughts at once, and her head throbbed terribly. Babies, abortions, sorry-ass men. She had a platinum necklace and bracelet she needed to finish for a client who was less than patient. Adoption . . . Jade and how she'd never belong to Connie again. John would never come home . . . and Reesy . . . Reesy, goddammit!

"Connie—are you listening to me? Did you hear what I said? Momma lives in a town called Murphy, Kansas, halfway between Salina and Kansas City," she continued despite Connie's obvious agitation. "I wrote her a letter, Connie, and told her we were coming to see her."

"No!" Connie snapped angrily.

"Can I please turn on the light?" Reesy desperately wanted to see Connie's face. Because looking at Connie was like looking at Charlotte, and if she could just see her face, she'd know she hadn't dreamed that woman.

"No! You cannot turn on the fuckin' light, Reesy! This is my house! You came here to see me, and if I want to sit up in the dark in my own house, that's my goddamned business! You don't like it, then get the fuck out!" How dare Reesy come to her bringing this bullshit! "What makes you think I give a damn about ever seeing that woman again?" Connie glared at her sister.

"We need to see her, Connie! To confront her!"

"No!" Connie pointed at Reesy. "You need to see her sorry ass. I don't ever want to see that bitch again, and if you want to take your behind to fuckin' Kansas to see that heffa, then you go right ahead, but you go without me!"

Reesy wasn't listening. She fumbled through her purse and pulled out an envelope with Charlotte's picture in it. She held their mother's photograph up for Connie to see and made the mistake of getting too close. "This is her, Connie! This is our mother, and we need to—"

Connie grabbed Reesy by the collar of her coat and pushed

her back to the front door. "Charlotte can go to hell, Reesy! I don't ever want to see that woman again! She ain't shit to me! She ain't shit!"

Tears flooded Reesy's eyes and she wailed, "She's our mother, Connie! She's our . . ."

"She ain't shit, Reesy! She never was! Oh, God! How come you can't see? She left us! That bitch walked out on us and never—how come you can't . . ."

Reesy sobbed like a child, and Connie pulled her baby sister into her arms and held her tight. "She's nothing, baby! Charlotte's ass ain't shit to us!" Connie cried, too, and forgot all about how angry she was at Reesy. She forgot to feel sorry for herself, and all that mattered was protecting her baby sister.

Reesy wrapped her arms around Connie, and the two women slid slowly to the floor, into their twelve- and eight-year-old selves, crying into each other's shoulder, the way they'd done nearly thirty years ago.

"Shhhh," Connie whispered into her ear, rubbing Reesy's hair. "It's alright, Reesy. We'll be alright. I promise."

Chapter 10

ookie. That was what she called herself. And she was his guilty pleasure. Justin sifted between the tables and chairs, finding his usual spot in the back of the room, near the bar.

"What can I get you?" the cocktail waitress asked almost as soon as he sat down.

"Gin and tonic," what he always ordered.

Coming here was an obsession. Seeing her was a compulsion he couldn't let go of. He knew what nights she worked, what time she danced, and he knew that she'd look for him in that corner, and make her way over to him before he left for the night. For her, it was all about the money. For Justin, it was about the fantasy.

Everything in his life had always been ordered and disciplined. He was an accountant, and a soldier to numbers, facts, formulas, rules, and laws. He was a husband and father, responsible, dependable, and predictable. But with Cookie, and for just a few minutes of her time, Justin could allow himself to melt freely between the warmth of her thighs, in the pools of her eyes, and let himself go completely for a hundred-dollar bill, or two.

"You can't touch the girls, but they can touch you." A rule he didn't mind adhering to, and one he'd learned as soon as he walked through the door. Touching her would've ruined the fantasy of her, and it would've been cheating on Reesy. That's how he justified it. And it was ridiculous, but for the time being, it worked. And that was all that mattered.

She came out on stage, wearing white. Justin caught his breath and held it for a moment at the vision in front of him. The dress was full, flowing all the way down to the floor. Cookie looked like a debutante, beautiful and flawless, her long, wavy hair pulled back away from her face and pinned up, showing off her long, luxurious neck and soft, round, caramel-colored shoulders. Even from where he sat, there was no missing the rich chocolate brown of her eyes and the moist, full pout of her painted lips.

Justin adjusted his hard-on and leaned back, releasing an audible sigh. He glanced at the other men in the room, some of them looking noticeably bored at her entrance, others gawking as if in anticipation of what beautiful treats were waiting for them underneath that gown.

For a minute, he felt anxious, thinking of any of those fools putting their hands on her. But then he looked up at the stage and locked gazes with Cookie. She smiled and winked, and Justin suddenly relaxed and waited patiently for his Cookie to make time for him.

"You can't touch the girls . . . but . . ."

He never laid a hand on Cookie. The closest he'd ever come to touching her was to slip $300 into her g-string. He left it up to her to do the rest, in a private room—VIP, they called it, where the best kind of lap dances took place.

She handed him a condom and smiled. "How've you been, Justin?"

Justin was high on anticipation and adrenaline. God, she was beautiful, her brown skin glistening with glitter, long black hair spilling down her back, small, firm breasts brushing up against his lips.

"I'll be fine real soon, baby," he whispered.

In real life, women like Cookie never noticed men like Justin. Women like Cookie didn't see the way men like Justin watched them, too afraid to even entertain fantasies, knowing full well that even that would break his heart. But this wasn't real life. Was it? And in this world, a woman like Cookie wouldn't dare look past a man like him, because he was what she lived for.

She unzipped his pants and freed his dick from his underwear. "Ooooh." she rubbed her hand up and down his shaft. "Is all this for me, baby?"

He nodded anxiously and waited impatiently while she slipped a condom on him.

"I'm gonna work it over real good for you, baby," she said seductively, sliding her g-string over to the side and straddling his lap. "You let Cookie take care of you, and I promise, you won't regret it."

Warm sweet Cookie dough enveloped him, and Justin sat with his hands clasped together behind him, fighting every urge in his body to grab and hold her close to him. Cookie flicked erect, dime-size nipples in and out of his mouth while slowly rolling her thick, firm ass in his lap, and sucking his soul from him and into her. Justin's eyes rolled back in his head.

"Awwww, baby . . . ," he said, nearly crying. "Cookie . . . baby."

"Tell me this is some good, pussy, baby. Tell Cookie she got some sweet ass."

All he could do was nod. "Yes. Yesssss."

Sweet, hot juice ran down his balls. Justin imagined himself licking . . . licking and swallowing buckets of this woman, until he was full . . . until he was full enough to explode. "I'm coming, baby! I'm . . . Cookie! Baby!"

She didn't get up right away. He liked that about her. And sometimes she came, too. He liked that even more. But always, Cookie would put her lips to his, dip her tongue in between his lips to remind him again that he loved her, and that he'd have to come back no matter what.

"You come back and see me again, baby boy," she said, catching her breath. "Promise me?"

He looked into her eyes and nodded. "I'll be back, Cookie. You know I will."

On the drive home, he smelled her on him. It wouldn't be hard for Reesy to smell her too, but more and more, he didn't care. He wasn't a priority for his wife. Reesy had obsessions of her own and he wasn't one of them. It was late, and chances were she'd be asleep when he got home.

"You don't care, Justin. We both know you don't."

"That's not true, Reesy. I'm your husband. Of course I care, but I don't think you do. Not about us, anyway. Not about you and me."

"Do you hear yourself? Listen to what you're saying, honey. I've finally found my mother, the woman who left me and Connie sitting up in that apartment building all those years ago. Do you understand what that means? Can you possibly put aside your needs for one minute and comprehend the magnitude of what that means? It's overwhelming, Justin. It's mind-blowing, so forgive me if I'm not myself lately . . . if I'm a bit preoccupied because the woman who gave birth to me, who I thought might've been dead, is alive and well and living in the next state over."

He questioned himself sometimes. Maybe he was being self-ish. The impact of finding first her sister and now her mother was huge. But so was the affect it was having on their marriage. These days, he was an afterthought in Reesy's mind. Justin was a big boy; he could handle it—in the beginning. But lately, he'd become nothing more than the bread and butter, her own per-sonal Steppin Fetchit: "Justin, I need you to . . . Justin, can you please go . . . Justin, did you remember to . . . Not now, Justin. I'm in the middle of something. Not tonight, Justin. I'm worn out. No, Justin. I said no, Justin. Will you please leave me the hell alone?"

Never in a million years did he think he'd ever pay for sex. Justin pulled into his driveway and sighed. But for now, it was turning into one of the best investments he'd ever made.

Chapter 11

*L*eave it to instinct to kick in where reason failed him. She wanted him gone. The rest was easy. John occupied his mind with eight and a half hours of loading boxes onto a truck at the plant, and when his shift was over, he collected his last day's pay, pointed his car in the direction of Bueller, Texas, and never looked back. Connie knew what she was doing. She knew that if she ever put it out there like that, he'd take it and run with it. Sometimes he believed she knew him better than he knew his damn self.

Leaving now felt wrong all over, but it was also a relief. Settling down had always been easier said than done for a man like him, and settling down and having a kid was something he didn't want to know how to do. She'd pissed him off with this baby thing. Connie had made up her mind for both of them, and expected him to go along with it, when he knew this whole thing was wrong, for him and for her. But she was the one who kept her eyes open for miracles, hoping some magic shit might happen to change her into a creature like Reesy—perfect.

All of a sudden, Connie wanted a house, kids, a husband. Where'd that shit come from if it didn't come from Reesy? Even if she never said a word, John saw Connie trying to emulate her sister, wanting to step it up and walk on water. It wasn't happening, and she shouldn't want it to. Hell. He didn't. If he'd ever left any kids behind during his travels, he never knew he did, and that was fine with him. He was a coward, though, running away from a woman and a kid who wasn't even born yet, like he was running for his life.

Bueller had been the place he'd run away from back when he was that fifteen-year-old kid. He'd left because there was nothing there for him except bad memories and a dismal future. Things had changed, though, and he had family there. John had developed a relationship with his father, Adam, and he had to admit, spending time with the old man had gotten easier over time, and he cared for him. Adam didn't require a whole lot of work to be around. All John had to do was show up every now and then, sit with the old man, and listen to him sing off-key to Sam Cooke songs and talk about Mattie, the woman he still loved even though she'd been dead more than forty years. She was still alive to him, though, still young and beautiful, that dark-skinned girl who promised to marry him.

John dialed Moses' number on his cell phone. Moses was Adam's brother and he took care of him. Moses was good people. Mean as hell when he wanted to be, but good people. He was close to Moses, mainly because he wasn't mentally disabled, and he and John were alike in that they could give a shit about most things. Moses just instinctively seemed to understand him without John ever having to say a word. He dug that about him.

"Moses. This is John."

"Hey, boy. How you doin?"

John decided not to say how he was doing, because he had no idea. "Is he up?"

"Naw. He's sleep. Want me to wake him? You know he'd get up to talk to you."

"No, don't wake him. Just tell him I'm heading down to spend some time with him. Should be there in a few days."

"Sure, son. I'll tell him. Is everything all right? You bringin' your girl with you?"

He'd been promising to bring her down every time he went down there, as a matter of fact. But something always seemed to come up. "No. Not this time, man."

"Man, you need to bring her down here to meet your daddy. You know he keep asking 'bout her."

"I know. Maybe next time," he lied.

"All right, then. Well, I'll let him know you comin'."

"Night, Moses."

"Night."

All he wanted to do was to get back to the sanctuary of Bueller, Texas, and to get back to a retarded and crippled old man, and that old oak tree he liked to sit under near the river, talking about the first time he'd made love to a girl.

It was funny how life turned around sometimes. Years ago, he'd wanted nothing to do with the old man. Fool. Everybody called Adam that when he was younger. John would kill anyone who dared call him that now. He'd kill them with his bare hands.

Chapter 12

S
he looked afraid when she walked in. Lost and searching. The club was packed, but there was no sign of him. Uncle watched her from the corner of the room, smoking a cigar, sipping his signature Black Velvet. Sam had done his good deed and left town like he was supposed to, leaving Uncle a gift to make up for all the frustration he'd caused him.

That pretty girl wandered over to the bar and spoke to Leroy, the bartender, who just shook his head and shrugged that he didn't know nothing.

"You seen Sam?" Uncle imagined her asking in that sweet voice of hers, wrapping those pretty lips around his name.

Nobody knew where Sam was. No one had seen him scurrying his scared rat-ass out of town in the middle of the night, hoping and praying that Uncle wasn't hot on his trail, grateful that he would live to see another day. Uncle gazed up through the cloud of smoke as she made her way back toward where he was sitting, admiring her from the ground up: big, pretty legs; full, rolling hips; and small waist. Her titties were on the small side, snack-size. He grinned.

Charlotte hesitated when she saw him, and then approached him cautiously, trying to smile, and to hide the fact that she'd been *crying.* Don't cry over that sorry mothafucka, baby girl, *Uncle thought, squinting at her.* Uncle's gonna make you forget he was ever born.

"Hi," she said apprehensively, stopping at his table. He nodded. "You're a friend of Sam's, right?"

He squinted through smoke.

Charlotte shifted nervously from one leg to the other. "Have you seen him around tonight?"

He heard the quiver in her voice. Saw the desperation in her eyes, the uncertainty in her smile. This kitty was his for the taking. Her man had run out on her, left her stranded a million miles from home, and Uncle would be her savior. It was too easy.

"Naw," he said, blowing smoke in the air. "I ain't seen him."

Charlotte stood still for a moment, waiting and hoping for more. Sam had left the night before and she hadn't seen or heard from him since.

"Thank you," she said, on the verge of tears again, and then turned to leave.

Uncle watched her go. He could've stopped her, but now was not the time. Money would come due soon on that room she was staying in. She'd need to eat in a day or two. Loneliness would set in. Fear and panic would take over. And that's when he'd step in. Right when she needed him the most.

The room was a mess. Charlotte turned over the mattress, stripped the sheets from the bed, and pulled the drawers out from the nightstand and dresser looking for spare change. The motel manager told her she'd have to pay up or be out of this room by morning. Charlotte hadn't eaten anything but pork skins with hot sauce since yesterday, and she hadn't had a cigarette in days.

*"Fuckin' Sam, man!" she sobbed, desperate to find some money.
She needed to take her ass back to Denver, that's what she needed to
do. She should've never left in the first place. Charlotte had walked
away from everything for that man. She'd left her home, her
friends, and yes, Lord, her children, chasing after a dick that had
her seeing double. She'd done some dumb shit in her life, but nothing like this. Charlotte collapsed on the floor in the middle of the
room, on a heap of dirty clothes, desperately wondering what in
the world she was going to do now.*

*She'd walked the whole way, her feet throbbed and swelled in her
shoes, but what choice did she have? Finally, she made it to the bus
depot, waited in line, and then made her way to the clerk behind the
counter.*

"How much is a one-way ticket to Denver?"

*She looked a mess. Charlotte knew she did. The clerk looked at
her funny and told her, "Forty-five dollars."*

*Where in the world was she going to get forty-five dollars? She
left as defeated as she was when she walked in. Charlotte didn't
know a soul in Kansas City. Sam's friends were his friends, and she
never even bothered to remember their names when he introduced
her because after all, they were on their way to Memphis, and just
passing through.*

*Back in the room, she showered and then put her feet up until
the swelling went down. She'd thought long and hard enough to give
herself a headache, thinking of ways to get her hand on some
money. And every idea led back to the same inevitable conclusion.*

*Uncle pulled up just in time to see Charlotte stroll into Dante's.
It was all just a lucky coincidence, really. He owned Dante's like he
owned several clubs in the city, and it just so happened, as he was*

making his rounds tonight, Dante's was next on his list. He watched her go inside, then climbed out of his black Lincoln Mark IV and followed her. Charlotte wasn't hard to spot. She peeled off her coat and stood in the center of the room, looking absolutely luscious, wearing skintight jeans, high-heeled shoes, and a sleeveless halter top, out of season, and out of sight. Every male neck in the room snapped in her direction, and Uncle had to fight back the urge to laugh out loud at the whole Looney Tune-ish scene before him.

She had her hustle on tonight. Honey Pie was desperate for some action, and some sorry mothafucka was going to have to come up off some big bills to get some of that action.

"Hey, Uncle," Bruce, one of his bouncers, said, meeting him as soon as he walked in.

Uncle handed him his hat. "I'll be in back if you need me," he said, never taking his eyes off Little Bit strutting her stuff. "And let me know when she looks like she's 'bout to leave."

The bouncer nodded, and Uncle went upstairs to his office.

"Hey, baby." Some fool sashayed up to her and said, looking all down her blouse. "Can I buy you a drink?"

She was hungrier than she was thirsty, and Charlotte knew that drinking on an empty stomach wouldn't lead to anything but disaster all over this idiot's shoes. But she needed to play it cool, so she did. "Gimme a beer."

He guided her to the bar and sat down next to her as he ordered. "So." He looked as cheesy as he sounded. "What's a fine woman like you doing up in a place like this all by herself? Where your man at? I know you got one."

Charlotte looked around the room, then back to him. "Really? Well, if I got a man, where he at?"

Cheesy threw his had back and laughed. "That's all I need to know, girl!"

Charlotte let him whisper toxic promises in her ear, rest his hand on her thigh, and blow stale gin from his breath in her face while she pretended to laugh, and not look hungry, and hide the contempt she had for him and for herself, knowing what she'd be willing to do for him, if he had the money.

One of the waitresses walked past them carrying chicken wings and fries. Charlotte's mouth watered. "You know, I'm starting to get a little hungry," she said, rubbing her finger down his arm. "And that chicken smelled damn good."

He grinned, showing a space on the side of his mouth where a tooth should've been. "You want some chicken, baby?" He flagged down the waitress and ordered her some food. When it came, Charlotte wolfed it down so fast, he couldn't help but to laugh. "Damn, girl! Ain't you gonna share with a brotha?"

Reluctantly, she pushed the food, what was left of it, closer to him. "I'm sorry. I just—love chicken."

He frowned, looking down into the near-empty Styrofoam container. "I can see that."

His name was Lester. Lester had a wife. He had kids. He was ugly as hell, and so horny for her he couldn't stand it. He dragged her slowly back and forth across the dance floor, kissing the side of her neck, and grinding on her so hard, she was sure she had a bruise on her thigh. "Where you stay?" he asked, breathless.

This was it. Charlotte needed money and she needed it bad enough to fuck Lester's brains out if he had it. She swallowed hard before answering, thankful that she was full for the first time in days. " 'Cross the street in the motel."

His eyes lit up like stars as he stared deep into hers. "I really wanna be whichu, baby. Know what I mean?"

She took a deep breath and nodded. "I figured you did."

He shrugged and stopped dancing. "So, can we go?"

Charlotte knew better than to take him back to her room and then ask for the money. He could get crazy all over her, and it would be the second dumbest thing she'd ever done in her life. "Can you pay?"

His expression went cold, and blank, but his eyes gave away his desire. "How much?"

"A hundred dollars."

He pushed her away from him and looked at her like she'd just lost her mind. "A hundred goddamned dollars? What the hell? You must got diamonds down there, ho, 'cause I ain't never paid no hundred dollars for nobody's pussy!"

All eyes were on her, and Charlotte felt her face burn red. She hurried past ugly Lester, picked up her coat at the bar, then headed toward the door. Bruce, the bouncer, caught up with her just as she was about to leave.

"Hold on."

Charlotte was nearly in tears. "What? What did I—"

He grabbed her by the elbow and then led her upstairs to Uncle's office.

Charlotte struggled to get free. "I didn't do nothing! Let go!"

He knocked softly on the door, and then opened it. "She was 'bout to leave, boss."

Uncle leaned back in his big leather chair, laced his fingers together in front of him, and waited for Bruce to push her inside.

Charlotte was stunned. She looked at Bruce and then saw Uncle sitting across the room. "What? I didn't do nothing," she said, desperately. "Why'd he bring me here?"

Uncle motioned for Bruce to leave. He closed the door behind him.

"Because I asked him to."

It took a moment, but Charlotte remembered where she'd met this man before. Before Sam left, he'd introduced her to him in another club across town.

"Sam's friend?" she asked him.

Uncle smiled and nodded. A shimmering gold tooth caught the light and twinkled. "Sam's friend."

"Have you seen him?" This time, she didn't try to hide tears swelling in her eyes. "Have you heard from Sam?"

"You asked me that already, and I told you I hadn't."

Charlotte was beside herself. She started to cry uncontrollably, frustrated and trapped by a situation she saw no way out of. "He left me here," she sobbed. "He just up and left me—I have no money! No food! And—no way home!" Finally she looked at Uncle. "I just want to go back—home."

Uncle stood up, came around to the front of the desk, and stretched open his arms. "Come here, girl," he said, soothingly. "It's gonna be all right."

Charlotte stumbled haplessly into his arms. Uncle wrapped her up inside him. "I just wanna go home. Can you help me? Please?"

He patted her back, ran his long hands over her hair, and tenderly kissed her head. "Of course. Of course I can, baby girl."

Uncle's low, deep, raspy voice burrowed its way into her core. Charlotte raised her arms and wrapped them around his long, lean torso, and rested for the first time since Sam had abandoned her.

"You just trust in Uncle, baby."

Uncle. Yes. That was what Sam called him. Uncle.

"Let me take care of you."

And that's all she wanted, was for someone to take care of her. Charlotte loved being taken care of. She loved being held in a man's arms, and made to feel special, and for him to make sure she was safe, and ate well, and had cigarettes. Maybe he could get her home. Maybe this Uncle could help her to get back home where she belonged.

She melted like butter against him. Uncle put his hand under her chin and slowly raised her face to his. Charlotte never opened her eyes. He kissed her lightly on the lips at first. Just a peck, sweet and harmless. Charlotte's eyes fluttered open, still wet with tears, and this time Uncle kissed her again, slipping his tongue deep between her lips. She groaned, but didn't fight. She wiggled against him, but didn't struggle to break free. She pressed her body firmly against his, and he knew this pot of honey belonged to him now.

Uncle's moves were fluent and quick, like a dancer's. He was tall, lean, muscular, and strong, and in one swift movement he'd spun around behind Charlotte, his lips moving from hers to the side of her neck.

"Awwww," she heard herself cry.

Uncle's hands expertly untied the back of her halter top and cupped her breasts in both his hands. Charlotte's nipples grew erect to the touch. With one hand he reached down and unbuttoned the top of her jeans, then unzipped them, and slid them and her panties down low on her hips. One long finger disappeared into the moist crevice in the space between her thighs, and Charlotte shivered and convulsed against him.

"Bend over, baby," he said in her ear.

Charlotte obediently did as she was told, stretching out both arms and clutching the edge of the desk.

Uncle stood up, admiring her golden, round, bare ass, licking his lips. Large callused hands caressed her behind, and Uncle knelt down, and kissed it.

Charlotte shuddered in anticipation at the sound of him slowly unzipping his pants.

"I'm a nasty man, honey," he told her, rubbing his stiff cock against the moist folds of her pussy. "I can do some nasty things, girl."

"I like it nasty, Uncle," she whispered. "I like it real nasty."

He slapped her ass, hard, then rubbed it where he knew it stung. "My, my, my . . . that's the prettiest ass I've ever seen." He smacked it again, then pushed himself deep into her.

Charlotte grimaced at the pain, and savored it, too. She rolled her hips against him.

"That's it, baby doll." He grabbed hold of her hips, and held on tight. "Give Uncle some of that hot, nasty snatch! Give it to me, baby. Make my dick blow up!"

He braced himself behind her, salivating at the reality that she was actually his.

Uncle was bigger than she thought he'd be, long, and hot. He pumped slowly, in and out, slopping her juices down the insides of her thighs. "Hit it again, Uncle," she demanded. "Hit it again!"

Uncle did as he was told.

Charlotte balanced on her toes. "That's good, baby! That's so . . ."

"This my pussy, girl? This ass belongs to Uncle. Don't it?"

"Yes! Oh, yes!"

He grabbed a handful of her hair and pulled her head back. "Shit, I'm bout to cum, girl! Awwww . . . shit!"

"Harder! Please! Harder!"

Charlotte was coming, too. A nasty, sweet come that would make her scream. "That's it! Uncle! That's my spot! That's my—"

"Ssssssssssssssss! Awwwww, girl!"

"Uncle! Unc . . ."

Chapter 13

*M*omma—no!”

Cammy had no business—“What I tell you about my things, Camille!” Charlotte was livid. Her full-moon face was red and her eyes bulged angrily, burning into Cammy.

Camille had been curious. Ever since Charlotte had gotten that letter from Clarice, she'd kept it hidden away from Cammy.

“I just wanted to see it! Momma!”

She'd never even heard Charlotte come into the house, and before Cammy knew what was happening, Charlotte grabbed a handful of her hair, and dragged her off the side of her mother's bed, and pulled her down onto the floor.

Her baby! Cammy held her hand underneath her stomach, and avoided falling on it by drawing her knees up to protect herself.

“She didn't send it to you, Cammy!” Charlotte screamed like a madwoman. Her hair was wild on her head, and spit foamed at the corners of her mouth. “It ain't yours! It ain't yours! It's mine!” Charlotte stomped her feet like a child throwing a tantrum. “It belongs to me! It's mine!”

Cammy curled into a ball at her mother's feet and held her

breath. This wasn't new to her. Charlotte had always had a vicious temper, and Cammy bore the brunt of it her whole life. But now she was pregnant. Charlotte hadn't gone off like this since before Cammy became pregnant, and she was afraid that Charlotte wouldn't care, and would hurt the baby.

"I'm sorry, Momma!" Cammy gasped. "I'm sorry. I didn't mean to—"

"How you gonna go in my shit? How you gonna go in my shit like it's yours! It ain't yours, Cammy! You damn fool! This ain't got nothing to do with you!"

Charlotte kicked Cammy viciously in her thigh just below her hip.

"Momma!" Cammy kept her head tucked in and one hand protecting her stomach. "Momma—I'm sorry!"

Charlotte kicked her again and again until all Cammy could do was cry, and Charlotte fell exhausted down onto her bed.

"Get the hell outta my room, girl!" she commanded, out of breath. "Just get out."

Cammy slowly stood to her feet and limped out of Charlotte's bedroom to her own, then quietly closed the door behind her. She didn't cry long. The baby was okay, and so Cammy hurried and dried her face. Her leg hurt like hell, but she'd been through worse. Her baby was all right, and that's all that mattered.

It was late when she called. Cammy knew he'd be asleep, but she needed to hear his voice. Charlotte had long since fallen asleep, and the house was dark and quiet. Cammy missed him so much. "Hey, baby," she said, softly. "You sleeping?"

He sighed. "What time is it?" he asked, groggily.

She glanced at the clock. "A little after one. I couldn't sleep."

"You all right?" he asked, concerned. "Want me to come get you?"

Cammy smiled at how sweet he was. "No, baby. It's late, and you need your rest. I know you got to get up early."

"I do, but I can come by if you need me, Cam. You know I will."

"I just wanted to hear your voice, Ty." Cammy closed her eyes, wishing she could curl up next to him tonight and sleep until noon tomorrow. "You get some sleep, and I'll call you tomorrow," she promised. "Okay?"

"Okay, Cam." He sounded disappointed. "I'll holla at you tomorrow."

Cammy held the phone until after he'd hung up. She was too old for this. Cammy was too old for her momma to still be kicking her ass, and too old to be saying good night to her man over the phone in the middle of the night. Cammy was a grown woman, about to have a child of her own. She loved this baby already, and bringing it up like this was not something a good mother would do.

Chapter 14

Evelyn Turner had spent most of the afternoon staring at the back of Reesy's head. She'd gone out of her way not to make eye contact with her mother, begrudgingly answering Evelyn's probing questions using as few words as possible. Reesy sat a cup of hot, steaming tea down in front of Evelyn, then turned her attention back to the dishes. "You think I'm jealous, but that's not it," Evelyn explained, then blew on her tea to cool it. "I just don't think it's a good idea for you to go to Kansas City alone, Clarice. You have no idea where you're going or what—what you might run into."

Reesy stood over the sink, washing the last of the dishes, glancing outside every now and then at her boys, playing football in the yard, and at Jade, bundled up sitting on the swing, hollering "Touchdown!" every time one of them caught the ball.

"I'm a big girl, Mom. I'm not scared of Kansas City, and the only thing I'm going to run into is Charlotte."

Evelyn was beyond frustrated with Clarice. Her child could be so headstrong and stubborn, and when she set her sights on something, no amount of reason could get through to her. Reesy's obsessions took her over, and left little room for anybody else.

"I think the children need you here," she explained carefully. "Your family needs you here, Clarice."

Reesy sighed agitated. "My family will be fine, Mom."

"And what about you, Clarice?" Evelyn had to slow this girl down. Reesy was moving too damn fast, thinking she was running off to a fairy tale when she could be headed straight for disaster. "How are you going to be when you finally see this woman, and you discover she's not the woman you remember?"

"Mom!" Reesy finally turned to her mother. "Why are you doing this to me? Why won't you at least try and understand that I need to do this?"

"What little I know about your mother isn't good, Reesy," she said desperately. "She walked out on your and your sister. What kind of woman walks out on an eight- and a twelve-year-old and not think anything of it?"

"That's what I want to know. And that's why I have to go. I need answers and she's the only one who can give them to me."

"And if she hurts you? You want her to say the right thing and make it all right, but what if there isn't an acceptable answer, Reesy? What if she was just a selfish woman who didn't want her children anymore? Then what?"

Reesy swallowed hard and turned away from her mother, watching her own children playing outside in the back yard. "Then at least I'll know," she said quietly. "And knowing is better than guessing or speculating, Momma."

"Maybe you can talk to Connie again," her mother nagged. "Maybe if you just talk to her, she'll change her mind and—"

"She doesn't want to go." Reesy turned abruptly to her mother. "Connie has her own reasons for not going, just like I have mine for feeling like I have to, Mom. And there's nothing I can do to change her mind."

"Well, then, take Justin. At least take your husband with you if you absolutely insist on going, Clarice. Does he even know about this trip?"

Just then, Justin walked into the kitchen, home early from work. "What trip?" he stared at Reesy, who turned her back to him.

"I knew it," her mother muttered under her breath.

"Hey, Mom." He kissed his mother-in-laws' cheek. "Reesy?"

"She's going to Kansas City to find that woman," she said, frustrated.

"Mom." Reesy's own frustration was beginning to show through.

"She wants to go alone, Justin. Talk some sense into her, please. Because Lord knows I can't."

"Kansas City," Justin asked perplexed. "When were you going to tell me about this, Reese?"

"Certainly before my mother had a chance to blurt it out." Reesy faced her mother and glared angrily at her. "You know I have to go, Justin."

"We hadn't talked about this," he said, starting to become angry himself.

"What was there to talk about? I found my mother." She caught a glimpse of her adoptive mother flinching. "I know where she is, now I have to go and see her. I thought that was understood. What was the point of me finding her if I had no intention of going to see her, Justin?"

"I have no problem with that," Justin gritted his teeth. "But I do have a problem with you making assumptions where I'm concerned. You assume that I am supposed to know that my wife is taking off to Kansas City without even considering the fact that I might like to know about it before the flight takes off."

"I was going to tell you."

"When?"

"You know what?" Reesy dried her hands on the dish towel and threw it onto the counter. "How about now, Justin. Now I'm telling you that I'm catching a flight to Kansas City to find my mother, despite the fact that I don't need your permission to go any damn where! How's that?"

"Clarice, you need to calm down!" her mother shouted. "He's your husband, and he's just concerned about you, like I am."

"No, Mom. He's not concerned. He's feeling slighted." She looked at her husband. "Ever since I started this search, all you've done is complain—I'm not giving you enough time. I don't want to make love. I'm not paying attention to you. Like my whole damn life is supposed to revolve around you. Well, this is something I need, and for once, it would be nice if the two people who claim to love me would have my back instead of trying to make me feel bad for doing the one thing I need to do more than anything if I'm going to be able to get on with my life!" Tears streamed down her cheeks. "I've found my mother. Don't you understand what that means? And I need to see her. I need to talk to her. I need—"

Reesy ran past both of them, headed upstairs.

Justin and Mrs. Turner stood next to each other for a moment, speechless.

"I'd better go," she told him quietly. "I'll call later on to check on her."

Justin didn't budge. Once again, Reesy had manipulated this whole situation and turned everything around, leaving her looking like the victim, misunderstood and unappreciated, making Justin out to be the bad guy. He understood how much finding her mother meant to her. But from the day she'd started looking, she'd pushed him aside and ventured out on this trek alone, leaving him and the kids wondering what the hell had happened to their mother and his wife. Everything and everyone else had taken a back seat to finding Charlotte. Whenever he asked why, she accused him of being selfish and uncaring and jumping to the wrong conclusion. When he didn't ask anything at all, she accused him of being selfish and uncaring and uninterested.

"Hey, Dad." His oldest son, Alex, brushed past him, headed toward the refrigerator. "You home early."

"Yeah," he said, quietly. "Thought we could all go out and get something to eat."

The boy's face lit up. "Really? Awright! Can we go now? Where's Mom?"

Justin hesitated before answering. And then finally just told him. "Mom's not feeling well. It'll just be us."

He saw the disappointment flash quickly in the boy's eyes. Unfortunately, Reesy was upstairs pouting and feeling beat up by the people who loved her, so—she missed it.

"I'm afraid of how much I still love her," she said quietly into the phone. The room was dark, and Justin and the kids had left more than half an hour ago. No one else seemed to understand the way he did. No one else seemed to even want to listen the way he listened.

"You were so young when she left, Reesy," Avery told her. "Of course you still love her."

"Yeah, but why so much, Avery? Why can't I have a healthy dose of hatred for her the way my sister does? At least—at least I'd have a balance if I could feel angry or loathing. But my heart is relieved that I've found her, and that she's alive, and I can't wait to see her, and to put my arms around her, and to know that she still loves me, too. Does that make any sense at all?"

"I've seen a lot of things in my line of work, Reesy, and what I've learned is everything and nothing makes sense when it comes to reunions. There is no right way or wrong way to re-unite with someone you've lost and now found, honey."

He flinched at the word slipping past his lips unexpectedly— *honey.* Avery needed to pull back and watch himself before his true feelings slipped out and spewed all over that woman. She was someone he hadn't expected to come into his life. And now that she had, she was someone he wasn't too anxious to have leave it.

"Nobody gets it, Avery. Not like you. And nobody wants to hear it. Every time I try to talk about it—her, they all look at me like I'm crazy for wanting to see my own mother."

"I think they're all afraid, Reesy," he explained calmly.

"Of what?"

"Of the same thing you're afraid of. I think they're all afraid of how much you still love her, and that maybe they'll lose you to her."

"And they'd be wrong, Avery. I love my mother, and my fam-ily. I would never leave them to—that's just crazy."

"You know it, but maybe they don't. In any event, you're go-ing to have to do what you feel you have to do, and at the same time, try and get them to understand that it has nothing to do with them."

He was right. Reesy couldn't help herself, and she smiled. "How come you understand me so well, Avery?" She chuckled. "Strange how empathy can sometimes come from where you least expect it. Huh?"

"I just care, Reesy. I can't help myself. I just do."

They talked for a few minutes more and then said their good-byes. Avery hung up the phone feeling a little lonelier all of a sudden than he'd been before she called. Clarice Braxton was a beautiful woman, soft and full where it counted. Or maybe Avery had made the mistake of working too much and playing too little. He was a workaholic, no doubt about it, so much so that his last two wives had left him over it. He'd been so busy working on this case for Mrs. Braxton, and others, that he'd forgotten what it was to find someone, fall in love, and get so caught up with a woman that nothing else mattered. But the moment he saw her, he knew that right there was the possibility of love happening. Never mind that she was already married. Since when did that ever stop two people from following their hearts?

Chapter 15

John called. He didn't leave a message, but his number showed up on her caller ID, and Connie stared at it with mixed emotions, trying hard not to read any more into it than it was—a phone number. For a moment, she thought about calling him back, but why? Just to give in to how messed up she was over him the way she always did? To forgive him, and condone him one more time the way she'd become so adept at doing?

She'd just gotten home from the store, and Connie was more exhausted than usual. She knew the signs, hell, she'd been pregnant enough to know all of them. Fatigue, nausea, more fatigue, and hormones running rampant and turning her into an emotional jelly mold. She cried for no reason and all of them. One moment her thoughts were clear and precise, and undeniably on point, and the next she was a ball of confusion, dumbfounded, and upside down in her world. Nothing made sense anymore. Nothing felt right or was right, and all she wanted to do was turn off time and make it stand still long enough for her to get her act together—whatever that meant.

Connie slipped out of her shoes and crawled across the bed fully clothed, closing her eyes and trying not to see his face behind them. He'd called. Knowing that meant the world to her, but these days, the world obviously wasn't enough. She was losing her mind. That's all there was to it. Connie was going insane, and the events that had unfolded in her life over the last couple of weeks had only served to make her spiral out of control even faster.

Twice in the last week, she'd picked up the phone to call and make another appointment for another abortion, and both times, she'd hung up the phone as soon as the receptionist answered. An abortion was the easy way out. It always had been. So how come she wasn't so anxious to get off easy? She'd asked herself that question a thousand times and every answer that came to her sounded as ridiculous as the last.

Because I want a baby.

Because this might be my last chance to have one.

Because I'm a woman and that's what women do.

Because I could be a good mother.

Because . . . because . . . because . . .

And then Jade's name would come into her thoughts, and then her face. She missed that little girl. Even as Aunt Connie, she missed her. Connie ached so much sometimes to touch her, and to kiss her small face, and to gobble her up, and whisper to her, "I'm your mommy, baby." But she'd given up that right years ago. She gave her away because she was afraid of the baby, and she was afraid of letting her down, and she was afraid of trying to be someone she wasn't able to be. She was afraid that she was more like Charlotte than she ever wanted to be: selfish, incapable, wicked.

She talked herself out of Jade. Connie didn't want to make the same mistake this time. She didn't want to let her fears get in the way of the one thing she wanted more than anything—to prove to herself and everybody else that she was better than her own mother had been. And that she was as deserving as any woman who'd ever wanted children.

Reesy and John didn't think so. How could they not think so, and say that they loved her? What the hell kind of monster was it that they believed they loved, then? And what if—what if they were right?

"I found Momma, Connie. I found Charlotte."

Reesy should've just let it go. Finding Charlotte was the first step in finding disaster, and she should've just let it go.

Right on queue, the phone rang. Connie answered it and it was Eddie, her piece of mind and calm in the center of the storm. Eddie was psychic and always managed to call right at the moment when Connie needed someone to save her life.

Connie was a fourteen-year-old runaway when she met Edwina Freeman behind that old soul food restaurant she used to own.

"I was torn between a drumstick and selling my body that night for some real food and a warm bed," Connie had told Eddie once.

"Sometimes sleeping with rats was better than letting some strange fool slobber all over you for a few dollars, baby." Eddie used to smile and put her arm around Connie, and she understood. "I ain't never been a ho, but I've slept with a few rats in my day," she'd laugh.

Eddie stepped in and became a mother of sorts to Connie, filling the shoes too big for Charlotte. She took Connie off the streets and gave her a job and time to finish growing up without having to sell her soul to do it. The three years she lived with

Eddie and worked in that restaurant, Connie felt more safe than she'd felt her whole life, and more loved. When the old woman finally retired and moved to Vegas, it was all Connie could do not to pack up and move with her.

"*This is my retirement, lil' girl.*" *Eddie continued packing, ignoring the begging and pleading from Connie to let her come along.* "*I worked too hard to save my money so I could move to Las Vegas and be a free woman. That's my reward.*" *She looked at Connie, and ignored her pouting.* "*You got to earn yo own.*"

Connie was seventeen when Eddie left. She had a job and her own place, and as far as Eddie was concerned, she was old enough to take care of herself. But she'd called every week since then, like clockwork.

"How you doin, Lil' Bird," she said, softly. Connie could hear the age in her voice, and she smiled and swallowed the sob swelling in her throat.

"I've been better, Eddie."

"Well, what's that supposed to mean?"

Any other time, she'd have been overly concerned with putting on airs, and reassuring Eddie that she was better than she actually was. But not this time. Connie was too tired to play those games, and too vulnerable to pull them off anyway. Eddie was her mother. She was the best one Connie ever had, and right now, she needed her mom.

"I did it again, Eddie," her eyes clouded with tears. "I messed up and got myself pregnant—and I don't know what to do."

Eddie was quiet for a moment, then sighed heavily. "What do you want to do, baby?"

She sat for a moment, pondering that question. "I don't know."

"Oh yes you do," Eddie said emphatically. "'Cause if you don't know, then who else does?"

Connie dried her eyes and sat up in bed. Eddie had a way of oversimplifying things sometimes, and circumstances in Connie's life were anything but simple at the moment. "It's not that easy, Eddie. I don't want to make the wrong decision."

"Okay," she said calmly. "And how do you know what that is?"

"I don't. That's the problem."

"You wanna keep this baby, Connie?"

Connie didn't answer.

"'Cause I think you should."

Nobody had ever said that to her before. Nobody ever believed Connie should keep a child. Not really. Even before Jade was born, she could see reservations and doubt in Reesy's eyes over Connie's ability to raise a kid. She'd never admitted it, but it had always been there—always.

"I'd like to," she answered quietly. "But—"

"But—what? What else is there? You havin' a baby, Lil' Bird, and you want the baby you havin'. It's not hard."

"John doesn't want it, though," she said, sadly.

"He don't?" Eddie sounded surprised at first, but then she seemed to remember who they were talking about. "Well, I guess I can kinda understand that about him. He never did seem like the type to want kids."

She'd never met him in person, but Eddie had spoken to him on the phone a few times, and sensed something about him that straight-armed people from getting too close to him. She liked him, but she could sense some selfishness in him, too, that didn't set too well with her.

"He's gone, Eddie," Connie confessed.

"He left you?" Eddie asked stunned.

"I told him to leave," Connie's voice quivered. "I told him—it just wasn't working anymore."

"You have to do what's best for you, baby." Eddie sounded sad. She was so hoping that Connie had found the right man this time. Someone who would love her the way she deserved to be loved, and cherish her like Eddie knew she should be cherished. That girl had had such a hard time in life, with people coming through it, reminding her of how bad she should feel about who she was. What pissed Eddie off was how often Connie seemed to let that happen, and how much she beat herself up after they'd finished beating her up first.

"Yeah," she said quietly. "I know." Connie wanted to change the subject. She hadn't spoken to Eddie since last week, and she didn't want to spend the whole time talking about all the mess going on with her. Eddie was her friend. And she wanted to at least enjoy this conversation with her friend. "How are you doing, Eddie? Give up that old nasty gambling habit you developed when you moved to Vegas?" Connie chuckled.

"Now, why should I give it up?" Eddie asked, surprised. "When I keep winning money all the time?"

"You still playing slots?"

"Girl, no. Slots is for suckers. I'm a blackjack ho now, *forgive me, Lord!*" Eddie laughed out loud. Since Connie had known her, Eddie had always cussed, and she'd always praised the Lord or begged for forgiveness immediately after. "I been winning so much they done banned me from two casinos in the last month! I can't help it, I tell 'em! I can't help but to win!"

"Good for you, Eddie! You keep doing, you! And I'm so happy for you."

"I know you are, sweetheart. You need anything? You need money? I got plenty and you know I don't mind sharing."

"No, I'm fine. You keep your money. I'm cool."

"How's Jade? How's your sister and her family?"

Eddie always talked about Jade like she wasn't part of Reesy and her family. Connie tried correcting her at first, but over time, she recognized the stubborn streak in Eddie, and realized that the woman was just doing what came naturally.

"Jade's good. She's real good," she said solemnly. "And Reesy's fine, too. She, uh—she found Charlotte." Connie swallowed hard, saying the name that sometimes got caught in the back of her throat. "I told you she'd hired some detective, and, well—he finally came through and found her. Reesy's elated."

"And you?"

Connie rolled her eyes. "Shit, you know me, Eddie. I could give a damn about Charlotte, and why Reesy spent all that money looking for that woman is beyond me. She's not worth it. Never has been."

"She's worth it to your sister, Lil' Bird."

"Yeah, well, Reesy has grand delusions about our mother. All she remembers about Charlotte is bouncing on her knee, and falling asleep in her lap. She's blocked out all the rest of that shit. But not me. That's all I remember about her is the shit she used to pull. It wouldn't have bothered me the least little bit if she'd fallen into the ocean."

"You two talked to her yet? You going to see her?"

"Reesy's going. I'm not interested."

"But you should be interested, Connie."

Connie was surprised to hear Eddie say such a thing. "Why should I be? Charlotte is nothing to me, Eddie. So why should I want to go all the way out to Kansas to see nothing?"

Eddie laughed. "Yeah, ain't shit in Kansas. *Thank you, Jesus!*"

"You know what I mean."

"I do, and you need to go see your mother, Connie."

"Why, Eddie? What good would it do?"

"It would put your mind to rest, Lil' Bird."

"I'm not losing sleep over Charlotte."

"You lost you over Charlotte, and the woman you might've been had she done right by you."

"What are you talking about?"

"Ever since I known you, you been down on yourself and feeling less than what you should feel like, Connie."

"No. No, I—"

"This is me, baby, and I don't appreciate you sitting there calling me a liar."

"I'm not."

"She left you in some unfair circumstances, and I know you wouldn't have had to go through half of what you went through if she hadn't."

"You don't know that."

"I do too know that!" Eddie snapped. "If she'd been there you wouldn't have had to be sent to that home, or living on the streets, or—youda had a momma, Lil' Bird. A bad one, but at least youda had a place to finish growing up in, and maybe you coulda gone off to college or something nice like that. You need to go see that woman if for no other reason than to cuss her sorry ass, *Hallelujah!*, out and tell her to her face she was a bad momma! She need to know it, and you the one who need to tell it, Connie. I know what I'm talking bout, Lil' Bird. It'll make you feel better. And just so you know, Reesy ain't the only one that woman hurt. She hurt you, too, but you just feel like you deserved it more than Reesy. That's the difference. And you didn't deserve it, Connie. You never did."

Chapter 16

Reesy stared at the phone sitting in front of her on the coffee table with Charlotte's letter spread out next to it. The kids were gone to school. Justin was at work. The letter had arrived in the mail yesterday and included her mother's phone number, with a message for Reesy to please call her.

She wrung her hands together, noticing for the first time that her palms were sweating. Three decades stood between her and a phone call, and she had no idea what to say or how to feel. In all this time, the challenge had simply been to find Charlotte and then to confront her, but until this moment, Reesy hadn't even considered fully the impact of what that might mean. What was she supposed to say? What would Charlotte say? And in the end, what would it all mean? A reunion to fix what had been broken when she was eight years old. What if it couldn't be fixed? Or, more importantly, what if it could? She took a deep breath just thinking about it, pondering the possibilities that she could forgive her mother for leaving and welcome her back into her life, into her family.

She picked up the phone and slowly dialed each number, hesitating a moment before finally pushing the final digit. She squeezed her eyes shut when the phone started ringing, and willed her heart to stop beating so fast.

"Hello?" the woman answered.

Reesy opened her mouth to speak, but the word caught in her throat and she froze, wanting all of a sudden to hang up.

"Hello?" the woman asked again. "Hello?"

"He-hello," she finally responded nervously. "Hi, I'm calling for—" For Momma. For Charlotte Rodgers. For my mother.

"Reesy?" she asked hesitantly. "Reesy, is this you?"

Reesy searched her memory for the sound of something familiar in the woman's voice. Of course it was her. The way she said her name confirmed that it was her.

"Reesy?" Charlotte stifled a cry, covering her mouth with her hand. "It's Momma, baby," she sobbed. "It's me."

Reesy cried, too, forgetting the resentment she'd grown up with for her mother, the anger she'd held sacred all these years. And all that was left was the sound of her mother's voice, saying her name as only she could.

"Momma? It's me, Momma. Oh God! Mom!"

Charlotte felt as if she would faint, and so she had to sit down before she fell. Cammy wasn't here. Lord, Jesus! How she wished Cammy was here to sit next to her and hold her hand. She was shaking, but Charlotte was relieved and felt herself falling in love again, for the first time in a long time. "I know, baby," she said soothingly, wishing she could stroke her little girl's hair the way she used to when Reesy was small. "I know."

"I thought I'd never find you," Reesy hiccupped. "I thought—" that her mother was dead or that she'd forgotten.

"Shhhhh, Lovebug," she smiled, and stroked the receiver with her other hand. "It's all right now, Reesy. Momma's here, baby, and it's all right now."

"I missed you, Momma. I can't tell you how much I've missed you."

Charlotte laughed. "You don't have to, baby girl. Because I know. Because I've missed you even more."

"Why'd you leave, Momma?" Reesy sniffed, remembering the reason she called, and the reason she'd paid a detective thousands of dollars to find her mother. "Where did you go?"

Two very loaded questions Charlotte wasn't prepared for so soon compounded with answers she didn't even want to think about, because she was too consumed with the sound of her daughter's sweet voice. Yes, she was there. Her pretty little chubby baby girl, sweet as candy and so full of love for her mother, was still there, all grown up, but still the baby. Charlotte warmed all over, and basked in the love emanating from this girl, even now.

"Are you coming to see me, Reesy? You promised you'd come to see me."

"Yes." She sounded so small. "Yes, Momma. I'm coming to see you. I need to see you."

"And I need to see you, too, Lovebug. My baby girl. My lovely little baby."

Reesy leaned back on the couch, pulled her knees to her chest, and recalled the image of curling up in her mother's lap, rocking slowly back and forth until she finally fell asleep. Hours later, she'd wake up in that same place, with Charlotte asleep, too. Reesy would nuzzle her face against her mother's chest, and drift back off to sleep.

"I need to check on flights." She dried her face with the back of her hand. "But I can be there soon—maybe in a week?"

Charlotte nodded. "A week seems so far away," she said lovingly. "But it's all right, baby. I have waited a lifetime for you.

One more week won't hurt. You get here as fast as you can, Reesy. Momma'll be here."

Reesy didn't want the phone call to end, but instinctively she knew that nothing more needed to be said at the moment. Both of them were too overwhelmed to say much more. But before hanging up, Reesy blurted out the one constant that had been in her heart her whole life. "I love you, Momma."

Charlotte was quiet for a moment, but then finally asked solemnly. "How much, Reesy? How much do you love your momma?"

Hot tears burned trails down her cheeks, and she said, almost whispering, "This much. I love you as big as this room, Momma."

Charlotte dialed her friend Lynn's number as soon as she hung up the phone. "Lynn," she could hardly catch her breath. "She found me, girl. My baby found me. Yes. Yes. In Denver. She's coming to see me, Lynn. She'll be here soon. I can hardly believe—Reesy'll be here soon."

Lynn asked about Charlotte's other daughter, Connie. Was she coming, too? Reesy didn't mention Connie. And Charlotte didn't ask about her, either. Reesy was the one—the only one who mattered. She was coming to see Charlotte on her own. And that was fine. That was just fine.

Chapter 17

Cammy stood in Tyrell's doorway, still wearing her uniform from work. "Can I stay with you tonight?" she asked softly.

He stepped aside and let her in. His apartment was small, but neat and tasteful. T didn't ask questions. He just helped her out of her clothes and into the shower. He washed her back and rubbed soap over her breasts and stomach, between her legs, and gently over the bruise on her hip. When they were finished, he dried her off first, and helped her into one of his shirts.

Cammy didn't want to talk, and instinctively he knew that, so he hardly uttered a word. The gentle rhythms from one of Kem's CDs played softly in the background, saturating the small apartment with soothing melodies and the hope of love. Cammy lay securely in his arms, her back to him, his strong hands caressing the baby inside her. This was heaven, and the only place she ever wanted to be anymore.

He kissed the side of her face. "Did you eat?"

She nodded slightly. "Yeah, I ate earlier."

Something told him she hadn't. But Tyrell didn't push. He'd get her to eat something in the morning, though. "You wanna tell me about it?"

Cammy was quiet at first, and he was beginning to think he shouldn't have even bothered asking. Finally she spoke up. "You know how she can get sometimes, T. Flipping like a coin somebody tossed in the air—you never know which side she'll land on. It's been like that my whole life, and—"

"You getting sick of it?"

"Yeah. I'm getting real sick of it."

"Then why you keep putting up with it, baby? Why don't you leave? You know you got a spot here with me. You know that, Cammy."

"I wish I could, T. I do." She turned to him and tried to smile. "I love you so much."

"I love you, too, which is why it's stupid for you to be any-place else but here."

He made it sound so lovely and right. Cammy turned back over on her side and sighed. "She'll die if I leave her. She ain't got nobody else."

"That ain't your problem, Cammy. She's your mother. You're not hers. She's made you her whole world and left you feeling like you responsible for her, and shit. That's not how it's sup-posed to be."

But that was how it was. As angry and hurt as she was right now, she knew she'd have to go home eventually. And Charlotte would bake her something, then spend the rest of the week apologizing and explaining and begging Cammy to forgive her, until finally Cammy would. Then the shit would start all over again, and she'd be back here, in his arms, escaping from that madness even if it was only for a night. Crazy. Her worst fear was coming here one of these nights and T deciding he was through, and refusing to let her in. He wasn't far from that now. She knew it. He knew it, too.

He waited awhile before saying anything else, but he had to know. "Did you call your mom?"

Cammy backed closer to him and kissed his arm. "No," she whispered.

"She's gonna be worried."

She shrugged.

T shrugged, too, and resigned himself to the moment with his woman. Charlotte had put that bruise on her hip. He struggled with shit like this because Charlotte seemed to do or say whatever she wanted to Cammy, and Cammy let her. Cammy even came to her defense whenever he tried to call her on it, so he had learned to back off, and let the two of them do their thang. All she ever had to do was choose him. The minute she did was the minute he'd step in and put that old woman in check—respectfully, but she needed to be checked. Cammy only chose T when bullshit went down at her crib and she needed a place to hide. Charlotte was no doubt blowing up the girl's celly, and he wouldn't be the least bit surprised if she showed up kicking down his door in the middle of the night looking for her baby. Best to sleep with one eye and one ear open tonight, he concluded. Best to be ready for anything.

It was after nine and Cammy still wasn't home. She'd gotten off work at seven. Charlotte had called to make sure. And she wasn't answering her phone, either. Charlotte had been calling all day and the girl wasn't answering her—

She paced back and forth in the living room, anticipating the sound of her baby's keys in the door, ready to get down on her knees if she had to, begging for her forgiveness. Damn! Why'd she have to get so mad? And why'd she have to get mad and hurt her little girl that way? Charlotte wrung her hands together, oblivious to the swelling in her ankles from spending all that time on her feet, pacing.

"Come home, Cammy," she muttered worried to herself. "Come home to Momma."

Momma was sorry. Yes. Oh yes, Momma was so very sorry. But then she should've said that last night. She should've waited up until she wasn't mad anymore and apologized before it was too late. Before Cammy got up and went off to work this morning, and had time to think—to forget how much her momma loved and adored her, and how sorry she could be sometimes when she lost her temper. If she'd just apologized last night . . .

"She'd be home," she stared woefully at the door, hoping to see her Cammy walk through it.

But deep down, she knew Cammy wouldn't be home. She knew where Cammy was, too. Any excuse! Any excuse to lay up with Tyrell's broke ass! That's where she was. With Tyrell, fucking or sucking that nasty dick of his, dumb over his ass, and stupid to think he'd want her fat ass, as pregnant as she was!

Cammy was naïve. Too damn naïve to be as old as she was, and that was Charlotte's fault. She'd been too protective of the girl, trying to keep her safe and away from all the sick mothafuckas out there just looking for an opportunity to take advantage of her dumb ass! Tyrell thought he was slick. He probably told her to come to his place, begged her. He was the one putting all those silly ideas into her head, that she should leave her momma and move in with him. That idiot brought that mess, too! Cammy would believe anything you told her, and ever since that slick Tyrell had put his thing to her, she'd lost her damn mind over him.

Without hesitation, Charlotte grabbed her purse and bolted

out of the front door of her house wearing her house shoes, nightgown, and robe. She stopped cold in the spot where the car should be. Cammy had the goddamned car. Cammy had the keys. Her chest heaved angrily up and down, and all of a sudden Charlotte felt trapped. She felt as if her feet were cemented to the ground and her legs weighted down by lead. Somebody had to go get Cammy's ass and bring her home. Somebody had to— where could she go? How would she get there? Cammy was gone. Her pretty baby girl was—Charlotte was all alone.

"Oh—God! Oh—God!" She dropped her purse and pressed both hands to her cheeks, burning hot with panic and fear.

She was all by herself out here. She looked up the road one way, then back down in the other direction. The nearest neighbor was more than a mile away. There were no street lights where they lived. Lord! When had they taken down the lights? Charlotte couldn't breathe. She couldn't stop her heart from beating so fast. She couldn't stop the sweat from beading on her forehead and the bridge of her nose.

"What am I going to do?" she said, breathless. "What am I going to do without my—Caaaammmyyyyyy!" she screamed at the top of her lungs. "I'm sor—Momma's sor—baby . . . Caaaammmyyyyy!"

Her worst fear in the world was being alone. Sammy had left her alone. He had left her alone in that wretched Kansas City. Charlotte thought back to the moment, years ago, when she realized he was gone. He'd snuck out in the middle of the night . . . in the middle of the goddamned night! No money! No food! No car! His ass left her! Alone in a strange place where she knew no one and nothing about how to get home.

"I'll take care of you, baby girl," he stroked her. He stroked her and held her close. "Whatever you need, sweetheart . . . all

you got to do—" Charlotte shuddered thinking about him and
fought back memories of what he'd done to her. It wasn't good
to be left alone. Nothing was more frightening than knowing
she'd have to sleep in that house all night by herself, or that
Cammy was gone—and might never come back to her. She
willed her stiff, heavy legs to move and carry her heavy frame
back inside the house. Charlotte crumbled down onto the sofa
and wailed like a baby. "Cammy! Momma's sorry! Momma's
sorry—baby!" She picked up the phone and dialed her baby's
number again . . . and again . . . and again . . .

Chapter 18

I'll go with you, Reesy, if you give me a chance, but I can't just drop everything and fly off to Kansas on such short notice. I need to check with my boss and see if I can get the time—"

Maybe Justin meant well. Then again, maybe he was just trying to think of a way to keep her from going. Whatever the case, it didn't work. Reesy found her seat on the plane, thankful to be sitting next to a window. Murphy, Kansas, didn't have an airport, so she'd have to fly into Kansas City, then rent a car and drive the rest of the way.

It all seemed so surreal and sudden. And it was—sudden, that is. One morning after dropping Jade off at school, she called the airlines to price a ticket. Before she realized it, she was reciting her credit card number to the clerk on the phone, and had actually purchased one. Reesy was caught up and riding the wave of her life, flowing with a momentum powerful enough to hold that plane up in the air and set her down in the place where she'd find her mother.

Finally, the plane took off, and Reesy watched Denver, Colorado, fade away. A new phase in her life would begin the

moment this plane landed, or rather, the continuation of the
first and most significant phase in her life.

She leaned her head back and closed her eyes, remembering
one of the most magical times in her life, before adoption and
troubled marriages and doubt.

Reesy was six. Pigtails on the sides of her head were gar-
nished in pink and white ribbons, matching her favorite pink-
and-white sweater. She was angry about something, but as hard
as she tried, grownup Reesy couldn't remember why. Her feet
were too short to reach the floor, and the room she shared with
Connie was such a mess. They had bunk beds and Connie slept
on top. Reesy wasn't allowed on top, because she was too small
and Momma was afraid she'd fall off and hurt herself.

Charlotte came through the door, looking beautiful and
smiling.

"Hey, Lovebug." She knelt down at Reesy's feet and tapped
her on her bottom pouting lip. "Where were you? I came
through that door after being gone and my Lovebug wasn't there
to welcome me home."

Charlotte's eyes sparkled like precious amber gems, hypno-
tizing Reesy, making it impossible not to stare into them.

"I'm mad," she said clutching Miss Polly to her chest. Miss
Polly was a pink stuffed pig Charlotte had won for her at the
amusement park throwing footballs through a tire. It was
Reesy's favorite toy, and she slept with it every night.

"I can see that," Charlotte said gently. "What in the world
would make my pretty girl so upset?"

"Connie did it," she said angrily. And that's all she needed to
say. Charlotte scooped her up in her arms, then sat on the side
of the bed, cradling Reesy like a baby in her arms and close to
her heart.

"That mean old Connie," she quipped, kissing Reesy on the head. "If she ain't good for nothing else, she sure is good for making Lovebugs mad. Know what I mean?"

Reesy nodded and Charlotte tickled, and they laughed together and cuddled for what felt like hours until Reesy could hardly keep her eyes open anymore, and she lay curled up in her mother's arms, until the two of them drifted off to sleep in her bed together until morning.

"Ladies and gentlemen, the captain will begin his descent into Kansas City in a few moments. Please restore your seats to their upright positions and stow all carry-on items underneath the seat in front of you. Flight attendants, prepare for landing."

Nobody back home gave a damn that she'd found her mother. Not Justin, Mom, or Dad, and especially not her sister. But all of a sudden none of that mattered anymore. Reesy was where she was supposed to be, one step closer to her roots, her foundation, and the end of a long journey that threatened to leave part of her empty if she hadn't completed it. Now that it was nearly over, she was starting to feel more whole than she'd ever felt before in her life.

I found no magic potion, no horse with wings to fly ...
My fantasy is over, my life must now begin

ANITA BAKER, *"Fairy Tales"*

Chapter 19

Sweat rolled down the back of her neck and soaked through her blouse. Lynn sat on her front porch next to Uncle staring out into the neighborhood, trying to ignore the sounds coming from inside the small, rundown house she shared with her man, Arnel.

"Got to be damn near eighty degrees out here today." Uncle said casually, dabbing sweat off his brow with a white handkerchief. He'd removed his white fedora and perched it on his knee.

"Yeah." Lynn inhaled desperately on her cigarette. "It's too hot for April."

"Umph! Umph! Umph!" Arnel grunted from inside the house.

"You still doing nails over at Barbara Lee's shop on Walnut?" Uncle asked casually.

Lynn hadn't noticed her knee bouncing up and down, or that she'd been biting on her bottom lip hard enough to leave a red mark just underneath it. She nodded. "Yeah. I'm there every day 'cept Thursdays and Sundays. Those are my days off."

She tried to smile. Uncle was the kind of man who liked to see a woman smile. "Ain't nothing sweeter than a friendly woman," she'd heard him say before, but she couldn't remember when or who he said it to. She just remembered that whenever she was in his company, she'd do her best to smile. No matter what.

"Umph! Umph! That's—enough! Man! That's—" Arnel screamed.

"I got a friend of mine," Uncle continued, unaffected by the sounds coming from inside the house. "A good friend. I'm gonna send her your way at the shop. She wanna get her nails done. Told her I'd see what I could do."

"Shut the hell up, niggah! I ain't done!"

Lynn winced. "She work for you?"

He smiled. "No. She ain't no ho. And I want you to take good care of her. Make her hands up real nice."

Uncle shook his head and sighed. "It's a good thing Arnel's family," he said, solemnly, staring straight ahead. "I'da shot his ass a long time ago if he wasn't family."

Lynn swallowed hard and nodded. "You been good to him, Uncle," she said nervously, hoping he'd miss the condescending sound of her voice. "You been good to both of us."

Arnel was his half brother. They had the same daddy but different mommas. He'd been born an idiot and dope fiend like his momma, and Uncle couldn't help but to feel sorry for him. But even pity had its limits. He glanced over at the white girl sitting next to him, Lynn. She was as dumb as Arnel, but shit, she loved his sorry ass. Been loving him ever since she set foot in Kansas City chasing behind him. Poor white trash and poor black trash made mud. And Uncle prayed silently that these two fools never procreated. It would be a hell of a mess if they ever did.

"Umph! Man! Please!—" Arnel cried from inside the house. "Please! Umph! I can't—take—umph! Please—you got to stop!"

Lynn nervously rubbed her brow and took slow, deep breaths, fighting the natural instinct to cry and beg and plead Arnel's case with him. "He ain't never gonna learn." She shook her head. "I just wish he'd—"

Uncle reached over and tenderly patted her thigh. "Don't you worry 'bout it, girl. It ain't your problem. Your man got problems. Maybe you should think about that, and go find yourself somebody else."

She shook her head and choked back her frustration. "I can't leave him, Uncle."

"Please! Man—stop! You—killin'—"

Uncle sighed. "I guess it's my fault, too, he's the way he is. Arnel got a weakness. He's one of them addicts, can't help hisself. But when he come to me looking for a job—he ain't worth a damn. Carry this to Blue Lou on Fourteenth, get the money, and bring it back to me. I'll give you a hundred bills, I told him." Uncle rolled his eyes in disgust. "Damn fool. Stole half my shit, took half my money, then gonna act like I'm the one that's crazy. What the hell did he think I was gonna do?"

Lynn bolted up from the step and walked to the front yard. This wasn't her business. This was between Uncle and his half brother, and it wasn't her place to butt in. Otherwise, it could just as easily be her in that house with a train being pulled on her ass.

"Y'all please! I'm beggin'—I'm beggin'—"

She turned to Uncle and pleaded with her eyes. "Can't you make 'em stop, Uncle? Please?"

Uncle stared unemotionally at her. "I can. But I won't. He took my dope, my money, and then lied to me dead in my face." He shrugged. "Like I said, if he'd been any other niggah, he'd have a bullet in him by now."

"Aaaaah! Oh—shit! Shit! Uncle! I'm sorry—man! Umph! Uncle! Please!"

Half an hour later, Arnel stopped screaming and three men emerged from the house, sweating, tucking in their shirts and adjusting their belt buckles. Uncle stood up to leave. "I swear, I think that mothafucka likes getting fucked in the ass," he said more to himself than anyone else. Uncle headed down the steps and over to the silver Cadillac parked in front of the house. "Go see about your man, baby. Tell him to call me when he feeling better."

He'd moved her out of that nasty-ass motel weeks ago, and into a nice apartment on the other side of town. Teaching Arnel's junkie ass a lesson had taken a lot out of him, and all he wanted to do was wrap Charlotte's pretty self around him, help him take his mind off the bullshit.

She met him at the door with outstretched arms and a smile, wearing some yellow hot pants, a white halter top, and high-heeled sandals showing off them pretty legs of hers.

"Hey, baby." He leaned down and kissed her slow. Uncle had never fancied redbones until this one came along. Two yellow people together don't do nothing but glow in the dark, he always said. That's the main reason he married Sherrell. She was as dark as he was light, and he figured they'd make some decent-looking brown-skinned kids. Of course, it didn't work out that way. Of the five kids they had, only one had come out brown-skinned. Two were high yellow like him, and two were black as night like her.

Uncle sank down into the leather sofa he'd bought, pulled off his shoes, and patted his lap for her to come sit on. "Bring it to Daddy, baby."

Charlotte bounced over to where he was and found her spot. She crossed her thick legs and kissed him passionately. "Mmmm." She ran her finger down the front of his unbuttoned shirt. "You hungry, *baby? I baked a chicken, and it wouldn't take long for me to make you some mashed potatoes and homemade gravy."*

Uncle couldn't help but to smile. Damn! "You trying to get on my good side, girl?"

She laughed. "I think I'm already on your good side, Uncle. I just don't wanna lose my place."

She knew he was married, but Uncle had taken care of her in a way no other man had ever done before. He'd set her up in a nice place, paid the rent, and bought some real nice furniture, too. He was even talking about getting her a little piece of car. In the weeks since she'd taken up with him, it had been like "Sam who?", sorry-ass sucka, running out on her and leaving her stranded like that. Charlotte had never been so afraid. Sammy had walked out on her without a word, took all his belongings and left Charlotte stranded in that dirty motel room, with no money, no food, and no way to get home. But then she met Uncle, and he knew how to make it right. If it hadn't been for Uncle, she'd have ended up hoing or lying dead on the side of the road somewhere trying to hitch a ride back to Denver. Not only had he been kind and generous with her, but he'd been one hell of a lay, too, with a dick as long as her arm and the skill to know how to use that magic wand, too.

"Why don't you go fix me a plate, then come back here and rub my neck for me, honey," he said wincing. "I got a mean crick I can't get rid of."

He called her honey because he said that's what she reminded him of, sticky, sweet honey.

"You want Kool-Aid, or a beer?"

"What kinda Kool-Aid?"

"Red," she called back over her shoulder, switching her wide behind hard just for him.

He noticed. "*Careful, girl. You gonna put a crick in the other side of my neck if you keep shaking that ass like that.*"

Charlotte smiled. He was her savior. All she had to do was ask, and Uncle provided. Yes. This was how it should be. This was how it should've been all along. Glodean might've been cool with rotting in the projects with a houseful of kids, but thank God, Charlotte had gotten away from all that before it was too late.

Chapter 20

"Walking away is second nature to you. Isn't it?" Connie said to John over the phone.

"You told me to leave, Connie," he responded unemotionally. "What the hell was I supposed to do?"

"Stay," she whispered. "You're a coward."

"Yeah. And you're delusional. So what's that going to make the kid?"

"Fuck you, John," Connie said under her breath.

"I'm just telling it like it is, baby girl."

He'd gone back to Bueller and gotten himself a room in a rundown motel just outside of town. Like it or not, it was home, and instinctively he'd come back to it when he realized he had nowhere else he wanted to go to. John had been back in town for nearly two weeks now and had been holed up in that motel the whole time, coming out of his room every now and then to eat at the greasy diner just off the interstate. He'd called Moses to tell him to let Adam know he was coming. But he hadn't called him and told him he was in town.

Connie sat inside a coffee shop near the boutique where she worked, staring out the window at traffic whirring by. Getting used to him being gone had been difficult, and it had been a relief. The threat was always there that one day she'd wake up and he'd leave for good. She'd spent the last year in a relationship with a man who seemed to be biding his time, waiting for the right moment to take off and move on to the next destination in his life, whatever that was. Her being pregnant was the right opportunity for both of them to do what came naturally to a man like John—leaving—and to a woman like Connie—being left.

"Well, then, I guess it really is over." She cleared her throat. "For real this time."

John didn't say a word.

"I am going to keep the baby, John."

"You said that already."

"Yeah. I guess I did. And I guess we've both made up our minds then. I want a kid, and you don't, which is why I'm here and you're not."

"I didn't call to argue."

"Then why did you call?"

"To let you know where I am. That's all. In case you—"

"Need you?" She chuckled. "Like I don't need you now."

"You wanted me gone, Connie."

"I wanted you to want this baby, John. That's what I wanted."

"You wanted me to fake the funk."

She sighed, disappointed that he'd ever have to fake wanting her and the baby she was carrying. "No, John," she said quietly. "I didn't want you to fake anything."

"Which is why you're there, and I'm not," he said, sounding almost disappointed.

Connie traced circles on the table with her thumb. "Yeah. I guess so. I'd be lying if I said I weren't disappointed." She swallowed hard. "I wish this could've worked out, King. I really do."

He was silent for a moment before finally responding. "It

worked out, baby," he said in a low, sad tone. "Just not the way we would've liked."

"What *we* would've liked?" she asked quietly. "Or what *you* would've liked?"

"Like I said, Connie, I didn't call to argue."

"We're past arguing. Arguing would mean there was still a chance for us, and I think we both know that's not the case anymore."

Connie was baiting him. John could feel it, trying to get him to say something—right or wrong, good or bad, to confirm shit she'd already made up her mind about, or to discredit him. Whatever the case, this conversation was going nowhere and he decided it was time to cut this call short.

"If you need anything," he said quietly, "you know how to reach me."

"And what would I possibly need from you, John? Why would I ever call you when I already know where you stand with all this?"

"I'm just saying."

"I know what you're saying," she said irritably. "And thanks. I'll keep that in mind." Connie hung up the phone, leaving John alone with the dial tone.

The food at the diner was giving him gas and the runs, and John headed to his uncle's spot hoping to get some real food made by somebody who didn't wear a hairnet. Connie was never far from his thoughts though he wished she could've been. From the very beginning he made it clear what kind of man he was, and the word *family* wasn't a word that fit well with who he was at all. In the beginning, they'd been careful. Connie was all high-strung and worried about giving him the herpes some cat had infected her with years ago, and he'd been leery about catching that shit, too. He could hardly kiss her without having to put on a rubber. But eventually they'd settled into a routine and each other, and they got comfortable. John got comfortable, and spending the next twenty, thirty years with this woman didn't seem like such a bad idea, so—yeah. They lost track of the need for safe sex all the time, and condoms weren't always so readily available, and besides, he loved the hell out of her fine ass. It never dawned on him that there were other possibilities besides STDs. Shit, she'd never mentioned wanting any other kid but Jade, and as far as he knew, she didn't want any. Now her ass was pregnant and wanted him to be pregnant, too, and happy about the idea of bringing some kid into the world to be raised by two people who'd spent most of their fucked-up lives being fucked-up. It just wasn't a good fit. She wanted him gone. And he wanted to be gone. Yeah, he was a mothafucka for it. But that just proved his point. Didn't it?

Adam was standing in the front of the house waiting for him to pull up as usual, excited to see him, like some big kid standing in line waiting to see Santa Claus or something. And damn if he wasn't just as happy to see his old man, too.

"Hey, Pop," he said, getting out of the car, going over to Adam, where the two embraced and John lifted him up off the ground. Moses told him once that the only time Adam ever came out of the house on his own was when he knew John was coming.

"B . . . b . . . boy!" Adam patted John hard on the back. "My boy! G . . . g . . . good!" John finally sat him back down on the ground. Adam nodded and grinned. "G . . . g . . . good!"

"Yeah," John grinned back. "It's good to see you too, man."

Adam was a crooked old man who walked using crutches. Years ago, he'd been almost beaten to death for raping a little girl, but he never raped anybody. She was young in years, but he was younger in his thinking. He was a sixty-year-old man who'd never mentally be more than six, but he knew love. He'd found it in Mattie King, a teenage girl, too fast for her own good, who'd done things she had no business doing. She claimed she loved him, though, but only in secret, in the letters she wrote, and in the conversations between the two of them.

Some crazy woman claimed she'd seen Adam following behind that girl, and that he'd done terrible things to her.

Moses, Adam's younger brother, saved his life. "I heard what they was about to do, and I got in my old truck, and found 'em in that old barn," he said in his deep and heavy voice. Moses was a mountain of a man, so big, if you stood just right, you could get lost in his shadow. "I don't remember too much of what happened." He stared reflectively ahead, into the open field across from the porch. "Shit, I was mad. And don't nobody want to be 'round me when I gets mad," he laughed. "They tried to kill 'im, and they almost did. But I got them first," he nodded. "Yeah. I got 'em all."

Chapter 21

Kiss me," Justin whispered to Cookie perched on his lap. He'd just come, and so had she. Time between visits was getting shorter, and he was one of the few tricks she didn't mind doing.

Cookie obediently did as she was told, and folded her tongue into his mouth. She let him break rules with her, touching. Hell, yeah, his handsome ass could touch her any way he wanted. She broke the seal of their kiss and stared into his eyes. "That was delicious, baby," she said softly, flicking her tongue across his lips. "It's been forever since anybody's gotten me off like that."

He cupped her full, firm ass in his hands and squeezed.

"That's a shame, baby," he responded, lightly kissing her shoulder. "A woman like you should be treated like a queen. Like she's special."

Reesy's flight had taken off that morning. She'd left with hardly more than a good-bye to him and quick kisses to the kids, promising she'd call when she landed in Kansas City. Maybe she had called, but Justin didn't wait around to find out. He'd left the office early, dropped the kids off at his mother's house, and made a trip to the bank before it closed. He got himself something to eat, caught a movie, and then headed straight for her, where he knew she'd be waiting.

"I'm gonna have to be getting back to work soon," she said apprehensively. "Burt's gonna be knocking on that door any minute." Burt was the watchdog, big, ugly, mean, making sure the girls were safe, and making money.

"I need some time to myself, Ma," he'd woefully explained to his mother earlier that evening. "I know this is short notice, but . . . I had no idea she'd just take off like this. I offered to go with her, but—"

"Don't worry about the kids," she reassured him. "They'll be fine here for a few days."

"I've got more money," he quickly said as Cookie climbed off him.

She looked at him and chuckled. "Don't you think you'd better catch your breath first?"

"No. No, I mean . . . for the weekend." Justin stood up and hastily pulled up his pants and tucked in his shirt.

Cookie hooked her bra and stared at him, confused.

"I want you to—" Justin sounded panicked and desperate. He took a deep breath to calm himself down. "A thousand dollars, Cookie," he said, more calmly.

"What?"

"Twelve hundred," he offered too quickly. "For you to spend the weekend with me . . . starting tonight."

He knew it sounded crazy. Hell, he felt crazy just saying it. She was a prostitute. He was married, but he wanted her like he hadn't wanted anything or anybody his whole life. Reesy's leaving the way she did pissed him off, but it also left a window of opportunity open, one that he knew he had to take advantage of now, or miss it forever. Did he call himself being in love with this woman? He had no idea. He just knew he needed her—close and for more than twenty minutes. Justin was missing something he couldn't put his finger on, but in all the years they'd been married, Reesy had never been able to satisfy it. It wasn't until he was here, with her, that he could give in to satisfaction and contentment, and he was desperate to grab even more of it, and hold onto it for as long as he could.

"Are you serious?" She stared at him in disbelief. Cookie wasn't an idiot. She made it a rule never to get with johns outside of the club. Burt was in the club, and he made sure she and all the other girls were safe. Alone with a client—a girl just wasn't sure. But twelve hundred dollars was some good-ass money, and she sure as hell could use money like that. "I don't know, Justin," she said hesitantly.

"Fifteen," he countered. He hadn't planned on spending more than a grand, but—he wanted to fall asleep holding her in his arms, and wake up with her in his arms, make love to her until he couldn't anymore, and, just for a few days, forget about marriage, kids, accounting, marriage. Justin had spent his life following rules, blending into them, becoming them. For once, he just wanted the freedom to break a few and not give a damn.

"I'll have to tell Tommy—" Tommy managed the club.

"I'll wait," he said anxiously. Justin took her hand in his, pulled her close, and kissed her softly. "I just want more time, Cookie. That's all."

He managed to get a room at the Radisson in northeast Denver. It wasn't the best, but on such short notice, it was decent enough. Warm water ran over the two of them, lathered in soap, kissing passionately in the shower. God! She was beautiful. He could hardly take his eyes off her. He ran his hand across her wavy black hair that clung to her back. Rich brown eyes stared back into his.

"What do you want me to do?" she asked softly.

He was caught off guard by the question and he chuckled, embarrassed. "What?"

Cookie pressed against him, running her hand down the small of his back. "You paying me a lot of money, Justin." She put her lips to his nipple, flicked her tongue against it, and tugged slightly. "I'm all yours this weekend, so . . . whatever you want." She shrugged and smiled. "All you got to do is ask."

"You're doing it." He sounded like some young-ass school-boy with a crush. "I just wanted you here with me, Cookie. That's all."

Cookie put her hand between his thigh, then slowly eased it up to his balls and began to massage them. "Well," she said seductively, "I'm here, baby. And for the next two days, I belong to you. However you want me to. Just . . . tell me what it is you really want, and I'll be your fantasy."

He thought for a moment, digging deep to reach down inside himself and pull out desires he'd never bothered to entertain before in his life. This beautiful woman had just promised him the world, and all he had to do was reach out and take it.

"I want you to treat me like I'm your man, Cookie. Like . . . I'm your only man."

He could feel embarrassment burning his face, but if she noticed, she never said a word.

Cookie smiled. "That's all you had to say, baby." Sliding down the length of him to her knees, she took his dick in her hand, batted lovely brown eyes up at him, then eased it between two of the most luscious lips he'd ever tasted.

Justin had always wondered what getting his dick sucked would feel like. Reesy would never even think of doing such a thing. Justin heard his cell phone ring in the other room, and ignored it. It was probably his mother or his wife . . . but he didn't care. And as streams of water pummeled against his back, he closed his eyes and gave in to the fantasy who called herself Cookie.

Chapter 22

"Hi," Dr. Gwen Dennis greeted Connie, sitting on the examination table. "I'm Dr. Dennis." She smiled.

Connie started to speak, but had to clear her throat first. "Connie. Connie Rodgers."

She'd put this off long enough. Connie was just over two months pregnant and this was her first exam. She'd come to her appointments when she was carrying Jade only because Reesy had insisted on it. Reesy had pretty much gotten her through that whole pregnancy back then. But this time, Connie had to do it on her own. She and Reesy were barely talking to each other, and the last thing she needed was to have to deal with her sister's disapproval and doubts in Connie's ability to raise this kid. Besides, Reesy would just think this was some scheme Connie had come up with to make up for not being able to raise Jade. She'd have devalued this pregnancy and Connie's role in it, believing Connie was the same confused, scared woman she'd always been, incapable of taking care of children. To Reesy, she'd have been John in a dress.

Dr. Dennis read through Connie's chart. "I see you're about two months along, based on your last period."

Connie nodded. "Yeah, that sounds about right."

"This is your first examination?"

No. They'd examined her at the abortion clinic, but Connie decided it wasn't worth mentioning. "Yes," she said, nervously.

"You're . . . forty?"

Connie nodded.

"First baby?"

She shrugged. "Sort of."

Dr. Dennis stared back quizzically. "Sort of?"

Connie cleared her throat again. "I had a daughter." She nervously scratched the back of her neck. "But I gave her up for adoption to my sister . . . about eight years ago."

"I see."

She saw. What? Connie tried to read her expression and the tone of her voice, but Dr. Dennis wasn't expressing much of anything.

"You plan on keeping this one?"

Connie looked surprised that she'd ask a question like that. Would she have asked it if she hadn't known about the adoption? "Yes," she said sternly. "I do."

The good doctor noticed Connie's defensiveness and quickly added, "I only ask because there are plenty of good families out there who'd be willing to adopt this one, too, if you were interested."

"Well, I'm not." She felt herself on the verge of tears. Damn hormones!

Dr. Dennis smiled warmly, and patted a warm hand on Connie's thigh. "Good." She pulled out her stethoscope to begin the examination. "Now, let's get this show on the road."

———

At the end of the visit, Connie emerged from the examination room and met Dr. Dennis at the nurse's station, busy making notes in Connie's file. "Lois," she called out to the receptionist. "Will you please make sure Miss Rodgers has an appointment scheduled for next month before she leaves."

Connie was caught off guard. "Next month? So soon?"

The doctor nodded. "Oh, you'd better get used to me, girl-friend," she smiled. "You'll be seeing me every month through your second trimester, and then biweekly, and then weekly, and maybe even every day," she laughed.

"Why?"

"Because as lovely as you are, my dear, you're forty."

"I'm not old!"

Dr. Dennis flipped open her file. "You're certainly not old." She snapped it closed. "I just want to keep a close eye on you and that baby of yours, Connie. At your age, there's a higher risk of certain chromosomal disorders in the baby, and we just need to make sure we don't miss anything." Second thoughts threatened to creep in, but Dr. Dennis seemed to sense that, too. "Don't you dare worry," she said reassuringly. "This baby is go-ing to be fine. Cross my heart."

Connie said good-bye to the doctor, set up her next appoint-ment, then headed toward the elevator. Once inside, she pulled a photograph from her purse and stared at it, hardly believing what she was seeing.

"Do you want to know what it is?" Dr. Dennis's question came back to her in that elevator.

"It's a boy, Connie. A little boy."

She lightly ran her finger over the photograph where his face was, and gave in to a smile. This was her baby. Her son.

———

Normally, she wouldn't bother Connie while she was at work. But Evelyn Turner was at her wits' end, worried sick over Reesy and the way she'd been acting lately. She'd picked up and just taken off without telling anybody where she was going to be staying in Kansas or when she'd be home. Poor Justin was just as frustrated as she was over his wife's unpredictable behavior. He'd come home from work early to find her packing and barking out commands on what he needed to do while she was gone.

She went to Connie hoping that she knew something about where Reesy was going and how to get in touch with her. Evelyn and Justin had tried calling her cell phone, but Reesy hadn't answered.

All she knew about Connie's job was that she made jewelry, and that she helped to run a quaint little store on Broadway. As soon as she walked through the door, Evelyn felt as if she'd been transported into some remote African village far removed from the busy street outside. The room smelled of sandalwood, decorated with abstract and boldly colored artwork she found much too dynamic for her taste.

Evelyn waited patiently in the back of the store, casually browsing while Connie waited on a customer.

"Oh, this is lovely, Connie." The woman at the counter crooned over the piece Connie was showing her. "Is this amber?"

"No, actually it's heliodor, which is a yellow or green variety of beryl. It's a gorgeous stone, very durable, found in places like Madagascar and Brazil."

"I love the ring, but could you make earrings to match it?"

"Absolutely." She pulled out a pad of paper, and began going back and forth with the lady with her ideas.

Connie waved to Evelyn, acknowledging that she'd seen her. "So, is this going to be cash or charge?"

"Charge, of course."

Connie rang up the order, and as hard as Evelyn tried not to be nosy, she couldn't help but overhear the price.

"That'll be eight-fifty."

Not bad, Evelyn thought to herself. Maybe she'd help the poor girl out before leaving and buy a piece of her jewelry, too.

Evelyn waited for the customer to leave, then smiled as she approached Connie sitting behind the glass display cased counter. "How are you, Connie?"

"Fine, Mrs. Turner," she responded curtly. "What brings you all the way down here?"

Reading Connie was difficult for Evelyn to do. She had a way of saying one thing to Evelyn, but always seeming to imply something else. Reesy had told her she was making something out of nothing, but Evelyn had an instinct when it came to people, and when it came to Connie, she knew that the woman didn't like her. Reesy never told Evelyn, but she knew Connie blamed her for separating them when they were children. Reesy had even asked Evelyn once, "Mom, why did you take me, and not my sister?"

Reesy was too young to understand. Both of the girls were. Adoption wasn't an easy decision for Evelyn and her husband, Matt. They'd tried everything to have children of their own, but they were never blessed that way. Reesy was adorable, and she smiled easily, and seemed so ready to be loved. But Connie— Connie was an angry older child, defensive and distant. Evelyn saw it in her eyes the first time they were introduced to the girls. Adoption was a stressful situation. "Connie is too much for us, Matt," she explained apologetically. "I don't think we can help her."

"Well, I . . . I wanted to talk to you about Reesy, Connie. Have you spoken to her?"

Connie shrugged indifferently. "I spoke to her last week."

"Did she tell you she was leaving? Did she call you yesterday before she got on the plane?"

That got Connie's attention. "A plane? To—"

"To find her mother," Mrs. Turner interrupted. "She didn't tell you she was going?"

Connie sighed irritably. "No, she didn't. But she's a grown woman. She doesn't have to tell me anything."

Mrs. Turner looked overly concerned. "I'm not surprised. She didn't even tell Justin she was leaving until the last minute. Ever since she became consumed with finding that woman—"

Connie tried not to chuckle. "That woman is her mother." Granted, Connie wasn't all that hyped about this obsession Reesy had with finding Charlotte, either, but she had good reason. She hated Charlotte. Reesy never did, and that was the problem, but Connie understood that. What she didn't understand was this woman, Reesy's adoptive mom, looking like someone had stolen her puppy, who wasn't even trying to feel where Reesy was coming from.

"That woman—your mother abandoned the two of you when you were just children," she said, as if Connie didn't already know it. "Why on earth would she want to find her? I don't understand it, Connie. I've done everything for Reesy. I took her in, loved her, her father and I have given her everything she could possibly want. That woman hasn't lifted a finger for her in almost thirty years, and . . ." Evelyn had held back her frustration for too long, and it was starting to burst through in the last place she'd ever wanted it to, in front of Connie. "I love my daughter." She blinked away tears. "I only want what's best for her, and Charlotte Rodgers is not it."

Connie stared blankly at her, realizing the selfish nature of this woman and seeing it fully for the first time since she'd known her. Reesy had it honest. That was for damn sure. First, Charlotte made her the apple of her demented eye, and then Ma Turner picked up where she left off, and crowned her the Princess of Perfection to finish the job. Shit. Girlfriend never really had a fair shot at humility. Poor, poor overprivileged Reesy.

"So, why are you here, Mrs. Turner?" Connie asked unemotionally.

Evelyn looked a bit wounded by the tone of Connie's voice. But she was desperate for answers, and Connie might be her only hope. Her husband had accused her of overreacting, and he'd waved off her concerns and turned his attention back to the news before she left the house to come here. "I want to know where my daughter is," she responded quietly. "And to know that she's all right."

"Call her."

"I tried," she said quickly. "Justin tried, too, but—"

"Well, maybe she'll call you, then. Just be patient," she said condescendingly. "I'm sure you'll hear from her soon."

"I don't want to lose her," Evelyn blurted out as Connie stepped from behind the counter and walked away. Connie stopped and slowly turned around. "I don't want to lose my daughter."

"Lose her?" Connie asked, surprised. "What makes you think you're going to lose Reesy?"

Evelyn Turner's hands trembled. "What if she finds Charlotte and—what if she doesn't need me anymore, Connie? What if she—"

Connie shook her head, amazed. "Are you for real?" she said in disbelief. "I don't think you have anything to worry about, Evelyn. Reesy's a grown woman, and believe me when I tell you that there's no reason for you to worry."

"I can't help it." Her voice quivered.

Connie folded her arms in front of her. "If you're worried about some happy, heartfelt reunion taking place and Reesy being swept up in a cloud of her biological mother's love and whisked off to some happy place in the sky, it ain't gonna happen. Charlotte will see to that. And once Reesy finally decides to get her head out of her ass and opens her eyes, she'll see that woman for what she truly is. Believe me. It won't take long."

"I don't know, Connie. Reesy loves Charlotte."

Connie rolled her eyes. "Reesy's an idiot over Charlotte," she said irritably. "Always has been."

"How come you're not? How come you can see her for the kind of woman she is?"

Connie just shook her head. "Because I wasn't the favorite. Reesy's everybody's favorite."

"If she calls, Connie . . ."

"I'll let you know."

She glanced nervously at the display case and saw one of the prettiest bracelets she'd ever laid eyes on. And besides, maybe if she bought something, she'd be helping Connie too, in some small way. "That's lovely." She turned to Connie and smiled, pointing at the bracelet. "May I see it?"

"Sure." Connie unlocked the case and set the bracelet on the counter.

"Did you make this yourself?"

Connie nodded. "Yeah."

Evelyn Turner reached into her purse and pulled out her wallet. "I'll take it," she said proudly. "It'll be a lovely addition to my collection of costume jewelry. How much is it?"

"Fifteen," Connie said, smirking.

Mrs. Turner pulled out a twenty-dollar bill. "Oh, that's very reasonable."

Connie stared at her money, and then back at her. Evelyn Turner always did have a way of underestimating Connie. "Fifteen hundred, Evelyn."

Evelyn stared at her blankly. "Dollars?"

Connie shrugged.

Suddenly, Evelyn looked embarrassed and slid her money back into her purse. "Oh, well—I—"

Connie closed the case and locked it. "Don't worry." She wrinkled up her nose. "I can't afford it either."

Mrs. Turner lowered her head and walked dejectedly to the door. Connie walked behind her. Then Evelyn stopped abruptly, wrapped her arms around Connie, and smiled. "She might need you," she whispered. "If she needs you . . . please . . . go."

Connie watched Evelyn Turner disappear out the door and down the street toward her car. Reesy was doing exactly what Reesy wanted to do. And deep down, Connie knew she needed this, for closure if nothing else. Would she go if her sister needed her to confront their mother? Connie managed to find her closure the day she realized that woman wasn't coming back. But yeah, after all, it was Reesy. And everybody always made sure to take good care of Reesy.

Chapter 23

"U ncle surprised me with this place one day when we were just driving around town," Charlotte said smugly to Lynn, busy doing her nails. "He parked in front of the building and told me he had something to show me. When we walked inside, he handed me the keys and told me this was my place, and not to worry about the rent and heat because he'd take care of it." Lynn wasn't listening, but Charlotte didn't notice. "He even pays my phone bill, girl, and groceries? All I have to do is tell him what I need and he gets it to me the next day."

He'd given her a better life than Sammy promised. Charlotte would've had to work when they got to Memphis. She'd promised Sam she'd get a job as soon as they got there, before they took off from Denver. But Uncle said he didn't want her working.

"He told me I didn't need a job, and that a woman like me had no business flipping burgers or mopping floors." He'd sent this woman over to do her nails and toes. Here she was, sitting in her own apartment like a rich woman, having somebody come to her.

It was the way she'd always dreamed her life would be. Glodean had worked her ass off for next to nothing, for a janitorial service cleaning office buildings, and they were still on welfare and food stamps, she still got fat and kept having babies, and men came and went so fast, Glodean looked like a revolving door. Charlotte thought Dwayne would take care of her, but his sorry ass disappeared a year after Connie was born, and Charlotte had to crawl back to Glodean's house to stay with her.

"The sucka left yo fast ass. Good, goddammit! You reap what you sow, Charlotte. Yo ass reap what you sow."

She couldn't stand being in that house, and Charlotte promised herself she wouldn't have any more kids. Two and a half years later, she meet Reesy's daddy, Frederick. Short and round, Frederick drove a sharp car, dressed like he made a million dollars, and talked her right out of her panties. Frederick had his own place, and Charlotte packed up her shit and left before Glodean came home from work.

"Don't worry 'bout nothing, baby doll." Frederick's big lips damn near covered her whole face when he kissed her. "I'ma take good care of you and that little girl."

"Even though she ain't yours?" Charlotte asked sweetly, batting her eyes at him.

Connie was almost three at the time. "She mine 'cause she yours, baby."

The day she found out she was pregnant, Charlotte broke down crying, and for three days, that's all she did.

"What is it, girl?" Fredrick asked over and over again. "C'mon now. What the hell is wrong with you?"

"I'm pregnant," she wailed. Connie sat on the floor staring up at Charlotte.

Frederick shook his head, sucked his teeth, and waved her off. "Is that it? Shiiiit, girl! Why you acting like it's the end of the world? A baby ain't nothing."

Seven months later, Reesy was born. Frederick didn't live to see her third birthday. His dumb ass got shot trying to rob somebody.

"Later on in the week, Uncle's taking me shopping for some new clothes, and then taking me to get my hair done," she continued boasting to Lynn. The woman concentrated intensely on Charlotte's cuticles. She had hardly said ten words in the two hours she'd been there. "I used to wear a size twelve, but I girl—none of my clothes fit me anymore," Charlotte sighed. "I think I'm about a size ten now, or maybe even a eight. Uncle digs it, though. He just told me not to lose too much because he don't want no bony woman. And then after that, I'm going to ask him to buy me a car, so I can get around. I need to be able to come and go when I need to."

This fool had no idea who she was dealing with, but Lynn wasn't the one to tell her. Uncle was generous to a fault when he wanted to be, and when he didn't want to be, well, he could be other things that Lynn tried not to think about. He had this girl twisted around his finger, though, and she was too dumb to know it. He had her right where he wanted her, and Lynn knew Uncle would never buy her a car.

Charlotte stopped bragging long enough to notice the small diamond ring on Lynn's left hand. "You married?"

Lynn glanced up at Charlotte and saw her looking at her ring. "Engaged." The truth was that she'd been engaged for the last five years, wearing a ring Arnel had bought for her not long after she'd moved in with him. It was the one thing that belonged to her that she'd refused to let him pawn.

"Really?" Charlotte smiled. "What's his name?"

Lynn wasn't in the mood for small talk. She'd been working her ass off to get in and out of this chick's place so fast she'd never know what hit her dizzy behind. "Arnel."

Charlotte waited for more, but it was obvious Lynn wasn't offering more. "So, when's the big day?"

Lynn shrugged. "Haven't set one yet." She finished up with

Charlotte's nails, then leaned back and sighed. "There. All done."
Lynn just wanted to grab her shit and go, but it was almost as if
Charlotte knew it.

"Wanna get high?" she asked, blowing her wet nails. "Uncle left
me a couple of joints on the nightstand near the bed. Why don't you
go get them for me? I don't want to mess up my nails."

They'd finished one joint, and immediately started the second
one. Lynn and Charlotte sat on the living room floor leaning back
against the sofa, passing dope back and forth between them. Lynn
looked through the pictures Charlotte had given her. "You don't look
old enough to have kids this big." Weed made anybody bearable as
far as Lynn was concerned. Once Charlotte stopped going on and
on about the virtues of Uncle, Lynn actually liked the woman.

"Those are my babies, though," Charlotte gloated. "And as soon
as I can get on my feet, maybe get a job and get a bigger apartment,
I'm going back to get them."

Lynn handed the Polaroids back to Charlotte. "Who's keeping
'em?"

Charlotte hesitated before answering, her memory temporarily
clouded by the marijuana. They'd be all right, she told herself the
day she walked out and left them both standing there. Yeah, they'd
be fine, and they were fine. She could feel it down in her bones. "My
momma's got them," she lied. "They staying with her."

Time passed in slow motion while they lay on that floor talking
like old friends. A box of chocolate donuts and a bag of potato
chips seemed to appear out of nowhere, next to them on the floor.

"Damn, this shit is good," Charlotte said with her mouth full,
munching on potato chips.

"I love Arnel," Lynn said sincerely. "But I swear to God, it ain't
easy. I left my family behind for him."

"I guess they ain't so liberal. Huh?"

"Girl, please! My daddy told me not to even come back for his funeral when he died, 'cause he'd curse my niggah-lovin' ass from the grave if he had to."

"Damn! That ain't cool."

"Naw, but back then, the idea of living without Arnel wasn't cool either. He had me hooked the first time he smiled at me, girl. I just . . ."

"That sounds like love at first sight."

"Oooh, it was. And in a mean, hard kinda way. In a losing my eva-lovin mind kinda way. That good, bad, nasty kinda way," she laughed.

Charlotte laughed, too. "Sounds like some damn good dick if you ask me."

"Damn good!" Lynn yelled.

"I ain't never been in love like that," Charlotte said reflectively. "I mean, I've been close, but . . . well, no, I take that back." She thought about Sam. "I don't know if it was love, but it was something."

"Good dick," Lynn said matter-of-factly. "That's all it takes."

"No, now, that ain't all it takes, Lynn. Sam had the good dick, but his ass didn't have no money. Now with Uncle," she took another hit of the joint, "I got good dick and money. I mean, look around. He did all this shit. Sam left my ass stranded in some cheap-ass motel on the other side of town, and Uncle picked me up and sat me down right here. That's what it's about."

Lynn didn't say a word. Charlotte only saw Uncle in the light he wanted her to see him. But Lynn had seen him in the dark, just the other day as a matter of fact. Arnel still couldn't walk right.

"I always wanted a man to take care of me. Someone who treated me good, and just gave and gave without even thinking about it. I could fall in love with him for that," Charlotte said quietly. "I'm falling in love with Uncle already."

"Just 'cause he gives you shit?" Lynn reached across Charlotte for the box of chocolate donuts. "What kinda love is that?"

"Shit." Charlotte rolled her eyes. "It's the best kind as far as I'm concerned. Just be my man and take care of me, and I'll love your ass to death."

"Well, he ain't your man." Lynn wanted to take it back as soon as she'd said it. "Shit."

Charlotte turned to look at her. "What's that supposed to mean?"

"Nothing." She took a big bite of donut and sat up to wash it down with a long sip of Schlitz. "Don't worry about it. Nothing."

Charlotte could see the panic in Lynn's bloodshot eyes and she sat up, too. "Lynn. Don't play, girl. What are you saying?"

Lynn searched her thoughts for a way out, but instinctively she knew it was too late. Hell, the woman couldn't have been that dumb anyway. Could she? She'd been bragging all afternoon about her man, and all the good things her man had been doing for her. If he was her goddamned man, why the hell wouldn't he have just moved her in with him, or be living here with her instead? "Uncle's married, Charlotte," Lynn said matter-of-factly. Charlotte stared at her, dumbfounded. "Come on, girl. Don't act like you didn't know. Why you think he set you up like this? And why you think his ass don't live here with you? Everybody in town knows Uncle's married, and you'd better be careful and be glad he got you locked up tight in this one-bedroom castle, 'cause if Sherrell ever found out about you . . . she'd kill your size-eight ass."

Charlotte tried to keep a straight face, but failed miserably. "I hear some people think she might even be a man."

Lynn stared in disbelief at Charlotte. "You did know."

She smacked her lips and then grabbed a chocolate donut. "Of course I know. You think I'm stupid? Uncle told me about her.

Showed me pictures of her, too, and of his kids. Girl, I know every-thing."

"Well, Sherrell's pictures don't do her justice. That woman is six feet tall and got shoulders like a linebacker. She looks like a man in a dress in person."

"Well, ain't no secrets between me and my man. I know all about his woman, Lynn. I know damn near everything there is to know about him, and I'm fine as wine sitting up here like a queen," she winked.

Lynn stared at her for a moment, then spoke quietly. "You don't know everything, Charlotte. Just what he wants you to know."

Chapter 24

You look so pretty, Momma," Cammy told Charlotte, apprehensively emerging from her bedroom. She wore the prettiest blouse she owned, and some nice slacks Cammy had brought her last Christmas that still had the tag on them. She'd gone to the beauty shop earlier that day to get her hair pressed and curled the way she used to wear it years ago, and Cammy had made up her face, too, even going so far as to put some lipstick and rouge on her.

"You sure I look all right?" she asked, nervously smoothing her hand down the front of her blouse. "I'm so much bigger than I used to be," she said, disappointed. "And my face—" Charlotte raised her hand to her face, and tried hard not to cry. Charlotte used to have such a beautiful face, but now she looked like a monster. "She's not gonna recognize me anymore, Cammy."

Cammy rushed to her mother's side and put her arm reassuringly around her shoulder. "Sure she will. And she'll think you're as beautiful now as you were back then. I promise."

Reesy was on her way. She'd taken a flight into Kansas City, rented a car, and spent the night in a hotel. This morning she called and finally, Cammy got her own chance to speak with her sister.

"I'm Cammy," she'd told Reesy over the phone before giving her directions.

"Cammy? Are you a friend of my mother's?"

Cammy laughed before answering, letting it sink in that the two of them were sisters and strangers. "You could say that," she said quietly before clearing her throat. "I'm your sister, Reesy."

You could've heard a pin drop between them.

When they heard a car pull up in front of the house, both Cammy and Charlotte froze, then stared at each other, afraid to move and more afraid not to. "That's her, Momma." Cammy's eyes grew wide. "That's Reesy."

Murphy, Kansas, was a two-hour drive from Kansas City, and rural. But the drive had been a blessing, giving her time to help calm her nerves and get her thoughts in order. She'd spent the night in a hotel near the airport in Kansas City, but she'd hardly slept a wink. Finding out that she had another sister had kept her up all night, raising all sorts of new questions she hardly had space for in her head. Like, how old was this sister? What was she like? Would the two of them get along? And why hadn't Charlotte abandoned her?

At one point during the night, she'd picked up the phone to call Connie and tell her the news, but then hung up, knowing full well that Connie could've cared less. She did try calling Justin, though. Several times, as a matter of fact, but he didn't answer the phone. So she called his mother first, hoping she'd get answers from her, so that she wouldn't have to call her own mother.

Sophia Braxton sounded irritated with her when she called. "The children are spending the weekend with me and Lou," she told her. "Justin's . . . he needs time, Reesy."

So he was still pissed, and refusing to take her calls, pouting because he couldn't have his way. To hell with Justin.

A million questions for her mother came to mind on the drive to Murphy, and just as quickly, a million questions vanished and Reesy had no idea what she would say or how she felt. The inevitable grew in her stomach the more she drove, though, sitting there like a rock made of dread and anticipation and confusion. Most of all—confusion. Why did she leave them? Reesy remembered that day, most of it. She remembered getting up early and turning on the television to watch cartoons. Connie was in the kitchen, making them something to eat. Reesy wanted cereal. She always wanted cereal, but Connie told her she couldn't have any, and they argued.

"Shhhhh, Reesy," Connie commanded. "You're gonna wake up Momma."

But Momma was already awake, and surprised them both coming from her room, fully dressed and smoking a cigarette. And then she disappeared. She walked out, and she never came back. Why didn't she ever come back? That was the only question that really mattered, she thought, taking a deep breath and following Cammy's directions and turning down the street where they lived.

She slowly pulled the car up in front of a small, cornflower-blue framed home in need of paint, with a yard that probably got watered only when it rained. A white Ford Escort was parked in what was probably the driveway. Reesy turned off the engine and then noticed her palms sweating and wrung them together, taking slow deep breaths. The front door of the house opened and a young pregnant woman stepped out onto the porch, followed by a shorter, portly woman all made up, looking as if she were going to church. Both of them stared at her, waiting patiently for her to get out of the car.

Reesy willed her body to move, finally opened the door and slowly stepped out of the car, and stared back at them. The older woman was the woman in the picture Avery had showed her. A lump swelled in her throat at the realization that she was seeing her mother for the first time in real life since she was eight, and Reesy stifled a cry. It was her, all right. It was Charlotte.

Slowly, Charlotte stepped toward the edge of the porch, looking for that precious little girl inside the beautiful, stylish woman climbing out of that car. Her hair was long, straight, parted on the side. Soft doe eyes blinked back at her, probably looking for her, too. Reesy slowly approached the porch, tears pooling in her eyes. Oh, she was so beautiful and so perfect and yes, yes! Charlotte descended the steps and stretched out her arms as the two of them finally met in front of the house, and embraced.

"My baby!" she wailed, squeezing Reesy tight in her arms. "It is you! My baby girl! Oh, Lord! It is you!"

Reesy held her arms firmly down by her sides, unwilling to return her mother's embrace so easily. "Momma?" She inhaled deeply without meaning to, recognizing the everlasting scent of the woman she used to love more than anyone else in the world. Suddenly Reesy broke down sobbing, angry and happy at the same time, relieved and yet full of resentment. "Is it you, Momma? Oh God! Is it really you?"

"Shhhh." Charlotte reached up and stroked Reesy's soft hair. "Hush, baby." She reassured her the way she used to when she was small. "It's okay, Reesy. Momma's here now. I'm right here."

The sound of her voice was like the sweetest song, and the words fell on that part of her that needed to hear them most, the part that was still small and afraid and missed her mother. Instinctively, Reesy wrapped her arms around Charlotte and held onto her, too. "I missed you, Momma," she sobbed.

"But we're together now, Reesy," she smiled. "We're together again, baby."

Chapter 25

She'd recognize that broad, strong back in her sleep with her eyes closed. She walked up behind him, standing at the deli counter in the grocery store. "I swear, John King." He turned, surprised to see her, and smiled. "Why don't you just go ahead and move down here? Seems like I see your behind every other month."

He was happy to see her, too, but then, who wouldn't be? Racine Cook was finer now at forty then she was at fifteen when she called herself his girlfriend. John's second home was deep between that girl's thighs back then. "Hey, girl!" He hugged her every time like it was the first, time, savoring every luscious inch of her luscious self.

Racine moaned. "You what's up. What brings you here this time? Back to check on your daddy?"

She wore her hair cropped close to her head. It looked good on her, framing her pretty face and big brown eyes. Thick red lips always compelled him to lick his every time he looked at them, wishing he could be licking hers instead. She was smaller on top than she was on the bottom, pear-shaped, jiggling like Jell-o from the waist down, and watching Racine walk was like watching a sporting event, with both cheeks bidding for the best spot on the field. Yeah, he still had a crush on her. Probably always would, too.

"This is my hometown, Racine. What's wrong with a man coming back to his hometown every now and then?"

"Nothing. You just down here more than you seem to be anywhere else. Makes me kinda think you should think about staying. Save some money on gas," she winked.

Racine had a way of making it clear, without saying a word, that she was interested in John for more than just friendship. Most of the times, he waged an internal battle to ignore it. After all, she'd married his childhood best friend, Lewis, and had three kids by the man. "How's Lewis and the kids doing?" he asked, dousing the fire that always threatened to get out of control between them if they weren't careful.

The glimmer from her eyes seemed to fade. "Kids are fine. My oldest graduated last year and is getting ready to leave for college in the fall, and the two youngest . . . they bad as hell," she laughed.

John laughed, still waiting on her to mention Lewis.

"How's your daddy?"

He nodded. "He's good."

"Glad to see you, I'll bet."

John shrugged. On one of his trips back, he'd stopped by to see Lewis and Racine, engulfed half a slab of ribs and a six-pack, and told them the truth about his father and what he knew of Mattie.

"For my whole life, I believed what everybody else believed and I hated him for it," he told them.

"So, he didn't rape Mattie?" Lewis asked, surprised at hearing it for the first time.

John shook his head. "Naw, man. She loved him. I read the

letter myself. When she came up pregnant, everybody wanted to believe that he'd raped her more than they wanted to believe that a pretty little fourteen-year-old girl loved a retarded man."

Lewis shook his head. "That's fucked-up, man."

"Tell me about it."

John took his package from the clerk at the deli counter and headed toward the checkout lane. Racine walked next to him.

"So, how long you here for this time?" she asked.

"Don't know."

"While you're here, you should come by the house for dinner one night. You know how much you love my cooking," she laughed, playfully bumping her shoulder into him.

John frowned. "Your cooking? Hell," he huffed, "Lewis is the one who can cook. "You can't burn water, girl."

She laughed. "I've gotten better, believe me."

"Uh-huh," he said, dryly.

"I've had to." Her tone changed suddenly. "Lewis and I are separated."

John stopped and looked at her. "When did this happen?"

"Back in October."

He looked surprised. "October? Didn't I stop by the house in October? And weren't y'all still together?"

She shook her head. "Not really. He was staying there, but . . . we slept in separate rooms, and he was looking for a place to live."

"Damn!" He paid for his steak. Racine trailed behind him. "Where's he staying?"

"In Corpus," she said, staring hard at John. He turned and looked at her. "So I'm going to ask you again." She cleared her throat. "Why don't you come by the house for dinner before you leave?"

Racine's message was loud and clear. John took his change, and the two walked out to his car in the parking lot. All kinds of thoughts crossed his mind, skidding and crashing into each other. Loving Connie. Respecting or disrespecting Lewis. Drowning in Racine's pussy.

"It don't have to mean anything, John," she whispered, standing close. "Just . . . two old friends having a good time. That's it. You used to enjoy my company," she smiled.

"I loved your company," he said menacingly.

"Well, why don't you try loving it again before you leave town this time? And give me the pleasure of enjoying yours again, too."

He hesitated before answering, looking for one good reason to turn down her offer, but at the moment, his mind came up blank. "When?"

"Friday? I can send the kids to my mother's, and Lenae, my oldest, will probably be spending the night with some friend of hers anyway. I can make you something good to eat."

Her implications were loud and clear. Racine stood too close. She smelled too good, and that boner of his was tugging hard on his brain stem.

Connie. Her name came to mind, then her face, reminding him that the right thing to do would be to decline Racine's tempting offer.

Racine stepped closer to him and pressed her small breasts lightly against his chest. "Is six o'clock good for you?" she asked seductively.

"Yeah." Shit! "I'll be there."

He drove home thinking about Racine's fine ass the whole way. Every now and again, he thought about Connie's fine ass, too, but like Racine said, it didn't have to mean a damn thing, just dinner between friends. His dick had been hard ever since she came up to him in that grocery store. When was the last time he'd had some? Shit. Felt like forever. Tony Bennett had said he'd left his heart in San Francisco; well, John had left his in Denver, but his dick was alive and well in Bueller, Texas, with him, and Friday had better hurry the hell up to get here, or he'd bust open all over every goddamned thing.

She met him at the door wearing black lace and high-heeled shoes, and after he slipped on a condom, everything else became a blur. Sweat burned trails down his back as John drilled deep into Racine's hot pussy from behind. He balanced himself on his knees, bracing her legs against his sides with his arms, pressing her down on the bed with one hand in the middle of her back.

"Ah! Oh, yesssssss!" she called out. "Oh, yessssss! Ah!"

She raised her wide ass as high as she could, then dropped it in circles and back toward him, giving him some of the best-looking and -feeling ass he'd ever had. John leaned forward, pushing his weight down on her, then sucked and kissed the sensitive space down her spine.

"Ah! Shit!" She wrestled beneath him, and her eyes rolled up and disappeared into white space. "Fuck! Dammit . . . John! Shiiiit! Oh . . ."

Moments later, John lay on his back, staring up at Racine's wild ass, fucking him and looking evil, like she wanted to draw the life right out of him. He cupped her small breasts in his hands, grazing his thumbs over erect, black nipples, that he desperately wanted to suck.

"Come here," he growled, wrapping one arm around her

waist and pulling her toward him. She leaned forward and fed him titties like they were delicacies, flicking her nipples against his tongue until, one at a time, they disappeared between his lips.

John held on tight to mountains of ass with both hands, pushing himself even deeper inside her than he ever thought he could go. And Racine met him, stroke for stroke, the room permeated with sweat and sex, until she bucked hard, arching her back, "Oh, John! I'm cumming, baby!" she said, breathless. "My ass is cumming!"

Yeah. His ass was coming too, dammit! This shit was supposed to happen. Most people never came at the same time, but damned if the two of them weren't caught up in this dance of climaxing themselves into a froth, about to lose their damn minds and dizzy, ready to pass out in the chaos of sperm and cum, collapsing, finally, her on top of him, with neither one of them able to move.

Racine lay resting her head on John's chest, recalling how much smaller it looked at fifteen and how much she believed she loved him back then. Seemed like he was always running out her back door or jumping out of her bedroom window just before her parents walked in the door to catch them. She used to fantasize back then about what it might be like if she wasn't fifteen and they didn't have to hide from her parents.

"Would you like to stay all night?" she asked quietly. But John didn't answer. He was already asleep.

Chapter 26

The house was small and musky smelling, outdated. But Reesy couldn't take her eyes off her mother sitting across from her at the small kitchen table, covering Reesy's hands with hers. Cammy made coffee, glancing back at her older sister occasionally, awed by how pretty she was, and how much she favored Charlotte. Reesy was darker, even her eyes. She had arm-length lashes and soft understated features that formed a subtle beauty, unlike Charlotte's bold good looks Cammy had seen in pictures of her mother when she was a younger woman. But the resemblance to Charlotte was there.

She'd tried everything to look her best. Charlotte nervously ran her hand over her freshly pressed curls, smoothing them down the nape of her neck, pursing her lips together, and turning her face slightly away from Reesy, hoping to minimize her disfigurement. Cammy had done a good job, or at least, she'd done the best she could, Charlotte thought woefully. He'd made a mess of her that day she left Kansas City. Charlotte had come to terms with that years ago, but today, what he'd done to her seemed more unfortunate and cruel than ever.

"You look good, Momma." Reesy seemed to read her mind, and reassure her when she needed it most. Just like always, her special girl knew just what to say and when to say it. "I can hardly believe I'm sitting here," she sighed. "After all this time. I was starting to think that—"

Charlotte pressed her hand to Reesy's cheek. "I always knew, baby," she said tenderly, smiling warmly. "I always knew I'd see you again. I never doubted it."

Charlotte got down on her knees every night and prayed to God to let her see her children again. And when she'd finally gotten that letter from her daughter, telling her she'd been looking for her all this time, she realized that He'd been listening after all.

Cammy set three coffee cups down on the table and began filling each of them. Her hands were trembling with excitement and anticipation at being close to her sister.

"Cammy," Charlotte said sternly. "Reesy and me need to talk, baby." She stared unblinkingly at Cammy, who seemed a little caught off guard at her mother's tone.

"Oh, no," Reesy interrupted. "It's okay, Momma. She can stay."

Cammy could see in Charlotte's eyes that she couldn't stay, no matter what she or Reesy thought. "It's all right, Reesy," she smiled. "I'll leave you and Momma alone for a while so you two can catch up."

Reesy reached out and touched her arm, then pulled her hand back. "But you should be here."

Charlotte squeezed Reesy's hands. "Let her go, Reesy. It's all right."

Cammy disappeared into the living room, leaving Reesy alone with Charlotte. Moments later, they heard the sound of the front door closing, and the car pulling out of the driveway.

"How old is she, Momma?"

Charlotte's gaze never left her daughter's face. "Who? Cammy?

She's too old to be living at home, but she's got it in her mind that I can't live by myself, and no matter how many times I tell her she needs to get out on her own, she fusses and argues, and tells me she'll think about it," Charlotte chuckled.

"When's her baby due?"

No. No. No. Charlotte didn't want to spend this reunion talking about Camille's ass this whole time. "We'll talk about that later, Reesy." She patted her hand. "I want to know all about you, and how you been doing. You turned out fine, baby," she said proudly. "You look absolutely beautiful, just like I knew you would. But I still see my Lovebug in that pretty face. My baby girl."

Reesy blushed. As much as she wanted to be angry or give in to feelings of betrayal by her mother, seeing her now, Reesy couldn't have conjured up those feelings if she wanted to. Relief was the emotion she gave into. It was the only one that mattered. Relief that she'd finally found her mother, and was sitting here with her, face to face, and comfortable in the realization that she was complete again. But some pieces were missing, and only Charlotte could fill in the blanks for her. Reesy had left her children and her husband behind for those answers, and she couldn't leave without them.

"I need to know what happened, Momma," she asked quietly. "Why'd you leave us the way you did, and why didn't you come back?"

"I wanted to," Charlotte said earnestly. "Lovebug, I tried to come back."

"But why'd you leave in the first place?"

Charlotte sat quietly for a moment, stirring cream into her coffee, trying to remember the woman she was back then, and the reason she'd left her children behind. "Back then," she said, almost whispering, "it seemed like something I had to do."

"Something you had to do?" she asked, appalled. "How can abandoning your children ever be something to do, Momma?"

Charlotte was caught off guard by her daughter's tone. It sounded judgmental and condemning and it didn't set well with her. "I didn't abandon my children, Clarice," she said austerely. "I left."

Reesy stared at her confused. "What's the difference?"

Charlotte bolted up from the table, and paced back and forth in the kitchen. No, this wasn't the way it was supposed to be. Reesy was too hung up on the wrong thing. It didn't matter why Charlotte left that day. The important thing was that the two of them were together now.

"I loved my girls," she mumbled to herself, wringing her hands together in front of her. "I loved you and Connie more than my life, Clarice."

Reesy fought back the anger and resentment building inside her. But she felt herself losing the battle. "Then why'd you leave us?"

It was so long ago, she thought back, tracing steps she'd lost track of back through time to a place that didn't seem so important anymore. Reesy was asking all the wrong questions.

"Momma?"

"Hush, Reesy." She scolded Reesy like she was a child. Sam. Sam made her leave. He'd messed her mind up. Talked her into . . . into . . .

"It's not you I'm leaving, Charlie. I'm leaving Denver."

"Then let me come with you," she pleaded.

No. No, that's not what happened.

"Please, baby. Come with me to Memphis," Sam pleaded. Yes. He begged her to come with him.

"And what about the kids, Sammy? I can't leave my kids. I just

can't do it. I won't." The years twisted some memories, but Charlotte was sure about this. It was Sam who begged her to leave her kids for him. Charlotte didn't want to . . . he was leaving, and she felt trapped. Those damn kids had her feeling old and caged like an animal, and she—

"*If you promise to take me with you . . . we . . . don't have to take the kids, Sam . . . I'll figure something out.*"

"Connie said you didn't care about us," Reesy blurted out. "Connie said that you never loved us, Momma. That you didn't love us, and that you left because you didn't want us anymore," she cried. "But she was wrong. Wasn't she? I need to know! Connie was wrong, Momma?"

Charlotte turned to Reesy. "Why would Connie tell you things like that?" she asked softly. Connie was the one. She was always the one, and if Charlotte had left anybody behind, it had been Connie. Reesy just happened to have been too young.

"Is it true?" she yelled.

"Don't raise your voice at me, Clarice!" Charlotte screamed back, balling up her fists and pinning them down at her sides.

"Then tell me!"

"Connie's ass lied!" she spat, glaring deep into Reesy's eyes. "How the hell would she know?" Charlotte pounded her fist hard against the table. "How the hell would Connie know anything about me?"

"Then tell me why the hell you left, Charlotte! Because as far as I know, Connie was right!"

"She lied!"

"Then prove her wrong and tell me the truth!"

This woman standing in her kitchen wasn't her baby anymore. Charlotte backed away slowly, losing sight of the little girl she'd left behind, trembling at the grown woman standing before her, unwilling to back down and stop talking back at her mother. Connie had lied. She had told Reesy things that just weren't true, and Charlotte couldn't let her get away with lying on her like that.

"I had to leave," she said to Reesy. "Because . . . because I was afraid."

"Afraid? Afraid of what, Momma? Who?"

This fine, upstanding woman in her kitchen had children of her own. She was a mother, and surely she knew what it was like sometimes. She knew how hard it could be taking care of people who depended on you for everything, and how disappointing it was when she had to let them down.

Charlotte swallowed hard before answering. "Of you and your sister."

"What?"

Tears flooded Charlotte's eyes, and Reesy blurred out of focus. This woman would understand how hard it was raising kids, and doing the best you could only to realize it wasn't ever going to be good enough. Reesy understood, and right at this moment, Charlotte was depending on that. "Of not being able to do right by you . . . and your sister, Reesy."

"Take me with you, Sammy. Please—baby! I can't stay here. Take me with you to Memphis."

"That doesn't make sense!"

"I didn't think I was doing a good job as your mother, Reesy." She spoke softly now, sounding more sincere and tender, the way she used to when she held her little girl close to her on her lap. "It was hard for me, baby. Harder than you'll ever know, being by myself and taking care of two kids all alone. I didn't have a nice husband like you. All I had was me, and the two of you to take care of, and I was so young, Reesy." Charlotte's knees grew weak, and she slipped back into her chair. She sobbed. "I was young, and I was scared that I wasn't doing the best I could by you and Connie."

"You were doing fine, Momma," Reesy said sadly. "You were doing the best you could."

Charlotte shook her head and grabbed a napkin from the napkin holder in the center of the table, then dabbed her eyes. "Not good enough, baby. Every day was a struggle."

"I'm getting old too fast, Sam. The kids will be fine. Momma will take care of them for me. Just don't leave without me."

Reesy sat down quietly next to her mother.

"Welfare wasn't hardly enough to live off of, and there were times when I wasn't sure if we were going to be able to eat from one day to the next."

"I . . . I had no idea it was that bad."

Charlotte tried to smile. "No. Because I didn't want you to know, baby. It was up to me to take care of you. And one day," she shrugged. "I realized I couldn't. Not the way I needed to."

"Well, maybe if you'd gotten a better-paying job."

"Who was gonna hire me? I didn't have a degree—hell, I didn't even have a high school diploma, and it was all I could do to get the little piece of job I had. I was fifteen when I had Connie, too young to work, and I needed to stay home and take care of my baby girl. And just when she got old enough for pre-school, and I had decided to go back and get my GED, you came along, and—"

Reesy reached across the table and held her mother's hand.

"Every year I kept thinking things were going to get better, and every year they never did, until one day . . ." Charlotte sighed. "I thought y'all might do better without me, Lovebug. In fact," she sniffled, "I knew you would." Charlotte smiled proudly at her lovely daughter. "Look at you, baby. You got a nice man, kids, probably got a big house, too. Don't you?"

Reesy smiled. "It's all right."

Charlotte laughed. "Child, please! I know you must be living nice out there in Denver, and Connie, too." Her voice trailed off. "How's she doing?"

"She's all right, I guess."

"You guess? The two of you used to be thick as thieves when you were little."

"Connie's had it harder than me, Momma. After you left . . . well, she had a hard time, and sometimes she can't seem to get past everything that happened to her."

"What happened to her, Clarice?"

Clarice thought for a moment before answering, realizing that it wasn't her place to tell her sister's business, and that if Connie wanted Charlotte to know, she'd have to come to Murphy, Kansas, and tell her herself. So, she decided to change the subject. "So, did you ever get married, Momma? Did you marry Cammy's father?"

Charlotte blushed momentarily, but then grew solemn. "There was somebody," she smiled. "Somebody I loved very much. Cammy's daddy. He was special."

"Really?" Reesy smiled, too. "Tell me about him. What was his name? Where's he now?"

Charlotte shook her head. "Oh, I can't talk about him, baby. He passed away before Cammy was born, and it's still hard on me."

"Oh. I'm sorry, Momma."

"Me too. Every time I look at that girl, I see her daddy, though. Sometimes that's good and other times . . . he was the one, though, and if he was still alive, he'd be here . . . with me."

"I wish I could've met him."

"I wish you could've met him, too, Reesy. He was a good man. A very good man. Best I ever knew."

Hours passed at that table. Reesy showed her mother pictures of her children, and of Justin, and even some of Connie. Seeing Connie's face took her breath away, and Charlotte felt as if she were seeing her younger self for the first time all over again.

"I can't believe that's her." Charlotte covered her mouth with her hand and gasped. "She's so lovely, Reesy."

"Yes, she is," Reesy said fondly. "She's beautiful. Connie's never far from sadness, though. No matter how good things might be going in her life, you always get the feeling that there's something going on inside her that keeps her from appreciating it."

"Is she married too? Got kids?"

Reesy shook her head.

It was late when she finally found and checked into a local motel. Charlotte had insisted that she stay at the house and sleep in Cammy's room, but Reesy needed to be alone for a while. She needed time to sort through the events of the day, and to gather her thoughts, to try and make sense of everything she'd learned and the things she and her mother had talked about. She'd learned one very important lesson, though. Reesy had learned that her mother wasn't infallible, never had been. And that the woman she'd idealized when she was a child had been just a woman, one who was too young and too vulnerable to continue coping on her own without the support of a network of people around her who loved her. She and Connie were so much alike in that respect. Of the three of them, Reesy had been the fortunate one. She'd been loved and shielded her whole life from the ugliness of the world, and the Turners had picked up the pieces where Charlotte left off without missing a step. All of a sudden, Reesy felt blessed and grateful and loved, and very, very selfish.

It was late, and she knew he'd probably be asleep, but she needed to hear his voice. She let the home phone ring until the answering machine came on, which she found strange, but then again, maybe he was just sleeping.

"Justin." She spoke softly. "I know it's late, baby, but I just wanted to . . . I saw my mother today, and it helped. It really did. We talked, and she . . . well, we'll talk when I get home. Kiss the kids for me, and—I love you, baby. I love you so much."

Chapter 27

*J*ustin sat on the side of the bed slipping on his shoes when he felt her hand on his back.

"So." Cookie eased up behind him and wrapped her arms around his shoulders. "Was it just me, or did we have a fly-ass time this weekend?"

He took a deep breath, inhaled her perfume, closed his eyes, and leaned back against her. "It wasn't just you, baby. We both had a damn good time this weekend."

Cookie's kisses set him on fire, and if he didn't put a stop to it, the two of them would never get out of this room. "We've got to go," he reluctantly insisted.

She groaned. "I know, I know."

She slid off the bed, then found her shoes underneath it. Tricking was business. That was all it had ever been, and Cookie was old enough to know better than to let herself get all messed up over any of these fools. They paid for pussy, and that's all she was to them. Cash money was all they were to her, and once one had been exchanged for the other, she went her way, he went his, and that was that.

She watched Justin standing in front of the dresser mirror, adjusting his tie, looking every bit like a fucking accountant.

Shit, he wasn't even her type. Cookie had a thing for thugs her whole life, and never in a million years would she have given a clown like Justin the time of day. Clean-cut, the man wore Dockers. Justin was thin but muscular. He neatly hung up his clothes and folded his bath towels. Hell, she'd even seen him floss. He was handsome in a way she wouldn't have noticed passing him on the street. Justin's good looks came across in less obvious ways, like in the way he held doors open for her, and genuinely seemed to care about her. But that was the kind of handsome man women like Cookie didn't notice until it was too late.

So how come she felt like she was all in love and shit? How come she found herself looking for him to walk through the door of the club every night, feeling her heart leap inside her chest when he did, and horny as hell to get some personal time with him, even if it was just a straight-up lap dance on the floor?

She was almost twenty-five years old now, and in the beginning, dancing was a way to make some money. Dancing was all she did, until she found out how much more money the other girls were making going that extra mile. She had two kids to take care of, and sorry-ass men in and out of her life, one right after the other, who weren't about shit, except giving her grief, heartache, and more babies if she let stupid slip in the sheets between her and whatever fool was the flavor of the day at the time.

Lola at the club set her straight, though. "Girl, you got to take care of you and those kids. Who the hell you think gonna hire your dumb ass with no skills? And even if they do, how you gonna feed them kids on eight-fifty an hour?"

"Tricking ain't my thing," Cookie had told her.

"Oh, like it's mine? Shit. Tricking pays my bills and then

some. I dance, get some good-ass tips, and then I do a few hard-
core lap dances for horny-ass men who'd rather do me than
themselves. You do it here, you're safe. Ain't no mothafucka
gonna get out of hand with Wide-Ass standing outside the door.
A couple of tricks a week, girl, please! I can make a thousand
bills in a week, and not lose one bit of sleep over it. And when
my conscience starts to bother me, hmph! Last time it did, I
went out and made myself feel better with that Louis Vuitton
bag I been wanting. Six bills! And I didn't bat an eye."

The first time was hard. But now, two years later, it was as
routine as brushing her teeth.

"What's on your mind, sweetheart?" Justin stared at her
through the mirror, looking concerned. "You all right?"

She smiled, and nodded. "I'm fine."

He smiled back. "Well . . . duh!"

See, he was different. Like somebody she wished she had for
real. Like somebody who cared that something might be on her
mind, and he really wanted to know what it was. All weekend,
he'd been like that. Considering her the whole time. "Do you
like this? Are you hungry? You cold? Let me know if my snor-
ing keeps you awake."

Hell, yeah, it did, but in the nicest way. She'd nuzzled up
next to him while he slept, and pretended that she'd been the
one to put that ring on his finger, and that the kids were asleep
in the other room, and that he hadn't actually hired her ass for
the weekend. And in the morning, he surprised her, turned over
on his side, kissed her softly on top of the head, and held her in
his arms, until he got all worked up, and she did, too, and they
made love like people who cared about each other made love.

"Want me to call down and order some breakfast?" she
asked while he held her.

"No," he sighed. "Now let's just lay here for a while. It feels good having you this close to me, and I'm in no hurry to let you go."

Shit like that made her toes curl. And it reminded her of how she'd always wanted to live her life, instead of how she was actually living it. The last thing she wanted to be was a forty-year-old ho.

"You been thinking about what I said?" he asked, kneeling down in front of her.

She nodded.

"I'm serious, baby. You don't belong in a place like that, do-ing . . . well . . ."

"I know, Justin."

"Metro is a good college, and it's affordable. You could apply for grants, loans, maybe even land a scholarship or two if you're not careful." He squeezed her hands in his.

"What if I'm not smart enough for college?" she asked, shamefully lowering her head.

He laughed. "Please, girl. Of course you are, and . . . if you're not, well, college will make you smart. That's what you'd be paying them for. The least they can do is earn their money."

"I don't even know what I'd take. I mean, I don't even know what I want to be."

"Well, you go until you do know, Cookie," he said encourag-ing her. "See, that's the beauty of it. College is the kind of place where you can better yourself and figure yourself out at the same time. You're still young, Cookie. Hell, you won't be but thirty when you finish, and I guarantee you, your life will be so much better for it. And," his voice softened, "you won't have to keep putting yourself out here like this, for me, or any other man."

Shit like that made her hot. Damn, she hated that they had

to leave. She threw her arms around him and kissed him passionately.

"Damn, baby," he said, falling backwards onto the bed, taking her with him. "We don't have time."

"Yes, we do." She fumbled at his zipper. "We've got time, baby. Trust me."

He insisted on dropping her off at her apartment building, instead of letting her take a cab home. Justin blew her one last kiss as he drove away, right after promising that he'd see her again . . . soon. She watched him disappear down the street and around the corner. This had been one of the best weekends she'd had in her whole life. Cookie went inside her building and stood waiting for the elevator, trying to calm the butterflies tickling her insides. Thank goodness the elevator was empty when she got on. Cookie reached into her purse and pulled out a slip of paper with Justin's cell phone number on it. No, she wasn't going to fuck up his world by being a bugaboo and harassing his wife or blackmailing him or no shit like that. That wasn't her style.

"Call me if you . . ." He never finished what he started to say. "You know."

She smiled and tucked it back into her purse. Yeah. He was cool, and right now, just being cool was plenty.

Justin listened to the messages Reesy had left, replaying the last one several times. He'd just picked up the kids, who were running wild through the house like they'd spent the last two days caged.

"Is that Mommy, Daddy?" Jade asked, hearing her mother's voice and crawling into his lap.

"Yes, sweetheart," he said tenderly. "That's Mommy."

"When's she coming home? Can we call her?"

"How about we call her tomorrow? It's a little late now, and tomorrow would be better."

" 'Kay. Can we have pizza?"

Pizza was the buzzword in the house, and the boys stopped wrestling on the family room floor at the mention of the word. "Pizza!" they said in unision. "Yeah, Dad!" J.J. bolted up. "I'll get the phone book!"

He ordered the pizza, then sent them all upstairs to their rooms until it came. He played through Reesy's message one last time.

"Well, we'll talk when I get home. Kiss the kids for me, and—I love you, baby. I love you so much."

Pain stabbed at his heart. Things had gone terribly wrong between him and Reesy. She'd gotten caught up in this journey of a lifetime back to her past, and he'd gotten caught up in things he had no business messing with. The whole thing was just crazy, and Justin couldn't help but to shake his head and sigh quietly to himself until finally the doorbell rang, the kids bolted down the stairs, and Jade stood in front of him, asking for twenty bucks and wondering what was wrong.

"Nothing, baby," he said, quietly. "I just miss your momma. That's all."

Chapter 28

ammy?" Just the sound of Reesy's voice calling her name was enough to set her nerves on edge. As excited as she'd been about finally meeting her older sister, Cammy was more intimidated than anything by her. There was something about Reesy, Clarice, that regal, expensive thing about her that reminded Cammy of how small she really was in the world.

"You need me to help you with the dishes?" Reesy appeared beside her, and Cammy about shot through the roof at her being so close.

"No," she said, her voice shaking. "I got it, Reesy. You go back in there and talk to Momma."

Reesy raised her hand and rested it on Cammy's shoulder. She smelled so good. Her hair was perfect, like she'd paid somebody a lot of money to keep it that way. Cammy had to be careful. Momma had been giving her those looks when Reesy wasn't looking, warning her to keep moving. Warning her not to sit too long, to not say the wrong thing, or much of anything for that matter.

"I think it's time I got to know my sister, too," Reesy said tenderly. "It's been me and Connie for our whole lives. And now," she smiled, "we've got you."

Cammy looked at Reesy, catching her breath at how beautiful she was. "Is Connie as pretty as you?"

Reesy threw her head back and laughed. "Girl, please! Connie is fine!" She coaxed Cammy to face her, and Reesy put her arms around her baby sister and hugged her. "You wait. You'll see. That girl's got it going on for real, and I hate her for it. Always have."

Cammy closed her eyes and put her arms around Reesy's waist. "I'm so happy to finally meet you, Reesy. I've been dreaming of this my whole life."

"We've got a lot to talk about, sweetie." Reesy let her go, then reached for the dish towel on the cabinet. "And we can start by finishing up these dishes. You wash, I'll dry."

"What's all that cackling I hear?" Charlotte came through the door of the kitchen.

Instinctively, Cammy felt the urge to leave, but then Reesy stopped her. "Nothing, Momma," she said over her shoulder. "Go on back in the living room, put your feet up, and watch the news. My little sister and I," she leaned in close to Cammy and whispered, "I always wanted to say that," then turned to her mother, "are getting to know one another."

"No, Cammy can do it," Charlotte insisted, trying not to look concerned. Cammy had a big mouth sometimes. She talked too much about things that weren't her business, and Charlotte knew the girl was more than capable of saying something stupid.

"Momma's right, Reesy."

"Momma," Reesy said sternly to Charlotte. "Let me and

Cammy do these dishes in peace, and you go back in the living room and rest." Her tone left no doubt in Charlotte's or Cammy's mind that Reesy was staying put, and Charlotte needed to take her place in the living room.

Cammy smiled, and gave her sister a mental high five.

After they finished the dishes, it was Reesy who insisted on Cammy taking her into town for a cup of coffee at the local Starbucks. Charlotte, of course, wanted to tag along, but Reesy wasn't having it.

"When's the baby due?" Reesy asked on the way to the coffee shop.

"June."

"Do you know what you're having?"

Cammy nodded. "A boy."

Reesy struggled to find the right way to ask the question about the father, but then determined that there was no way to ask that wouldn't sound insensitive. "Is the father involved?"

To her surprise, a smile stretched across Cammy's face a mile wide. "Oh yes! He's all excited about this baby. His name is T, well, Tyrell, but most people call him T, and he owns his own repair shop fixing cars. Makes good money, too. He's saving up so that we can go shopping and get the baby a crib, a stroller, some clothes, diapers."

"The two of you getting married?"

Cammy hesitated. "Well . . . we've talked about it."

"Sounds like you love him. And I'm guessing he must love you, too."

"Oh, he does. And I do."

"So, marriage seems like the next logical step."

You run your damn mouth too much, Cammy! Stop telling everybody all my business!

But this wasn't Momma's business. Not really.

"I'd like to, but it's kinda hard with Momma."

"Why is that?" Reesy's strategy was working. She'd managed to get Cammy to open up a little at a time, and getting her away from Charlotte was the key. It didn't take a Sigmund Freud to see that something wasn't quite right in this relationship between Cammy and Charlotte. Reesy was just curious. That was all. And besides, she had a sister to get to know, and to be there for her, if that's what she needed. Cammy seemed lonely to Reesy. She reminded her a lot of Connie in that respect.

"Well, you know." Cammy looked at Reesy for affirmation.

Reesy shook her head and shrugged. "I haven't seen Momma for nearly thirty years, Cammy, so I don't really think I do."

"She needs me," Cammy said finally. "I mean, she needs somebody around, and I'm all she's got . . . well," she looked at Reesy and smiled. "Until now. I think she's been scared that she'd end up all alone, and I couldn't ever see myself leaving her that way."

"I understand," Reesy nodded. "But that doesn't negate the responsibility you have to yourself, too, and now this baby. You still have to do what's best for you, too, Cammy."

"And I am." She sounded as uncertain as she felt, and from the look in her sister's face, Cammy knew Reesy had noticed. "I plan on moving out eventually. You know, when the time is right."

"And when is that?"

Cammy never did answer that question, and Reesy didn't push her to. But she'd left the girl with plenty to think about, and for the time being, that was plenty.

Ten minutes later, they sat in a booth at the coffee shop. Reesy had ordered herbal decaffeinated teas with honey for both of them.

"What happened to Momma's face?" She had wanted to ask the question to Charlotte, but it was clear that Charlotte was embarrassed by the disfigurement, covering the bottom half of her face with her hand when she spoke or laughed most of the time.

Cammy shrugged. "I don't know. It's been that way for as long as I can remember. Somebody hit her, I think. She never talks about it."

Reesy looked appalled. "Do you know who?"

"I don't know if it was my daddy or some man she calls Uncle. When I was little, I heard her talking about it on the phone to her friend Miss Lynn, but I can't remember the details."

"It's funny," Reesy said solemnly. "There's so much she hasn't told me. Every time I ask her about specifics in her life, she skirts around them, and changes the subject, turning back time to remind me of something that happened between us when I was a kid."

"She doesn't tell me anything, either."

"The thing is, I'm not a kid anymore, and I just wish she'd . . . I wish she'd open up more, and tell me everything. She's been gone a long time, and so much has happened to all of us. Thirty years is forever when someone you love disappears."

Cammy knew Charlotte better than anyone, and Charlotte never talked about her life before moving to Murphy. Every now and then, she'd talk to her friend Miss Lynn on the phone, and maybe Cammy would get bits and pieces of her mother's life, but never more than that. It was frustrating, but it was her way. Cammy had come to accept it a long time ago. Reesy would just have to try.

"You were her favorite," Cammy winked. "I think you still are."

Reesy shook her head. "I was the baby for a long time, but I wouldn't say I was her favorite."

"No, it's cool. It is. I ain't hatin'. But I can see why she'd feel that way." Cammy stared at Reesy and nodded. "I'm glad you're my sister. Now I'm gonna brag to everybody I know, and they can stop thinking I'm lying."

Reesy laughed. "Aw, that's not good. You mean to tell me everybody thought you were just making me and Connie up?"

Cammy laughed. "My whole life. I've been going around telling everybody I got two sisters, and they live in Denver." She mimicked a child's voice. "And they'd come back with . . . well, where they at, then?" She and Reesy laughed. "Shoot! I didn't know what to tell them. To this day, they all think I was making it up."

"Well, we'll just have to prove their asses wrong, then. Won't we?"

"Oh, can we?" Cammy pleaded. "Tomorrow's Wal-Mart day and everybody I know will be shopping there, Reesy. Can we go?"

Reesy almost fell out of her seat, laughing so hard. "Girl, yes! And let's go early too, so we don't miss anybody."

They sat in Starbucks for another hour before the store closed and they had to leave. Cammy was just about to start up the car to leave when Reesy pulled out her cell phone and stopped her.

"Wait," she said, hitting speed-dial on her phone. "There's someone I want you to talk to."

It was late, but it didn't matter. This was important, and Connie needed to wake her ass the hell up.

"Hello!" she answered, half-asleep, and obviously agitated.

"Hey." Reesy crossed her fingers that this woman wouldn't hang up on her, but even if she did, she'd call back until she drove her sister absolutely insane if she had to.

"What? What is it? Reesy?" Connie sat up in bed, turned on the light on her nightstand, and looked at the clock. It wasn't even ten yet. "Where are you?"

"Murphy, Kansas, of all places." Reesy rolled her eyes. She expected Connie to start cussing, but she didn't.

"Call your husband and your mom. Especially your mom, because that woman is driving me up the fucking wall."

"I have someone I want you to talk to, Connie."

Connie wasn't fully awake yet, but she was conscious enough to put two and two together, and she wasn't having it. "No, Reesy! Don't you even think about it! You wanna get all warm and fuzzy with Charlotte's ass, that's your business! But I'm not about to talk to that woman, and . . ."

"It's not Momma, Connie," Reesy said calmly. "I wouldn't do that to you. I swear I wouldn't."

"Then . . . who is it?"

"Her name is Cammy," Reesy reached over and took Cammy's hand in hers. "And she's our little sister, Connie. And she's got your eyes."

Cammy's eyes clouded over with tears as she hesitated before taking the phone from Reesy and putting it to her ear.

Reesy smiled. "It's okay, sweetheart. It's just Connie."

"H . . . hello?" Cammy's voice shook.

Connie sat stunned in bed, not quite sure if she was awake or dreaming this whole thing. Sister? What sister? Where the hell did they get a . . .

"Hello? Who is this?"

Cammy cleared her thoat. "This is Cammy. I mean, Camille. Me and Reesy just left Starbucks." She felt like an idiot as soon as she said it. Reesy looked at her and chuckled.

Cammy? Camille. Connie pinched her thigh. It hurt, so

yeah, she was wide awake. Do the math, Connie, she told herself. Yeah, it's possible, and plausible, and just like Charlotte to go out and have more kids, with names that all started with Cs to fuel her egotistical ass, and fuck them up just like she'd fucked up the first two. But give this girl the benefit of the doubt. Maybe, just maybe, she was spared. Not.

"Cammy. How old are you, Cammy?" she asked bluntly.

"Twenty-six, almost twenty-seven."

Connie sighed, then lay back staring up at the ceiling, half expecting it to cave in on her all at once and put her out of hormonal misery. "Charlotte's your mother?"

"Yes."

Connie rubbed the sleep from her eyes and groaned. "Is she there?"

"No. Momma's at home. It's just me and Reesy sitting in the parking lot at . . ."

"Starbucks. Yeah," she said dryly. "I know.

"Cammy?"

"Yes, Connie?"

"Put Reesy back on the phone."

Cammy did as she was told and handed the phone to Reesy.

"I take it you're as shocked as I am?" Reesy asked.

"To say the least. What's she like?"

Reesy looked at Cammy. "More like you than me, but sweeter and with an accent."

Connie laughed. "That's messed up, Reese."

"She needs us, Connie."

"Yeah?"

"Yeah."

"Charlotte mess her up, too?"

"Maybe not as much, but . . . yeah," Reesy laughed.

"Damn. Well, good. At least she didn't play favorites. Well, except for you."

"That's so wrong."

"You're the favorite, Reese. Take it like a man, girl."

Reesy laughed. "Go back to sleep."

"How can I? You keep insisting on uprooting my little firm foundation of abandonment and bringing me new sisters and shit like that. Who can sleep?"

"I'll be home day after tomorrow, Connie. We'll talk."

"There's a lot to talk about, Reesy. You bringing what's her name?"

"I don't know. Let me check." She spoke to Cammy. "You wanna come back to Denver with me to meet Oscar the Grouch?"

Cammy's eyes grew wide. "Oh, I don't think I . . ."

"Not this time," she said to Connie. "But I'll get her out of this hick town sooner or later."

"And away from Monster, I mean, your momma."

"Stop it," she said affectionately. Times had been tough between them lately. They rarely talked anymore, and when they did, the things said between them were seldom nice. Tonight wasn't about anything else but being sisters, and the new bouncing-baby, almost twenty-seven-year-old pregnant addition to the fold. It was hard for Reesy not to feel sentimental by it all. "And we'll talk when I get home, Connie."

Reesy hung up and looked at Cammy.

"I don't think she liked me, Reesy."

Reesy sucked her teeth and rolled her eyes. "Don't be silly, Camille," she said, waving her hand in the air. "She adores you."

Chapter 29

"Mmmmm." Charlotte broke the seal of her kiss from Uncle's lips with a wet smack. "Did I thank you properly for my new fur coat, baby?" She batted her eyes at him, and ran her finger lightly across his bottom lip.

Uncle grinned. "A couple of times, as a matter of fact. My ass is exhausted, girl!" He turned, facing the mirror, and finished buttoning up his shirt. "But that's a compliment, though," he winked in the mirror at her standing behind him. "Not a complaint."

Damn, he was good to her. Ugly men were the best kind of men, she'd learned. Uncle's piss-yellow complexion wasn't her taste. Neither were the million freckles, gold tooth, and big-ass gap between his teeth, but he made up for ugly in every other kind of way, including being one of the best lovers she'd ever had. Even better than Sam, as a matter of fact. He did shit that left her clawing and ripping the bedsheets into shreds. When he finished with her, Charlotte came so hard, she nearly cried.

"Don't! Don't . . . ," she'd say, sweating and out of breath, when he was finished, and he'd reach over to hold her and kiss her. "Don't touch me, Uncle! I can't . . . Ooooh! Damn!"

He'd laugh, and sometimes touch her anyway, just to fuck with her.

He had it bad for her, though. Even worse than she had it for him. Charlotte wasn't a fool. She knew what he was, and the kind of man he was, even though he insisted on calling himself a businessman. Business. Yeah, right. He was a bad guy, a crook, a pimp, drug and gun dealer, and Lord only knew what else. He was the kind of man people were scared enough of to respect, and to practically bow down at his feet whenever he walked into a room. And when he took her with him, they bowed at her feet, too, waiting on her hand and foot like she was his queen, which she was. Yeah, Sherrell was his wife, but Charlotte was his honey, his sugah, his But baby, I'm feenin for you, girl.

If he was in a bad mood before he walked through her door, he wasn't in one when he left. All she had to do was ask, and whatever she wanted was hers. And if she pouted, or pretended to be hurt, he'd give her two, and some money to go along with it. She'd asked him once how come he didn't turn her out and put her to work after Sam ran out on her.

He stared at her without blinking and said with a straight face, "Who the hell you think ran that sucka out of town, girl?"

She could hardly believe her ears. "What? You mean to tell me you made him leave me here by myself? Sam wouldn't do that, Uncle. He loved me."

"Yeah." He inhaled on his cigar. "He loved you fierce, girl."

He left it at that.

Sometimes she'd let her mind wonder about what it would be like to have him all to herself. Uncle kept her on the other side of town, put away nicely and out of reach of Sherrell. Not that he was all that worried about her finding out. Charlotte was his arm candy, and he flaunted her around town, in and out of clubs and parties, like she was his wife. But then she'd think about how good she had it already, and wonder why the hell would she fuck that up? Living like this was a dream come true. The only thing missing sometimes, when she thought about it, were her girls. She'd told him she had kids. He said he liked kids. She told them she missed them, and that her momma was giving her a hard time about coming home to get them. He promised to get her a bigger place so that she could have room for them. She squeezed his neck, kissed his face, and squealed thank-you's until his eardrums nearly burst. And then they'd fuck, and she'd forget all about her kids for a while, until enough time passed for her to miss them again.

"You still gonna get me a bigger place, Uncle?" she asked, laying across the bed wearing the red satin nightgown he'd brought her.

Uncle adjusted his tie and stared down at her beautiful ass. "I said I would."

She stretched like a cat and sighed. "I think they're gonna like it here. Get them into school, buy them some new clothes." She smiled at him. "I can hardly wait to see them again."

Uncle stood over her with his hands in his pockets, taking in every inch of her to save in his memories until the next time he came by. "Yeah. I can't wait to see 'em, either."

She kissed him good-bye at the door, and then locked it behind him. Charlotte curled up in one corner of the sofa, and called her friend, Lynn.

"Girl, whatchu doing?" She giggled. "My baby just left, so you know, I'm sore as hell."

Sherrell sat in her cousin Coco's car, parked right out in front of the apartment building, watching her man strutting out looking fresh and flashy with his ugly ass. Uncle climbed into his car and drove off. She smirked. His ass thought he was so damn smart, but that mothafucka didn't have a goddamned clue. She'd seen him and that ho, kissing and pawing all over each other, through the window. Nasty-ass bitch! Didn't even have the decency to keep the mothafuckin' windows closed so any fool looking up could see all her dumb-ass business, and her half-naked ass bouncing around like the fool she was.

Sherrell climbed out of the car, closed the door, and leaned up against it long enough to light up a cigarette. Good thing Coco had washed that raggedy-ass car of hers, because if the shit had fucked up her fox fur, she'd have had to beat that bitch's ass, too. She stood over six feet in her black platform heels. Red velvet bell-bottom hiphuggers looked painted on her wide hips and bubble behind, and a gold chain belt hung loosely around her waist. Sherrell's favorite one hundred percent silk, red-, gold-, and pink-striped blouse was tucked perfectly into her slacks, and she felt as bad as she looked. She'd just come from getting her nails done, painted blood red to match her mood.

Yeah, the sucka had a tendency to fuck around, mostly with one of them bitches he had working for him. Sherrell had no problem with that. Shit. She couldn't fault the man for checking out his merchandise, making sure the shit was worth what he was charging for it. From time to time she'd sampled his wares, too, because pussy was just good, and good pussy was damn good, and why should she be denied if she was in the mood? Getting his nut every now and then wasn't the problem. But getting his nut and calling his ass being in love, setting the bitch up in an expensive-ass place, buying her funky ass an expensive-ass coat, and strutting around town with the ho on his arm like she meant something in front of every goddamned body, now that shit was a different story.

"When the hell is these bitches ever gonna learn?" she muttered, heading toward the building.

"She lives in 404, and it's nice, too, girl. Uncle had me go in to do her nails."

Everybody knew that if you ever wanted to know anything, ask Lynn. And if she wasn't talking, threaten to kick Arnel's ass. She'd sell you her soul to save that dumb-ass mothafucka.

She wasn't going to kill the bitch. She was just going to make her ass wish she would.

"Oh, hold on, girl," Charlotte told Lynn on the phone. "Somebody's at the door."

She'd seen pictures of Sherrell. Heard about her. So there was no need for a formal introduction.

"Yeah, bitch! I hear you been fuckin' 'round with my man!"

Charlotte didn't have to see her fist coming at her to know she'd been hit in the face with it. The world suddenly went black, and Sherrell hit her with such force, she was airborne, flying through space, and landing in a crash on top of and through the new coffee table Uncle had brought her.

". . . don't play that shit! You . . . who you fuckin' . . ."

Charlotte levitated off the floor, her legs flailing wildly in the air. The pain of being pulled up by her hair didn't register right away, but when it did, she reached up and instinctively grabbed Sherrell by the wrist.

"Oh, you don't know this game, bitch! See." She backhanded Charlotte hard across the face, once, then again, then dropped her back into the broken heap on the floor, and kicked her hard in her ribs with her platform shoe.

"See, this is what happens when you mess round with shit that don't belong to you! My shit, bitch! That ugly-ass mothafucka belong to me! And I'll be damned if I'm gonna turn him over to the likes of yo ho ass! Oh, hell naw!"

Charlotte struggled to catch her breath, but before she could, Sherrell kicked her again in the side. Then, when Charlotte curled up to protect her precious ribs from the onslaught of this madwoman, she kicked her hard in the ass.

Blood and drool snaked from her mouth, pooling onto the beige carpet.

"You think yo shit is all that, bitch? You think you bad enough to steal my man from me? Lemme tell you one goddamned thing, ho! Uncle ain't . . . What? Get off me, mothafucka! Get the hell . . ."

"Who you think you swinging on, bitch?" He balled up his fist and buried it in her midsection.

"Mothafucka, I . . . umph!"

Sherrell would fight his ass like a man if he gave her the opportunity. He'd seen her big ass get out of that car across the street as soon as he'd turned the corner, then he made his way back around, knowing full well where she was headed. Uncle stepped over Charlotte, writhing on the floor, unable to breathe, bleeding from her mouth and nose, and picked up the receiver laying on the couch. "Hello?"

Whoever it was hung up the minute they heard it was him. He glared suspiciously at Charlotte, who probably didn't even know his ass was in the room. Two minutes alone with Sherrell's big ass had that effect on people. He dialed a number. "Yo. I'm at the apartment. Get on over here."

"Mothafucka!" Sherrell managed to pull herself up off her knees, clutching her stomach, gasping for breath. "How you gonna . . . set this bitch . . . up with my goddamned . . . money? How you gonna fuck 'round on me with this ho?" She charged at him, but Uncle was too quick for her, and he hit her in the pit of her stomach again.

"Yo money? Bitch! Since when has yo black ass ever made me any money?"

"I'ma kill yo piss ass, Uncle! And then . . . I'ma kill yo bitch!"

Uncle bent down and pulled Charlotte up by her elbow, then helped her to sit on the couch. He chuckled. "What's the matter, baby girl? Can't take a punch?"

"Get . . . yo fuckin' . . . hands . . ." Sherrell made it to her feet again, but Uncle wasn't the least bit surprised. He'd hit her as hard as he'd ever hit any man, and Sherrell's ass didn't know how to stay the fuck down. A long time ago, he'd come to realize that was one of the things he loved about her. Pussy would come and go, even Little Miss Pretty sitting over here on the couch with her swollen eye would fade into a nice memory someday, but Sherrell was the only woman he'd ever known who'd actually had the heart and soul for him. Shit, maybe in another life she'd even had a set of balls. If he hadn't already gotten his nut earlier this evening, he'd be hard as hell right now, and the two of them would probably end up fucking like maniacs all damn night, scratching and clawing and cussing each other out. Shit, in this marriage, physical abuse was fucking foreplay.

"You making me hard, baby," he teased.

"Shut the fuck up, mothafucka!" She pointed a long, manicured finger at him. "This bitch is mine, Uncle! You wait . . . you wait . . ." Once again, she started to charge in his direction, but Leon, one of Uncle's associates, came up behind her and wrapped two massive arms around her, the way he always did whenever he was expected to pull Sherrell's vicious ass off somebody.

"Let go of me!" she screamed, and kicked, trying to stab her lethal heels into his shins. "Mothafucka!"

Leon held onto Sherrell, and calmly turned and left the apartment, carrying her kicking and screaming all the way down the hall to the elevator. Somehow, he managed to get her on it and finally out of the building.

Charlotte wanted to cry, but she was in too much pain to do it. Her face felt as if it had been caved in, and her ribs had to have been broken.

Uncle knelt down in front of her and pulled a clean handkerchief from his lapel. "If I could take it all back, sugah," he said softly, "you know I would."

She quietly started to sob. He kissed her head. "Don't cry, honey baby. I can't stand to see a woman cry."

He motioned to Zoo, another one of his employees, a young brotha who barely looked old enough to drink, standing in the doorway, to come inside. "Take care of my baby."

Zoo shrugged. "You want me to take her to the hospital?"

Uncle shook his head. "Naw. She'll be fine. Ain't that right, baby?"

Charlotte whimpered.

A few minutes later, he left, laughing like he'd just had the time of his life.

Chapter 30

*I*f I didn't know better, I'd think you were trying to avoid me," Reesy said half-jokingly to Justin on the other end of the phone. She'd been out of town for nearly three days and had left at least three messages, none of which he'd seen fit to return. This time, she'd just gotten lucky, and he'd answered the phone.

"You should know better than that," he responded dryly. "I've been busy with the kids."

He was lying, and she knew it. But more than anything right now, she wanted to avoid the argument. "I've had an interesting trip."

"I'll bet. You want to tell me about it?"

A sense of relief and ease set in at the sound of his voice. As bad as things had been between them this past year, Justin was still the love of her life, her mate for life, and she wouldn't have it any other way. His lack of understanding had come between them, though, and more than anything she wanted to share this whole experience with him. But not until she'd looked it in the eye and faced it head-on herself first, and now that she'd done that, she knew that she needed her husband back.

"I do want to tell you about it, Justin," she said warmly.

He sat quietly on the other end of the phone, and she tried to imagine what he might be thinking. He'd turned inward lately, and she'd come to realize that she had done the same, diverting all her time and attention to the quest to find Charlotte. Now she needed to bring her family together wholly and fully, because she was finally at peace inside.

"Momma's the same, and she's different," she explained, hoping he was listening. "She's guarded, only telling me what she wants me to know, but I can tell that there's so much more she isn't telling. But I guess, it'll all come in time."

"Well, it's been almost thirty years, Reese. She's probably as overwhelmed as you are, and maybe doesn't even know where to begin, baby."

She smiled at the word *baby*. "I know. It's tough, but I'm glad I did it, Justin. I know I haven't been easy to live with and this whole ordeal has been hard on us, but . . . I needed to do it. I needed to find her, and I needed to close the circle. It might've come across as selfish to you, but . . ."

"No," he lied. "Not selfish, Reese. Sometimes it just felt like you were pushing me away. Almost as if you didn't want or need me to come along for this ride, and that's been hard to take."

"It probably seemed that way."

"Yeah. It did. You're my wife, honey, and it felt like every time I reached out to you, to remind you of that, and that I'm here for you, you got angry and turned your back on me."

Now was not the time or the place to pursue this discussion. She felt herself growing defensive and apprehensive at his suggestion that she'd been the selfish one and he'd been victimized by all of this. Reesy decided to change the subject. "How are the kids?"

Justin sighed exasperated and frustrated. "Fine, Reese. The kids are fine."

"I'll be home day after tomorrow. Tell them I miss them, and that I'll be home soon."

"Sure." He spoke too quickly. "Anything else?"

"No, Justin." Her disappointment filtered through the receiver. "I'll see you soon."

Something about the way he sounded left her feeling uneasy and doubtful. Where was her patient and understanding man? Was it her imagination, or was Justin really changing into someone bent on pointing the finger at her for the problems building between them? It almost seemed as if he didn't want to see where she was coming from. Like he wasn't interested in the effect her mother's leaving her and Connie all those years ago still had on her to this day.

"You've got people who love you, Reesy," he'd argued. "You ended up with two good parents who would walk through fire for you, me, and I love you more than my own life. You've got three kids who adore you, and of course Connie."

"It's not about all that, Justin."

"Then help me to understand, because I don't get it. She walked out, leaving you and Connie to fend for yourselves, and you want this woman back in your life, because?"

Because her memories of Charlotte before she left them were some of the most precious she could remember. Charlotte had loved her from the moment she was born in a way that nobody else ever could. Despite her shortcomings, it was the sound of her mother's voice she held dear to her heart, the scent of her hair that still lingered in her dreams, and the softness of her touch that felt warm on her skin. Connie might've hated her, Momma and Daddy could never justify her actions, and Justin simply refused to give her the benefit of the doubt. And she deserved at least that much. If nothing else, Reesy could give her that.

Cammy had conveniently left Reesy and Charlotte alone after dinner. The relationship between those two just didn't make sense to Reesy, but the dynamics of it seemed to work for the two of them, however dysfunctional it might've seemed to her. Charlotte was a master at skirting around confrontational questions. Reesy had thrown them at her like rocks, but she'd managed to duck and dodge every last one of them like a pro.

As evening settled in, they wandered out onto the porch and sat next to each other, admiring the beautiful scene of the sun setting out in the horizon. Charlotte reached out and took Reesy's hand in hers, kissed it, and placed it lovingly in her lap.

"It feels like you've just gotten here," she told her, glancing quickly at her baby girl, then turning away. "I wish you'd stay."

Reesy smiled, touched by her mother's sincerity. "I've got a family to get back to, Momma. They need me. No telling what kind of damage my kids have done to my house," she joked.

"I'll bet you're a good mother, Clarice. So much better than I ever was to you and your sister."

Reesy squeezed her mother's hand. "You did the best you could, Momma. That's all any of us can expect to do. The odds were stacked against you, being single with no family to help support you and no husband around to help." She looked at Charlotte. "I understand that now."

"Do you think your sister will ever understand?" her voice cracked. "Connie's always been the hardest on me. Harder than anybody. I doubt there's anything I could say to her to . . ."

"Connie's had it tough, Momma. Being the oldest, she kind of took it in the gut and . . . I don't think anybody will ever know what she went through all those years before I found her."

Charlotte dug deep inside herself, looking for a thread of sympathy for that girl, but it just wasn't there. Connie had had it hard, but then so had Charlotte. Of course, Connie was hers too, though. And she couldn't help but to think of her, and to wonder and even to miss her oldest daughter. "I hope I can see her, too, one of these days." She meant that. She truly did.

Reesy smiled. "I think you will. She just needs time. That's all."

Time. She'd waited almost thirty years for this moment, thinking it might never come, but it did. Time wasn't so big and bad after all. And now that she had her baby back, time didn't mean a damn thing.

Chapter 31

So, I'm asking." Yolanda talked a million words a minute, hardly taking time out to breathe since she'd gotten back from her last trip to South Africa. "Do you want to buy me out, or what?"

They'd been friends and business partners for years, and even best friends, but in the last two years, her trips to Africa had become more frequent.

"Are you serious?" Connie asked, stunned by the offer and Yolanda's news.

"Seriously in love, yes!" she said, dramatically. "And don't act like you didn't see this coming, girl. I've been going on and on about him for the last year, and you know how long and hard I've been digging him."

"But—marriage, Yo? And moving to Africa?"

Yolanda sat across from her in the coffee shop, wearing a red and gold scarf wrapped around her head, a string of large wooden ebony beads circling her neck, and she looked good enough to eat wearing that traditional matching African dress. "It could work, Connie, I'm telling you. You keep the shop going here, and own it outright. And I'll be your distributor on the other end, girl. Just tell me what you need, and I'll send it to you. I think it could work. I do. And I think you can run this place better than I ever could. Hell, you're doing it now. Or haven't you noticed?"

Damn hormones.

"What?" Yolanda asked, looking as perplexed as Connie felt. "Connie? Girl!"

That ceiling had decided to cave in on her after all, only it had waited until having coffee with Yolanda to do it. The floodgates opened up, and Connie spilled tears out all over the coffee shop.

"I'm pregnant, Yo, and King left. Reesy and I damn near hate each other. She found Charlotte. We have a sister. You're leaving. Eddie's too far away. And I'm falling apart." Tears flowed like rivers down her cheeks and into her coffee cup. Yolanda struggled to piece it all together in her mind, and Connie put her head down on the table, oblivious to the stares and bewilderment from everyone in the room because she was too busy having a nervous breakdown.

"Damn," Yolanda reached across the table and rubbed her shoulder. "I've only been gone a month, Connie. Good thing I came back when I did. Huh?"

Yolanda coaxed her out of the restaurant and into her car, where they could carry on the rest of the conversation in private.

"So, he left when you told him about the baby?" she asked Connie, sitting in the passenger seat, sobbing.

She shrugged. "I told him to leave," she admitted.

Yolanda looked surprised. "You told him to . . . Why would you do that, Connie?"

"Because he would've left anyway, Yolanda," she sniffed. "He wasn't interested in having a baby, and shit—it was only a matter of time before he'd have taken off. Holding onto John was like trying to hold water. I just got tired."

"You're optimism truly amazes me," she said dryly. "So you throw the man out because you're hormonal and you figured he'd leave anyway one of these days. Sounds like a relationship doomed from the start."

Connie sniffed.

"Are you and Reesy at odds over the baby?"

Connie shook her head. "Not this one." She looked at Yolanda. "Over Jade. We were arguing over whether or not to tell Jade that I'm her mother, and I let it slip out in front of her that I was." Yolanda's disappointment showed through. "I didn't know she was there, Yo. The last thing I wanted was for her to find out like that."

"And Reesy's pissed."

"Reesy won't even let me see her."

"How can she stop you from seeing your own kid?"

"Legally, she's not my kid," Connie sighed. "But it's a relief, Yo. I mean, if you could've seen the look on that child's face . . . I don't think I'm in any state of mind to see her now anyway. I mean, look at me."

Yolanda stared back sympathetically.

"Then last night Reesy calls me from fuckin' Middle-of-Nowhere Kansas, telling me she's been spending quality time with Momma, and that we have a sister. A damn grown-ass sister, Yolanda. That cow abandoned us, walked out on us, then went out and had the nerve to have more kids? What the hell? What kind of sense does that make?" Connie started crying again. "And I've missed you, and I miss Eddie."

"You miss John?"

She nodded and blew her nose. "I miss the hell out of him. You know how hard I love that man?"

"Yes. I do."

"But it was all one-sided, Yo. More and more, I was starting to see that, and I couldn't keep doing it. As much as it hurts, I couldn't continue to let myself love him more than I knew he loved me. That shit just wasn't fair."

"If I tell you that I don't think that's the case, will you get mad at me?"

Connie nodded. "Yeah. Because it's a lie, and you know it, and I know it most of all. And I don't feel like being consoled or lied to at the moment."

"Then I'll keep my mouth shut."

"And your ass wants to move to Africa to get married and leave me to run this place all by myself. What kind of shit is that, Yo?"

"You've been running it by yourself, Connie. C'mon. I'm hardly ever there, and you've been doing a damn good job, I might add. If you hadn't been, then I wouldn't have been racking up frequent flier miles back and forth to the motherland like I've been doing."

"But I can't keep doing it."

"Sure you can. Why can't you?"

"Duh! I'm going to have a baby."

"Duh! Like other women don't have babies and run successful boutiques."

"And since nobody gives a shit but me, I'm going to have to get this single parent thing down within the next seven months so that my kid doesn't grow up all fucked up like his parents."

Yolanda laughed. "Hmmmm . . . I don't think seven months is enough time."

Connie sucked her teeth and rolled her eyes, but she couldn't help but to laugh. "Don't make me mad."

"Oh, here we go. You wanna try and fake like you can fight again, Constance? We both know you don't have it in you to whoop up on me, or anybody else for that matter, so draw in your little claws and take it back to that corner over there."

Connie hissed.

The two sat quietly for several minutes while Connie dabbed her eyes dry and caught her breath. "That's been happening a lot lately," she explained quietly, looking out of the window.

"What?" Yolanda stared out of the window on her side of the car.

"Emotional outbursts, girl. You know that ain't me."

"Maybe that's the problem. You keep shit so pent up inside you, maybe it's time to let it all out."

"I'd rather not."

Yolanda started the car. "Yeah, I know. But you gotta cleanse that soul of yours some kind of way. Especially before that baby gets here. If you ask me, old folks shouldn't have babies in the first damn place."

Connie surprised herself and laughed. "I'm not old."

"Modern medicine is remarkable these days, though, girl. Women can have babies well into their forties and even their fifties. So you hang in there, Momma. Senior citizens make some of the best parents anyway."

"Kiss my ass, please."

"Godmomma. No. Momma Yo. I like that. The kid can call me Momma Yo, and he can come stay with me every summer . . . well, maybe not every damn summer . . . but every once in a while in Johannesburg." She headed toward Connie's house.

"Oh, you just going to take it for granted that you're going to be my child's godmother. How you gonna act?"

"Shit, you ain't got no other friends. I'm the only one left. Be real, girl, and stop fighting the inevitable. The mighty and beautiful Momma Yo has spoken, and I'll be damned if I'm going to let you come between me and my godchild."

Connie chuckled.

Yolanda pulled her car up to the curb in front of Connie's house. "I'm serious about leaving, Connie," she told her. "You are a brilliant businesswoman, and design some of the baddest jewelry in the country—in the world! I wouldn't sign over my business to just anybody. I want you to have it, and I'm not bull-shitting."

"Yolanda." Connie started to tear up again.

"Get out of my car before you make me cry, and I'll make an appointment with my attorney to draw up some papers. Cool?"

Connie hesitated before getting out of the car. Cool? No. She wasn't cool. Nothing was cool at the moment, but she gave Yolanda a shaky thumbs-up before going inside.

She and Yolanda had met in a parking lot, of all places. Connie was working for the electric company and Yolanda complimented her on a necklace Connie was wearing that she'd made herself. The next thing she knew, Yolanda was selling Connie's jewelry on consignment and the rest was history.

She'd lost one best friend in John, and now she was about to lose another. Connie locked the door behind her and spent the rest of the day curled up in bed with a box of Oreos, some tissues, and the Lifetime channel. Some businesswoman.

Chapter 32

Where's your woman, John King?" Racine's shoot-from-the-hip approach made him laugh. "What did you say her name was?"

They walked down old Jackson Road, headed toward the lake. The walk had been her idea, like everything else between them, and John just sort of followed along blindly because he didn't have shit else to do, and because it was easier than trying to figure out what the hell he was going to do. He'd walked away from a decent-paying job, Denver, Connie, the way he'd done most of his life, without looking back or giving it a second thought. Something he once thought he'd grown out of came all too easily, reminding him that that familiar rhythm of his life was nothing more than second nature and routine.

"Weren't you two living together? Or are you *still* living together?" she probed.

Shit, he loved this place. Bueller was warmer than Denver, the air thicker, and he felt like a fish swimming around in his own little private pool where everything was perfect every time he came down here.

"Would it make any difference?" he said, looking at her, taking in how pretty she looked with the wind blowing gently through her dress.

Connie was never far enough away. He loved her, regardless of what she might've believed. But spending time here, with another woman, John had to admit that maybe he didn't love her enough after all.

Racine smiled. "No. I guess it wouldn't." She looped her arm in his as they continued walking. "You ever think that maybe you and me were meant to be together all along?"

He chuckled. "No. I've never thought that."

Racine threw her head back and laughed. "Damn, John! Can you at least humor a sistah and lie?"

"All right. I think we're soul mates."

"Well," she said, rolling her eyes at his sarcasm. "I think about it sometimes. Always have. If you hadn't left when you did, I'm convinced I'd have married you instead of Lewis."

"Why did you marry Lewis?"

"Because he was as close as I could get to you. Rebound, baby. You left and he stepped in saying all the right things."

"Lewis liked you first anyway."

She laughed. "I know. But I liked you."

"No accounting for taste."

"Oh, please, man! Every damn girl from here to New Orleans was digging your ass, and you know it."

"I had no clue."

"Well, I'm telling you. And the fact that I'm the one that landed you made me the envy of every female under the age of thirty in this town and a few towns over."

"Thirty?" he asked startled. "Damn."

"Grown women used to cry themselves to sleep worrying

over you, boy. Big, strong, strapping young man, with the pretty dark eyes and wide shoulders."

If he'd been anybody else, he would've blushed. "Then I was a fool for leaving," he laughed. "Think I still got it like that?"

"Even if you did, I wouldn't tell you. I'm trying to get you all to myself."

He looked down at her arm, clutching his. "Looks like you got a head start."

Sex outside was some damn good sex. Racine was uninhibited and free underneath that tree by the lake, ass bucking up and down in the air, pussy wet and wild sucking in his dick, pulling the kind of orgasm from him that made his head spin. Nipples tasted like fresh fruit in the open air, and when it was over, there was nothing left but the sound of the birds singing in the trees, gentle waves rippling in the lake, her soft, warm hand on his chest, and the unmistakable longing for the woman he'd left behind in Colorado.

"I hope you decide to stay here once and for all, John King," Racine whispered quietly. "I promise to take good care of you if you do."

He kissed her head and stared up at the leaves above them. "I know, baby. I know you would."

Adam was waiting on the porch for him after he came home from dropping off Racine. "S . . . s . . . supper's ready," he said, waiting for John to climb the stairs.

"Smells good," John said, smiling.

"You got a n . . . new girl?" Adam asked with a mischievous look in his eyes.

John shook his head. "No, Pop. She's just an old friend."

Adam smiled broadly. "G . . . g . . . g . . . good, 'cause I likes . . . that other one. The n . . . n . . . nice one."

Connie and Adam had spoken several times over the phone, and the old man fell head over heels in love with her.

"L . . . L . . . lemme talk to that w . . . woman," he'd demand, and the two of them would spend the next twenty minutes talking about absolutely nothing.

John held open the door and let his father walk through it first. "They're all nice, Adam. Every last one of them."

"You go . . . gonna bring her . . . n . . . next time?"

John smiled. "Let's eat. I'm hungry."

Chapter 33

I'm gone less than a week and miss my little bigheads like crazy." Reesy slid in bed next to her husband. "Feels so good to be home," she sighed. "Sleeping in my own bed."

The tension between them seemed to go unnoticed most of the evening. Reesy had been so busy with the kids, who were happy to have her home, and Justin sat back, watching in awe the perfection of his family blending together like some painting from an artist's imagination. He loved being a part of this picture. Family, to Justin, had always been the prize that made living worthwhile. His wife was the flip side of him, and until recently, the two of them had balanced their small world flawlessly. He'd been silly to let his own selfishness get in the way. He'd been an idiot to risk it all for sex and to feed his own ego.

He reached out and took her hand in his, toying with the wedding ring he'd placed on her finger all those years ago. "You should let me get you another one," he said, quietly. "Something bigger."

She laughed. "Don't even think about it."

"I've got a real job now, Reese," he joked. "I can afford a bigger one. Something blinging and blanging and brilliant."

Reesy was touched by his sincerity. "No," she said simply.

"But I want to."

She raised her hand and stared at her small diamond on her ring finger. "This ring meant the world to me when you gave it to me, Justin. That hasn't changed and it never will. You gave it to me because you loved me and you wanted me to be your wife. Why would I want to replace it with something else just because it was blinging?"

Soft brown eyes stared back at him, and slowly, he felt himself sink deeper into them. She was all the woman in the world he wanted, and until this moment, he'd made the mistake of forgetting that.

"I've been an asshole," he said, quietly.

She shook her head. "No more than I've been, Justin."

"I should've known how much finding your mother meant to you, Reese, and I should've been more supportive."

She turned to face him. "I didn't have to be so obsessive about it, though, sweetheart. I tuned you out. I tuned everybody out because of my tunnel vision, thinking I needed to do this alone, when that was never the case."

"No, it wasn't. You've never had to do it alone, baby. We're a team, Reese. Everything, absolutely everything, that happens in this relationship—we face together. That's how it's supposed to be."

"I know, baby."

"This isn't any different, but for some reason, we let it come between us and that didn't need to happen."

"I know, Justin. And I'm sorry."

Justin didn't want her apologies. He pulled her face to his and kissed her passionately. Reesy reached around him and slid his shorts down his hips. He let go long enough to slide them the rest of the way and kick them off onto the floor, then rolled her over on her back, raised up her gown, and slid it off over her head. She smelled so good. She felt so good. All he wanted to do was to taste his wife. He slid down her torso, spread her legs open, then buried his face full in the folds of her, probing and making love to her with his tongue. Reesy raised her knees to her chest, cupped his head with her hands, and let Justin do what he did best. They made love the way they used to years ago, giving and taking, changing positions, on top, from behind, side by side, on the floor, until they were exhausted and lay in each other's arms at the foot of the bed.

"That was impressive," he said into the crumpled sheets underneath her head.

She laughed, and kissed his cheek. "Yeah. I'd say."

Justin raised himself up on his elbows and gazed lovingly into her eyes. "In case you hadn't noticed, I missed you, too, Reesy."

"I noticed, honey," she smiled. "And I'm so glad you did."

"Hello, Avery." Reesy had been dying to call him to fill him in on the reunion with her mother.

Avery leaned back in the chair behind his desk and relished the moment more than she'd ever know. "Well, hello there. Are you back?" He knew the answer to that question before he'd even asked it.

"Yes. I got back yesterday, as a matter of fact."

"Well, from the tone of your voice, it sounds like things went pretty good."

"Better than I'd hoped," she said glowingly. "I can't tell you how much this whole experience has changed my life, Avery. Finding my mother again after all these years, well . . . it's been amazing, and terrifying, and enlightening, all at once. And I feel like a weight has been lifted off me. You have no idea."

He was genuinely touched by her enthusiasm. "I think I do, Reesy. And believe me, I'm as excited by all this as you are."

"You've been a good friend, Avery," she said sincerely. "I know we started out as business partners, but I truly believe that if it weren't for you, I don't know how I'd have made it through this. You believed we'd find her, even more than I did, and if it weren't for you, I'd have given up a long time ago."

Avery was the kind of man who didn't put too much stock in miracles. Most of the time, people hired him to find people who didn't want to be found, and very rarely did things ever work out the way some of them had hoped. From the sound of her voice, he was pulling for her, and maybe, just maybe, Reesy and her mother would be the exception and not the rule. In any event, he'd managed to burrow into a soft spot in her heart, and he didn't mind one bit.

"I'm glad to have helped, Clarice," he said, tenderly.

"We should keep in touch, Avery. Maybe you can come by one night for dinner?"

"Sure. I'd like that. Just let me know."

"I will."

He hung up the phone, missing the sound of her voice, and the promise of her that was nothing more than a figment of his imagination. Sweet woman. Beautiful. Genuine. Maybe too good for the likes of him. Then again . . .

He opened up his file drawer and pulled out a manila envelope filled with photographs. Avery loved photography. Back in the day, he'd even tried to break into the industry, photojournalism, freelance, weddings, birthday parties. His best work, though, was the shit he pulled out of his lens with visions of shit nobody else seemed to notice. He flipped through some of his favorites: a perfect red rose near the highway. How the hell did that one rose get there? he recalled wondering when he pulled over to snap the picture. Two beautiful children, playing marbles, oblivious to the drunk laying sprawled out not less than twenty feet from where they played. A lovely young woman, staring across the atrium, with her arms folded, her hair flowing, wearing a frilly pink ruffled dress, and a wicked-looking skull and crossbones tattooed on her upper arm.

And then there were his other photos. One of a woman terrorizing her five-year-old behind the Wal-Mart, where she thought nobody would see her. Her husband wanted custody, and thanks to this picture, he got it. Another one of a kid stealing from the cash register of the convenience store where he worked. The manager suspected as much, and thanks to this photograph, that kid lost his job, and landed on probation. And finally, a picture of his baby girl, Avery's daughter, dressed in white, her long hair hanging loosely down her back, and her angelic face looking even sweeter than her mother looked more than twenty years ago, when they first met. He hadn't seen his daughter in years. She had to be, what? Twenty-four, twenty-five years old now? They'd never been close. In fact, neither of them knew much about the other at all, except that they were related, and so far removed that it still amazed him that they were connected by blood.

Avery leaned back in his chair and sighed. She had no idea he'd taken this picture. And he had no idea, when he walked into that joint, that she'd end up in his special collection of photographs of unfaithful husbands, particularly the ones in which he had a vested interest. If she wasn't fucking him, she sure as hell looked like she was. From the expression on Justin Braxton's face, it didn't matter if it was the real deal, or if she was just faking the funk. The mothafucka came.

Camera phones. Technology can be a bitch.

Justin played hard while his pretty wife was away. Avery wondered if she had any idea. He stared at the picture, then thought of Clarice Braxton and shook his head. Naw. She didn't have a clue. Not yet, anyway.

Chapter 34

The baby was craving greens, corn bread, and fried catfish, so Connie talked Reesy into meeting her for lunch at the Welton Street Café.

"It was like seeing a ghost, Connie," Reesy explained, toying with some delicious-looking macaroni and cheese. "She looked different, but not completely. Know what I mean?"

No. She didn't know what she meant, but that was neither here nor there. It didn't matter to her what the woman looked like, or what she was doing, or that she was even still alive, for that matter. But it mattered to Reesy. And maybe, for her sister's sake, she could pretend to give a damn long enough to let Reesy have this moment.

"She seemed like she really was happy to see me." Reesy's eyes twinkled. "And it was good knowing that, because I wasn't sure she would be. You know? I didn't know if she left because she hated us, or . . . or what, but she missed us, Connie."

It was the *us* part that made Connie squirm in her seat.

"I know you don't believe it," Reesy continued woefully. "But she missed both of us, Connie, and . . . she'd like to see you, too."

Reesy's coercing fell on deaf ears, as Connie sprinkled hot sauce on her fish and licked her fingers.

"I'm not saying today," she continued. "I'm just asking you to keep an open mind—and heart. That's all."

Connie continued eating for a while before finally responding. "You've always had a good relationship with Charlotte, Reese. From the time you were a baby, I mean, the two of you just fit together like two puzzle pieces, and I've never doubted for a moment that she loved you more than anything in the world."

"She loved *us*," Reesy quickly added.

"She adored *you*, Reese. But for every beautiful memory you have of her and of the two of you together, I have twice as many bad ones of her and me."

"Connie," Reesy started to interrupt.

"I'm happy that you've found your mother, baby." Connie reached across the table and squeezed Reesy's hand. "Even though I haven't been the most supportive person in all this, I know how important it was for you to find her, and to get the answers you needed. And nobody knows more than me, Reese, how much you love her, how much you've always loved her."

"I can't help it," she shrugged. "I know she was wrong for leaving. No mother, no good mother would ever think to do such a thing, Connie, and I know that, but after seeing her and talking to her, it would be impossible for me not to forgive her and give her the benefit of the doubt."

"Yeah, Reesy," Connie smiled. "I know. And I would never ask you to hold a grudge against her. But I'm not you, honey. And I have no desire whatsoever to see her again, or to make amends, or to listen to anything she has to say. And it has nothing to do with holding a grudge," Connie quickly added. "She and I have never seen eye to eye on anything, Reese. Even when I was a kid, we could hardly stand to be in the same room with

each other, and that was long before she ever walked out on us."
Hope faded from Reesy's eyes as she stared back at Connie. "I
don't like my mother," Connie admitted. "I never did, and I never
will. There," she sighed. "I've said it, and I mean it. And I don't
want to have to sit here with you, or spend the rest of my life
feeling guilty for not caring about someone who I felt never
cared about me. So no, Clarice," she said with finality. "I don't
plan on ever seeing Charlotte again for as long as I live."

"I think you'd feel differently if you'd just heard what she
had to say," Reesy persisted. "After listening to her, I could understand how she must've felt, Connie. A single woman, overwhelmed at raising two girls alone. Do you know what she told
me?"

Connie tried not to let her exasperation show through. "No,
Reesy."

"That she was afraid she wasn't good enough for us. She was
afraid that she was failing us as a parent."

"So she walked out on us and left us to fend for ourselves,"
she said sarcastically. "That makes sense."

"I think she panicked. I think she didn't see any other way
out, and I honestly don't believe she meant to leave us perma-
nently."

"She had luggage when she left, Reesy," Connie said, calmly
spreading butter onto her cornbread. "Miss," she flagged down
the waitress. "Do you have peach cobbler?"

"Yes, ma'am."

"What about ice cream?"

"We sure do."

"Bring me some peach cobbler with a scoop of vanilla. You
want one too, Reese?"

"No," she said bluntly, watching Connie slather half a pound of butter on that bread, then fill her mouth with greens. "You're making a pig of yourself."

"I'm hungry."

"If I didn't know better, I'd think . . ."

Reesy stopped in midsentence. Connie stopped midway between the fork and her mouth.

"The last time I saw you eat like this, you were pregnant with Jade," Reesy said, stunned.

Connie leaned back and tried to swallow, washing her food down with a gulp of iced tea.

"Connie?"

Connie stared at her.

"Oh my God! No!" she said in a hushed voice. "Tell me it's not true. Tell me your not pregnant again."

It was the way she said it that hurt the most, like dumb-ass Connie had messed up again. "Yeah. So?" Was that the best she could do? On the receiving end of Reesy's judgmental and disapproving glare—yes.

Reesy sat back and rolled her eyes in disgust. "I don't believe it. I don't believe you—"

Connie's feelings were beyond hurt, but then, this was the reason she hadn't said anything to Reesy about it. Because Reesy knew her better than anyone, and better than anyone, she knew how to make her feel small without even trying.

"What? You don't believe that I could want to have a baby, too, Reesy?" The threat of tears burned her eyes, but Connie willed them back.

Reesy glared at her. "Why? How could you let this happen—again, Connie?"

Connie dug deep to try and salvage her pride and self-esteem. She'd prepared herself for this argument and the day

Reesy did find out, but all of a sudden, she couldn't find the speech she'd prepared in the conversations she'd had over and over with herself and Reesy in her imagination.

"It just happened," she shrugged. "We got careless."

Reesy shook her head in disbelief. "You've got herpes, Connie. You don't do careless."

"What difference does it make?" she asked defensively. "It just happened."

"Birth control pills! Shots! Rings! IUDs! Patches! Condoms!" She counted each one off on her fingers. "It can't happen if you don't let it, Connie! Sounds to me like you did this shit on purpose."

Connie stared back, wounded, at her sister. "And so what if I did?" she asked quietly. "What if I did do it on purpose, Reesy? If a woman is going to have a kid, shouldn't she choose to have one on purpose? Shouldn't she just want one?"

"This is about Jade. Isn't it?" Anger shot from her eyes and straight into Connie's heart. "You can't have her, so—you go and do this. Trying to replace one baby with another one? Does that seem right to you?"

The waitress returned with Connie's peach cobbler and ice cream, but suddenly she wasn't so hungry anymore. Connie pulled out her wallet and laid a twenty-dollar bill on the table.

"If I were any other woman, Reesy," she started to say, "would you be happy for me?"

Reesy didn't bother with a response, but them Connie didn't expect one. She got up and left Reesy sitting in the restaurant alone.

Chapter 35

*S*ugar daddies don't always stay sweet. Uncle's kindness and
patience seemed to be fading and turning into something
bitter and impatient.

"Sometimes he's cool," Lynn had told her. "But Uncle's got some
strange ways, too. And you never know when he's gonna flip over
and change on you. One minute he's fine, and then the next," Lynn
puffed on a cigarette and shrugged. "I never know how to take
him."

Two months had passed since her encounter with Sherrell, and
Charlotte hadn't seen the woman since. Uncle had moved her into
another place, smaller, and further out toward the country, but she'd
heard Sherrell was looking for her ass, and she'd better hope Uncle's
woman never saw her out in public somewhere.

Now when he'd come to see her, he'd pile Charlotte up in the car,
fur coat and all, driving for hours at a time, all over the city, han-
dling his business, and Charlotte saw for the first time just how
ugly it was. And how ugly he could be.

"I ain't holding nothing back, Uncle. I told you that already." The
girl didn't even look like she was eighteen years old yet. Charlotte
trailed behind Uncle, into a seedy little apartment smelling like pee,

cornflakes crushing under her feet, and cartoons blasting from the television stared at by two wide-eyed little boys.

The girl glanced at the kids. "Y'all go in the bedroom," she demanded, trying to sound brave.

"But we wanna watch cartoons," the oldest boy protested.

"Go in the other room, I said!"

Uncle stalked her, unrelenting, staring her down and finally backing her into the corner of the room.

"I told you," he said in a low and steady tone, "I told you that if you ever needed anything, all you had to do was ask." Uncle breathed down hot and heavy on the girl pinned in that small corner of the apartment.

Charlotte's heart beat so hard it felt like she'd swallowed it. Her palms sweated as she glanced nervously back at the two goons standing behind her blocking the entrance, looking bored and unimpressed.

"If you need something for yourself or them boys, ain't I always told you to ask me, Gail? You remember me telling you that?"

Gail nodded convincingly. "Yeah, Uncle." Her voice dissipated into sobs. "I remember, and you been good to me." She tenderly reached out and pressed her hand to his chest. "Which is why I'd never steal from you, baby. You know I wouldn't. You know me. You know I wouldn't do that to you."

Gail raised up on her tiptoes and kissed him seductively.

Charlotte gasped. "What the—"

One of Uncle's henchmen caught her by the arm and dared her to move.

"Whatchu doing to me, girl?" he said in a husky growl.

The girl tried to smile and slowly descended down to the floor on her knees in front of him. "Whatchu like best, Uncle."

Charlotte watched horrified as the girl unzipped his pants, pulled out his Johnson, and slipped it into her mouth, sucking and licking furiously, while Uncle extended his arms, placed his hands flat against the wall, and braced himself, "Shhhhhhhiiiit!"

"No . . . no . . . no!" Charlotte screamed, lunging at him and Gail.

"Wait till he's done, girl!" one of the men behind her said, grabbing her around the waist and lifting her off the ground, with Charlotte kicking and screaming the whole time. "Don't fuck with a man while he's getting sucked!" he laughed. "Shit like that ain't proper."

"Let go! Let me . . ."

Uncle seemed to forget she was even in the room, grabbing Gail by the back of the head, thrusting in and out of her luscious mouth, loving the way she loved him. Gail knew how to suck a dick better than any woman he'd ever known. Better than any ho he'd ever had, and Uncle felt himself swelling up and getting ready to explode in her mouth like he was a fucking volcano.

"That's it, baby girl," he whispered.

Charlotte was crying. When had she started crying? Watching this shit was unbelievable and disgusting. She didn't realize how disgusting it all was until she happened to glance in the direction of the bedroom door and saw four sets of eyes peering out through the crack, snickering and watching their mother with her pimp's dick in her mouth.

"Awwwwwwww!" he groaned as he came. Uncle threw his head back, closed his eyes, and stumbled back as his knees buckled underneath him.

Charlotte had stopped fighting as the big man put her back down on the ground, looking at his partner and slapping him a five.

And then Uncle turned to Charlotte and the audience watching him, winked, and smiled as he zipped his pants. "It don't get no better than that," he laughed, satisfied.

"What the fuck is yo problem?" Uncle asked indifferently, sitting in the back of the car next to Charlotte. Rocky and Bullwinkle sat in the front, one driving while the other rode shotgun.

Charlotte was appalled that he'd even had the nerve to ask that question. "What the fuck do you think my problem is?"

"If I knew I wouldn't be asking," he said flippantly.

"You just fucked another bitch right in front of my face, Uncle, and you wonder what the hell my problem is?"

Uncle stared out the window. "Well, technically, she fucked me. I never laid a hand on the ho."

More and more lately, Uncle was showing her a side of himself she'd never wanted to believe existed. Lately, he seemed to be hell-bent on shining a bright light on his business dealings and it was getting to be too much.

"I wanna go home," she said quietly, gazing out into the still-unfamiliar streets of Kansas City. Sometimes this place was too fast for her, too hard, too mean. Yeah, Denver had been boring, but it was her home, the place she knew better than she knew the back of her hand, and it suited her so much better than the world she'd stumbled into out here.

"Say what?" he asked indignantly.

"I've been thinking about it ever since Sherrell and me . . ." She swallowed hard, gathering the courage and conviction to say what she'd felt these last few months. "I don't belong out here, Uncle." Charlotte finally turned to him with tears in her eyes. "I mean, I care about you and everything, but tonight . . . this shit was the last straw. I got my kids back home who need me, and . . ."

"That bitch fucked me, honey! You talking craziness, girl. Hmph!"

He'd taken good care of her ever since Sam left. Bought her nice clothes, set her up in a bad-ass place, paid her electric, heat, anything she wanted; he'd made sure she had it, like he'd cared. Really cared, and deep down, she knew he did, but all this shit was beginning to take its toll, and Charlotte saw signs everywhere, looking like Sherrell's fist, one of Uncle's bodyguards, or Gail down on her knees, sucking Uncle's dick while her kids watched, warning her that she needed to come to her senses and go back to Denver where she belonged before she drowned in all this bullshit.

"This shit is too much for me," she sobbed. *"That girl's kids were watching her do that to you! And you didn't give a damn! You didn't care and neither did she, that those kids saw the whole thing or that . . . that I saw it, too, Uncle! And I'm supposed to be your woman?"*

"Those damn kids know their momma's a ho! And you know what I do, girl! What you saw tonight was part of my job, honey. Part of one of many jobs." He sat back, noticeably irritable. *"You better check yourself, girl,"* he grunted.

"No, you'd better check yourself, because I'm leaving, Uncle. I'm leaving and there's nothing you can do about it."

She'd saved some money. She'd thought it out. All she needed was a bus ticket out of town, and in a day she'd be back at home where she belonged.

"Is that right?"

"I'm a grown-ass woman, Uncle. And if I want to leave, then I'm getting my ass the hell up out—"

Uncle grabbed her by the hair.

"Ow!" She screamed.

He pulled her head down into his lap, flipped her facedown, lifted up her coat, and hit her hard on her ass, repeatedly, with an open hand.

She screamed again in disbelief. "Uncle!"

Uncle raised his hand up high, then brought it down full force, stinging and burning Charlotte's ass, setting it on fire. Then he jerked her up and threw her back against the car window, grabbing her viciously by the ankles, spreading her legs and pulling her toward him.

"You wanna play with Uncle, bitch!" he spat, taking his long wooden cane and pressing the handle hard between her legs. His eyes were like fire, his face red-hot.

Charlotte grimaced. Tears streamed down the sides of her face.

"Turn your monkey ass back around, mothafucka!" he growled at the big man in the passenger seat.

Uncle turned his attention back to Charlotte, who was terrified at what he might do. "My bitches don't leave unless I tell them to leave," he said coldly. Charlotte shuddered. With one finger he slid her short pants to the side, then her panties, relishing the sight of her hot pussy trembling before him. He slid the handle of his cane on to her soft flesh and rubbed it up and down, his mouth watering at the juices glistening on top. Then he brought it to his lips and licked off the essence of her, his honey baby, smacked his lips, and moaned. He gazed down at Charlotte and smiled wickedly.

"I'll be damned if I let you take that sweet, sticky shit from me." His eyes twinkled, and then Uncle did something he'd never done before, for any woman, not even his own wife, Sherrell. He leaned down and kissed that delicious pussy, slicing his tongue between the folds, flicking it against her swollen clit, and swallowing every drop of the nectar flowing like water into his mouth.

It was a sensation like none she'd ever had before. Charlotte's eyes rolled up into her head, and she grabbed handfuls of his coat and wrapped her legs over his shoulders, raising her hips to meet his lips, staring at the driver and passenger in the front seat, watching them staring at her, and Charlotte could give a damn.

Chapter 36

The day was gorgeous, cool, breezy, and bright. A perfect day for watching the kids play in the park and spending time with her husband. Justin rested his head in her lap, relishing the softness of his wife, and wallowing in the rebirth of their devotion to each other. The trying times between them were over. He was convinced of it, and rather than dwelling on past transgressions, Justin found it more important to focus his attention on the future with the people most precious to him.

The music of Reesy's laughter resonated in his heart. She called out to her son J.J. "Not so high, J.J.," she scolded him as he pushed his sister high in the air in the swing.

Jade squealed the whole time. "Higher! Higher, J.J.!"

"Leave them alone," Justin admonished her. "She's all right, Momma."

"She's going to flip right over the top of that bar if he pushes her any higher, Papa."

"And she'll hold on tight and love every minute of it."

Justin was right, of course. Jade had a bit of a daredevil in her, much to Reesy's chagrin. A risk-taker, adventurous, so much like . . . like Connie.

Or was Connie just a fool? Pregnant again and as confused as ever. Reesy had seen it in her eyes. And where was John in all this? Connie hadn't mentioned him in ages, but did she really have to? Chances were, he'd left Connie without so much as a second glance. This time, Connie was on her own. Really on her own, because Reesy had no more time or energy to come to her rescue and adopt this kid, too. Connie should've known better. Connie did know better. Only Connie had a hit-and-miss relationship with common sense sometimes, and Reesy was sick and tired of it, and of Connie.

"So, did you get the ticket yet?" Justin asked.

Reesy smiled and rubbed her thumb lightly across his forehead. "I booked the flight yesterday."

"She excited?"

"Excited, and scared to death to fly. She's been wanting to come home for years. I think she was beginning to believe she'd never get a chance to."

"Cammy's not coming?"

Reesy shook her head. "She's too far along in her pregnancy, but she wants to come after the baby is born. Besides, I think she wants to spend time with her boyfriend."

This was like a dream come true. Charlotte was going home, finally, she was going home to be with her baby girl, and to meet her grandbabies, and Reesy's husband, a good man, Justin, who loved Reesy the way she deserved to be loved.

She sat on the side of her bed, folding the clothes she planned to take with her, trying to remember what spring in Denver was like, and finding her best things, her prettiest things, to make the best impression on everyone.

Reesy was throwing a dinner party in her honor. Charlotte's heart beat hard and fast every time she thought about it. A fancy dinner where she'd be the guest of honor, and everyone could see how much she loved her daughter, and how sorry she was for leaving her, and how glad she was to be home.

Cammy interrupted her excitement, standing in the doorway, sobbing. "I wish I could go, too, Momma." Her eyes were red and swollen from crying all damn day. That big belly of hers shook as she hiccuped through pathetic tears. "Reesy said I could come, too, after the baby comes. She's my sister. They're my family, too."

Sometimes she just couldn't help herself. As hard as she tried, and as much as she'd regret it afterward, Charlotte couldn't help lashing out at Cammy the way she did. Cammy just seemed to beg her to. She seemed to provoke her mother on purpose, and compel Charlotte to say and do such ugly things.

Charlotte adamantly shook her head and pursed her lips together, trying to hold back menacing words threatening to escape and hurt poor Cammy's feelings even more. "This is my time, Cammy," she said sternly. "I've been waiting for this day almost thirty years, and—"

Cammy hurried over to where her mother was sitting and knelt down at her feet, pleading up to her with sorrowful eyes. "I know, Momma. But after the baby is born I want to go to Denver, too. I wouldn't do anything to ruin this for you, but . . . . They're my sisters, and it's my family, too, Momma."

The sound of her voice, whining and sad, threatened to ruin Charlotte's spirited mood. Charlotte had been more excited than she'd been in years, and Cammy's begging and pleading, trying to make her feel bad, threatened to cloud her anticipation. Cammy was a pain in the ass, threatening to get in the way. She always got in the way. Even before she was born—she got in the way. And here she was now, doing her damnedest to ruin the best thing to happen to Charlotte since she left home.

"I said no, Cammy." Charlotte glared into Cammy's wet eyes.

Cammy clutched Charlotte's housecoat in her fists and started to cry again. "Please, Momma! Reesy said I could come! Please!"

It happened before either of them had a chance to brace themselves. The back of Charlotte's hand landed hard across Cammy's cheek, sending her tumbling backward onto the floor.

Rage. Regret. Charlotte stood over Cammy, who lay curled up on the bedroom floor, her knees drawn to her chest, sobbing uncontrollably.

"This ain't your party, Camille!"

Charlotte reached down and grabbed a handful of Cammy's hair, hating this girl more and more for making her act this way. She shook her head back and forth with all her strength. "You ain't going!" Charlotte cried, too. "You ain't going to ruin this for me, bitch! I swear! You ain't messing this up!"

Moments later, Cammy was gone, and Charlotte sat alone in her room, on the side of her bed, wiping away her own tears. Her life had been too hard, her misery lasting too long; her hopes and dreams for some peace were back home in Denver, Colorado. She knew it. She just knew it. Cammy had come from a history she'd just as soon forget. She was a reminder of the most tragic and terrible incidents in her life, and most days, she couldn't even stand to look at the girl.

She could hear the girl crying most of the night, through the thin wall that separated their bedrooms, but it didn't matter. She didn't need Cammy the way she once did. Reesy was back, her baby. Her real baby. And she would be the one who took care of Charlotte from now on. Cammy could go to hell.

Chapter 37

Every instinct in her body told her not to dial the number, but since when was the last time she'd paid attention to instinct? Connie sat alone in her dark apartment, fighting back panic threatening to take her over. Keeping this baby had been a mistake. It must've been, because her world felt like it was off balance, and turning the wrong way, and spinning way too fast.

It was late, and even later in Texas, but she dialed John's cell phone number anyway, hoping in the back of her mind that he'd surprise her and say something remarkable and life-changing.

"Yeah?" he said, sounding half asleep.

Connie hesitated before responding, wondering why she called in the first place, and searching for something, anything, to say that would fix what was broken between them. "I didn't mean to wake you," she said softly.

John didn't say anything at first, and for a moment she thought he might hang up on her. "You all right?" he asked, almost convincing her that his concern might be real. There was a time when she seldom questioned his sincerity. Too bad that time wasn't now.

"I'm—okay," she answered. Lying. Of course she wasn't okay. He was there and she was here. He was there and she was pregnant. He was there, and she'd been the one to tell him to leave. No. She wasn't okay at all.

"So, what's going on?" he asked indifferently.

She ran her hand through her hair, tangled and nappy, desperately needing to be picked. A lump swelled in her throat, but she swallowed hard and choked it back. "Do you at least wonder about the baby, John? Do you at least think about it?"

It seemed like forever before he answered her question, and because she knew him so well, she knew he would've done everything he could to dodge it and dance around it if they were face-to-face.

"I'll send money, if that's what you're asking."

She shuddered at how cold he sounded, and his tone reinforced the thoughts drilling into her head lately. Thoughts that she'd kept at bay long past the opportunity to have an abortion, and into the space in time where the baby was gray matter, and she was numbed by it all.

"No," she said quietly. The invisible tether between them was no longer there. It no longer tugged at her heart, and from the sound of things, it didn't tug at his, either. Connie had been prepared to spend the rest of her life with this man. But in a matter of months, they'd become strangers to each other, with nothing in common but the child she was carrying, and wasn't so sure she wanted anymore. Not because of him, or the fact that he was gone, but because she was gone, too, disappeared, somewhere in the whirlwind of all the bullshit in her life.

"You still plan on keeping it?" he asked.

Connie sighed, ignoring the tiny flutter inside her, because it was easier than acknowledging it, and getting excited over it. "I don't think so," she confessed.

He didn't respond.

"Well," she said, accepting the fact that this would be the last time they spoke to each other. "You take it easy, King. I'm going to sleep now."

She hung up before he could say good-bye. Connie settled down into bed, staring up at the dark ceiling and at a future that was all too familiar to her, but comfortable. She breathed a sigh of relief, and for the first time in months felt a twinge of optimism and hope. Maternal instincts didn't come so easily to her. She'd been trying to make this baby thing work for all the wrong reasons, every last one of them selfish. Connie had no business being anybody's momma. And John King wouldn't fare so well as a daddy, either. Connie rubbed her hand over her swelling stomach. What kind of chance would this baby have with parents like the two of them?

"You deserve better than us, kid," she said quietly. "Trust me. And neither one of us deserves you."

Racine slid her hand across his chest, then nuzzled up next to him. "Any other woman might jump out of bed raising holy hell about her man getting phone calls in the middle of the night from some other woman."

John ignored her comment. Connie wasn't some other woman. Up until a few months ago, she'd been the only woman in his world who meant anything to him.

"She trying to get you to come back?"

He glanced down at her, then sighed. "No."

"I'm not stupid, John," she said, rubbing her foot up and down his shin. "You never talk about her, but I know you love her. In fact, you go out of your way not to talk about her, so I know it has to be pretty serious."

Racine slid her hand down his torso and underneath the sheet, then wrapped her long fingers around his dick, feeling it grow hard in her hand.

"And you all right with that?"

She moaned. "Yeah, I'm cool with it. Know why?"

Racine raised her leg over John, then positioned herself above him, straddling him, and easing her self slowly down onto his shaft.

John sucked in his breath. "Why?"

She stared mischievously into his eyes. "Because I have the advantage."

"How's that?"

Racine pushed herself down on him as far as she could go, then slowly raised her hips until she was sitting on top of him, and gradually engulfed him again. "Because you're here with me, and her ass is in Colorado." She leaned down, parted her lips, then slipped her tongue in between his. "Now fuck me hard, Daddy, and put my ass back to sleep."

Coming was synonymous with sleeping, but he fought it. Racine lay passed out on her stomach next to him, but John's mind wouldn't let him rest. Hearing the sound of her voice had done something to him. What exactly? He wasn't sure. But it had awoken some part of him that he thought he'd buried the day he left. Cutting ties, leaving the past behind, never looking back, were the kinds of things he'd mastered back when he was fifteen and his grandmother, Agnes, told him to get out of her house. He'd mastered them because he had to, or else how in the hell was he supposed to survive?

"Do you ever wonder about the baby?" Connie had asked.

No. He never did. And he never believed he could ever do a kid justice.

John felt his eyes start to close as he began to drift off to sleep, finally. He'd been spending the night at Racine's almost every night for the past month, and she'd put it on him, damn good, too, keeping him filled up with sex and good food. But tonight, for the first time since he'd left Denver, while Racine pumped her full ass up and down on top of him, he'd closed his eyes, grabbed Racine by the hips, and came hard at the vision of Connie riding him, and not Racine.

Chapter 38

*D*addy's little girl. It was hard for him to watch his daughter slithering down a pole in the middle of that stage, spreading her legs to drooling maniacs, and jiggling ass in their faces. And it was hard for him not to. Avery had crossed the line of shame a long time ago, back when he first found out she was dancing and when she told him he wasn't her goddamned daddy, and he needed to get his ass out of her face before she called security.

Cookie, she called herself. Her real name was Lisa. He'd named her and then he'd lost her. Avery and Lisa's mother, Felicia, argued all the time. Hell, they loved each other long enough to make a couple of kids, then woke up one day only to find they couldn't stand sharing the same space. He left, never intending on leaving his kids. Just her. But time got away from him. He visited every now and then, he met somebody else, Felicia married some fool who'd put his hands on Lisa and turned her into what she was now. And Avery was nowhere to be found. She believed he'd forgotten her, but that wasn't the case. He'd just gotten busy, and with every intention he had of going to see about his kids came another case, another failed relationship, even a heart attack.

Eventually, he came to his senses and set out to find his kids. His oldest, Anthony, drove a car he shouldn't have been able to afford, wore gold chains around his neck big enough to be shackles, and had a warrant out for his arrest.

"Where you been, man? Hmph! Like I need you now."

And here was his little girl. Shaking ass and titties with the best of them, filling up her panties with dollar bills, while they licking their lips for her like she was food on the table.

He sat in his car and waited for her to come out of the club. She looked so much like Lisa now, young, like she was heading to college or something. He'd had no idea his daughter was being molested growing up. She told him the first time he found her, and he told her he wanted to pick up the pieces with her and her brother.

"Where were you when I needed your ass?" she spat in his face. "When momma's fucking husband was busy fucking my eleven-year-old ass? Get the hell away from me, Avery! I don't need a daddy! At least, not one who can't pay for my ass!"

He looked for the man who'd defiled his daughter and his son. Of course, he never found him. But to this day, he kept his eyes open, hoping to stumble across his sick ass in the grocery store or at the gas station and beat the shit out of him, until the mothafucka begged to die. After all, it was the least he could do, and besides, maybe it would ease his conscience just enough to live with himself.

"What are you doing here?" she asked, startled, watching Avery climb out of his car.

"How you doing, baby?" he asked, sincerely.

Cookie rolled her eyes, and headed for her car. "Go to hell, Avery," she muttered.

He couldn't help but to laugh. Lisa was stubborn, more like him than she'd ever want to know.

"Give me a minute, Lisa," he said, following her. Out of the corner of his eye, he saw a dark, massive shadow appear at the entrance of the club, a bodyguard for the ladies to keep stalkers at bay.

She noticed him, too. "It's okay," she shouted to the man. "I know him." Cookie turned her attention back to him, annoyed. "Say what you got to say, Avery. Otherwise, I might just sic him on you."

And she would, too. He could see it in her eyes, and he wouldn't blame her one bit. Avery pulled a picture from his pocket and showed it to her. "Obviously you know him," he said sarcastically.

She glanced at it briefly, then handed it back to him. "So?"

"You see a lot of him?"

Cookie rolled her eyes, and pushed past him. "That's none of your goddamned business."

"I'm asking," he said, hurrying behind her. "Because he's married."

"Who isn't?"

"I know his wife."

She stopped and turned to him. "She hired you to take these pictures?"

He lied. "Yes."

Cookie turned away, disgusted, and unlocked the door to her car. "You and her need to get a life, Avery." She climbed in the car and shut the door.

"He's cheating on her. And it's going to eat her up when she finds out, Lisa. I'd have to say he's her life."

Cookie sat in her car for a moment, remembering Justin and the wonderful weekend she'd spent locked up in a hotel room with him. He'd been nothing but kind to her, tender, patient, maybe more than any man she'd ever known. But he wasn't her man, and she never made the mistake of thinking he ever would be. The last thing she wanted to do was cause trouble for him. He just didn't deserve it.

Cookie started up her car. "You tell whoever she is that it was a one-time thing. He came here with some friends, they got a little drunk, and things got out of hand. That's all."

He could tell she was lying, but Lisa had her reasons, and he knew better than to push the issue. "You sure you doing all right?" he asked, turning the conversation back to her. "You need anything?"

She shook her head, disgusted. "I don't need anything from you, Avery," she said icily. "I never did."

Avery watched her drive away, disappearing into the city. Her words cut him deep. But then, they always did.

Chapter 39

Zoo was young, twenty-two, maybe twenty-three, with smooth, glossy black skin, a short 'fro, big, soft lips that he licked all the time, and he blushed easily. Charlotte liked that most about him. He'd been the one to nurse her back to health after Sherrell had beaten her ass, spending the next week at her place, making sure she ate, keeping bags of ice available for her face to help take away the swelling, and staying up late at night just to talk if she felt like talking. The last few months, they'd become good friends, and more and more, she was beginning to enjoy the pleasure of his company over that of Uncle's.

Zoo was a glorified errand boy. He wasn't hard like the rest of Uncle's cohorts. But he'd known that boy since he was a nappy-headed kid running barefoot through the neighborhood, when Uncle used to send him to the store to get him some cigarettes, and Zoo's role hadn't really changed a whole lot over the years. Except now he not only picked up Uncle's cigarettes for him, he might be sent to collect money, take his car to get washed, or look after his bruised and battered girlfriend, bringing her groceries and dropping her off to get her hair done every now and then.

Uncle had no idea what he'd done, though, putting that innocent and sweet boy in Charlotte's path. He was everything Uncle wasn't anymore, attentive and kind, romantic and tender, and so hard to resist when a woman set her mind to it.

The two of them lay on the sofa, Charlotte pinned underneath Zoo, her leg wrapped around him, his lips wrapped around hers. The music played in the background, incense burned on the table, and they kissed, playing games with each other's tongues and lips, like teenagers necking while their parents were out of the house, fully clothed, but grinding against each other, wanting what they knew they shouldn't have.

Charlotte ran her manicured fingers up and down his muscular back, wanting him the way she hadn't wanted anything in her life. "Mmmm," she moaned. Was it love she felt for him? Or admiration? She felt at home with him, comfortable and cared for, and unafraid. With Uncle, the longer she was with him, the more afraid she was becoming of him. He was a volatile man, a dangerous man, once so protective of her; now he was getting careless.

Zoo was the kind of man she always wanted, but never thought she'd have. He did little things for her, things she never thought would matter but did, like bring her flowers for no good reason, or come by and spend the night with her when she called him because she'd woken up in the middle of the night and needed him to crawl in bed with her. Zoo never pressed her for sex, though she knew he wanted her as much as she wanted him, but there was a sweetness between them and she wanted to preserve that innocence for as long as possible, so she would only let him go so far, and then she'd send him on his way. Obedient and obliging, he'd leave, disappointed, but looking forward to the next time they were together.

"I love you, Charlotte," he whispered between kisses. He said it like he meant it, like more than anything he wanted her to believe him.

She opened her eyes long enough to see him staring down at her, and Charlotte smiled, pressed her hand to his cheek, and smiled. "I know you do, baby. You don't have to keep saying it."

"Yes I do," he insisted. "Because if I stop, then you might forget how much you mean to me."

He'd say the kinds of things that set butterflies free in her stomach, and made her wish she'd met him first instead of Uncle.

"I wish it was just us, Zoo," she told him. "Just you and me, and . . . nobody else."

He nodded thoughtfully. "Too bad things didn't work out that way. But I'm here now, Charlotte. And we just have to make the most of what we can get when we can get it."

He nuzzled his face in the side of her neck, and the two of them just lay still, letting the minutes tick quietly away, prolonging an evening that would end too soon.

"I want to make love to you, Charlotte," he said, quietly.

"You know we shouldn't," she mildly protested.

"I know. I guess we'll have to wait, then."

Sherrell stood in front of the television with her hand on her hip, purposefully blocking his view, wearing her leopard-print satin robe, opened and exposing a nylon negligee two sizes too small.

Uncle rolled his eyes. "Mind moving your big ass so I can see?"

"What?" she said smartly. "You getting tired of your bitch already, Uncle? Ain't had her long. You ready to put her out to pasture already? Might make you a little change if you put her ass on the right corner. That is, if I don't find her first," she winked, laughed, then walked away.

He hadn't thought about putting her on the street, but it was an option. Shit, Uncle was in a mood, bored, and yet addicted to her little yellow ass like a junkie, but, most times, she got on his damn nerves. *Sort of like a wife.*

Take me here.

I want this. I want that.

Where've you been?

How come you didn't call me?

I thought you said you were coming over?

Blah! Blah! Blah! Uncle took a long drink from his beer, realizing that it wasn't so much her he wanted, as much as he didn't want anybody else to have her fine ass. She was a trophy, and if he could just put her up on the shelf and tape her whiny-ass mouth shut, she'd fit perfectly into his world. Every now and then, he'd take her down long enough to get him some, then put her back where he found her.

Business was getting to him, though. Seemed like every goddamned body who worked for him had lost their damn minds. Knuckleheads who were supposed to protect him and watch his back were sneaking around behind it, getting free pussy from his hos. Hos were holding back, claiming they just weren't making as much and swearing up and down that what they'd given him was all the money they'd made in the world. Dope money was coming up short, cops were watching his damn house night and day, and to top it off, Sherrell's black ass was fucking around with some sucka 'cross town who drove a goddamned cab for a living. If he didn't have so much on his mind, he'd go in that bedroom right this minute and beat the shit out of her ass.

No sooner did he think it did she emerge from the bedroom fully dressed, wearing that diamond necklace she'd bought with his money, a short-ass miniskirt, and a red halter top with her titties bouncing around all over the place.

"You gonna put some clothes on before you walk out that door?" he asked sarcastically.

She rolled her eyes and sucked her teeth as she picked up her purse and put on her coat to leave. "Don't wait up," she said indifferently, disappearing out the front door.

Uncle turned his attention back to the television he wasn't watching and finished off the last of his beer. "I won't."

Instinctively he picked up the phone and dialed Charlotte's number, but there was no answer, which was odd. He looked at the clock. It was late, after eleven. Uncle calmly hung up the phone and turned the channel to watch the late news. Baby Girl obviously wasn't getting enough attention. The next time he saw her, he'd just have to make it a point to give her more attention than she knew what to do with.

Chapter 40

eesy had been leaving messages for Connie at the store, at home, and on her cell phone, but Connie wasn't answering. But that was no reason for Reesy not to try one last time. "Connie," she said pulling up in front of the hotel where Charlotte was staying. "You're being dumb. I know you're probably listening. Fine. Don't pick up the phone. I just called to remind you that dinner's at six. And you need to be there, Connie, just like I need to be there. We need to do this. Six. You bring the wine!"

Charlotte had flown in that morning, and Reesy and Justin both agreed that it would be best to put her up in a hotel instead of having her stay at the house. It wasn't her plan to disrupt her family's lives all at once, just a little at a time, which was the best way to dole out Charlotte, especially where Reesy's adoptive mother and father were concerned. Evelyn wasn't happy about any of this, but she needed to understand that Charlotte was as much a part of Reesy's life as she was, and that was all there was to it. Whether or not she wanted to believe it, Reesy certainly understood how Evelyn felt. She understood her mother's insecurities and doubts as well as anyone, because she herself was in the same situation with Connie and Jade. And as much as she hated to admit it, as selfish as she sometimes felt about it, the truth of the matter was, she did feel threatened having her daughter know that Connie was her real mother, and not just her aunt. Jade was crazy about Connie, and she missed her. Connie hadn't been around in months, and not a day went by that Jade didn't ask about her. The issue of telling that little girl the truth had surely put a wedge between Reesy and her sister, and Connie's pregnancy wasn't helping matters any. They needed to sit down and talk, really talk, and come to terms with each other once and for all. When all the dust settled around Charlotte, they surely would.

Charlotte rubbed her palms together in her lap underneath the table, staring wide-eyed at all the beautiful children, her grandchildren, sitting around the table for dinner, and at Justin, Reesy's handsome and successful husband, doting over Reesy and the children so lovingly. The scene took her breath away, and she blinked away joyful tears trying not to make a fool of herself.

"What should the children call me?" Charlotte asked Reesy on the way from the hotel.

Reesy thought for a moment before answering, and then she smiled. "How about Miss Charlotte for now?"

Looking at these beautiful babies, it didn't feel right having them call her that, but she would respect Reesy's wishes for now. In time, though, she'd be Grandma, or Nana. Something safe, and sweet. The boys were handsome, but it was hard to take her eyes off that little girl. Jade was her name. Such a pretty name. The child smiled at her, and Charlotte saw the indelible image of Reesy when she was that age, that same smile, but then she blinked, and she also saw someone else, especially in the girl's eyes. She saw Connie staring back at her, glancing at the position of her mouth, which was out of place and not where it should've been.

"Momma, why don't you let me do this," Reesy coaxed Evelyn gently. "Go sit down. I can finish up in here. Dinner's just about ready."

Evelyn hadn't hardly said two words to Charlotte since she'd come in. She nervously dried her hands on her apron, and reluctantly gave in to Reesy's suggestion. "I guess the least I could do is sit down and have a conversation with the woman," she said as nicely as she could.

Reesy hugged her, and laughed. "It would be a start." She stared deeply into her mother's eyes, realizing that there was no better moment than now to reassure her. "Everything's going to be fine, Mom. I love you now more than ever," she smiled. "You should know that."

Evelyn nodded. "I'm being silly. I know."

"No, you're not," Reesy reassured her. "You're being my mother, and I can always forgive you for that."

Evelyn tried to smile, but she still had a feeling about Charlotte she couldn't shake, and Reesy's notion of the two of them getting together and ever being friends was something she just couldn't fathom.

Just then the sound of the doorbell ringing interrupted them. "That must be Avery." Reesy hurried out of the kitchen and rushed to the door in time to see Justin answering it and letting Avery in. "I'm so glad you could make it," she said excitedly, giving him a quick peck on the cheek.

"Well." He handed Justin a bottle of wine. "I appreciate the invitation."

Justin reached out to shake his hand, more than willing to put aside the tension that had always been between them since Reesy hired him to find Charlotte. "Glad to have you, man."

Avery shook his hand, and tried his damnedest not to recall the memory of his daughter straddling Justin's lap. "Thank you, Justin."

"Come." Reesy grabbed Avery by the hand and practically dragged him into the dining room. "I want you to meet her."

He felt like a kid with a crush, hoping the hand she was holding wouldn't break out in a terrible sweat from nervousness.

"Everyone, I'd like you to meet a special friend of mine." Reesy's elation couldn't be kept at bay. She was so glad to see him and had been excited about this moment all day. "Avery," she looked at Charlotte, let go of his hand, and walked over to where she was sitting, "this is Charlotte." She shrugged and squeezed her mother's shoulders. "Momma?"

"Yes." Both Charlotte and Evelyn answered in unison. Evelyn shrunk away embarrassed and hurt when she realized Reesy wasn't talking about her.

Charlotte glanced at Evelyn and stood up proudly, smoothing down her blouse. "Hello?" she said, feeling proud that she'd been introduced as the mother, and not that snooty woman who'd been trying to keep Reesy to herself all evening. She extended her hand to the nice man.

"He's the one who helped me to find you," Reesy said softly in her ear. "If it weren't for him, I don't think I ever would've."

"It's a pleasure to meet you, ma'am." Avery smiled.

"It's truly a miracle, Momma." Reesy continued talking to Charlotte.

Evelyn fought the urge to leave the room, holding on tight to her husband, who held on tight to her.

"It is a miracle, baby," Charlotte said. "And a good one, too."

"You're part of my life again." She looked around the room. "My family, and . . . I feel so complete now. Like everything is as close to perfect as perfect can get."

The two women embraced and cried.

"All right now," Justin interrupted, and came over to put his arms around both of them. "You've got the rest of your lives to make up for lost time." He kissed Charlotte on the forehead, then his wife. "But I've got a table full of kids here who look mighty hungry."

Everyone laughed. Reesy dried her eyes and headed toward the kitchen, with Justin trailing behind her. "Then come on, Mr. Man of the House, and help me serve these here chillun'!"

Reesy outdid herself on dinner, ham, greens, macaroni and cheese, corn bread, and fresh string beans. For the next forty-five minutes after being served, the only thing to be heard was the sound of lips smacking and fingers being licked.

When she was finished, Charlotte pushed back from the table and patted her full stomach. "Oh, that was so good, baby. Child, where'd you learn to cook like that?"

Reesy laughed. "Momma taught me." She looked at Evelyn and winked.

Evelyn blushed.

Charlotte rolled her eyes. "Well, it sure was delicious. I don't think I've ever been so full in my life."

All of a sudden, Reesy felt a small hand on her thigh. She

looked at Jade, who stared back with a confused look in her face.

"Yes, baby?" Reesy asked.

Jade leaned over, and asked her in a quiet voice, "You got two mommas?"

At first Reesy laughed, but then she realized how all of this must appear to this child too young to really understand everything going on around her, especially since the seed of doubt and confusion had been planted in her own head by Aunt Connie.

"Yes, Jade. I do."

Jade studied each woman for a moment before finally taking solace in Reesy's answer. For the rest of the evening, she was unusually quiet.

After dinner, the women stayed behind to help clean up, while Justin, his father-in-law, and Avery disappeared into the family room.

Avery tried to let down his defenses, but it was difficult. Justin, on the other hand, seemed more at ease than he'd ever been since Avery had first met him. Justin led Avery out back to the patio, where he seemed to want to get something off his chest.

"Look, man," Justin started to say. "I know I haven't been the easiest brotha to get along with."

Avery chuckled. "No. You really haven't been."

"Well." Justin shrugged. "I just wanted to say thank you for what you did for my wife. Honestly, I didn't think it could be done, and I wasn't all that sure I wanted it to be, but she's happy. In fact, I don't think I've ever seen her happier, and I owe it all to you."

Avery shrugged. "I was just doing what I'm paid to do, man."

Justin nodded. "Yeah. Paid an awful lot of money to do, bro. Anybody ever tell you that your ass is expensive?"

Avery laughed. "Every now and then. Yeah. But I work hard, man. Believe me."

"I do, Avery man. I believe you one hundred percent."

It was getting late, and Avery was getting ready to leave. Justin walked him to the door, and Reesy came out just before he said good-bye.

"I know you're not going to leave without telling me good night?" she fussed.

Avery smiled. "Where are my manners?"

"Obviously you don't have any." She walked over and hugged him. "Did you get enough to eat? You want to take any home? There's plenty."

"No, no. I'm fine. Dinner was delicious, Reesy."

"Well, thank you. And I look forward to you coming back another time. You're a friend of mine, Avery, and I hope we can keep in touch."

"Of course," he nodded. "Good night, all."

Avery felt a sense of regret as he sat in his car, getting ready to pull away from the curb. Justin was a man like any other man, who loved his wife, his family, but who'd made a terrible, terrible mistake. Avery was a firm believer that people shouldn't have to pay for one mistake for the rest of their lives. He started his car and slowly drove down the street. He was in love with Reesy. That's all there was to it. But she was in love with her husband. That much was painfully obvious.

Evelyn Turner was beyond uncomfortable. Her husband had dozed off after dinner in the living room, Justin was upstairs helping the children to get ready for bed, and Reesy was in the kitchen, pretending to put away food and dishes, leaving Evelyn alone in the family room with this woman.

The silence between them was deafening as they sat facing the television that wasn't on, listening to music they couldn't hear, sipping on cups of coffee, and trying as hard as they could to ignore the fact that the other existed. It was Charlotte who spoke first.

She cleared her throat. "Dinner was delicious. Reesy really outdid herself," she said, feeling as proud as any mother would about having such a daughter.

Evelyn sipped on her coffee, then cleared her throat to respond. "It was nice. Too much cheese in the macaroni for my taste, but she says that's the only way the children will eat it."

Her smug tone naturally rubbed Charlotte the wrong way, but she fought hard to hide it. "Well, I certainly enjoyed it."

Evelyn stiffened, willing that woman not to say another word to her, but of course, Charlotte Rogers seemed to sense her distain and was bound and determined to provoke her even more.

"I wanted to tell you," Charlotte carefully sat her cup and saucer down on the table, then stared warmly at Evelyn, who refused to look at her, "that you have done a wonderful job raising my daughter."

The words "my daughter" cut into Evelyn like a hot knife cuts through butter, and she shuddered uncontrollably, but Charlotte either ignored her reaction or didn't seem to notice it.

"She's grown up into such a lovely woman," she continued sincerely. And she meant every word of it, too. Evelyn was classy and sophisticated, and it was obvious that Reesy had taken after the woman. Charlotte couldn't fault her for doing a good job, no matter how snooty the woman was. She'd taken her baby girl in, raised her right, and given her everything

Charlotte never could. The least she could do was thank the woman.

"No thanks to you," Evelyn muttered taking another sip of coffee.

Charlotte was caught off guard by the remark, but tried hard to hide the effect the insult had on her. "Well." She sat with her hands folded demurely in her lap, squashing every urge in her body to reach over and slap the hell out of that bitch. "I did the best I could," she replied humbly. "Maybe not as good as you, but—"

Finally, Evelyn turned to look at her, down her nose, like she was the better woman, and Charlotte felt small under the weight of her glare. "How could a mother abandon her children the way you did, and then have the nerve to sit here and try and pretend it never happened? That's something I don't think I can ever understand, Ms. Rodgers, and something I don't know how *my* daughter can bring herself to forgive."

Of course, Charlotte was hurt, wounded, and disappointed that Mrs. Turner wasn't even trying to get along. She held her gaze, though, refusing to back down or buckle under the weight of this woman's judgment. She had no idea what Charlotte had been through, or what made her walk out that door, leaving her daughters with no one but themselves to look after them. Guilt consumed her still, to this day, and it always would until the day she died, but this heffa had no right to judge her. Because Reesy had forgiven her, and that was all that mattered.

"My daughter has forgiven me, Evelyn," she said smugly, pressing her shoulders back proudly. "And that's all I care about."

Evelyn shook her head, and turned away.

"I did the best I could," she continued.

"Well, it wasn't good enough."

She clenched her hands into fists and gritted her teeth. "She was mine before she was yours," she growled under her breath. "I started out raising Reesy, and I'm the one she loved first. You may not like it, but her love for me was strong enough to send her looking for me all the way to Kansas. And now I'm here! In my daughter's home, because she wanted me back!" Charlotte leaned closer to Evelyn, who leaned away from her. "Do you honestly think she'd come looking for you the way she did for me if you left?"

Just then, Reesy walked in to the room. "Hi, ladies," she said, smiling, oblivious to what was going on. She sat down in the leather chair across from them, then stared at each one of them. "You two getting along all right?"

Charlotte turned to her daughter and smiled. "We're getting along just fine, baby." She looked at Evelyn, who also tried to smile.

"Just fine," Evelyn said calmly. "It's getting late, dear, and I need to get your father home to tuck him into bed." She stood to leave, and so did Reesy.

Reesy put her arm around her mother's shoulder and squeezed. "I think Dad has an OFF switch somewhere on him that he pushes right after he eats."

Evelyn laughed.

"Good-bye, Evelyn," Charlotte called after them. "It was nice meeting you."

Chapter 41

How many times had T told her it was time for her to grow up? Cammy was a grown woman, and if she wanted to make dinner for her man at her house, then why shouldn't she? She paid most of the bills while Momma barked out most of the orders, and Cammy was getting sick and tired of it.

She'd been hearing things about T and Tonya. Like that Tonya had been hanging around his shop more than she should for a woman who didn't have a car. And that she'd caught up with him at the basketball court a couple of times when he was playing with his friends. At first, she was ready to be mad at him, but then she had to realize that if he was spending time with Tonya, it was only because he wasn't spending it with her because she was always working or cooped up in the house all the damn time taking care of Momma.

She'd been cooking most of the afternoon, frying chicken, his favorite, making homemade mashed potatoes and gravy, and peas. Cammy was exhausted, and her ankles were starting to swell up. Lately she'd been more tired than anything, working double shifts at the restaurant to put away some extra money for when she would be out having the baby. Momma had been gone for three days now, and she hadn't even bothered to say good-bye before the cab came and picked her up. Reesy had paid for everything, including the cab, some new clothes, and a nice hotel room in Denver for Charlotte to stay in. She'd practically begged Cammy to come along, too, but of course she had to tell her no. It broke her heart, because more than anything she wanted to see Reesy again, and to meet Connie, and to visit Denver.

"Oh, no, Reesy," she remembered telling her. "The doctor says I can't fly. She says I'm too far along and it would be best for me to stay here."

"Well, then, you can come after you have the baby," Reesy assured her. And she would, too. After Cammy had this baby, Charlotte wasn't talking her out of going again. She'd go even if she had to walk to Denver.

Just then, the doorbell rang. Cammy stopped in front of the mirror by the door to fix her hair and adjust her top. She looked so fat. Too fat. Maybe Tonya was right. Maybe she really was having twins.

He looked so good standing in the doorway carrying flowers. "Hey, baby," he said, stepping inside and kissing her lips. "You look beautiful."

Of course she blushed, and he was lying through his teeth. "Why you lying, boy?" she teased.

He grinned. "Because I could smell that food all the way out in the yard and I'm hungry as hell."

Cammy rolled her eyes and sucked her teeth, turning her back to him like she was mad.

"Come here, girl." He turned her to face him. T put his arms around her and pulled her close. "You know I'm playing. I mean, I am hungry, and the food does smell good, but—I ain't lying, girl. You do look beautiful."

She led him into the kitchen and fixed his plate for him, then sat down at the table next to him.

"When's your momma coming home?" he asked, stuffing mashed potatoes into his mouth.

"Day after tomorrow."

"She call?"

Cammy shook her head. Charlotte had no use for her now that she had Reesy back in her life, so why would she call? She'd been thinking about it ever since Charlotte left, thinking about how easily she could discard Cammy, and act like she was invisible all of a sudden, when before she almost made it seem as if she couldn't live without her.

And it was all good, because maybe Cammy needed to see how Charlotte really felt about her, and it took Reesy coming here to make it clear as day. All her life, Cammy felt like she was the one who needed to be here, to take care of her mother. Now, she realized, she never needed to be here after all.

After dinner, they curled up on the couch together and watched movies. Cammy had been waiting for the right time to talk to him about Tonya all night, and now was as good a time as any. "So, what's this I hear about you and old greasy Tonya?" she asked smartly.

T looked at her, then stared back at the television and shrugged. "Don't know. What is it that you hear about me and greasy Tonya?"

"I hear she's been spending a lot of time at the shop, and anyplace else she thinks you might be."

"I can't tell the woman where to be, Cammy."

"You seeing her?"

He looked like it might be a trick question. "Yeah, if she's where I'm at. I'm sure I see her."

T was taking this whole conversation way too lightly for her taste. "I'm being serious, T."

"So am I, C."

"Are you cheating on me?"

He turned down the volume on the television set and stared at her a moment before answering. "Not yet. But you make it real hard for me not to."

Cammy looked hurt and appalled. "So, you been thinking about cheating on me?"

"Tonya might be greasy, but she fine, Cammy. And she's all up in my face all the time, and yeah . . . I've been tempted."

She couldn't believe what she was hearing. Here he was sitting in her living room, after having eaten up most of her food, admitting that he had been planning on cheating on her when he claimed to have loved her?

Cammy stood up and marched to the front door, opened it, and propped her hand on her hip. "Get out!"

T just sat there and turned the volume back up on the television.

"You heard me, T! If you want somebody else, then you need to go get you somebody else and leave me the hell alone! If you want that greasy heffa, then don't let me stop you!"

"Close the door and come here," he said calmly.

"I ain't coming over there, but you are getting out of my house!"

"Cammy!" He turned to her. "I said I'd thought about it. I never said I did it. I don't even want to do it."

"You just said . . ."

"I just told you the truth. Which is, if I wanted greasy Tonya, I could've had greasy Tonya a half-dozen times already. But instead, I'm trying like a mothafucka to be true to you, my girl, my woman, the mother of my kid. I'm putting up with your crazy-ass momma, seeing you only when you have time to see me, and . . . damn, baby! I miss you."

T turned back to the television, frustrated, and full, and ready for her to just sit her ass down, and be quiet so that he could digest his food in peace.

Cammy's expression softened. In her heart, she knew he was telling the truth. That's how T was, honest to a fault, and, for some odd reason, crazy as hell about her, even when it didn't make sense. She slowly walked back over to the couch and sat down next to him.

"You miss me?" she asked softly.

T rolled his eyes and sighed in frustration. Lord, why the hell did he have to say that? Now there was no way she'd let him watch TV. "I said I did, Cammy."

Cammy smiled and snuggled up against him. "You still want to get married?"

"That ain't never gonna change."

Cammy sat up and looked deeply into his eyes. "Then let's do it."

He studied her for a moment. "When?"

She shrugged. "I don't know. When do you want to do it?"

"Tomorrow," he said, making it sound like a dare, fully expecting her to make up some excuse as to why she wouldn't be able to.

Cammy looked shocked, but she knew instinctively that if she said anything but okay, she might not get this chance again. "Okay, T."

Now it was his turn to look stunned. "You serious?"

She nodded. "I am if you are."

He swallowed hard. "Of course I am, Cammy. I've been serious about you since . . . since . . . I first met you, baby. And I want you to be my wife for real."

It happened so fast. First thing the next morning, he piled her in the car, drove to Wal-Mart and bought rings, then Cammy and T drove to the courthouse, said their vows, and were married. She hadn't had a chance to really think about what she was doing or how it had changed her life.

"We'll go back to the house, get your things, and . . ."

"No," she said suddenly.

T looked confused. "What do you mean, no, baby? We're married, Cammy. Which means you live with me."

Cammy felt herself start to panic. This was all happening so fast, and Momma . . . Lord, what would Momma say? How would she . . . "I need to tell Momma first, T," she said desperately. "She can't just come home and find me gone."

"Fine." His frustration was starting to show through. "Then tell her from the phone at my crib, baby. Our crib."

Cammy had tears in her eyes, realizing she'd made a terrible mistake, been too hasty and done something drastic without first talking to Charlotte. This wasn't how she wanted it to be. She loved T, but she loved Charlotte, too, and she needed Charlotte in a way she couldn't understand or explain.

T recognized that familiar look of regret in her eyes, and he knew that no marriage license, no ring, not even the fact that he was her husband now was strong enough to lure her away from the hold her mother had over her. So he drove her home, and left Cammy standing in front of the house as he drove away. This was it, as far as he was concerned. The final straw that had broken his back.

Chapter 42

S o far so good," Dr. Dennis said, smiling, after completing Connie's latest examination. "Sixteen weeks and counting, Momma, and that boy of yours is growing like a weed."

Connie sat up on the table, and pulled her gown closed.

"You still tired?" Gwen asked, jotting down notes in Connie's file.

Connie shook her head. "No. Not as much."

"Taking your vitamins?"

Connie chuckled. "Yes, ma'am."

Gwen laughed too. "Good. Now." She looked at Connie. "Got any questions for me?"

"As a matter of fact," she hesitated. "I do."

"Shoot."

She felt comfortable enough with Gwen to consider her a starting place. Connie couldn't keep this baby. And she'd finally come to terms with that. "Know anybody interested in adopting a kid?"

Gwen stared at her, unblinking, taken aback by the question, but not totally surprised. She'd sensed apprehension in Connie the moment she met her, believing that maybe Connie was concerned because of her age. Looking at her now, the woman looked absolutely terrified. "Why?" Gwen asked reservedly. "You know somebody planning to put one up for adoption?"

Connie shrugged and took a valiant deep breath before finally answering. "I can't keep this baby, Gwen."

"Why not?"

"I just . . ." A tear escaped down her cheek, and she quickly wiped it away. "I don't know the first thing about taking care of kids."

"Who does, Connie? I've got teenagers who come in here, don't know the first thing about taking care of themselves, let alone children, and none of them are talking about giving up their children."

"I'm not talking about them," Connie said defensively. "I'm talking about me. I can't do this, and I just . . . do you have the names of any agencies, or . . . some patient who might . . ."

"What are you afraid of, Connie? And don't tell me nothing, because I can see it in your face."

Connie jumped down from the table and reached for her clothes. All Gwen had to do was give up a goddamned name, not psychoanalyze her. "Forget it," she said, frustrated.

Gwen stood up, turned Connie to face her, and asked her again. "What are you afraid of?" she asked softly. "Connie?"

Connie looked at the woman, then told her what she was afraid of. "I've had more abortions than I care to remember." Her voice quivered. "I've given birth to one kid that scared me so bad, I gave her up for adoption to my sister. I've been homeless, a prostitute, I've got herpes, dammit! That's what I'm so afraid of, Dr. Gwen. And I can't do that to this—I won't do this to my son!" Connie broke down crying, and Gwen put her arms around her and held her.

"It's all right, Connie," she said tenderly. Gwen stepped back and looked Connie square in the eyes. "Talk about a mother's love," she said endearingly. "Girl, I don't think I've ever met a woman more deserving of having and raising a child than you."

Connie looked shocked. "Did you hear what I just said?"

Gwen laughed. "I heard every word. The question is, did you hear what you just said?"

"I'm a mess, Gwen. A crazy mess. And I don't have any business having a kid. In fact, after I have this one, I want you to tie my shit up."

"No problem. I'll double-knot it if I have to."

"Good."

"Because if nothing else, you're fertile."

"Yeah, well . . ."

"In the meantime, I have something I want to give you. Go on and get dressed. I'll be right back."

Connie waited for Gwen to leave, and then started getting dressed. Something about this whole conversation confused the mess out of her, and all she could do was shake her head, trying to make sense out of what had just taken place. "Did I hear what I just said?" Connie mumbled to herself, recalling Gwen's comment. "Of course I heard what I said. I know what I said, and I don't have no business . . ." The tears threatened to come again, but Connie fought them back. "I can't do this," she said, breathless. As much as she wished she could, inside, she fought a losing battle. Her heart was willing, but common sense was kicking her ass, reminding her of all her shortcomings, let-downs, disappointments, every time she got a whiff of being happy about having this child. If Gwen wouldn't give her the names of any agencies, then she'd just have to find one the old-fashioned way, and look in the Yellow Pages.

Moments later, Gwen came back into the examination room, carrying something behind her back.

"Don't know what it is about you, girl. But I liked you the moment you first walked in here, and, well . . ." She held out a large baby blue gift bag with yellow tissue paper shooting out from the top like flames.

"What's this?" Connie asked, taking the bag.

"Look and see."

Connie sat the bag down on the examination table and pulled out everything ever made for a newborn baby boy; booties, bibs, t-shirts, rattles, a stuffed brown bear, and a blue knitted baby blanket so soft the first thing she did was press it to her cheek.

"Why'd you do this?" she asked, turning to Gwen.

"Because you looked like you needed me to," she smiled. "Connie, I've got two kids of my own, and I used to have a husband, too, but, well . . . now I just have a really fine boyfriend." She and Connie both laughed. "I have a feeling you kept this one because you felt it might be your last chance to have one. Am I right?"

Hell, yeah, she was right. Too right. Connie nodded.

"And maybe it is, so don't blow it. Whatever happened to you in the past happened, and you can't do anything to change it. But if you keep letting it beat you up, then how are you ever going to be able to put it behind you for real?" Gwen picked up Connie's file and got ready to leave. "There's no such thing as a perfect parent. The best we can do is love them, and the rest will come." Dr. Gwen smiled, "See you next month," and then she left.

Connie squeezed the little brown bear in her arms, took a deep breath, and laughed out loud.

Chapter 43

I can't believe how much everything has changed," Charlotte said, walking arm in arm with Reesy through the Cherry Creek shopping district. "The whole city has grown so much, and . . ." She shook her head in dismay. ". . . it's just not the same place at all."

Reesy laughed. She'd spent the day with her mother, driving through their old neighborhood, through the new neighborhood where the old airport used to be, and finally for a drive around the city, stopping in Cherry Creek to do some shopping and grab a bite to eat.

"It's so fancy here," Charlotte continued. "Cherry Creek wasn't nearly as fancy when I used to live here."

"It's fancy, and expensive. But there's a restaurant here that has some of the best jalepeño corn bread you'll ever taste in your life."

The two of them talked over lunch, about life thirty years ago and today. Charlotte felt young again here, fresh like the air, and happy for the first time in so many years. The city moved so fast, but in a place like this, she wasn't a woman old before her time anymore. She was Charlotte Rodgers, the same one she was before she'd left, only better, because she appreciated this place too much now to ever want to leave it again.

"What's wrong, Momma?" Reesy asked, noticing the sudden change in Charlotte's expression right in the middle of their conversation. She reached across and touched her hand. "Are you alright?"

Charlotte felt so silly, and she blushed. "Of course I'm all right, Clarice." She chuckled. "I'm home again. And I wish I never had to leave."

Reesy saw regret in her mother's eyes.

"I was a young woman when I left, Reesy," she explained quietly. "Dumb enough to think there was something so much better waiting for me someplace else, and it took leaving for me to see how wrong I was."

Charlotte had been walking around like Dorothy in Oz ever since she'd been here. Her elation hadn't been missed by her daughter. Charlotte missed home. Charlotte wanted to come home, and to never leave again. Her heart went out to her mother, and Reesy made it up in her mind to find a way to make that dream come true for her. She'd talk to Justin as soon as he got home from work about it. He'd become so supportive about all this, and between the two of them, Reesy was sure they'd be able to figure out a way for Charlotte to stay.

Justin sat relaxed in his office with the door closed, half-listening to a conference call he'd been pulled in on, marveling at the transformation his marriage had taken these past few weeks. He and Reesy had made love this morning before dawn, and even showered together afterward, savoring the private and intimate moment before kids invaded it. She was all he needed.

Justin's short-sightedness had nearly gotten in the way of the best thing to ever happen to him, and the thought that he'd ever believed he could replace the woman he loved with a hooker amazed the hell out of him. Who was that man? The one shelling out hundreds of dollars to a woman he didn't even know, consumed by her to the point that he'd lock himself in a hotel room with her for an entire weekend, sulking and pouting like a damned baby because his wife was busy tying up loose ends to her own life. He'd been selfish, and even heartless in his actions. And blessed, thankful that it started and ended and he was no worse for the wear. On his way home from work, he'd stop and buy flowers, her favorite, white tulips, and maybe pick up a bottle of wine for the two of them to share after dinner, after the kids had gone to bed.

Her mother was supposed to come by and pick up the kids. She'd called her, and . . . how come she hadn't come to get the kids . . . how come she . . .

Reesy heard the garage door open and then close. That anxious feeling had come back again. The one that made her feel as if she'd throw up.

She heard the sound of muffled voices coming from downstairs. The kids. Justin. Laughing. "Where's your momma?" she heard him ask.

"Upstairs," they all seemed to say in unison.

And then the sound of heavy footsteps coming up the stairs, two at a time, the way he always took them. "Baby?" he asked, opening the door. Justin looked so happy, carrying flowers in his hand that he held out to her. He smiled as he approached her, bent to kiss her cheek, then placed the bouquet lovingly in her lap.

Reesy froze.

He crossed the room and sat down on the bed, kicking off his shoes and loosening his tie. "We having leftovers?" he asked. "With that size of that ham you bought, we'll be eating it from now until Christmas." Justin looked at her when he didn't hear her laugh, and his expression changed to one of concern. "What's up, babe? Is everything all right?"

She couldn't take her eyes off him. She couldn't blink away the image of her husband sitting across the room from her. He was a stranger all of a sudden. Someone she thought she knew, but really never did. Someone she thought she loved, but now wondered how.

"Reesy?"

"I got a letter in the mail today," she said, nearly whispering. "From who, baby?"

Reesy slowly shook her head. "Doesn't matter who."

Confusion shown in his eyes.

Reesy stood up, letting the beautiful flowers fall to the floor, and walked over to him, carrying something in her hands. She stopped and looked down at him, then to the object she clutched, as if to make sure it was really the same man, but she already knew it was.

He reached up and apprehensively took it from her. All the color faded from his face when he saw the photograph of Cookie sitting in his lap, and then his world turned blood red as the fire from Reesy's palm burned the side of his face. She hit him once, and then again, and again, and she sobbed uncontrollably, then fell to his feet on the floor.

"Get the hell out of here," she demanded, gritting her teeth.

His heart sank into his stomach and Justin searched for explanations and excuses in his mind to make her understand that this picture meant nothing. That this woman meant nothing to him.

"Reesy," he reached out to her, but Reesy jerked away and slapped him again. "Baby, I . . ."

"Get out!" Reesy leaned back on her hands and kicked up at him, landing blows to his shins. "Get out! Get out!" She crawled backward in a crabwalk into the corner of the room, drew her knees to her chest, and cried uncontrollably into her hands.

"It wasn't like you think, Reesy." Justin was disgusted at the sound of his own pitiful voice. "Reesy." He stepped toward her. "Reesy, it was just . . . it didn't mean anything, baby . . . it was just . . ."

"Just what?" she growled, rising to her feet. "What the hell is *it*, Justin?" Reesy's eyes burned holes into him. "It's you with somebody else!" She pushed him hard in the chest. "It's you fucking somebody else!"

This wasn't happening. Justin couldn't believe this was happening. A soft knock at the bedroom door came from their son Alex. "Mom? Dad? Is everything all right?"

"Yes!" Justin blurted out.

"No, Alex!" Reesy retorted. "Go back downstairs! Go back and . . ."

"Get downstairs, son."

"How could you do this to us, Justin?" The look in her eyes cut him into a million pieces. "What were you thinking!" Reesy pointed across the room to the picture lying on the floor. "What were you thinking doing that to us!"

He couldn't respond.

"Do you know what you've done?" she cried. "Do you realize what you've done to this family? To . . . you and me? Oh my God! Oh, God!"

"I'm . . . sorry, Reese!" He was at a loss. He had lost. There wasn't a thing he could say to make a difference. He knew it, and he knew she did, too. "I'm . . . so sorry."

He waited for the kids to go to bed before leaving. Reesy sat alone in the dark in the living room. He had no idea where he was going or when he'd be back, or more importantly, *if* he'd be back. Justin stood in the doorway of the living room, staring at Reesy, sitting staring at the fire burning in the fireplace.

"I'll call you," he said, quietly.

She said nothing. She felt nothing. And everything she loved and valued and prided herself on was gone. Just like that.

Chapter 44

"Where's Momma?" Racine's oldest daughter, Brenda, had no problem letting John know she wished he'd dry up and blow away in the wind. Brenda was a brain, graduated at the top of her class, and was headed to Spelman in the fall. He was in the living room watching the basketball game when she came in.

"She went to the store," he answered without bothering to look up, but the sound of the girl sucking her teeth and rolling her eyes damn near drowned out the sound of the announcer's voice.

". . . sitting up in here like he owns the place . . . ," he heard her muttering when she walked away. He didn't know if she didn't like him because he was sitting in her daddy's chair and watching his TV or what. But the beer was his, goddammit. He'd bought it himself.

He didn't have too much to do with her kids. Honestly, he felt uneasy around them, since they'd only seen him in passing, and they knew he'd known their father. Kids weren't stupid. They knew something was going on between John and their mother, and nobody seemed to be cool with it except for Racine. John just tried to ignore it. After all, he was just here for a short while, passing through like he always did. It wasn't like the two of them were serious or getting married. What was it the young people called it today? Friends with benefits? Sounded right to him.

Racine had pulled some hellified shit in her days, but this one beat all of them put together. Brenda had called him, telling him all about Racine and the new man in her life.

"I think you know him, Daddy," she said, trying to sound all sweet and clueless. Lewis knew that girl better than she gave him credit for knowing her. Brenda was a smart one. Too smart. And as much as he didn't want Racine's skank ass anymore, he certainly couldn't let John's ass get away with fucking her in his own goddamned house, right under the noses of his goddamned kids.

John didn't hear either of them pulling up outside. He heard voices, though, first Racine's. "What the hell are you doing here?"

Then Lewis's. "Is he here? Is the mothafucka in my house?"

"Your house? Since when is this your house, Lewis? When's the last time you paid the mortgage? And where's my child support? Lewis! Lewis! Don't you go in—"

Hell, he didn't even get a chance to say hi before Lewis's bony ass pounced on him like a cat. John almost had to laugh. Lewis's fist flew like bullets into the side of John's head, and bounced off just as easily, hardly leaving a mark. John stood up with Lewis hanging on for dear life, grabbed his beer from the table, and walked out of the house and into the front yard with Lewis still hitting him and screaming.

"Mothafucka! Mothafucka!"

"Lewis! Get off him!" Racine screamed behind them.

John laughed, imagining how funny this shit must've looked to the neighbors.

"Lewis! John! Don't hurt him! John!"

John leaned forward, bending at the waist, and shook Lewis off him, sending him tumbling to the ground, where he immediately jumped to his feet, took on a boxing stance, and started punching John hard in the stomach. Lewis had stopped growing around the age of fifteen, maybe sixteen. John towered at least a foot over him, and outweighed him by a good eighty pounds at least. He gulped down the last of his beer, threw the can aside, then faced Lewis in a boxing stance of his own, grinning wickedly at his opponent.

"Kick his ass, Daddy!" Brenda shouted from her bedroom window upstairs.

"Yeah, Daddy," John said, mockingly. "Kick my ass!"

Lewis ducked his head and lunged his shoulder full force into John's midsection. John reached over, grabbed Lewis around his narrow waist, and lifted him off the ground, turning him upside down and threatening to pile-drive him into the sidewalk.

"Aw, hell!" he screamed, all the blood rushing to his head, turning his eyes red. "Put me down!"

"Don't you hurt my daddy!" the girl shouted again.

"John!" Racine's voice pierced into John's sense of reason.

Hell, he was about to kill Lewis. Must've been that second six-pack he'd just finished consuming.

"Put me down, man! John! C'mon, man!"

John carefully turned Lewis around and set him safely back on the ground. Lewis was livid. He looked at John, then at Racine, then back to John. "How the hell you gonna do that, man?" He looked like he was about to cry. "How you gonna do that to me man? I thought we was best friends?"

John furrowed his brow. "Lewis, man, we ain't been best friends since we were kids."

"That ain't the point, bitch!"

John laughed.

"You know me, man!" Lewis patted his hand against his chest. "You know—me! And . . . a man don't do no shit like that to a man he knows. Not in my own house, man."

"This ain't your house!" Racine shouted.

"Shut the hell up, bitch!" Lewis spat.

"Leave my momma alone," Brenda shouted.

"Shut up, Brenda!" Racine shouted back.

"But Momma," Brenda started to protest.

"Brenda," Racine's eyes narrowed. "If you say one more word, I swear I'm gonna put my foot in your little narrow ass."

Teeth-sucking, eye-rolling Brenda disappeared into the house.

John looked at poor Lewis, and all of a sudden, he did feel bad. "I'm sorry, man."

"Sorry?" Lewis stared at him appalled. "Sorry for what? For fucking my wife?"

"Almost ex-wife," Racine corrected him.

"Or for that fact that I found out about it?"

John had to think about that one for a moment before answering. "Actually, I'm not sorry about fucking Racine."

Lewis looked like he'd just been shot.

John shrugged. "Sorry, man, but I'm not."

"Thank you," she said, smartly.

"But I am sorry things had to end up like this."

Lewis paced back and forth, mumbling incoherently to himself, frustrated and angry that he'd been disrespected like this by someone he considered his friend. "Man?" He stopped and turned to John. "Them my kids, man."

John looked confused. "What?"

"My kids, King! My fuckin' kids!"

"I didn't do anything to your kids, Lewis."

"Awwwww, man!" Lewis clutched his stomach and doubled over, then straightened up again. "You disrespecting me in front of my kids, man! How you gone do that? It's bad enough she do it, John, man, but you? Them my kids! How you gone disrespect me in front of them?"

John turned to look at Racine, who all of a sudden looked sheepish and embarrassed. Then he looked at Lewis, who looked wounded and defeated. The kids. Had he missed something? "I'm not . . ."

"They think you they uncle, man," Lewis said wearily. "I told them about you all the time, Uncle John, man. Uncle fuckin' John."

"Uncle?" John was shocked. "Why the hell did you tell them some shit like that?" He turned to Racine. "Did you tell them some shit like that, too?"

Racine shrugged.

"Well?" John asked again.

"That was when they were little, John," she explained. "We haven't told them you were their uncle since . . . since . . ."

"Since last year about this time when he swung through here," Lewis shouted.

"That's a lie!" she argued.

"You a lie! And a ho!"

"Fuck you, Lewis!"

"That's your problem, Racine! Always going around fuckin' everybody!"

She leaped over the three steps leading down from the porch toward Lewis, leaping high in the air to land on his head, but not before John caught her around the waist and sat her back down behind him. Racine swatted at Lewis, trying her best to get him in the face with those long fingernails of hers.

John stood like a barrier between them, wondering what the hell had happened to the happy little couple he'd seen the last time he was down here, because these two fools obviously weren't them.

Eventually everybody got tired. Lewis got in his car and drove back down to Corpus. Racine folded her arms, pouted, and disappeared inside the house, and John climbed into his car and drove back to the house. Uncle John. That was some shit. No wonder that girl kept cutting her eyes at him every time he so much as breathed. She thought he was a mothafuckin' pervert or something.

Moses was sitting on the porch smoking a pipe when John made it home. Adam sat at the foot of the steps, happy as always to see him. As soon as John sat down, Moses handed him a newspaper with a want ad circled.

"What's this?" John asked.

"It's a job, boy," Moses said, flippantly. "What you think it is?"

John leaned back and read through the ad needing construction workers for a new subdivision being built on the other side of town.

"Friend of mine works there," Moses explained, huffing and puffing on his pipe. "Pay good money. Need folks with experience. I figure that must be you."

John lay the paper down on the porch. "What makes you think I need a job?"

"Every man need a job."

"I . . . I . . . I . . . had a j-j-job one time," Adam interrupted. "B . . . b . . . bag . . . gin' grocccccries at the store."

"I got money, Moses," John replied.

"It ain't bout you havin' no money."

"Then I don't need a job. I ain't stayin'."

"Where you goin', then?" Moses probed.

John didn't answer right away because he had no idea where he was going.

"Time fo' you to grow the hell up, man," Moses told him matter-of-factly.

John was trying not to get frustrated. All the drama with Lewis and Racine, and then he had to come home to being talked to like he was a teenager, it was frustrating, and he wasn't in the mood.

"I'm a grown man, Moses."

"Then act like one, son." Moses turned to look at him. "You runnin' 'round town with this woman and that one, pullin' off in that car of yours and goin' to the next town doin' the same thing."

"That's just how I live my life, Moses. I ain't hurtin' nobody."

Moses chuckled. "You hurtin' yo'self son. Don't even know it." Moses stared straight ahead, reflecting back on his own youth and how much it resembled John's. Only Moses had come to his senses a long time ago, not long after he'd committed the worst transgression of his life, leaving Adam to pay the price for it. "You 'bout forty now. Is that right?"

John didn't answer. He knew where this was going, and he wasn't interested. He started to get up, but Moses stretched his arm across John's chest and held him in his chair.

"Thought you had a woman back up there in Colorado."

"I had one."

"Y'all break up?" He looked at John, who again didn't respond. Moses chuckled. "Always something wrong with somebody. Ain't it, boy?"

It was the way he said the word *boy* that made John uneasy.

"Women ain't perfect. Ain't nobody perfect."

"Never said I was looking for perfection, Moses."

"Then what is you lookin' fo'?"

"Nothing."

Moses thought for moment, then sighed. "Then you is one pitiful soul, son. And I feel sorry fo' you more than I ever felt sorry for anybody. You got good looks. Probably fuck a good fuck with the best of them. Plenty of women willing to take you in at the moment. Then, one day, it's jus' you. And you might look back one day, think about all them women, see that there was some good ones in there, too, and you miss 'em. Wonderin' what it might be like if you'd jus' stayed a while longer, swallowed some of that pride you got, and let her jus' be yo' woman."

Moses was trying to make a point, one that wasn't new to John. He'd thought enough about growing old alone to know that was probably how he'd end up. The thing was, he'd come to terms with that thought a long time ago.

"My wife don't always know it, but I love her," Moses said reflectively. "Love her more than I ever loved any woman. Wished we coulda had kids. I know she wanted some. Deep down, I did, too."

"I . . . I got kids," Adam said excitedly, pointing to John. "That's my sssssssson!" He laughed and clapped his hands. "My b . . . b . . . boy! Ain't nothin' like it! Ain't nothin' better than . . . my . . . boy! M . . . mattie . . . she made him . . . and gave him . . . to . . . to . . . me. 'Cause she . . . love me.

"Y . . . you should . . . get you a boy . . . John." Adam smiled radiantly at his son. "G . . . get you one . . . too, so you won't . . . never . . . have to be lone . . . some."

Moses laughed. "'Cause she did love you, Adam. And she gave you this boy." Moses stood up, tapped his pipe on the porch railing to empty it, and headed inside.

Moses and Sara had never had kids of their own. He always supposed it was penance he owed God for all the sins he committed when he was young. Back in his day, he was hell to deal with, and he saw a lot of himself in John. Sometimes too much. Reckless, selfish behavior was second nature to both of them, and if John wasn't careful, he could end up an old man full of too many regrets. Moses' biggest regret was one he'd only confessed to his wife, five years ago when Adam had that heart attack and they weren't sure he was going to make it. His older brother had been frail and weak ever since those three fools tried to kill him that night in that old barn, accusing him of raping that girl.

"Somebody took that girl and hurt her," he told his wife in the hospital waiting room of the ICU. They'd been up all night long, wondering if Adam was going to live or die. Moses was tired, and that night, this particular secret weighed heaviest on him.

"I was jealous of him, baby." He gazed into his wife's tired eyes, and tried to smile. "He was the kind of man I wasn't, even back then, and I resented him for it. Big, bad, black Moses— mean as hell and full of fire," he chuckled. "Had a chip on my shoulder big as a tree, and dared any fool to try and knock it off."

He was a hard man to love back then. But Adam never seemed to have a problem loving him. "Y . . . y . . . you my lil' b . . . brotha," he used to say. "Even if y . . . y . . . you is bigger. Ima l . . . look out for you."

Moses had seen him with her. He'd seen the way Adam made that girl smile and the way she looked at him despite the fact that he was Fool to everybody else in town. He wasn't a fool to her. He'd seen his brother love that girl, hold her, and kiss her. Adam was tender and careful, and she held onto him like he was a dream she never wanted to end.

"I drank too much back then." His voice cracked. "I was mean. I was so mean."

"What are you saying, Moses?" Sara asked, squeezing her husband's hand.

"Adam didn't rape that girl," he told her. "He made love to her, but he didn't rape her." Moses swallowed hard, then lowered his head. "But I did."

John King was Adam's son. He looked so much like Adam before they beat Adam and nearly killed him. That boy was the spitting image of his half brother, but only on the outside. On the inside, he looked too much like Moses.

Chapter 45

His first inclination was to beat her ass, but then again, if he wanted to catch a fly, honey always worked best. Twice he'd called her and twice she didn't answer her phone. Honey Baby was up to something, or perhaps somebody. Could've been she was just out there on the prowl looking for trouble to get into. He'd find out one way or another, though. The world was too small for him not to find out.

"How's my baby girl doing tonight?" He kissed her cheek as she climbed into the car next to him, smelling all good.

"Fine," she answered smugly.

Good-looking women had an air about them. One that let a man know they knew they were good-looking whether he said she was or not. And men were fools, with their tongues hanging all out, panting behind them like stray dogs looking for someone to take them in.

"That you are, baby," he chuckled, fulfilling his role as admirer. "That you certainly are."

Uncle could've stayed home tonight and watched Baretta. Of course, there were more interesting things to watch than TV tonight. He sat in his spot at the club with Charlotte sitting pretty by his side bouncing in her seat talking about, "Dance with me, Uncle. C'mon, baby."

Sam strolled in, decked out in a black velvet suit, looking a whole foot taller than he did when he left with his dick tucked between his legs like a bitch. She hadn't seen him yet, and even if she did, Uncle doubted she'd even recognize his pussy ass. All of a sudden, Charlotte stopped bouncing and stared at Sam heading their way. He stopped in front of them, looking down his nose and hard into Uncle's eyes, then glanced indifferently in Charlotte's direction. She just sat there with her mouth gaping open as if he were a ghost. Uncle chuckled, inhaled deeply on his cigar, took a sip of E&J, and stared up at Sam.

"Look at what the cat dragged in," Uncle mumbled.

Sam reached into the inside pocket of his jacket, pulled out his wallet, then dropped a stack of bills down on the table.

Uncle stared at it, then at Sam.

"I think we even now," Sam said unflinchingly.

Uncle nodded, then picked up the money and fanned through it, mentally taking note of the stack of fifties Sam had put before him. He handed it to Charlotte.

"That's a mighty honorable thing you did, son," he said, turning his attention back to Sam. "Honor in a man these days," he shook his head and frowned, "almost nonexistent."

Sam never said a word, just turned on his heels, walked over to the bar, and ordered a drink.

Charlotte's heart beat a million miles a minute at the sight of Sam. She'd have expected Jesus to come walking in that bar tonight before believing she'd ever see him again. How long had it been? Eight months, no, closer to a year. And she vowed that if she ever saw him again, she'd cuss his ass out for leaving her stranded the way he did. But seeing him tonight . . .

"Whatchu staring at?" Uncle asked, nudging her in the arm with his elbow.

"What . . . I . . . I wasn't staring at nothing."

It was as if she was seeing Uncle with new eyes, and he looked old to her, and worn. Uncle was never good-looking, but whenever Sam was in the same room with him, he looked even uglier than usual.

"I'm tired," he said, finishing his drink. Uncle dropped a twenty-dollar bill down on the table and stood up to leave. Charlotte followed.

They stopped by Wilma's Chicken House on the way back to her apartment and ordered two dinners to go. Uncle started eating his in the car, but Charlotte wasn't hungry. Sam had hardly even looked at her, and in the brief moment that he did, he seemed to be looking through her.

"You coming up?" she asked Uncle as they pulled up to the curb.

He wasn't in the mood to fuck tonight. Uncle was high, he was full, and he'd got him some earlier, so, "No," he said wearily. "You go on, baby." He leaned over and kissed her. "Good night."

She'd been in the house less than twenty minutes when a knock came at the door. Her first thought was that Uncle had changed his mind and decided he was horny after all. But when she opened the door, Sam stood on the other side of it, looking fine as hell and black as the night he'd just stepped out of.

"You gonna let me in?" he asked in that deep voice of his that rumbled low and deep like an earthquake.

Excitement over seeing him threatened to make her act like a fool and jump into his arms, but then she remembered what he'd done, and she quickly composed herself. "Give me one good reason why I should after what you did to me?" She hoped she looked good and pissed when she said it.

Sam's smile told her she hadn't.

"Because I missed you, Charlie. I been missing you every day since I left."

"Then why'd you leave in the first place?" she asked angrily.

He shrugged and shook his head. "It couldn't be helped, baby. I swear . . . I didn't want to leave you like that."

Her resolve was starting to shrink, and Charlotte knew she was destined to lose this battle of wills. Sam had that effect on her. He always did, and probably always would, too. The kind of effect that made her do stupid shit like let him in.

He closed the door behind him, admiring how lovely this girl was to him. Uncle hadn't turned her out into the street. He'd saved her for himself, and for that, Sam had to admire his ass.

Charlotte pulled her satin robe close around her neck, keeping him from getting a view of anything that was no longer his business. But Charlotte had him memorized, and she could've worn shoulder pads and a helmet and gotten a rise out of him.

"If Uncle knew you were here, he'd go crazy," she said, keeping plenty of distance between herself and Sam. But there wasn't enough room in this apartment to stifle the effects he still had on her. "No telling what he might do."

"But I am here, baby." He slowly stalked her around the room, wanting more than anything just to get close to her again, smell the scent of her, and recall how soft he remembered her being. "That should tell you that I don't give a damn about Uncle's sorry ass."

"Why are you here, Sam?" She sounded agitated. "Why now?"

Charlotte suddenly ran out of real estate and found herself backed into a corner in the living room. Sam stood in front of her, reached down, and untied the belt of her robe.

"You really got to ask me that?"

Sam's kisses made her weak. They made her head spin. Always did. Sam's kisses peeled off her clothes, slid her panties down past her thighs, calves, ankles, and finally to the floor. His kisses spread her legs wide open, throbbing in the center of herself, and thirsting for him, right there on the living room floor.

Uncle was no fool. Two plus two always equaled four, and that fool was back in town for one reason and one reason only.

"You want me to go up and get him?" his driver asked, looking into the rearview mirror at Uncle.

Uncle stared at the building Sam had disappeared into, envisioning the two of them together almost as if he were sitting in the same room with them. Charlotte's pretty booty spread wide and open on the man's lap, rolling and rounding the curves and corners of Sam's dick, slapping titties against his face, slurping spit from his mouth, and fucking nasty as only she could.

He was getting hard just thinking about it.

"Naw," he sighed, rubbing his hand against his dick. "I'm feeling hospitable this evening. Besides, he paid good money for that ass. Twice what he owed me. Take me to Flo's." Flo was a good friend. Always ready to feed a brotha in more ways than one. Not all that cute, but she had a good heart. "She ought to be home."

"We get him another time?"

Uncle just nodded. "Yeah. Another time."

Chapter 46

Connie had been up most of the night trying to put her life into perspective. She was forty years old, pregnant, still single, and still beating herself up over past transgressions.

"When does it end?" was the question she'd meditated on at two in the morning. She called Yolanda at nine to tell her she wouldn't be coming into the store today.

"Mr. Whitman called asking for you. He wants you to design something special for his wife and their thirtieth wedding anniversary."

Nice man, Mr. Whitman, romantic, thoughtful, doting. "I'll be in tomorrow," Connie promised. "Just tell him that if he calls back."

"You feeling all right?" Yolanda asked, sounding concerned.

Connie hesitated before answering. "You still moving to Africa?"

"You know I am."

"Then I'm not all right," Connie said woefully, "because I'm going to miss my best friend."

Yolanda was quiet on the other end of the phone. Then she

finally asked the question Connie had been hedging on for weeks. "So what do you want to do about the store?"

"I'd like to keep it, but—I probably won't."

"Why not?" Yolanda had a feeling the woman would say something like that. "Connie, that doesn't make sense. You practically run this place by yourself anyway. Why not keep it?"

Connie didn't bother to respond.

Yolanda sighed. "You're being ridiculous. Folks come to this place looking for you, girl, not me, shelling out small fortunes for your jewelry and artwork. It's your store, Connie. It has been since word got out about you, girl. Don't you see that?"

Connie surprised herself and blushed. "That's true, huh?"

Yolanda laughed. "Of course it's true. So stop being dumb about it."

"I'm not trying to be dumb, Yolanda," Connie retorted. "I'm moving away, too."

She tried not to snoop, but Charlotte couldn't help herself. Reesy and Justin had such nice things. Charlotte had to go home today. Reesy had picked her up early this morning from the hotel, brought her back to her house, and had to leave to run a quick errand, leaving Charlotte at the house alone. Sadness weighed heavy on her just thinking about leaving her beautiful hometown and her family to go back to that dreadful hole in Kansas. Living there was like living in a tomb, with no room to breathe and no wide-open space to stretch out in. Not like here, where everything looked brand-new, and the air was light enough to practically lift you up off the ground like a bird.

She looked at all the pictures on the mantle over the

fireplace of Reesy and her family, all of them smiling and happy to be together. They looked make-believe, too good to be true and real. Until now, Charlotte had never believed people could be this perfect and this happy. She never believed she could be either.

"I'm going to talk to Justin, Momma," Reesy promised her the other day. "And we'll see what we can do to get you back home."

It was a lovely promise she would live for until it happened. Reesy was a good girl, and she'd do it. She'd find a way to get her momma home. Of course, that Evelyn Turner wouldn't be too happy about it, but Charlotte could give a damn about that stuck-up woman. As much as she might've wanted to believe it, Reesy wasn't her child. Sure, she'd finished raising her and taking care of her, and for that, Charlotte was grateful. But Reesy had come from Charlotte's body. She'd been nurtured and loved in Charlotte's heart, and when she moved back here, that old Evelyn was going to have to step back and be the glorified babysitter she'd been in Charlotte's absence. The doorbell rang, and Charlotte wasn't quite sure if she should open it or not. Reluctantly, she decided it would be rude not to, and staring back at her, as shocked as she was, stood Connie, looking beautiful enough to take Charlotte's breath away.

Connie had come by to talk to her sister. To tell her she loved her, and that she understood Reesy's apprehensions of Connie where Jade was concerned. She had stopped by to tell her she was leaving town to start over, and to have her child and to do the best she could as a mother, to love him, too much, if she had to, and to leave the past behind her once and for all.

"I thought you'd left by now," she said, staring back at her mother. Charlotte's full face showed subtle signs of aging, but not as many as Connie might've imagined. She looked different by the mouth, off center and appearing disfigured despite her efforts to hide it with crimson-red lipstick. She was heavier than she'd been back then, and the vibrant light that had once been in her eyes had faded.

Charlotte smiled, and almost reached out to hug her oldest daughter, before catching and containing herself. "I was hoping to see you before I left," she said nervously, unable to take her eyes off the woman who looked the way she used to look. Men flocked to Charlotte when she looked like . . . she had so many who wanted her and would do anything to keep her. She was that honey-gold girl, that fine ass—that—that—oh, what she wouldn't give to look like that again.

Connie's initial shock faded, and she remembered who it was she was staring at. She brushed past Charlotte indifferently and went into the living room. "Is Reesy here?"

Charlotte followed nervously behind her, wringing her hands together. "No. No, she had to go . . . uh . . . run an errand." She tried to smile, hoping Connie would return the gesture. But she didn't. "She'll be right back, though. Gotta take me to the airport. I'm flying out today."

Connie nodded, searching for something to say that didn't include a cuss word or resentment. Seeing her mother now, what amazed her most was the lack of any feeling about her whatsoever. She was standing in the same room with the woman who'd given birth to her. The woman who'd raised her for the first twelve years of her life. The woman who she'd loved more than anything and hated more than she thought it was possible to hate anyone, and Connie felt absolutely nothing. She wasn't even angry, which surprised her most of all. And she'd always promised herself that if she ever saw Charlotte again, she'd at least be angry. But she wasn't. Charlotte was just a woman, could've been any woman Connie happened to have seen before. But that's all she was.

"Did you enjoy your trip here?" she asked, making polite conversation.

"Oh yes!" she said, excited. "I can't believe I'm here. Denver's gotten so big." She laughed nervously. "It doesn't look like the same place at all. But I'm glad to be back. In fact," she took a step closer to Connie. Instinctively, Connie took a step back, a move that didn't go unnoticed by Charlotte. "Reesy and Justin might see about me moving back here for good."

Connie stared at her. "You and . . . your daughter. What's her name?"

You're my daughter, baby, Charlotte wanted so badly to say, and hold her in her arms. *You and Reesy.* She loved Connie. As hard as that girl had always been to love, Charlotte loved her beautiful child more than she'd ever know. "Cammy. Camille. Her name is Camille. And no, I don't think she'll be moving here. She's engaged to marry a boy back home. Getting ready to have a baby, so she ain't coming."

Her arms ached to be around Connie. Her heart ached to make everything wrong right between them. If only she knew what to say. She'd say it a million times if she had to. She'd say it loud enough for the whole world to hear.

"Well." Connie started back toward the door. "You have a safe flight home." She opened it to leave. Charlotte didn't want her to leave.

"And tell Cammy I said hello."

Panic set in that she might not get another chance with this daughter. "Connie!" Charlotte called out, uncertain as to what she wanted or need to say.

Connie stopped and looked at her.

"I . . ."

Whatever it was Charlotte had to say was of no consequence to Connie. There was nothing she could ever say that would make a difference. Connie's mother had walked out on her almost thirty years ago, and as far as Connie was concerned, she'd walked far enough to fall off the edge of the earth and disappear forever.

"Good-bye, Charlotte," she said one last time, closing the door behind her.

"Hey, Eddie, it's me," Connie said into the receiver, smiling.

"Lil' Bird! Didn't I just talk to you?"

"And so what if you did? I can't just call and talk to my most favorite person in the world if I want to?" she asked teasingly.

"Who dat?"

Connie laughed. "Well, now, if you have to ask . . ."

"Baby, I'm just playin'. How you doing? How's my grand-baby doing?"

Connie felt sad for a moment. "Jade's fine, I guess. I haven't seen her in a while."

"Well, that's good. How's the other one?"

Connie smiled. "The doctor says he's fine."

"Good. I ain't letting you give this one away."

"I know, Eddie," she said, quietly. "I don't want to give him away."

"Then don't. God keep givin' you chillen, he obviously mean for you to keep at least one of 'em."

Connie laughed again. "I have something to tell you."

"Oh Lawd, what now?"

"What do you mean, Oh Lawd what now? What's that supposed to mean?"

"It means every time you start off a sentence with I got something to tell you, Eddie, I need to sit down and hold onto my girdle. What is it, Lil' Bird?"

"Remember just before you left for Vegas and I asked you, no, I begged you to let me come with you and you told me no? Something about you didn't want to have to keep taking care of me or something lame like that?"

"Well, no. I can't say that I do remember havin' that conversation, but if you say I did say something like that, then I'm sure I must've. Why?"

Connie hesitated before answering.

"C'mon now, girl. Spit it out!"

"Well, I've got my own money now, Eddie," she said carefully. "And I can get my own place and take care of myself."

"That's 'cause I raised you right. So what's your point?"

"My point is . . . I'm moving to Vegas, Eddie. And I'm not asking you this time, I'm telling you," she quickly added. "Because I'm a grown woman and I can move to anywhere I want to move and there's nothing you can say about it. And because I miss you and I love you, and because I'm going to need someone to teach me about raising babies, and because . . ."

"Hush, Lil' Bird." Eddie's voice cracked, and Connie could tell she was crying. "When you comin', baby, 'cause I cain't wait to see you, too."

All of a sudden, Connie realized why seeing Charlotte hadn't affected her one way or another. She realized why she wasn't angry or hurt or why feelings of betrayal didn't take her over and send her into a downward emotional spiral. It was because after Charlotte left, Eddie stepped in, and became a better mother to her than Charlotte ever could be. So how could she be mad at Charlotte, when by leaving she'd given Connie the gift of a lifetime? She'd moved over and made room for Eddie.

Chapter 47

ustin was beside himself. He'd spent the last two nights in a hotel room, calling Reesy like crazy, but she wouldn't take his calls. He'd gone by the house, only to find her and the kids gone. "Connie?" he said, hoping he didn't sound as desperate as he felt.

"Connie, hey. How've you been? Me? Fine. Yeah . . . Uh . . . are Reesy and the kids with you? No? Nothing. Nothing, I just, uh . . . Everything's—fine. Well—I mean—Look, I can't get into it right now, Connie. If you hear from her, tell her I'm looking for her. Just—tell her, Connie. Yeah."

Justin sat on the side of the bed, running his hand over his head. He hadn't shaved or showered since that night when that picture of him with Cookie had burned its image into his mind, and when he closed his eyes all he saw was that expression on Reesy's face when she told him to leave his own house. Never in his wildest dreams did he ever think she'd find out. She never needed to, because it meant absolutely nothing. It was a meager episode in his life that was never meant to disrupt his family. Just sex. That's all it was. Sex with a woman whose real name he didn't even bother to ask. A stripper. A prostitute. Shit like that wasn't supposed to come between him and his wife. It was too menial and meaningless. Justin still couldn't grasp the magnitude of what that short tryst had on what he treasured more than anything.

How could she have done him like that? And how come he hadn't seen it coming? Questions tumbled over each other in his mind as he tried to recall a moment when he and Cookie were together, that moment when he should've seen this coming. How'd she get his address? Who took the picture? When? He stood up and paced the room where he'd been pacing it since he got here. He hadn't disrespected her. Hell, he hadn't even heard from her since that weekend they were together. He'd given her his card with his work number on it, and she hadn't called. Not that he'd expected or even really wanted her to. But at least if she'd called, he might've felt warned that he needed to be careful. That he needed to consider that this woman might be the kind to make waves. There were no foreboding signs. No warning. She just . . . fucked up everything, out of the blue. For what? Spite? Did she want him? What?

He needed answers. Something to help him make sense of what was happening to him and his marriage. Reesy wasn't talking to him, but Cookie was going to have to. She'd been the one to fuck everything up for no seemingly good reason except to hurt him. Hell, if she'd called him up asking for money, that would've made sense. If she'd called him up wanting him to leave his wife and to be with her, maybe he could buy into that, too. But to just send Reesy that picture for no other reason but to break up his marriage, that made no sense at all.

It was Thursday night, and the club was nearly empty. That was the way it was sometimes, though, especially during the week. Justin scanned the dark, smoke-filled room until he spotted her standing at the bar, giving a private dance to a customer.

Cookie was topless. The small gold triangle of her g-string covered her pubic area, and the string in back formed a *V* at the base of her spine, then disappeared into her plump ass.

"Cookie," he called out as he got closer. She spotted him, smiled, but kept dancing. "Cookie! I need to talk to you."

"Not on my dime, man," the man protested, never bothering to take his eyes off Cookie's luscious behind. "Get your own girl, or wait till I'm done."

She winked. "I'll see you in a few minutes, lover."

Justin started to protest again when one of the bouncers came over to where he stood and, without saying it, insisted that Justin step back and wait until she was finished with the gentleman behind her.

In frustration, Justin left the building altogether and sat in his car outside, waiting. The longer he waited, the angrier he became. She'd fucked him over, then had the nerve to smile at his ass, winking and shit like she hadn't done a damned thing.

Hours had passed when he finally saw her. Cookie and the rest of the girls left in a pack, escorted outside and watched by one of the bouncers until they got in their cars and left. She drove a silver Pathfinder, and Justin followed her.

Cookie drove up Interstate 70, taking the 225 exit south into Aurora, where she finally exited off Mississippi Avenue, and drove for another ten minutes until she turned into her apartment complex. He came up behind her while she was unlocking the front door.

"Cookie."

She stifled a scream, then turned, surprised to see it was him. "Justin? What . . . what are you doing here?" For a moment, she looked afraid, but he didn't care.

"Why'd you do it?" From the way she was looking at him, he

must've looked like he was out of his mind. "Why'd you do that to me, Cookie?"

"What are you talking about?"

Her feigned ignorance annoyed the hell out of him. After the way she'd turned his world upside down, for her to play dumb was an insult. Especially since he knew. Of course she had to know what he was talking about.

"Don't play dumb, Cookie," he said, agitated. "You know what I'm talking about."

Cookie stared innocently at him, panic slowly building inside her. "No, Justin." She spoke carefully. "Maybe you need to leave." She turned to go inside, and Justin grabbed her hard by the arm, then pushed his way in behind her. She started to scream, but he covered her mouth with his hand before she could.

"Scream, and I swear . . ." His eyes watered, he was so pissed. He'd never been so livid in his life, and for a moment, he realized what he was capable of, what most men were capable of, given the right circumstances. "You fucked me up, girl."

Cookie tried to pull away, but Justin's fingers dug deeper into her flesh. "Justin," she said, staring to cry. "You're hurting me."

"You hurt me!" he growled. "You took away the most precious, the most—Why? Why the hell would you do some shit like that to me?"

"I don't know what you're talking about," she hiccuped. "Please. Let me turn on the light."

"I'm talking about that goddamned picture! The one you sent to my wife!" In a strange way, he'd trusted Cookie when they were together. Trusted that she wasn't the kind of woman to betray him, because of the way he'd treated her. "I treated you with respect! I never . . . I was careful with you, Cookie! I was fuckin' careful! And then you send that shit to my wife? How could you do that to me? When all I did was . . ."

"I never sent her anything, Justin," Cookie defended herself. "How could I when I don't even know where you live? I don't know your wife! How could I send . . ." And then it dawned on her, and her eyes glazed over as she stared back at him in disbelief. "Avery," she whispered. "Avery did it."

Justin's face twisted in anguish at what she said. "Avery?" His grip began to loosen. "Avery Stallings? The detective?" But no. That couldn't be true. Avery had been at his house. He'd sat down and had dinner with Justin and his family. The two of them had talked and . . .

"He's my dad, Justin," she confessed. "He came to me and showed me a picture of you and me a few weeks ago, and I . . . I didn't think anything about it, Justin!" Justin turned away, disgusted, rubbing his tired eyes. "I thought maybe your wife had hired him because she thought you was cheating on her. But I never said anything other than you were just someone who came into the club every now and then, and that's all! I swear! I wouldn't lie to you about that!"

Something about the way he recalled seeing Avery that night at dinner, watching Reesy's every move, staring at her longer than he should've, but none of those things meant anything until now. Even in the beginning, when he and Justin first met, Avery rubbed him the wrong way, monopolizing his wife's time, making up reasons for them to meet, usually when Justin was working.

"He's your father?" He turned, looking perplexed, at Cookie. She nodded. "Sort of. I mean, I don't have too much to do with him, and I don't even see a whole lot of him. Every now and then he pops up, trying to be Daddy, but . . . I haven't needed a daddy in years." She dried her eyes and tried to smile. "I wouldn't do nothing like that to you, Justin. You helped me, man." Cookie turned on the light near the sofa, then hurried over to the dining room table and came back over to Justin, showing him her college class schedule and course book. "I start this summer," she said excitedly. "I'm going to major in business, or maybe theater. I love acting," she smiled. "But I wouldn't even have thought about college if you hadn't said something. Nobody ever told me I could be anything other than a . . ."

Justin fought valiantly to care, and tried returning her smile with one of his own.

"Dancing pays good," she shrugged. "But that's all I'm going to be doing. Nothing else. Because I'm better than that. You taught me that."

When he left, Justin sat in his car, outside her place, awed by what he'd just heard. Avery had taken the picture, and he'd been the one to send it. And his motives were simple. He wanted Justin's wife.

Chapter 48

Charlotte had been on the phone with Miss Lynn all morning, telling her about her trip to Denver. "Girl, I couldn't believe how much it had changed. Oh my! It looked like a different place, but it felt like home. You know what I mean? I felt like I belonged there and like I fit there."

Cammy listened from the kitchen while she washed dishes. Charlotte hadn't told her much about the trip at all, shooing her away whenever she asked, complaining that she was too tired to talk about it.

"They treated me so good, girl. I stayed in a nice hotel room and . . . well, they just wanted me to be comfortable, Lynn. With all them kids they got, they didn't want the children to get on my nerves."

Momma seemed so proud of Reesy, and she seemed so happy to go home again, too. Ever since she'd been home, she'd acted so different and distant, as if Murphy, Kansas, wasn't her home after all.

"And my daughter's house is as big as a mansion. I swear to God it is. I think she had it decorated by one of those interior designers, too. Wouldn't surprise me one bit if she did. That's how Reesy does things, you know . . . classy. Oh, her husband is a handsome, handsome man, and the children . . ." Charlotte stopped talking when Cammy came into the room and sat down. Charlotte picked up the phone and got up to finish her conversation in the kitchen.

Cammy wasn't Reesy. It was painfully obvious that Charlotte only had eyes for Reesy now, and Cammy felt like an unwanted guest in her own house. Charlotte could be such a mean woman sometimes. Cammy had grown up with her mother's ways, distant and cold one minute, warm and needful the next. Most of the time, she'd just adjust accordingly, keeping her distance when necessary and staying close the rest of the time.

She went into her room and closed the door, then picked up her cell phone to call T. They hadn't spoken to each other in a week, ever since they were married. She still couldn't believe they'd actually gone through with it, but even worse, she couldn't believe the way she behaved when it was over. Cammy had a husband who wanted her and this baby, and she turned her back on him, and came running home to her mother like she was a little girl, scared to death she'd get in trouble. "Hey, baby," she said sweetly into the phone. Sadness crept over her as Cammy gave in to the thought that she'd finally pushed him too far away this time, and that he was finally finished with her. "Please pick up, T. I know you're there." Of course, he didn't answer, and maybe he never would again. "I wanted to come by, baby. I wanted to come see you so we could talk. So I could say I'm sorry for the way I acted. I love you."

"Reesy said she's going to talk to her husband and they're going to see about moving me back to Denver. I'm going to pray hard on that one, girl. You know I am. Cammy? No, she's staying here. She's not going. Said she doesn't want to. And that's fine. You know she's got that baby coming and that man of hers . . ."

Charlotte was a liar sometimes, too. Cammy had never told her mother she didn't want to go to Denver. Her mother had never asked if she wanted to go, either. Hurt feelings swelled inside her, and she quietly started to cry, feeling small and insignificant. She'd let him go for her. She'd chosen Charlotte time and time again over T, and he'd waited and been patient, hoping that one day she'd see that she was wasting her time. But Cammy didn't see it until now. Charlotte didn't want her. And now T didn't want her, either, and she realized how much of a fool she'd been her whole life.

Cammy flung open the door to her room and confronted Charlotte right then and there. "You never asked me if I wanted to go to Denver, Mom!" she cried, standing over Charlotte, sitting shocked on the couch with the phone to her ear. "You told me I couldn't go! Reesy invited me to come, too, and you didn't want me to go! Don't lie!"

Charlotte was aghast and embarrassed, knowing full well Lynn heard this fool screaming like she'd lost her mind. "Let me call you back, Lynn," she said calmly, hanging up the phone.

"Who you calling a liar?" Charlotte rose to her feet, planted her fists on her hips, and stared hard into Cammy's eyes.

Cammy's anger made her fearless. The fact that she was a married woman gave her the right to stand up to Charlotte. Her heart had been broken by her mother, and by T, and most of all by herself, and all of a sudden she realized she had to speak up, say what was on her mind, or never say a word.

"I want to go, too," she sobbed.

"You ain't going with me," Charlotte said maliciously.

"Why not? Because you don't need me anymore? Because you have Reesy now? It wasn't that long ago, Momma, when I was the one you needed. When I was the world to you and if I ever left you, you'd be lost. You told me that! Now you don't need me!"

"No, Cammy," Charlotte sounded cold. "I don't need you, baby. Not anymore." It felt good to say it and to know she meant it. Cammy was as much a burden as a blessing, and lately, the burden outweighed the blessing.

"That's so wrong, Momma." Tears streamed down her cheeks. "After all I gave up for you."

Charlotte threw her head back and laughed. "What you gave up for me? Little girl, please! What I gave up for you is more like it. Do you know how hard it's been on me, raising a grown woman? Do you have any idea how tired I get . . . Cammy, do this. Cammy, did you do that? Cammy, don't forget to . . . You're a fool and an idiot, Camille. Have been your whole life." Charlotte stared down her nose at her, then folded her arms across her chest.

Her words were cruel and cold, but more than any of those things, they were honest. Cammy could see in her eyes how much she meant them. Her mother's venomous words were meant to hurt and they did, and Cammy understood for the first time that she'd been used in the worst way by the one person she loved more than her own life. "That's not right, Momma." Anger and resentment swelled inside her. "How can you say that to me? How could you . . ."

Charlotte pointed in Cammy's face. "You're just like you're daddy, girl!" she spat angrily. "He was sorry, too. One sorry mothafucka! Weak! Helpless! Pathetic! I watched his ass die, girl!" Charlotte had finally said it out loud. Cammy needed to hear it, and she had spent years trying to figure out ways not to tell this girl the truth, but now it didn't matter, because Cammy didn't matter. Charlotte was going home. Finally. She was going home to her babies, and to hell with every terrible stray memory she'd picked up and been saddled with ever since she left.

"No!" Cammy shook her head in disbelief. "No, Momma!" Her daddy had died. That's all she knew. That's all she ever knew. Charlotte had loved him.

"He was precious to me," she'd told Cammy when she was small. "Just like you're precious to me, Cammy. Don't ever leave Momma, baby. I'd die if I lost you, too."

"He begged for his life." Vivid memories began to surface in Charlotte's mind of that day, the sounds, the smells. She looked through Cammy and back in time like she was seeing it all over again. "He cried like a baby."

"No, Momma."

"'Get up!' I told him. 'Fight! Fight for us! Get up!'

"They beat him and then they put the gun in his mouth.

"He was a coward!" she said callously. "And you're a coward, Cammy. Just like him. Too scared to do shit! To fight! My baby fought. Both my babies fought and they lived! And they are beautiful women! Strong women! Not sorry little bitches still clinging to their momma's tittie like your dumb ass!"

Cammy had had enough. Her scream pierced through the house as she lunged at Charlotte full force, releasing every frustration, fear, and disappointment that had been planted in her for as long as she could remember. She knocked Charlotte backward, but her mother didn't fall. Charlotte fought back, grabbing Cammy by the shirt and slamming her facedown hard against the oak coffee table. Cammy rolled over on her back and saw her mother standing over her. "Get the hell out of my house, bitch!" she huffed. Her face flushed, her eyes watering, she looked like a monster, and Cammy wanted no part of monsters.

She took everything she could carry and left the house.

Cammy headed to the only place she knew to go. It was late when she found herself standing at his door, pounding hard on it with her fist. "Let me in, T!" she cried. "Please! Let me come home!"

Finally the door opened. But it wasn't T who answered it. It was Tonya.

"Uh . . . he in the shower," she said smugly. "Is there something I can help you with?"

Cammy drove too fast. She rounded a corner and didn't see the other car swerving into her lane until it was too late.

Chapter 49

*J*ustin eventually moved in with his parents. Reesy reluctantly agreed to meet with him over coffee two weeks after she found out about the affair. The strain between them was thick enough to cut with a knife, and neither one of them could bear to look the other in the eyes.

"How are the kids?"

"You've spoken to them on the phone, Justin," she said shortly. "You know how they are."

Justin rubbed his tired eyes, trying his damnedest to avoid arguing with her. "Yeah, well . . . we can't keep telling them I'm out of town on business, Clarice. Eventually we're going to have to tell them the truth."

"I know that, Justin. Just . . . not now. I don't think they could handle it."

"They can't? Or you can't?"

She shot him a look, but not a response.

"I don't want to lose you, Reesy," he said tenderly.

"Well, it's too damn late for you to be thinking about that now." Reesy glanced around the room, hoping no one had overheard her. "I just want to know why, Justin." She leaned forward and finally found the strength to look at him. "Why would you do that to us?"

The answer escaped him. Justin had been asking himself the same question every day since she found out, but for the life of him, nothing he came up with made any sense. "I don't know, Reese."

"Bullshit!" she said in a hushed tone. "There is an answer, Justin. And you need to give me one today. Or else you can speak to me through my lawyer from now on, because I deserve better than that." She started to cry, but Reesy held her tears at bay with her anger. "Why?"

He leaned back and held her gaze to his, thinking back to that time, recalling what was going through his head and how he could've justified cheating on his wife. "I just remember feeling left out, Reese," he quietly explained. "You were looking for Charlotte, consumed with finding her."

"So it's my fault? I drove you to it because I needed to find my mother, you felt like you had license to . . ."

"I'm not saying it's your fault, honey. You asked me why, and I'm trying to tell you why."

"You felt left out," she said sarcastically.

Justin was offended by her tone, but knew better than to challenge it. Fighting would get him nowhere. Arguing would only lose the battle for him, and he could see from the look in her eyes that she fully expected him to lose this battle. Or at least to concede it.

"For the first time in our marriage," he swallowed hard, "I felt like we weren't connected, Clarice. Like you and me weren't even on the same page."

"And so you fucked a stripper?" she asked bitterly.

"I fucked a woman," he said simply. "Because I was lonely."

"You were horny, Justin."

He nodded. "I was horny as hell, Reesy, for you. But . . . you weren't feeling that way for me."

She looked appalled. "I needed to find my mother, Justin. How come it was so hard for you to understand that? And why . . . why in the world would you think I'd give a damn about sex when I had the weight of the world on my shoulders?"

"Because you never had to carry that weight on your own, Reesy. I never intended for you to, but once you set out to do this, you cut me off and out of the picture."

"That's not true!" she defended herself.

"That's how it felt."

"And so . . . you found her?"

"I didn't go looking for her."

"But you found her?"

He pressed his lips together and shrugged. "I needed a drink one night after work."

"At a strip club?"

"What difference did it make?" He looked defiantly back at her. "Whether I met her at a strip joint or in a dance club, Reesy, would it matter?"

She sat back, defeated. "No. I guess not."

"I was lonely, Clarice. While you were busy carrying the weight of the world on your shoulders, I sat back, watching, feeling absolutely useless, and jealous because all of a sudden your attention was anyplace and everyplace except on me."

Reesy shook her head in disbelief. "God, Justin! You sound like a woman."

He was hurt and insulted by her remark. "Why? Because I'm an addict for my wife? Because I need her, and I don't give a damn who knows it or what anybody else thinks? Maybe I do sound like a woman, Reese, but I can't help the way I feel. You weren't there. And looking back, I know that I wasn't there for you, either. Not the way you needed me to be. I had sex with another woman. And then it was over. It happened, and I can't do anything to change that or take it back, no matter how badly I wish I could. But I am still and will always be madly in love with you, no matter what happens from here on out. You can bank on that." Justin finished his coffee and got up to leave. "Oh, and just so you know." He stopped and leaned down close to Reesy. "You might want to talk to that private detective of yours about that picture." He kissed her tenderly on the cheek. "I have a feeling he might know where it came from."

Justin walked out of the coffee shop feeling as vindicated as he could possibly feel under the circumstances. All the "I'm sorry"s and "Baby, she didn't mean anything to me" in the world would only serve to make her hate him even more. The ball was in Reesy's court, and either she'd hang out and try and play this game until it was finished, or she'd get the hell off the court and walk away for good. Either way, he'd never stop loving her, and as long as she needed him, he was there. Always.

Reesy could tell from his demeanor that he was expecting her. Avery stood up behind his desk, pushed his hands into his pockets, and never said a word as Reesy walked over to him, laid the photograph of Justin and the prostitute down on his desk, and sat down across from him. Avery glanced at the picture, then back at Reesy. He sat down, too, struggling to read the expression on her face.

"I always said you were the best at what you do," she said. "Once again, you proved me right."

"This time it would've been nice if I'd been wrong."

"Lying doesn't set well with me, Avery. So please, let's just keep it real."

He chuckled, then stood up and walked around to the front side of his desk, just to be closer to her. A myriad of thoughts ran through his mind about how all of this would unfold once she knew the truth about Justin, and once she opened up and let Avery step into the void Justin would inevitably leave behind. Maybe not today, but eventually.

"He fucked up," Avery said easily.

Reesy nodded in agreement. "Yes," she said thoughtfully. "He did."

"I struggled with whether or not to give that picture to you, Reesy. Believe me when I say that. Because it's true. I don't have anything against Justin personally, but—well, a leopard can't change its spots, and I can't change what I do, and what I do best—according to you. But I wanted you to see the truth, because I'm your friend and I think it's the least you deserve."

Without warning, Avery leaned down close, gazed deeply into Reesy's eyes, and pressed his lips to hers in a sensuous kiss. He expected her to pull away, maybe even to slap him hard across the face, but Reesy surprised the hell out of him and kissed him back. The two of them sat in silence, absorbing this moment between them, wondering what the next move would be, if there was to be one. And there was. And Reesy made it first. She slipped the strap of her purse over her shoulder and rose to her feet.

"As tempting as it might be, Avery," she said sensuously, "as tempting as it's always been, I just don't have it in me."

He chuckled a little, expecting her to follow up with a punch line, but then realized none was coming. "I fucked up?"

She shrugged. "My husband was caught in the most despicable act of betrayal a man can make, and I hate him for it. But I hate you for looking hard enough to find it."

"I just thought you should know," he explained.

"Because you cared so much for me?" she asked. "Or because you thought you could slide into my life and pick up where he left off?"

Avery didn't answer.

"I don't know what's going to happen to my marriage, Avery," she said, turning to leave. "But I do know that it would take more than you to pick up the pieces a man like Justin leaves behind."

Chapter 50

Racine cozied up next to John sitting at the bar at Rosco's, a local nightclub in Bueller. "So how long are you going to be mad at me?" she asked, nudging her shoulder against his.

He looked over at her and continued drinking. "I ain't mad, Racine."

"Really?" She nodded introspectively. "So, how come you haven't called or come by?"

"Been busy," he replied indifferently. "Besides," John glanced at her again, "seems to me like you might have some personal matters that still need tending to. How is Lewis, by the way?"

Racine laughed. "Still crazy about me, when the mood strikes him, or when he thinks somebody else might be sniffing around."

"His ass never could fight."

"Never could. Even I've kicked it a few times through the years. He's like a Timex watch. Takes a lickin' and keeps on tickin.'"

"Ever think about giving the brotha another chance?"

Racine looked surprised. "Why? Lewis is the one who left me. It wasn't like I put him out. He wanted to go. Said he had some woman who worshipped the ground he walked on, or something to that affect. So, he left me, then she left him, now he calls himself wanting me back, and I call myself wanting to get with you. As the world turns on its ugly axis. Crazy, huh?"

John grunted. "Yeah."

"And what about you, John?" Racine asked, motioning to the bartender. "Absolut and tonic with lime, please. Who do you want? What about that chick up in Colorado? What's happening with that?"

"The chick put me out," he said matter-of-factly.

"Why?" Racine asked without hesitation. "What did you do?"

John looked at her and laughed. "Maybe I didn't do nothing."

She rolled her eyes. "Yeah, right. Of course you did. Why else would she put you out? And it had to be something serious, too, because the dick is all that." She smiled, and winked.

He felt flattered. "Thank you."

"So, what happened?"

John thought for a moment, trying to figure out what happened. In fact, he'd been trying not to ask himself that question since he'd left, believing that if he just let it go and turned his back on it, the whole Connie thing would disappear, go up in smoke like it had never happened. That was how it had worked for him in the past, and there was no reason to think it wouldn't work for him this time, too. But it wasn't working, and that Connie thing was as stubborn as she was and just refused to disappear like a good little episode should.

"We wanted different things." It sounded like a cliché, even to him.

Like she wanted a baby, and he didn't know what he wanted. But it started long before that. Didn't it? It wasn't just about the kid she was carrying, his kid. It was about trying to settle down when it wasn't ever in his blood to do so. And be the kind of man he'd never known, which she seemed to need so badly.

"Like what?" Racine asked, sipping on her drink.

He looked at her. "Like . . . normal shit. You know what I'm talking about."

Racine laughed. "Like . . . marriage? A family? A house with a white picket fence?"

"Something like that," he muttered.

"And your big ass couldn't go there?"

John shrugged. "Go where?" he chuckled.

"I tell you, John King." Racine shook her head slowly back and forth. "Why you gotta make it so damn hard on a woman?"

"I don't make it hard," he said defensively. "Y'all are the ones who make it hard. I'm just being me, living my life, and doing the best I can."

"Which ain't much, lemme tell you."

John had the nerve to look offended. "What's that supposed to mean?"

"It means that men like you are big pussies, scared of every goddamned thing."

"You got me confused with somebody else, baby."

"Afraid not. In fact, I'd say you're probably the poster child for the Scared Black Men of America Foundation. Oh, you talk tough. Walk around with your chest stuck all out, shoulders back, ready to throw down and fight any man who steps to you wrong." Racine sat next to John with her chest stuck out, shoulders back, swaying from side to side in her chair, like she was walking with a big dick stuck between her legs. John laughed. "You'll fuck a woman silly, pound on your chest like a big-ass ape when you're done, then strut around like the cock of the roost, breaking hearts and bathing in a pool of tears filled by all the pitiful, foolish women you leave behind in your wake. And then, when one comes along who you kinda dig, who gets to you, and expects more from you then just a screw and a pat on the ass, you take off running, looking back over your shoulder hoping and praying that she can't run as fast as you and catch your punk ass, and make you own up and do the right thing by her."

John just looked at her, shaking his head. "Yeah. Right. So . . . you here to try and get me to do the right thing by you, Racine?"

She rolled her eyes and waved her hand in the air. "Please. I've chased your ass as far as I'm going to chase you, John."

"I never asked you to chase me. In fact, I'd prefer it if you didn't."

She looked offended. "Well, to hell with you, too."

"I'm just saying, you're a pretty woman, baby. And you shouldn't have to chase any man. He should be chasing you."

"So, why don't you chase me?"

John gulped down the last of his drink, then motioned to the bartender to bring him another one. "Because I don't run fast enough, and I don't have the stamina, baby."

She laughed. "Oh, you got plenty of stamina. I just don't think you have the heart, baby."

"That neither."

"In fact," she continued, "I don't think you've got it in you to chase after any woman. Am I right?"

He shrugged.

"But maybe there's one you just can't get out of your system?" Racine probed, studying him intently.

John just looked at her, but didn't say a word.

"I'd hoped to make you forget her, which is why I damn near sexed you to death. But I don't think all the sex in the world could do that." He sat quietly while she spoke. "A woman can sense these things sometimes, that there's someone else who's just gotten so deep under a man's skin that nothing or nobody can wash him clean of her. You put up a good front, though. I think you've almost got yourself fooled into thinking you're over her."

"I think you must have me mixed up with Lewis, sweetheart." John smiled, hoping she'd change the subject.

Racine just stared at him. "You can make fun of Lewis all you want, but the two of you aren't really all that different. He has it bad for me, and you, baby boy, you still have it bad for Miss Colorado. And both of you are fools, because you didn't appreciate what you had when it was sitting nice and pretty right in front of your face. I'll never take Lewis back no matter how much he begs or how long he pleads. And if you wait too long, Mr. King, if it's not too late already, the love of your life might not be so eager to take you back, either."

John stared at Racine, awed and surprised at how this conversation was affecting him.

"You've never had to chase after a woman in your life, John King, because every last one of us has been tripping and falling all over each other chasing after you." Racine finished her drink, then stood up to leave. "Maybe this time you should break your own unwritten rule. Run fast, hard, and to the moon and back if you have to, and catch up with her this time."

"And what if I do?" he said, swallowing his own pride. "What if I do, and she doesn't want me back? Then what?"

Racine looked endearingly at him, then kissed him softly on the lips. "Then you'll finally be able to join the human race and be just like the rest of us pathetic, lovestruck, and broken-hearted fools," she laughed. "And if you play your cards right," she turned and winked, "I might just be waiting here when you get back."

Racine disappeared out of the club, and John knew he'd miss her.

He sat there nursing his drink, his mind reeling through the stages of his life, and the twists and turns it had taken in his forty years. John had learned the perils of a broken heart when he was a boy, loving harder than he should've, the kinds of women who could bury a man alive, condemn him for a life-time, just by turning away from him when he reached out to them as a boy. He'd been avoiding that kind of pain all of his adult life, and until now, he figured he'd done a damn good job of it.

John wanted Connie. There was no doubt in his mind and heart that she was the only woman he wanted. But what did Connie want? She wanted him to be something he wasn't. She wanted him to rise to the occasion and be some ideal of man-hood she'd imagined and needed her whole life. She wanted a kid. His kid. Any kid?

And what about the baby she was carrying? He had pur-posefully put aside any opinion of it one way or another. But one thing he couldn't deny, and he wouldn't be able to ignore it forever, either. If she went through with keeping it, his ass was going to be a father, and somewhere running around in this world would be a small version of him. John had grown up not knowing his father, only terrible rumors of him, lies, and distor-tions of a man he'd come to know and love. But the bottom line was, he had no idea how to be a father. He had no idea how to raise kids, and he'd never thought he'd ever have to.

Not that he'd raise this one. And not that he should, either. Hell, the last thing he wanted to do was fuck up a perfectly good kid. And he could, too. Then he'd feel like shit, and responsible, and guilty for screwing up somebody who could probably do so much better without him. He didn't like kids. Didn't have the patience for them, either.

"Shit," he muttered, finishing his last drink, then dropping money on the bar before leaving. The night air bathed his face, helping him to sober up from the slight buzz in his head. He had a kid on the way. The only way to ignore that was to stay drunk for the next forty years. Otherwise . . . he had to do something. Didn't he? Of course he did, but exactly what that was . . . was a mystery to him.

Right down to the wire
Even through the fire

—CHAKA KHAN, *"Through the Fire"*

Chapter 51

*C*onnie was just about to close up the store for the night when she saw Reesy running through the rain, headed her way. Connie held the door open for her as she hurried inside.

"Well, what brings you all the way down here in this weather?" Connie asked, staring at Reesy, who looked like a wet rat. The expression on Reesy's face warned her that something was terribly wrong. "What's wrong?" she asked, concerned.

Reesy caught her breath. "Momma called. Something's happened."

"Are the kids okay? Is your dad all right?"

Reesy shook her head. "Charlotte, Connie," Reesy corrected herself, once she realized Connie thought she was talking about Evelyn. "Charlotte called. There's been an accident." Connie sighed and started to walk away. Reesy grabbed her by the arm. "It's Cammy, Connie."

Connie looked confused. "Cammy? Who is—"

"Our sister," Reesy said, frustrated. "The one you spoke to on the phone? Cammy, Connie! How can you not remember her name?"

Connie turned and placed her hand on her hip. "Well, excuse me for not remembering that woman's name, Reese. I've never met her, so it slipped my mind." Connie pulled away from Reesy's grasp.

"She had an accident, Connie," Reesy explained desperately. "She had a car accident, and she lost the baby." Reesy started to cry.

Connie had barely even remembered that the girl had been pregnant. She saw how this was affecting Reesy, and of course she understood why Reesy was taking this so hard. She'd spent time with Cammy, gotten to know her. She'd had a connection to her. Connie had only spoken to her briefly on the phone. "I'm so sorry, Reese." She hugged her sister tenderly.

"We have to go see her, Connie," Reesy sobbed into her shoulder. "Momma says she's pretty bad off, and she needs us."

Connie backed up and looked at her sister. "You go, Reese. She knows you, and I'm sure she'd be glad to see you."

"We both need to go, Connie!" Reesy protested. "She's our sister, and we need to be there for her!"

"I don't know that girl, Reese!" Connie argued. "You do. So, go see about her, but I'm not—"

"You'd do it if it were me, Connie," Reesy said angrily, glaring at her sister. "She's your sister just like I'm your sister, and you know you'd be there if it were me up in that hospital, so what the hell is the difference?"

Connie stared back, realizing that Reesy had won this argument hands down. "So, when do we leave?"

They didn't say much on the plane. Connie and Reesy rented a car in Kansas City and drove to Murphy.

"How's the pregnancy going?" Reesy finally got up the nerve

to ask. Connie was showing now, but she put forth a lot of effort to hide her swelling stomach, almost as if she thought that if Reesy didn't see it, then maybe they didn't have to talk about it.

"Fine," she said shortly.

Reesy drove another mile before she spoke up again. "Do you know what it is yet?"

Connie didn't answer right away. "It's a boy."

For a moment, Reesy almost forgot and let herself get excited, but then she glanced over at Connie, sitting sulking and staring out the window, and remembered who it was she was dealing with. The last time Connie was pregnant, eight years ago, with Jade, she sulked a lot back then, too, wrestling internally with the impending thought of motherhood. In the end, motherhood lost out and Connie gave her daughter to Reesy to raise. What was she planning to do this time? And where the hell was John in all this?

"Is John happy?" Reesy knew the answer to the question even before she asked it. John wasn't the type of man to be happy about fatherhood, any more than Connie looked forward to being a mother. So, what was Connie planning for this baby, exactly? That was what Reesy wanted to know.

Connie knew where this was going. Reesy might've tried to be slick about it, but the bottom line was, she wanted to know what was up, without coming right out and asking what was up.

"We split up," Connie said matter-of-factly, still staring out the window.

Reesy started to say something that would probably piss Connie off, but Connie interrupted her before she could.

"He'd rather not have kids," Connie explained.

"And what about you, Connie?" Reesy probed carefully, trying to avoid another argument. "Are you going to keep this one?" For some reason, as soon as she asked the question, Reesy felt the urge to duck.

Connie looked at Reesy and smiled. "You know me, Reese," she said, tenderly. "I get skittish sometimes . . . scared that I'll fall on my ass again and mess everything up."

Reesy was surprised by Connie's tone and demeanor. She fully expected the woman to come back swinging on her for even going there, but there was something calm about Connie, something gentle and ready to be vulnerable.

"I thought about giving him up for adoption, too, but then . . ." Connie turned her gaze back to the scenic views outside. "He's my baby." Without thinking, she ran her hand gently over her stomach. "And I'm going to have to be brave this time . . . for him, because . . . it's time."

Reesy reached over to Connie and patted her stomach. "That's good, Connie," she said sweetly. "That's good."

Maybe this time, Connie could see this through. Reesy hoped she would. John was out of the picture, which didn't surprise her one bit. Something like this seemed like his M.O. Hit it and when it got pregnant, quit it and leave the scene of the crime. But Connie wasn't much better, either. Making the same mistakes over and over again, ending up back in the same dismal place, pregnant and alone. Reesy would play her role to the hilt, too. She'd be the supportive sister right to the end, when they handed Connie that baby, and panic set in, and Connie would hand him off like a football to someone else.

Charlotte sat across the room from Cammy lying in that hospital bed with tubes coming out of her. She'd lost that baby, which was a blessing in disguise as far as Charlotte was concerned. Her collarbone was broken; she had a concussion, and a dislocated hip. Resentment was all she really felt toward Cammy, causing all this commotion and upheaval in her life because she'd been an idiot about absolutely everything.

Cammy had been the one to start the fight between the two of them. Charlotte was minding her business, talking to Lynn on the phone, when that girl, for no reason, butted in on the conversation and got a good strong whiff of herself, bowing up to her momma like a fool.

She couldn't wait to get out of this hellhole and move back to Denver. Charlotte couldn't wait to get away from Cammy's dumb ass, too, finally. As old as that girl was, she should've been out there on her own, acting like a grown woman instead of an over-grown baby for once in her life. God took that baby because he knew that fool wouldn't be able to raise it. Hell, she didn't even know how to take care of herself, let alone somebody else. Which was why Charlotte had been staddled with her all these years. Cammy was helpless. She was needy and depended on Charlotte entirely too much for someone her age. Moving away was going to give Charlotte the relief she needed from having to take care of Cammy for the rest of her life, and it would help Cammy, too, to learn how to stand up on her own two feet and to grow the hell up.

"Momma?"

Charlotte smiled warmly, relieved to hear the sound of her voice, which sounded like an angel. She looked up and saw Reesy standing in the doorway of Cammy's room, and Charlotte's heart swelled ten times over with the joy of seeing her baby girl again.

Charlotte stood up to hug Reesy, then noticed Connie standing behind her. Both her daughters had come. Lord have mercy!

She could hardly believe it. Charlotte almost reached out to hug Connie, too, but the apprehension in her eyes was still there, and Charlotte knew it was still too soon. But it was just a matter of time. She could feel it down in her soul, the time would come when Connie would forgive her again, too, and the three of them would be united the way they'd been before.

"How's she doing?" Reesy asked quietly, glancing at Cammy asleep in bed.

Charlotte donned concern. "The doctors say she'll be fine. They've got her all drugged up right now, and she's mostly been sleeping."

"Excuse me," Connie said, brushing past the two of them, to get a better look at Cammy.

While Reesy and her mother whispered back and forth about the girl's condition, Connie went to her, and saw her youngest sister for the first time. Even in her current state, Connie could see how pretty she was. She looked so young, closer to twenty than twenty-six. Cammy was darker than Reesy, her features fine and soft. Her eyes fluttered open and she stared back at Connie.

Connie smiled and leaned down close. "Hi, Cammy," she said, quietly.

Cammy blinked.

"I'm Connie."

Cammy's eyes immediately filled with tears and she slowly raised her hand up in the air. Connie reached out and held it in hers.

A tear slid down the side of her face.

Tears burned Connie's eyes, too. "It's nice to meet you, sweetie." She kissed Cammy softly on the head and watched her close her eyes again to sleep.

Charlotte and Reesy stood back and watched as Connie pulled up a chair next to Cammy's bed. Reesy was touched. Charlotte could hardly believe that heffa would sit there like that, next to that girl she didn't even know.

Chapter 52

I haven't seen or heard from Sammy in weeks," Charlotte said to Lynn, sitting at the table eating ribs. She'd brought over some to Charlotte that Arnel had made over the weekend, but Charlotte just paced back and forth across the room like a tiger in a cage.

"Girl, c'mon and sit down and eat. You making me tired with all that walking back and forth. Sam's okay. He always is. Probably just went back down South or something."

"He said he wouldn't leave without me, Lynn. He promised he'd take me with him."

Lynn almost choked on a rib. "Take you away from Uncle's crazy ass?" She chuckled. "Girl, you gonna make me choke."

Charlotte stopped and glared at Lynn. "I ain't property, heffa. I can come and go when I damn well please. Uncle don't own me!"

"Uncle do too own your ass, Charlie. And if you don't know it, then you dumb as hell."

Who the hell was this bitch calling dumb?

"All I'm saying is," Lynn swallowed a mouthful of food, "Uncle ain't nobody to be messing around with, girl. And you need to be careful about who you bring up in here. You never know who might be watching."

Alliances were funny things. Charlotte was too caught up in how good she looked, all the pretty things somebody gave her, and who she was fucking to pay attention to what was really going on. Lynn liked her. She liked her a lot, even going so far as to consider Charlotte one of her friends. But Lynn had herself to look out for. And she had Arnel to think about, too, and both of them were pawns in Uncle's dangerous world, to use any way he wanted.

Charlotte told Lynn too many things, confided in her about more than she should've. Don't trust nobody around her, Lynn had warned her time and time again. But Charlotte was dense and never seemed to get the message Lynn tried giving her in a round-about way. Everybody had a price. Everybody had an agenda.

"Keep an eye on baby girl for me, Lynn, darlin'," he'd told her from the moment he realized the two of them had become friends. As far as Lynn knew, Uncle had designed that, too, knowing the two of them would get close. But that's the kind of man he was, seeming to have more than two eyes and an extra set of ears. Uncle was psychic or something, and she sometimes believed he could read minds.

"Where'd you get a name like Uncle?" Lynn had asked him once, back when Arnel first introduced her to him.

Uncle seemed so nice, generous with his smile, flashing eyes that twinkled like stars at her, lulling her into his trap.

"I was born on the seventh day, of the seventh month, at the seventh hour," he explained, almost as if he were telling a story. "Big Momma had a superstitious nature, and she took one look at me, and made everyone swear not to name me until she said it was time."

"So you didn't get a name when you was born?"

Uncle shook his head. "I didn't get a name until seven days after I was born. And it was my nephew who named me. Big Momma called him into the house one Sunday, and said, 'Cecil, this here is your uncle.'

"'My uncle?' the boy asked, looking at her strange. 'But he's only a baby. How can he be my uncle?'

"Big Momma slapped him on the back of the head because Cecil always was mannish. Boy got his ass whooped every damn day of the week," Uncle laughed. "But you see, Cecil was seven at the time. And he was the seventh son of a seventh son. So Big Momma decided with all them sevens going around, it seemed only fitting that he be the one to give me a name. So, she said, 'Cecil, now, you got to give this child a name, and you the only one who can do it.'

"'I got to name him?' Cecil asked, looking confused. Big Momma nodded. 'If you don't give him a name, then he won't never have one, boy. So . . .' Big Momma looked at him and everybody else in the room looked at him, waiting for Cecil's bad ass to give me a name worthy of royalty." Uncle's story was filled with drama and tension. And everyone within earshot who could hear it stopped what they were doing just to listen. Lynn sat mesmerized on Arnel's lap, caught up in the magic of this strange man.

"'Uncle,' the boy said. Big Momma said, 'What?' 'Ima name him Uncle' cause he my uncle and besides, I don't even like babies.' Then the boy ran back outside to play, and that's how I got my name."

Uncle had a thing for this one. Lynn halfway expected him to have her working the streets by now, but he kept her locked up in here like a princess in a palace, doting on her and spoiling her, keeping her away from everybody and everything. Charlotte didn't know how good she had it. But Lynn knew. And she knew how bad it could get, too, if Charlotte wasn't careful.

Just then the phone rang, and Charlotte hurried across the room to answer it, hoping it was Sam. "Hello?" From the smile on her face, Lynn knew it had to have been him. "Hi, baby. Oooh! Where have you been, Sammy? I've been so worried that you'd left without me."

Lynn watched Charlotte smile and nod. She giggled, blushed, and blew him a kiss into the receiver. "I'll be ready, baby. I'll be outside waiting."

She spun around the room like a dancer. "My baby's coming, Lynn." She stopped and stared at her friend. "And we're getting out of here tonight, girl. He's coming to get me, and when we get to Memphis," Charlotte laughed out loud, "we're getting married."

Lynn stopped eating and just stared at the woman talking all this nonsense.

"I think I'm pregnant, Lynn," Charlotte said, breathless. She placed her hands over her stomach, and grinned so hard, Lynn thought her face would split.

"Pregnant?"

Charlotte nodded.

"Sam ain't been here but a month, Charlie! How you gonna know you pregnant in less than a month?"

"It's not Sam's," she said, shrugging her shoulders, sitting down next to Lynn, and taking one of the ribs from her plate.

"Uncle got you pregnant?"

"I think Zoo did," Charlotte said, licking her fingers. "As long as Uncle and me been together, I usually use something. But I didn't use nothing with Zoo."

"Sam know?" Lynn asked, stunned.

"Of course he don't know, girl." Charlotte smiled mischievously. "How many men you know gonna take a woman who's pregnant with another man's kid?"

"What are you doing, Charlie?" This was too much for even Lynn to take. Charlotte had taken a trip out to the twilight zone all by herself, and all of a sudden, she didn't make sense. "What kinda game you playing with all these men?"

"I'm not playing games," she said defensively. "The only man I ever wanted was Sam, Lynn. And he came all the way back out here to get me, and he's the one I want to be with. Fuck the rest of them."

"Sounds like you did."

Charlotte was too full of herself to be offended. "I did what I had to do."

"You had to fuck around with Zoo right under Uncle's nose? Zoo's a kid, Charlotte. How you going to do that to him?"

"Zoo ain't no kid, Lynn. Trust me. But he's all in love and shit, and honestly . . . I need a man who can take care of me. Zoo ain't ready for all that. He thinks he is, but . . . besides, I don't even know if I am or not. Not for sure, anyway. Maybe I'm not. But whether I am or not, I'm leaving with Sam and getting my ass the hell up out of here before Uncle figures it out."

Uncle was born on the seventh day, of the seventh month, at the seventh hour, and named by the seventh son of the seventh son. And Lynn knew instinctively that he'd already figured it out.

"Get in the car, son," Uncle told Sam, coming out from the motel he'd been staying at. "We got business to tend to."

Instinct told him to run, but cars pulled around on either side of him, blocking any escape he might've thought of from being a possibility.

"I ain't got all night, boy," Uncle said gruffly, sitting in the back seat of a maroon Cadillac.

Reluctantly, Sam did as he was told, and climbed in the back seat next to Uncle. The big man sitting in front on the passenger side got out and climbed in back, too, pinning Sam between the two men.

Sam's heart sank into his shoes, and he knew that the business he and Uncle had might very well be the last bit of business he ever had dealings with again.

War was never easy. Uncle had taken Sam to a spot near the river, deserted and isolated, quiet, except for the sounds of fists meeting flesh, and bones crunching. You could hear a man trying to catch his breath out here in this place. That was how quiet it was. That was how come he'd chosen it.

Sam's jaw had been broken more than once. His eyes were swollen shut. Teeth were missing. Ribs were broken, or at least, they felt like they were.

"Sit his ass back up in that chair!" Uncle demanded.

Sam no longer felt the pain in his body as he was lifted off the ground, as if by air, and placed in a chair across from Uncle.

"Now," Uncle said with finality. "I'm through kicking your ass for a while, boy. Why don't you tell me why it is you trying to steal from me?"

Sam found the strength to shake his head back and forth. Spit and blood dripped from his bottom lip and pooled on the ground beneath him. "I—I—ain't—stealin,' man."

Uncle leaned forward, resting his elbows on his thighs. "You ain't?" he said sarcastically. "Then what the hell you call it when one man come to take another man's woman from him?"

Sam slowly raised his head to Uncle. "I—paid you back. Even more."

Uncle leaned back and thought reflectively. "Yes. Yes you did, son. But you didn't give me enough. You gave me the money you stole from me, and that's cool. I appreciate that. You even gave me a little extra, which," Uncle smiled wickedly, 'I consider interest. But that girl is expensive, boy. We talking rent, new furniture, clothes, shoes, got to get her hair done, her nails, feed her . . ." Uncle counted on his fingers. "I'd say all total I done spent, shit, fifty thousand dollars on that bitch, easily. Now, if you can give me that kind of money, son, I'll drive your ass over there to pick that ho up my damn self." Uncle took his walking stick, raised it up off the ground, and put it under Sam's chin, raising his head up with it. "Otherwise, your ass is stealing from me, and you know I don't take kindly to thieves."

A man ain't a man without his dick. "Cut that shit off" were the last words Sam remembered hearing before he died. He thanked God for that bullet.

Chapter 53

Tyrell had to hear about the accident on the news. He'd tried calling Cammy before coming by, but she wouldn't take his calls. He stared at her from the doorway, uncertain as to how she'd react to seeing him. Cammy sat in a chair in front of the window with her back to him.

He cleared his throat to get her attention, but she never bothered to turn around. T waited for a moment, then called out her name. "Cammy?" he said, stepping inside the door.

If she heard him, she didn't respond. There was another chair across from her, and T wearily made his way over to it and hesitantly sat down, seeing her face for the first time. It was bruised, swollen, but she looked all right for the most part. At least, on the outside. Cammy seemed like she was in a trance, oblivious to the fact that he was even in the room.

"Hey, baby," he said gently, watching for some kind of reaction from her that she knew he was there. "I'd have been here sooner, but . . . I didn't know, Cammy. I heard about what happened on the news, baby, and I . . ."

"The baby's gone, T," she said in a whisper. "He's dead."

T felt like he'd swallowed his heart hearing her say that. They'd said as much on the news, but they hadn't said it the way she'd said it, and it didn't have the kind of impact on him that hearing it now had. "I know, honey," he said sweetly.

T sat beside her, feeling more helpless than he'd ever felt in his life. He wanted to touch her, but something inside warned him that now was not the time. So all he could do was sit, and wait, and be there for her, if she needed him.

Cammy had never had much faith in anything. She'd spent her life wading through it, trying to stay on the shallow end of things and away from the deep parts, afraid she'd drown in them if she ever wandered too far away from what she could count on.

But those things had proven just as fragile as anything else in life. And all the things that mattered, that she always felt she could count on, had shattered into a million pieces in the course of an afternoon.

"I know you don't see it now," her mother told her after they took her baby from her. "But it's for the best, Cammy. You'll see. One day you'll see it's for the best that you didn't have it."

Charlotte was cold sometimes, and most times, Cammy could let it past and excuse her indifference to that just being her way. But not this time. She'd reeled Cammy in her whole life, then cast her away when it suited her, only to reel her in again when Cammy was just getting used to the idea of learning to swim. Charlotte didn't love her. She never had. And it had taken this . . . all of this for her to finally see that.

Cammy had wasted two lives, hers and her child's. She'd wasted T's too, only he'd realized that and moved on already with Tonya, or anybody else who could be there for him the way she never was. T felt sorry for her. Maybe he even missed his baby as much as she did, but the two of them were separated by an ocean of regret now, and Cammy was too tired to try and swim back to the other side.

"Do you need anything, baby?" he asked sorrowfully. "Can I do anything for you?"

He would've been the answer to her prayers now, if she was the same Cammy he'd married a few weeks ago. But Cammy was hollow inside, void of who she thought she was then. She needed absolutely nothing from anyone. Just to be left alone.

Eventually, the sky outside turned dark, and T disappeared out into it.

"Time for your medication, Cammy," the nurse said, handing her a small cup with pills in it, and a cup of water. She helped Cammy go to the bathroom, then helped her into bed.

"You might get to go home tomorrow, sweetie. I heard the doctor talking about it earlier today. But we'll just have to wait and see."

Home. Where in the world was that?

Chapter 54

He'd done all the right things. He'd called first to let her know he was back in town. He'd called again to let her know he was on his way over. He knocked on the door for three good minutes, letting her know he was there, on the other side of the door. And when he'd exhausted all of the proper protocols for calling the ex, he pulled his out his key and let himself in.

After taking a few minutes to look around, it was obvious she wasn't there. He'd dialed her cell phone number until he'd developed a blister on his thumb from hitting REDIAL, only to get the "Out of the area" message from her service. Connie insisted on no roaming, arguing that she wasn't going anywhere, so why bother. Apparently she needed to reevaluate that stance when she got back from where it was she'd disappeared to.

John sat down on the couch, wondering what his next move should be. He looked around the house. Nothing had changed. He got up and went into the kitchen, looking in the refrigerator hoping to find a beer, but there were none. Soy milk. Sierra Mist. Water. Leftover fried chicken. John pulled out the chicken, stuck it in the microwave, heated it up, then sat down at the table to eat.

Just then the phone rang. He started not to answer it, but then figured, what the hell. Maybe it was somebody calling Connie who might know why her ass wasn't here.

"Hello?"

"Who's this?" Eddie asked, surprised on the other end.

John smiled. "Who's this?" He knew who it was, but he'd always loved messing with Eddie.

"What the hell . . . *forgive me, Lord* . . . you doing there?"

"I've got a key," he retorted.

"That don't mean nothing," she responded angrily. "Do Connie know you in her house?"

John sighed. "No. She doesn't because she's not home."

"Then you need to get your ass . . . *thank you, Jesus* . . . out of there right this instant, John King! You know she don't want you up in there!"

"Where is she, Eddie?"

"How would I know?"

"So why'd you call?"

"That's none of your business, fool!"

"You calling to see if she made it back yet?"

"You need to get out of that house and out of that girl's business, boy!"

"Where is she, Eddie?" he asked again, taking a big bite out of a chicken leg.

"I ain't saying," she said smartly.

"But you know she ain't here, right?"

"What's it to you?"

"So, why you calling if you know she's not here? Is she supposed to be here? Is she on her way home?"

"Boy, I tell you . . . that girl can do ten times better than she did with the likes of you."

If it were anybody but Eddie saying it, he'd have been offended. But deep down, he knew that Eddie liked him.

"I just want to know where she is."

"Why? So you can hurt her feelings again?"

"I didn't hurt her feelings," he said, defending himself.

"You left her by herself with this baby."

"She threw me out!"

"She . . . well, if she did it's because she probably thought you'd walk out on her anyway."

Those words alone were powerful enough to shut him up. Leave it up to Eddie to help put Connie into perspective for him. "Shit, Eddie."

"You cussing me, boy?"

"No. No, I'm not cussing you. I'm cussing me."

Eddie was quiet for a minute, obviously trying to make sense of what he'd just said. "Now, why would you go and do something like that?"

He'd driven all the way from Bueller back to Denver to see Connie. And in all that time, he still hadn't figured out what to say to her, or even what he'd planned on doing once he got here. One day, instead of driving across town to see about a job at a construction sight, he passed right by it, ended up on the highway, and headed his ass straight here.

"She all right?" he asked, solemnly.

Eddie sucked her teeth. "She pregnant, fool. How you think she is?"

John thought for a moment before responding. "So, what do you think I should do, Eddie?"

"Whatchu mean, what I think you should do? About what?"

"About Connie. About . . . me and Connie and . . . this . . ."

"This baby?" she completed his sentence for him. "It's a boy, John King. Did she tell you that?"

John was surprised. "No. She didn't. A boy?"

"I suppose she didn't tell you she was moving out here, neither, after the baby is born? Did she?"

"No, Eddie." He was even more surprised. "She didn't tell me that, either."

"I swear, man," she said, irritated. "If you don't learn to get your head outta your ass . . . *praise God* . . . one of these days, your whole life is gonna pass you by and you won't even know what happened."

"Where is she, Eddie?"

Eddie sighed, then told John the whole story about Charlotte and Connie's new sister, Cammy, who'd had a car accident in Kansas, and lost her baby. Connie had let Reesy talk her into going out there to see about her, and that's where they were, but since Connie's cell phone didn't work out of town, Eddie told her she'd check on her by leaving messages on her home phone and Connie could call home every now and then to check them.

"Damn! I missed all that?"

"You sho did. Now, how much more you plan on missing?"

"I don't know about that whole kid thing, Eddie," he said apprehensively. "I'm too damn old for kids, and I don't know shit about them anyway."

"Boy, Abraham was older than you and God saw fit to bless him with one. Of course, Abraham wasn't as sinful as you, but the Lawd work in mysterious ways sometimes, and who know why he saw fit you make you a daddy."

"Thanks, Eddie," he said dryly.

"Connie's just as scared as you. Only this time, she ain't running from it, John. And it's time for you to stop running from it, too, 'cause that child's gonna be here sooner than you think, and he's gonna need good strong people willing to look after him, teach him, and love him. And if you'd stop being self-ish for one minute in your life, you might surprise yourself and Connie, too."

John hung up the phone and started to reflect back on his experiences with kids. He'd hung out with Connie and Jade every once in a while, but pushing a kid on a swing for half an hour wasn't the same as raising one. Racine's kids couldn't stand his ass, so he knew he had nothing to draw on from that whole experience, either. All he ever knew about being a father was to avoid the possibility at all cost. Hell, he didn't even know his own father until a year ago, and that was . . . Well, Adam was . . . He was cool. But he was mentally disabled. So, what kind of example of fatherhood could he possibly be?

John thought about this kid Connie was carrying, and all of a sudden he felt sorry for him. He wasn't even born yet and already had a big-ass strike against him. He had John King for a daddy. Damn.

Chapter 55

Cammy had gotten home from the hospital earlier in the day. It was such a strange feeling coming back to that house. Before the accident, when she'd left it, she never dreamed she'd ever come back to it again. But life just kept on playing one cruel joke after another on Cammy, and all she could do about it was nothing. Momma sat across the room from her on the couch, pretending to watch her stories, but cutting her eyes at Cammy when she thought no one was looking. Cammy didn't have to see her to know she was doing it. She could feel it.

Reesy and Connie had brought her home. Reesy was in the kitchen making lunch, and Connie had gone to the store to pick up some lemons for Reesy's iced tea. It felt strange having them both here. Strange in a good way. They were so nice to her, so patient, and gentle, calling her baby, and honey, and sweetie, and treating her like the little sister. Not like she was a woman neither of them hardly knew, but like she was one of them.

Charlotte could hardly believe what was happening. Her girls were here in Murphy, so close to her, and yet all they could do was dote over Camille the whole time, almost as if Charlotte wasn't even in the house. Cammy just sat there, staring at nothing, acting like she didn't see Charlotte either or even know who she was. She wouldn't look at her, and acted like she barely heard her if Charlotte did say anything to her. Cammy might've wanted to blame what had happened to her on Charlotte, but she'd be wrong for that. Charlotte wasn't the one to start the argument they'd had, and she wasn't the one to go running out of here like a maniac and drive that car into another one.

Connie walked into the house, carrying a small bag of groceries. She stopped at Cammy and asked, "How you doing, sweetie?"

But she walked right past Charlotte as if she weren't even in the room. Connie had been doing that shit since she got there, acting like she used to when Charlotte was raising her. Acting like she was better than Charlotte, superior, and like Charlotte was of no consequence. Charlotte had been trying to be good since they got here, smiling and being so considerate of poor Cammy and of her loss. But Connie and Reesy didn't know the truth. They had no idea how Cammy could be sometimes.

Reesy had made sandwiches and salads for lunch. The four of them sat at the kitchen table, eating.

"This is delicious, baby girl," Charlotte said, smiling at Reesy. "Real good. Isn't it, Cammy?"

Cammy had hardly eaten a thing, and Charlotte felt embarrassed by her.

"It's just sandwiches, Momma," Reesy said sheepishly. "You're not hungry, Cammy? You really should try and eat something."

Cammy nodded slightly and tried to smile.

They ate in silence for a few minutes, which made Charlotte uncomfortable. Someone should be saying something. After all, she thought looking around her, she had a table full of daughters. She'd waited almost thirty years for this moment to come, and it was hard to deny the joy she felt.

"So, Connie," Charlotte said hesitantly, not knowing what to expect from this one. "I hear you own your own store in Denver, selling pretty jewelry and other things."

Connie bit into her sandwich, and nodded. "Yeah."

Charlotte waited for her to say more, but Connie had a way of limiting her responses to Charlotte to one-word answers.

Reesy felt obligated to fill in the blanks. "She not only sells the jewelry, Momma," she said proudly. Connie wished she'd shut up. "She makes it, too. And it's beautiful. People pay lots of money for Connie's pieces. Look." She held her arm out across the table and showed Charlotte a bracelet Connie had made and given her for her birthday. "She made this for me. Isn't it beautiful?"

Charlotte glanced at it and smiled sweetly. "It's very nice."

"Can I see?" Cammy asked, awed by the bracelet. "It's beautiful, Connie."

Connie winked at Cammy.

Attitude. As hard as Charlotte tried to ignore it, Connie had too much of it. And she never minded flaunting it in plain sight of Charlotte, either. Charlotte silently took in a breath to calm her nerves. Connie was trying them. Charlotte could see it, even if nobody else in the room could. She glanced over at Connie, who happened to catch her gaze at the same time, and hold it.

After lunch, Connie helped Cammy outside to the front porch to get some fresh air. This one was pretty bad off and not just physically, Connie surmised. Losing the baby had to have been hard enough, but Connie had a feeling that there was even more to it than that. Cammy had no fight to her. No spirit. No guts. She reminded Connie of herself in that respect, after Eddie had found her behind her restaurant digging in the garbage cans looking for food. Cammy looked defeated, and beaten down by more than just this car accident, maybe by life. That was something Connie could relate to so much better than Reesy ever could.

"This is a hell of a way for us to meet. Don't you think?" Connie asked Cammy, sitting next to her.

"Yeah," Cammy said quietly. "I guess it is." Cammy looked over at the swell underneath Connie's blouse. "Are you . . . pregnant?" Cammy hoped she hadn't offended Connie, since maybe she was just fat and not going to have a baby after all.

Connie nodded. "Yeah." She studied Cammy for a reaction, wondering how her pregnancy would affect a woman who'd just lost one.

"How far along?"

"Eighteen weeks."

Cammy stared out in front of her, recalling how she might've looked when she was just past four months pregnant. Then she turned her attention back to Connie. "I have some clothes you might like," she said, her eyes twinkling.

Connie smiled. "Oh, really?" she said smartly. "You think I need some clothes?"

Cammy finally smiled back. "You need something cuter than that shirt you're wearing."

"Now what's that supposed to mean? You trying to say my shirt is ugly?" she teased.

Cammy wrinkled her nose and nodded. "You don't have to cover up being pregnant these days, Connie," she explained. "Nowadays, women kinda flaunt it, wearing tight shirts and showing off their stomachs, because . . . well . . ."

"Well . . . what?"

"Because being pregnant is sexy."

Connie threw her head back and laughed.

"I'm serious," Cammy said emphatically. "You're so pretty, and if you just . . . I have a pink top that would look so pretty on you." Cammy surprised Connie by taking her by the hand and leading her back inside the house to her room. She dug through her dresser drawer, and held the top up to Connie with the arm that wasn't in a sling. "This would look so nice."

"Girl, please!" Connie gasped. "That's two sizes too small."

Cammy smiled. "That's the point. Try it on."

Connie looked at her like she was crazy. "Cammy?"

"Go ahead," she coaxed. "Just try it."

Connie reluctantly did as she was told, peeling down that skin-tight shirt past her bulging stomach, like she was slipping on pantyhose from the top down. She stood in the mirror and all she saw was stomach, exploding all over the room.

Cammy gasped. "You look so good."

Connie frowned. "I look fat."

"Reesy!" Cammy called out.

"Cammy!" Connie protested.

Reesy stuck her head in the door. "What's up?" she asked, and then she saw Connie. "Whoa."

Connie propped her hands on her hips. "Go ahead, Reese," she said annoyed. "Finish the statement. Whoa . . . Nelly!"

Reesy laughed and huddled up with her sisters in front of the mirror around Connie. "You look so cute!" she squealed.

Connie rolled her eyes. "You playing, Reesy!" Connie pointed her finger at her sister. "Don't make me pinch you!"

"For real, Connie," Cammy said, laughing. "You don't look so frumpy and fat in this."

"I am fat, girl!"

"You are not," Reesy said defensively. "You look adorable. Like you should be a pregnant model or something. How come I never looked that good when I was having all them babies?" she frowned.

"I'll bet you did," Cammy told her.

"Girl, ignore her. Reesy's always complaining that she's the ugly one."

"You're not the ugly one, Reesy," Cammy exclaimed. "I'm the ugly one."

"No, actually, I'm the ugly one," Connie said with finality. "And damn proud of it."

"Fine." Reesy looked at Cammy. "Then you be the ugly one. Cammy and I will just have to suffer and be cute."

The three of them roared in laughter, not realizing that Charlotte was standing in the doorway, getting ready to erupt.

"I guess you ain't so sick now, Cammy," she said, her voice shaking. "Are you?"

Cammy seemed to shrink right before everyone's eyes as she sat down on the side of the bed and lowered her gaze to the floor.

"Well, of course she's not feeling well, Mom," Reesy said in Cammy's defense. She crossed behind Connie and sat beside Cammy on the bed, then put her arm over her shoulder, comforting her. "But at least we know she's feeling a little bit better." Reesy smiled at Cammy.

Charlotte stepped into the room and stared at the three of them, laughing and clowning without even bothering to include her. How come they hadn't asked her to come in? How come they couldn't . . .

"What was so funny?"

"Nothing." Reesy looked at her mother, trying not to snicker about the ridiculous conversation they'd been having. "Nothing, Mom. We were just being silly."

Charlotte's pinched expression bore into each one of them, daring them not to include her in on what had been so funny. They'd been in this room together, laughing and having a good time, but no one had asked her if she wanted in on the joke, too. In fact, they'd been ignoring her ever since they'd come here, petting and pampering Cammy the whole time, like she was the only one . . . the only one who'd . . . been hurt or lonesome. How dare they come here and not see about her, too. How dare they . . . Charlotte caught a glimpse of Connie standing in the mirror, looking back at her like Charlotte was crazy.

"What the hell you looking at!" she snapped, glaring at Connie.

Connie slowly turned around to face her mother, but as soon as she did, she remembered that Charlotte was of no consequence to her anymore, and nothing she said mattered one way or another. Connie brushed past her, and went back into the living room.

"Bitch!" Charlotte screamed out, and turned to go after her. She'd had enough! She'd had enough of this heffa!

"Momma!" Reesy yelled, following behind Charlotte.

"Shut the hell up, Reesy!" Charlotte stopped abruptly, turned, and pointed her finger in Reesy's face.

Connie surprised everyone and burst out laughing. "Is that the best you can do, Charlotte?" She propped her hands on her hips and mimicked her mother's tone. "Bitch!"

"You're the one, Connie!" Charlotte's face turned crimson-red, she was so angry. She walked up to Connie and pointed in her face, spitting and baring down on her the way she'd done when Connie was a child. "Why the hell did you bring your skank ass down here, girl? Why the hell did you bring your little black ass into my house?" Rage flowed down her cheeks in hot tears.

"Momma!" Reesy tried stepping between them. "Momma, don't!"

Charlotte pushed Reesy hard enough to send her stumbling back toward the couch. "I always hated you!" She clenched her hands into fists, fighting against herself to keep from hitting this woman.

"And I always hated you, too, Charlotte!" Connie screamed back. "So I'd say that makes us even!"

"I left because of you, little girl!" she spat.

"Momma?" Reesy cried, staring at the two women, stunned.

"Strutting around thinking you so much better than me! You ain't better than me, Connie! You ain't never been . . ."

"Better than you? Shit, *Momma!* Who the hell wasn't better than you?" Connie said venomously. "And don't stand here and tell that lie! You didn't leave because of me, Charlotte! No! You left because your ass was too sorry to be a mother. You were too goddamned sorry to be anything but a . . ."

Charlotte's hand seemed to come out of nowhere and land hard against the side of Connie's face. Connie stumbled back, her eyes blazing like balls of fire, and she drew back her own hand to return the blow, but before she could, Reesy stepped in front of her and slapped Charlotte so hard across her face, she fell backward into the chair behind her.

Charlotte stared wide-eyed at Reesy, standing over her, heaving in anger.

"Don't you ever put your hands on her again, Momma!" she growled in a low voice.

Charlotte was speechless and more broken than she'd ever been in her life.

While Reesy watched the scene unfold in front of her, images flashed in her head of moments just like this one, with Charlotte cursing and hitting Connie, while Reesy watched from the corner of the room or disappeared under the bed, pretending nothing was happening, until it ended, and she could curl up on Charlotte's lap again, smothered in kisses by her mother. Reesy recalled glimpses of Connie's blackened eyes, swollen lips, and bruised arms, but Connie never talked about it. She'd just tell Reesy she'd hurt herself and not to worry about it.

"She took care of me!" Reesy pointed hard into her own chest. Charlotte melted in a blur behind her tears. "Connie took care of me! Not you!"

"Reesy . . . baby!" Charlotte reached out to her to try and make her understand.

"No, Momma!" Reesy slowly backed away from Charlotte. "Connie . . . combed my hair . . . bathed me . . . she . . . made sure I . . . ate." All of a sudden, Reesy turned to Connie, standing behind her, staring in awe of her sister.

"I never said . . . thank you, Connie," Reesy cried, reaching out to her. "I never said . . ."

Connie held onto her tightly. "Shhhh . . . Reesy," she said, soothingly.

"I'm so sorry . . . Connie!" Reesy sobbed into her shoulder.

"For what?" Connie chuckled. "I did what I was supposed to do, Reese. You're my baby sister," she said lovingly. Connie looked over Reesy's shoulder at Cammy standing in the doorway of her bedroom staring at the two of them. "Cammy?" she called out. "Pack your things. We're leaving."

"No!" Charlotte said desperately, reaching out to Reesy.

"Reesy—baby! No!" Tears fell fast down her face. "What about—what about me?" Charlotte fell to her knees on the floor at her daughters feet. "You can't leave me here! You can't just leave me—"

Connie stepped toward her. "Being left behind is a bitch— ain't it, Charlotte? Cammy," she called out. "Hurry up, girl." Connie headed to her room to help her pack. "We've got to go."

Reesy stared down at her mother, crumpled on the floor, sobbing uncontrollably. "Now I can close the door, Mom, and I know exactly what's behind it."

Cammy followed her sisters out of the house.

Reesy smiled back at her and laughed. "Oooh, Connie! Can we keep her?"

Connie sighed. "Yeah, but make sure you feed her, or else . . ."

Charlotte watched her daughters disappear through the front door as if they'd been ghosts and none of them had ever been there in the first place. Cammy, the last one out of the door, turned to her one last time and blinked away tears of her own. "I love you, Momma. I always did." Reesy helped her down the porch steps.

Chapter 56

*L*ynn never told Uncle everything, but she made sure to tell him enough.

"I think she's still into Sam," she mentioned to him once.

"Oh, she into Sam all right," he said confidently. "So, what else is going on, sugah?"

Lynn genuinely liked Charlotte, so it was hard to betray her like this, but . . . she turned to look at Uncle and smiled. "She's fuckin' around with Zoo, too."

Sam had left without her. Charlotte had been sulking around for the last two days, jumping every time the phone rang, hoping it was him. But it never was. Zoo pumped slowly in and out of her, holding her close to him, licking and sucking on the side of her neck.

She slapped him on the back. "No hickeys, Zoo! What did I tell you about that?"

"Sorry," he said, breathless. "Sorry, baby."

She didn't want Zoo. Not the way she wanted Sam. But she wanted him more than she wanted Uncle anymore. Charlotte wanted to go home. She wanted to go back to her little apartment

346

on the Five Points, to see her babies again, and to be back in her old skin, doing all the things she used to complain that bored her, with no recollection of Uncle or Zoo or Sam. This place wasn't home, and it never would be. Sam had fucked up her life, and left her stranded while he went off to do whatever the fuck he wanted, when he wanted.

"Damn, Zoo!" she moaned, because he'd found her spot. Charlotte closed her eyes tight, raised her knees higher in the air, and thrust her hips wildly against him. "That's the way I like it, baby! Oooh!" Damn if she wasn't about to cum. "That's it! Shit! Baby!" she squealed.

"Is it good, baby girl?"

It was Uncle's voice she heard, not Zoo's. Charlotte opened her eyes and looked up at him, standing over the two of them. Zoo disappeared in a flash from on top of her, and Uncle gazed down on her naked body, licking his lips and unzipping his pants.

He leisurely crawled on top of her and eased himself down into her. "Somebody's got to finish the job," he laughed out loud. Two of Uncle's cohorts stood behind him. "Might as well be us. Ain't that right, fellas?"

One by one, they took turns with her in every way imaginable while they forced, Zoo to watch.

"Turn over, bitch!" The big light-skinned one Uncle called Leon pulled her head back by the hair, wrapped his arm around her waist, and lifted her up on all fours on the edge of the bed, then burned into her ass with a dick that felt like it was as big as her arm. Charlotte tried to scream, but he covered her mouth with his hand before she could. The other one, Dante, crawled onto the bed in front of her, unzipped his pants, and pushed himself into her mouth until Charlotte gagged, then threw up all over him and the bed.

"What the . . ." He slapped her hard across the face, then

laughed. *"Oh, we gonna do this till you get it right, ho!"* He grabbed her hair, then held back her head and filled her mouth again.

Uncle watched the whole time with Zoo sitting at his feet on the floor, holding the boy's head up, making sure he didn't miss a thing.

"I'm sorry, Uncle!" Zoo cried. *"Please! Please! I'm sorry, man!"*

Charlotte heard Zoo crying, sobbing like a baby.

Help me! she wanted to scream. *Zoo! Make them stop!*

"Aaaaaaaah!" Butch screamed from behind when he came, then slapped her as hard as he could on the ass, leaving a mark as big as his hand.

Dante ejaculated in her mouth, and Charlotte made the mistake of gagging again, and throwing up his seed in front of him.

He pushed her hard, flipping her head over heels, off the bed. Charlotte landed flat on her back.

"Nooooo! Uncle!" Zoo screamed, as Uncle pulled his bitch ass up by his nappy head.

Uncle slapped him over and over again, knocking Zoo around like a rag doll. Zoo's blood splattered all over the walls, the bed, onto Charlotte.

She watched him shrink into the child he was, too afraid to even try to fight back while this man kicked his ass. Charlotte's body convulsed in the pain that had been inflicted on it by the three men.

"This the kinda bitch you want for your man, Honey?" Uncle laughed as he swung the boy around like he was a toy?

Charlotte cried. *"Nooooo! I—don't—want him!"* she wailed.

Uncle looked at her and laughed. *"Course not, girl. But that brotha you want is long gone by now!"* he kicked Zoo hard in the pit of his stomach. *"Keep lookin if you want to, but . . ."* he kneed him underneath the chin, and Zoo's head flung backwards, carrying the rest of him with him. "Sam ain't coming back."

The gun came out of nowhere, and all of a sudden Uncle held the boy up by his hair, forced the gun in between his lips, and pulled the trigger.

Charlotte screamed, "Noooo!" Zoo's lifeless body fell backward in a heap. "Honey! Hush!" he screamed, laughing, and in one swift motion, Uncle swung his wooden walking stick far behind him, then rounded it to Charlotte's face, breaking her jaw.

He knelt down beside her. "I got about fifty mothafuckas been wanting to get in that ass since I met you, baby. You wait right here. We'll be back in a minute."

The room went dark, and Uncle disappeared. Charlotte woke up in agony and with Lynn hovering over her.

"C'mon, Charlotte!" she said, desperately trying to help Charlotte to her feet. "He'll be back soon!"

Charlotte struggled to get to her feet. Her head felt like it had been split in half. Zoo's body was gone, but the blood-spattered wall reminded her that he'd been there, and that she hadn't dreamed his death.

"Hurry, girl!" Lynn cried. "Hurry! We got to go! Before he . . . Charlie!"

She never saw Uncle again after that. And Charlotte never set foot back in Kansas City again. Lynn went back, though, because Arnel needed her.

"You seen my honey pot, Lynn?" Uncle asked her out of the blue one afternoon, shortly after it happened.

Lynn puffed nervously on a cigarette and shook her head. "No, Uncle. Haven't heard from her."

He leaned in close to her and gently pushed her hair back from her face. "But you'd tell me if you did," he smiled, showing off his gold tooth. "Wouldn't you, sugah?"

Lynn looked him straight in the eyes. "You know I would. I swear."

"On Arnel's life?"

She nodded, knowing that if it ever came to that, Charlotte would be in trouble. "Absolutely," she said convincingly. "Yes, Uncle."

Chapter 57

Tyrell looked up from the engine he was working on and saw Cammy standing outside his garage. He dropped the wrench into the engine and dug around until he found it.

"Hi, T." Cammy smiled at him, and his heart skipped a beat when she did.

"Hey, Cammy." She hadn't spoken to him since the hospital. She hadn't returned his calls. T decided maybe it was best that he stop crowding her, and step back until she was ready. Maybe he'd gotten lucky, and she was ready sooner rather than later.

"I came to say good-bye."

T looked confused.

She motioned over her shoulder at the white SUV out in front. "I'm going out of town for a while." She smiled reluctantly. "Going to Denver with my sisters."

T crumbled inside as his world seemed to be coming crashing down around him. He cleared his throat. "You moving to Denver?" he asked sheepishly

She stared tenderly at him, then nodded her head. "I'm going to spend some time with my sisters." Cammy turned to leave, then turned to him one last time. "Maybe I'll see you when I get back?" She started toward the car.

T smiled optimistically and called out to her, "When's that gonna be?"

Cammy waved, and T saw the shimmer of her wedding ring still on her finger. That was all he needed to know.

Reesy had already decided that Cammy would stay with her. After all, it made sense. She had more room.

"What do you think Justin's going to say about this?" Connie asked.

Reesy shrugged indifferently. "Doesn't matter."

"Of course it matters, Reese," Connie told her. "You'd probably better call him and let him know before you show up at the door with a new family member all of a sudden."

"It's all right, Connie." Reesy sounded agitated.

Connie realized something was up. "What's going on, Reesy?"

Cammy sat in the back seat watching the conversation unfold like a tennis match. Who knew having sisters could be such a hoot?

"Nothing."

"Liar."

"Nosey."

"I'm going to keep bugging you till you tell me."

Reesy knew Connie meant it, too. So she took a deep breath, then blurted it out. "Justin and I are separated."

Connie looked back at Cammy, then back at Reesy. "Separated? Since when? Why?"

"Since . . . I found out he was cheating on me."

Connie's mouth flew open in disbelief. "Justin! Girl, you lying!"

"Wish I was," Reesy responded.

"But . . . Justin doesn't cheat, Reese. It's just not possible."

Reesy looked at Connie and rolled her eyes. "Anything's possible, Connie. He's not perfect."

"He's not?" she teased.

They rode in silence for the next several miles, with nobody really knowing what to say.

"So, are you going to divorce him?" Connie asked apprehensively.

Reesy sighed. "I don't know what I'm going to do, Connie."

"But you still love him, though," Cammy chimed in from the back seat. "Don't you?"

Reesy glanced at her in the rearview mirror. "Yes. I love him very much, Cammy. And Connie's right. Justin is and has always been damn near perfect."

"And you know he loves you?"

Reesy nodded. "He does."

"Then give it some time, Reesy," Cammy said quietly. "And don't give up on him so easily. Damn near perfect or not, people make mistakes sometimes. The worst thing is having to pay for those mistakes for the rest of your life. That's not cool."

Connie stared out the window of the truck, nodding in agreement. "It's not cool at all," she said introspectively.

They'd finally made it back to Denver. Reesy picked up her car from long-term parking and dropped Connie off at her house.

"You sure you don't need help getting upstairs?" Reesy asked, concerned.

"No, I'm fine." Connie leaned over and kissed Reesy on the cheek, then reached back and patted Cammy on the leg. "Get some rest, baby girl."

"I will," Cammy smiled back.

"I'll give you a call later, Reese," Connie said, getting out of the car.

"Yeah," Reesy agreed. "We've got a lot to talk about."

Connie stared quizzically at her.

"Jade," was all she said.

Connie studied her. "You want to tell her?"

Reesy thought for a moment before answering. "Maybe not right away, but . . . the worst thing we could do is not tell her."

"We'll talk," Connie said, relieved.

She stood on the sidewalk in front of her house and watched Reesy drive away. "Whew!" Connie said, exasperated and exhausted. "One revelation after another," she muttered. "I need to pee."

Connie opened the door to her apartment, shocked to see John lying on the couch asleep. She stared at him for a moment, torn between feelings of joy and relief at seeing him, confusion, wondering what the hell he was doing here, and anger that he'd had the nerve to let himself in without permission. She dropped her suitcase down hard on the floor, startling him awake.

"What! Wha . . ." He forgot where he was for a minute, then looked up and saw her standing there looking as pissed as all get-out and fuckin' gorgeous!

"What the hell are you doing in my apartment?" she asked angrily.

John was speechless. Maps were spread out all over the coffee table and scattered on the floor. John clumsily stood to his feet, taking in the vision of this beautiful woman. "Looking for Murphy, Kansas," he said apologetically.

"What?" she asked, perturbed.

He motioned to the maps scattered in front of him. "That shit's not on the map, baby. I looked, and I couldn't find it."

"Why would you be trying to find Murphy, Kansas, John?" Connie asked, perplexed.

He looked a little embarrassed before he answered. "To find you."

Connie couldn't believe what she was hearing, or that it was coming from him. "Why?"

John just stared at her, trying to catch his breath, and to sound convincing, and serious, and real, and like he meant every word. His gaze traveled down to the swell in her midsection, and his stomach fluttered. "I . . . uh . . ." He couldn't take his eyes off her. And it seemed to hit him all at once. John's palms started sweating, he felt light-headed, and his knees felt a little weak. "Is, uh . . ." He motioned to her stomach.

"What?"

". . . the baby!" he blurted out. "Is that . . . the baby?" He nervously cleared his throat.

Connie saw pure unadulterated fear in this big, strong man's eyes, and she couldn't help but to laugh. "You'd better sit down before you fall down." She went over and helped ease him back down on the sofa. "You look a little flushed."

She was so close to him, and she smelled so good. John turned to her and stared into her lovely amber brown eyes. "I'm a little weak," he confessed.

She laughed again. "Want me to get you some water?" she asked, concerned.

"No, baby," he chuckled. "Just stay . . . right here."

Connie studied him for a moment, and realized she was glad to have him here, but her reluctance just wouldn't make room for optimism. "I'm keeping this baby, John. With or without you." She held his gaze. "I'm keeping him."

He nodded, and then cleared his throat again. "Yeah. Eddie told me."

Connie looked surprised. "Eddie? When did you talk to her?"

"She called when you were gone. She said you were planning on keeping it."

Connie looked at him a moment, then asked again, "Why are you here?" She hoped she knew the answer, but she needed to hear him say it, and she needed to see him mean it.

He took her hand in hers and kissed it. "I'm here because this is where I belong, Connie. I'm tired of running and got nowhere else to run to. And besides, what kind of man would I be if I can't be man enough for you?"